THUS BAD BEGINS

THUS BAD BEGINS

Javier Marías

TRANSLATED BY
MARGARET JULL COSTA

HAMISH HAMILTON
an imprint of
PENGUIN BOOKS

HAMISH HAMILTON

UK | USA | Canada | Ireland | Australia
India | New Zealand | South Africa

Hamish Hamilton is part of the Penguin Random House group of companies
whose addresses can be found at global.penguinrandomhouse.com.

First published 2016
001

Set in 12.5/16 pt Fournier MT Std
Typeset by Jouve (UK), Milton Keynes
Printed in Great Britain by Clays Ltd, St Ives plc

A CIP catalogue record for this book is available from the British Library

HARDBACK ISBN: 978–0–241–97280–9
TRADE PAPERBACK ISBN: 978–0–241–97281–6

www.greenpenguin.co.uk

Penguin Random House is committed to a
sustainable future for our business, our readers
and our planet. This book is made from Forest
Stewardship Council® certified paper.

To Tano Díaz Yanes,
after forty-five years of friendship,
for always being there to deflect
any charging bulls

And to Carme López Mercader,
who, most improbably, has still not tired
of listening to me. Yet

I

This story didn't happen so very long ago – less time than the average life, and how brief a life is once it's over and can be summed up in a few sentences, leaving only ashes in the memory, ashes that crumble at the slightest touch and fly up with the slightest gust of wind – and yet what happened then would be impossible now. I mean, above all, what happened to them, to Eduardo Muriel and his wife, Beatriz Noguera, when they were young: rather than what happened to me and them when I was a young man and their marriage was a long, indissoluble misery. The latter would, of course, still be perfectly possible: what happened to me, I mean, given that it's happening to me now, or perhaps it's all part of the same ongoing story. And I suppose what happened with Van Vechten and so on could also occur. There must always have been Van Vechtens and they won't suddenly stop existing, they will always be there, in real life and in its twin, fiction, because the nature of the characters never changes, or so it seems, they continue to be repeated over the centuries as if the two spheres lacked imagination or had no alternative (after all, both spheres are the work of the living, perhaps the dead are more inventive), sometimes it's as if, like very young children, we can only really enjoy one drama or one story, albeit with infinite variations that disguise both drama and story as either ancient or modern, but always essentially the same. Therefore, throughout the

3

ages, there must also always have been Eduardo Muriels and Beatriz Nogueras, and the same applies to the bit-part players too; there have been endless Juan de Veres, because that was and is my name, Juan Vere or Juan de Vere, depending on who is saying or thinking my name. There's nothing original about me.

Divorce did not exist then, nor was there much hope of it ever existing when Muriel and his wife married some twenty years before I became involved in their lives, or rather before they entered mine, the life, if you like, of a mere beginner. But right from the very moment we come into the world, things begin to happen to us, its weak wheel takes us up sceptically and dully, and reluctantly drags us along, because it's an old wheel and has unhurriedly ground down many lives by the light of its idle sentinel, the cold moon, which dozes and observes with just one eye open, and knows all the stories even before they happen. Someone only has to notice you – or cast an indolent glance in your direction – and there's no withdrawing, even if you hide away or stay very still and quiet and take no initiative or do anything. Even if you try to erase yourself, you have been spotted, like a distant shape on the ocean that you can't ignore, that you must either avoid or approach; you count for other people and they count on you, until you disappear, although, in the end, that wasn't true of me either. I wasn't totally passive nor did I pretend to be a mirage, to make myself invisible.

I've always wondered how people dared to contract marriage – and did so for centuries – when marriage was for life; especially women, for whom it was harder to find an escape route, or if they did, they had to be doubly or triply careful to conceal such escapades, and five times more careful if they returned carrying cargo and had to disguise a new being before it even had a face to show to the world: from the moment of its conception or detection or presentiment – not to say its annunciation – and to make it an impostor for the rest of its existence, often leaving that new being perennially unaware of its own imposture or its bastard origins, not even when he or she was old and on the verge of never again being detected by anyone. Innumerable children have believed someone to be their father who was not and believed half-siblings to be their true brothers or sisters, and they have gone to their grave with that belief and that error intact, or perhaps one should say the deceit to which their stoical mothers had submitted them from birth. Diseases or debts are the other two main things one can 'contract', all three share the same verb, as if all of them augured ill or presaged doom or were, at the very least, painful: but unlike them, there was definitely no cure, no remedy for marriage, no resolution. Or only through the death of one of the spouses, a death sometimes silently longed for and, less often, sought or induced or prompted, usually even more silently or in deepest secrecy. Or the death of both, of course, and then there would be nothing more, only the unwitting children they'd had, if any and if they had survived, and a brief memory. Or, on occasions, a story. A tenuous, rarely told story, since people tend not to tell stories about their personal life – mothers who remained stoical until the last breath, and many non-mothers too; or if they do tell their story, they tell it only in whispers, so that it isn't as if they had never existed, so that they do not remain with their grieving face pressed into the silent pillow, or visible only to the somnolent, half-open eye of the cold, sentinel moon.

Eduardo Muriel had a thin moustache, as if he had first grown it when the actor Errol Flynn was still around and had then forgotten to change it or allow it to grow more thickly, one of those men of fixed habits as regards his appearance, the kind who doesn't notice that time passes and fashions change nor that he himself is growing older – it's as if time did not concern him and so could be discounted, rendering him immune to its passing – and up to a point he was right not to worry about it or to pay it any attention: by attaching no importance to his age, he kept it at bay; by not giving in to it in external matters, he rejected it, and so the timid passing years – which make bold with almost everyone else – prowled and stalked, but didn't dare to claim him, did not take root in his mind or affect his appearance, merely casting upon it a very slow shower of sleet or shadow. He was tall, well above average height for a man of his generation, the generation just after my father's or possibly the same one. At first glance, his height made him seem strong and slim, although he didn't exactly conform to the manly stereotype: he had rather narrow shoulders, which made his belly seem larger, even though he carried no excess fat there or on his hips, from which emerged a pair of very long legs that he didn't know quite what to do with when he sat down: if he crossed them (and that, generally speaking, was his preferred position), the foot of the upper leg easily touched the floor, a pose also achieved – albeit by artificial means and with the aid of foreshortening and high heels – by certain women who are particularly proud of their calves and who prefer not to leave one leg dangling free or to become pushed out of shape by the supporting knee. Because of his narrow shoulders, Muriel used to wear jackets with carefully disguised shoulder pads, I think, or perhaps his tailor cut them in the form of an inverted trapezium (in the 1970s and 1980s, he still went to see his tailor or his tailor came to him, which was unusual even then). He had a very straight nose, with not a trace of a curve despite its good size, and his thick, predominantly dark brown hair (parted with a wet comb as doubtless his mother had done ever since he was a child – a tradition he had seen no reason to break with) had a sprinkling of grey. His thin moustache did little to diminish his bright, spontaneous, youthful smile. He tried to restrain that smile or repress it, but often failed, because there was in him an underlying spirit of joviality, or a past self that emerged easily and without the need to send a sounding line down very deep. Nor, on the other hand, was it to be found in very shallow waters, for in those there floated a certain bitterness, either habitual or unconscious, of which he felt he was not the cause, but possibly the victim.

The most striking thing about him, though, when one saw him for the first time or came across a rare full-face photo in the newspaper, was the patch he wore over his right eye, a classic, theatrical or even filmic eyepatch, black and bulky and held in place by a thin black piece of elastic. I have always wondered why such eyepatches have a rough surface, I don't mean the cloth ones intended only as temporary protection, but the permanent, fitted ones made of some stiff, compact material. (It looked like Bakelite, and I often felt tempted to drum on it with my fingernails to find out how it felt, not that I ever tried this with my employer; I did, however, find out what it sounded like, because sometimes, when he was upset or irritated, but also whenever he paused to think before uttering a sentence or embarking on a speech, with his thumb tucked under one armpit as if it were the tiny riding whip of a soldier or a cavalryman reviewing his troops or his mounts, Muriel did exactly that, drumming on his eyepatch with the fingernails of his free hand, as if summoning the aid of his non-existent or useless eye; he must have liked the sound it made and it was rather pleasing, toc, toc, toc; although until one got used to the gesture it did make one cringe slightly, to see him invoking his absent eye.) Perhaps the somewhat bulky shape of the patch is intended to give the impression that there is an actual eye underneath, when there might only be an empty socket, a hollow, a dent, a depression. Perhaps those patches are convex precisely in order to contradict the awful concavity that, in some cases, they conceal; who knows, perhaps the cavity is filled by a polished sphere of white glass or marble, with the pupil and the iris painted on with pointless, perfect realism, an eye that will never be seen, always covered in black, or seen only by its owner at the end of the day, when, standing before the mirror, he wearily uncovers or perhaps removes it.

And while the patch inevitably drew one's attention, his useful, visible eye, the left one, was no less striking, being of an intense dark blue, like the sea at evening or perhaps at night, and which, because it was alone, seemed to notice and register absolutely everything, as if it possessed both its own faculties and those of the other invisible, blind eye, or as though nature had wanted to compensate for the loss of its pair by making it more than usually penetrating. Such was the energy and speed of the left eye that I would, gradually and furtively, try to place myself out of its reach so as not to be wounded by its piercing gaze, until Muriel would tell me off: 'Move a little to the right, I can barely see you there unless I lean sideways. Don't forget, my field of vision is more limited than yours.' And at first, when I didn't know where to look – torn between that living, maritime eye and the dead, magnetic patch – he would have no hesitation in calling me to order: 'Juan, I'm talking to you with the seeing eye, not the dead one, so please listen and don't get distracted by the eye that isn't saying a word.' Muriel would openly refer to his halved vision, unlike those who draw an awkward veil of silence over any personal defect or disability, however conspicuous and dramatic: people who have had one arm amputated at the shoulder, but who never acknowledge the difficulties they face and do just about everything short of taking up juggling; one-legged people who scale Annapurna on crutches; blind people who go to the cinema and then make a fuss during the scenes with no dialogue, complaining that the image is out of focus; disabled people who pretend they're not wheelchair-bound and insist on trying to climb stairs rather than using the ramps that are available everywhere nowadays; men with heads like billiard balls, who, whenever there's a gust of wind, are constantly smoothing their non-existent hair and getting frustrated with their imaginary unruly mop. (Not that I'm criticizing them in the least, of course, they're free to do exactly as they like.)

But the first time I asked him what had happened to his eye, how his silent eye had been struck dumb, he replied as brusquely as he did sometimes to people who annoyed him, although he rarely did so with me, for he usually treated me with great kindness and affection: 'Let's get one thing straight: I don't employ you to ask me questions about matters that are none of your business.'

At first, there wasn't much that *was* my business, although this soon changed, and simply by dint of being there, willing and waiting, I ended up being entrusted with various tasks, some even created especially for me; and by 'there' I mean his apartment, although, after a while, it vaguely came to mean 'at his side', when I accompanied him on the occasional trip or visited him when he was filming, or when he decided to include me in suppers or card games with friends, more to make up the numbers, I think, and for him to have an admiring witness on hand. In his more extrovert moods, of which fortunately there were many – or perhaps I should say his less melancholic or even misanthropic moods, for he regularly went from one extreme to the other, as if his mind lived on a rather slow-moving seesaw that sometimes picked up speed in the presence of his wife, for reasons I couldn't understand and that must have gone back a long way – he enjoyed having an audience and being listened to, or even being egged on a little.

When I met him at his apartment in the morning to receive my instructions for the day, if there were any, or to allow him to hold forth for a while, I would often find him lying on his back on the floor of the living room or the adjoining study (the two rooms were separated by a folding door that was almost always left open, so that, together, the rooms formed a single ample space). Perhaps this was because of his difficulties in knowing what to do with his legs when seated and he felt more comfortable like that, lying full length, unimpeded, unchecked, whether on the living-room carpet or on the study floor. Obviously, when he was at ground level like that, he didn't wear one of his smart jackets – it would have become too wrinkled – but a shirt with a waistcoat or a V-neck sweater and a tie, yes, he always wore a tie, he was of an age when such an item seemed essential, at least when in the city, even though, at the time, sartorial norms had been blown sky-high. The first time I saw him lying on the floor – like a nineteenth-century courtesan or the contemporary victim of an accident – it caught me by surprise and I was alarmed, thinking he must have had a stroke or fainted, or bumped into something and fallen over and was unable to get up. 'What's wrong, Don Eduardo? Are you ill? Can I do anything? Did you slip?' I went over to him solicitously, holding out both hands to help him up. After a slight tussle (he had urged me, right from the start, to address him as 'Eduardo' or *tú*), we had agreed that I could continue to address him formally as *usted* or as 'Eduardo', as long as I omitted the courtesy title of 'Don', but I still found this very hard to do, it just came out naturally, spontaneously.

'Don't be ridiculous,' he said from the floor, giving not the slightest sign either that he was about to get up or that he felt in the least embarrassed by my presence; he regarded my two outstretched hands as if they were a couple of pesky flies buzzing around him. 'Can't you see I'm just having a quiet smoke?' And he brandished his pipe at me, holding it by its bowl. He mostly smoked cigarettes, especially when he was away from home, when he only smoked cigarettes, but in his apartment, he alternated them with his pipe, as though wanting to complete a picture that, otherwise, few of us would see (for he never smoked a pipe during the occasional, mostly spur-of-the-moment parties he threw), to complete that image for his own benefit: eye-patch, pipe, thin moustache, thick hair with a high parting, tailored suit, sometimes a waistcoat; it was as if, unconsciously, he had remained stuck with the image of the male leads from the films of his childhood and adolescence, in the 1930s and 40s, not just the image of Errol Flynn (par excellence, and with whom he shared a dazzling smile), but those of now slightly more nebulous figures, like Ronald Colman, Robert Donat, Basil Rathbone, even the rather longer-lasting David Niven and Robert Taylor; he had a touch of all of them even though they were all quite different. And given that he was Spanish, he occasionally reminded me of certain swarthier actors: the even more distinct and exotic Gilbert Roland and Cesar Romero, especially the former, who also had a large, straight nose.

'What are you doing lying on the floor, may I ask? Just out of curiosity, you know, not that I disapprove, heaven forfend. I just want to understand your habits, assuming this is a habit.'

He made a face expressive of resigned impatience, as if my reaction were all too familiar and he had often had to give the same explanation to others before me.

'It's not so very odd. I often do it. There's nothing to explain, but, yes, it is a habit of mine. Can't a person lie down on the floor simply because he wants to and because it suits him?'

'Of course, Don Eduardo, you can perform acrobatics if the fancy takes you. Why not? Or do a bit of Chinese plate-spinning.' I slipped in this remark deliberately, to make it clear that his posture was not as normal as he made out, not in a man of a certain age, and a father to boot, because crawling about on the floor was something adolescents or children did, and he had three children still living at home. I wasn't sure either that what I was thinking of was a particularly Chinese speciality, spinning several plates at a time with each plate balanced on the end of a long, thin, flexible stick and each stick balanced on a fingertip, I have no idea how they do it or indeed why. He obviously knew what I meant though. 'You have two perfectly good sofas over there,' I added and pointed behind me, to the living room, because he was lying down in the study. 'I wouldn't have found it at all alarming to find you on one of those, even asleep or in a trance. But on the floor, with all the dust . . . I'm sorry, but it's not what one expects.'

'In a trance? Me? In a trance? What do you mean?' He seemed positively offended, but the flicker of a smile indicated that he was also amused.

'It was just a manner of speaking. Thinking. Meditating. Or hypnotized.'

'Me? Hypnotized? Who by? What do you mean "hypnotized"?' And now he couldn't suppress a broad but fleeting smile. 'Do you mean I'd hypnotized myself? In the morning? *A quoi bon?*' he concluded in French, such brief incursions into French being not uncommon among the educated members of his own and preceding generations, since it was usually their second language. I had realized from early on that he rather enjoyed my little jokes, for he rarely cut them short, but tended to repeat them back at me, and the only reason he didn't linger longer was not because he didn't want to, but so that I didn't get too cheeky too quickly, an unnecessary precaution, since I admired and respected him greatly. He paused after that sally into French and, to emphasize his words, he again raised his still smoking pipe. 'The ground or, in this case, the floor, is the safest, firmest and most modest place there is; and, as well as providing the best view of the sky or the ceiling, it's an ideal spot in which to do some thinking. Besides, there isn't a speck of dust to be seen,' he added. 'You'll have to get used to seeing me here, because once on the floor you cannot fall over or, indeed, fall any lower, a great advantage when it comes to making decisions, which one should always base on the worst possible hypothesis, if not on sheer desperation and its usual companion, meanness, then there's no risk of your giving way to sentimentality or being disappointed by whatever decision you happen to take. Anyway, it's not a problem, so sit down, will you, I need to dictate a couple of things. And I've told you before, don't call me "Don Eduardo",' he said, imitating the way I had said it, and he was an excellent mimic. 'It makes me sound older than I am, like some character out of a novel by Galdós, a writer whose work, by the way, with two possible exceptions, I've always loathed, the kind of author you could almost accuse of being a literary despot. Come on, get writing.'

'You're going to dictate to me from down there?'

'Yes, from down here. What's wrong with that? Can't you hear me? Don't tell me I need to take you to an ENT specialist, that would be most unfortunate at your age. How old did you say you were? Fifteen?' He, too, was much given to jokes and exaggerated remarks.

'No, twenty-three. Of course I can hear you. You have, as you know, a strong, manly voice.' I was not always the one to start; whenever Muriel made a joke, I would return it or at least respond in the same playful tone. He again smiled involuntarily, more with his one eye than with his lips. 'But I won't be able to see your face if I sit in my usual place. I'll have my back to you, which would be rude, wouldn't it?' When we had business to conduct, I usually sat in the armchair opposite his, with his eighteenth-century desk between us, and he, at that moment, was lying near the door to the living room, behind my usual chair.

'Well, turn your chair round to face me, then. It's hardly a major problem, it's not nailed to the floor.'

He was quite right, and I did as I was told. Now he was lying literally at my feet, perpendicular to them; it was an eccentric arrangement, the boss horizontal on the floor and the secretary – or whatever I was – near enough to give him a kick in the ribs or the thigh if I made the slightest sudden or involuntary or ill-judged movement of my legs. I prepared to write in my notebook (I would type the letters out afterwards on an old machine of his that he had lent me and that still worked well, and I would then give them to him to check and sign).

Muriel, however, did not immediately begin dictating. His rather affable, covertly amused expression of a moment before had been replaced by one of abstraction or preoccupation, or by one of those griefs that you put off because you don't want to confront or plunge into it and which, nevertheless, always comes back, recurs, grows deeper with each attack, having failed to disappear during the period you were keeping it at bay or far from your thoughts: instead, it has grown in its absence and has not once ceased to stalk your mind surreptitiously or subterraneously, as if it were the preamble to a break-up that will inevitably happen, but which you still cannot even imagine: those feelings of coldness and irritation and boredom towards a much-loved person, feelings that come in waves, that linger, then depart; and with each departure, you try to believe they were pure phantasmagoria – the product of your own unease or a general discontent, or of some other minor annoyances or even the heat – and that they won't come back. Only to discover, the next time, that each new wave proves more tenacious and enduring, poisoning and oppressing the mind and causing it to doubt and complain a little more. That feeling of disaffection takes a while to appear and still longer to take shape in the mind ('I don't think I can stand her any longer, I've got to close the door on her, I must'), and even when our

15

consciousness has finally accepted it, there's still a long way to go before it's actually put into words and placed before the person about to be abandoned, and who neither suspects nor imagines it – because not even we deceitful, cowardly, dilatory, slow abandoners suspect or imagine it, but come up with all kinds of reasons why we should not: for the avoidance of guilt or to save her pain – the person whose fate it will be to languish incredulously and even pine palely away.

Muriel rested his hands on his chest, one hand still grasping the now extinguished pipe that he hadn't bothered to relight. Instead of beginning to dictate, as he had announced he would, he remained silent for a couple of minutes, while I gazed at him interrogatively, pen at the ready, until, fearing the ink would dry up, I replaced the cap. He seemed suddenly to have forgotten what it was he had been about to do, as though a thought or a problem had crossed his mind, or a much-mulled-over dilemma had swept away everything else, apart from me as a possible chance adviser or simply as an ear to listen to his anxieties: from his position on the floor, he kept shooting me doubtful or almost furtive glances, as if he had something on the very tip of his tongue – a few times he opened his mouth and took a breath, then closed it again – something he could not bring himself to say, that is, to have me hear, as though pondering whether or not it would be right to share with me a matter that troubled and disturbed him or even burned him inside. He cleared his throat once, twice. The words were fighting to get out, held in by prudence, a desire for secrecy or, at least, discretion, as if the matter were a delicate one and should not perhaps be aired in public, or even put into words, because once spoken it would instal itself in the atmosphere and be very hard to expel. I waited without saying anything, without insisting or urging him to speak. I waited confidently and patiently because even then

I knew – one learns this early on, in childhood – that the thing one is tempted to say, to tell or ask or propose, almost always bursts out, emerges, as though no force – no restraint or even reason – were strong enough to stop it, for we nearly always lose our battles against our own excitable tongues. (Or the tongue itself is angry, dictatorial.)

'You, who are from a different generation and will, therefore, see things differently,' Muriel said at last, still tentatively and cautiously. 'Yes, you, who are young and from another generation,' he repeated, thinking he was buying time and might still be able to interrupt himself and say nothing, 'what would you do if you heard that a friend you'd known most of your life . . .' He paused, as if he were about to reject what he had just said and begin again: 'How can I put it, how can I explain . . . that a friend of many years' standing had not always been what he is today? Not as you have known him and as he now is, or as you had always believed him to be?'

Given this succession of confused and vacuous questions, he was clearly still struggling. Muriel was rarely confused, on the contrary, he prided himself on being very precise, although sometimes, in his search for precision, he did have a tendency to ramble. Depending on my response, he still had time to retreat ('Oh, don't worry, let's just let the matter drop' or 'No, no, forget it' or even 'No, it's best you know nothing about it, it's not your business and, besides, it's an unpleasant affair; you wouldn't be able to help me and you wouldn't understand either'). And so I decided to wait and adopted an expression of intense interest, as if I were on tenterhooks waiting for him to speak and there was nothing in my life that interested me more; but when he continued to say nothing – entangled in his own tangled thoughts – I realized that it was up to me to give him a verbal cue and, before he could withdraw entirely, I asked boldly:

'What do you mean? Some kind of betrayal? An act of treachery against yourself?'

I saw that he could not allow my mistaken interpretation to pass, even though it was an interpretation of a mist, a darkness, a mere nothing, and I thought he would have no option but to continue, at least a little.

He put his pipe in his mouth, chewed the end and spoke from between clenched teeth, as if not wanting me to be able to hear too clearly what he had to say. As if what he was saying were, perhaps, pure bluff.

'No, that's the problem. If it were, I would know how to confront him, how to deal with the situation. If it affected me directly, I would have no hesitation in going to him and demanding an explanation. Or if it turned out to be something truly unforgivable, a *casus belli*, I would simply never speak to him again. But that isn't the case here. The matter doesn't concern me at all, it has nothing to do with me or with our friendship, and yet . . .' He did not complete his sentence, and withdrew into himself again, finding it hard to admit what he believed to be the truth.

I did not believe what I said next, but I either thought or sensed that it would help to draw him out, because, as soon as someone begins to tell or to insinuate something – something delicate or salacious or forbidden, some presumably grave matter, about which he is unsure whether or not he wants to speak – we immediately do our best to draw him out. It's almost a reflex reaction, largely for our own amusement, for what used to be called 'sport'.

'Why don't you just ignore it, then? Why not let it pass? It might not be true, a mere calumny or a simple mistake. After all, if it doesn't actually concern you, why get involved? Or you could, of course, ask him about it, ask him to confirm or deny it. If you're really good friends, then he'd tell you the truth, wouldn't he?'

Muriel removed the pipe from his mouth and raised his free hand to his cheek, although I couldn't say whether his cheek was resting on his hand or his hand on his cheek, it's hard to know when someone's lying on the floor. He turned his wise eye towards me; up until then, it had been staring at the ceiling, at the higher shelves in the library, at a painting by Francesco Casanova hanging on the wall of his study: he was very proud to be the owner of an oil painting by someone who was not only the younger brother of the famous Giacomo, but also Catherine the Great's favourite painter, as he told me more than once ('Catherine the Great *of Russia*,' he explained, as if doubting my historical knowledge, not entirely wrongly). He looked at me, trying to judge how genuine or how ingenuous my interest was, if I really wanted to find a solution or was merely being kind or, worse still, was eager for gossip. He must have given provisional approval to my response, because after several inquisitive seconds that made me very nervous and during which I myself was tempted to examine my conscience, he said:

'Not necessarily. No one would readily admit to something like that, anyone would deny it to whoever asked them, to a friend, an enemy, a stranger, a judge, not to mention his wife or his children. What would he say if I asked him? Was I mad? Who did I take him for? Didn't I know him better than that? He'd say these were malicious lies or the product of some vile settling of accounts by a spiteful, devious person who harboured an implacable grudge against him, the kind of grudge that never dies. No, he would demand to know who had come to me with such a story. And I would doubtless have to lose his friendship, on his insistence not mine. And then he would be the disappointed party. Or would feel justifiably insulted if it turned out to be false.' He paused for a moment, perhaps in order to imagine the absurd scene, that plea for sincerity. 'No, don't be silly,

Juan. There are many occasions on which a No is the only possible answer and such a No clarifies nothing, is useless. It's the answer one would get whether it was true or not. A Yes can be useful sometimes, but a No almost never, especially when the subject under discussion is something ugly or shameful or when it's a matter of getting what you want at all costs or of saving your skin. It's of no value in itself. Accepting it is an act of faith, and the faith is ours not that of the person saying No. Besides, faith is a fickle, fragile thing: it stumbles, recovers, grows stronger, cracks. And is lost. Belief can never be trusted.'

'What on earth has he been told about this dubious friend of his – or, rather, this friend who suddenly appears to be dubious – what can he have said or done?' I wondered, or thought. 'After half a life of utter clarity.' Or perhaps that isn't what I thought, but only how I remember it now that I'm no longer young and am more or less the same age as Muriel was then or perhaps older; it's impossible to recover the inexperience of your inexperienced youth once you've moved on considerably; once you've understood something, it's impossible to not understand what you once didn't understand, ignorance doesn't return, not even when you want to describe a time during which you either basked in or were the victim of ignorance, and never trust anyone who tells you something with a falsely innocent look on his face, feigning the lost innocence of childhood or adolescence or youth, or who adopts the gaze – the icy, frozen gaze – of the child he no longer is, and the same is true of the old man who speaks out of the years of his maturity rather than out of the old age that now dominates his entire vision of the world, his knowledge of other people and of himself; even the dead – could they speak or whisper – would distort the truth, putting themselves in the shoes of the foolish, unfinished living beings they once were, pretending they hadn't yet entered the realm of death and metamorphosis and had no knowledge of what they had once been capable of doing and saying, given that they have done and said everything and there is no possibility now of surprise or emendation or improvisation, that account is closed, never to be opened again . . . 'He said, "No one would readily admit to something like that", so it must be something very murky, some very dirty linen indeed, but what? Some "spiteful, devious person", yes, he said that too, and I assumed he meant a woman, although those two adjectives could easily be applied to a man as well, after all, why not, and yet when he said them, I instantly imagined a woman as the source of the information . . . He's wondering whether or not to tell me what it's about, this thing he has so painfully discovered. He's afraid that if he confides in me, it will seem still more real or more certain, that the more he speaks about it, the more validity he'll be giving it, the more he'll be condemning his friend, and it's only natural that he would prefer not to do that. But nor can he dismiss out of hand what he has heard, or perhaps the matter so worries and troubles him that he can no longer keep it to himself, it stalks his thoughts day and night, but he doesn't know who he can speak to about it without making the matter seem even more significant, even more serious. Perhaps he sees me as the least important of his acquaintances, precisely because of my youth, my inexperience and my complete inability to move in his world of the fully adult. And if I were to decide to blab about it, my voice lacks weight and credibility. That's why he has chosen me, because of my insignificance,' I thought. 'Telling me is the closest he can get to telling no one. He'll feel safer with me than with anyone else, I can be dismissed and never seen again, I can almost be cancelled out, sooner or later I will be a mere empty space. That means I can also inquire, probe, draw him out. I have no resonance, I bring no consequences.'

'I can't really give you an opinion, Don Eduardo, I mean, Eduardo,' I said, correcting myself, and that 'Eduardo' grated on my ears, sounded horribly disrespectful, 'if you don't tell me a little more. You asked what I would do, but since I don't know what the problem is, I can't really answer. And since you say that even if you went to see your friend, you still couldn't be certain he would tell you the truth, that he would deny the whole thing and that his No would be of no use to you . . . Well, I really don't know what you should do. Put pressure on the person who told you the story, try to get them to withdraw it, to retract? Although it seems unlikely, doesn't it, that someone would go back on what he'd said once he'd taken the step of uncovering something ugly that showed someone else in such a bad light? You could try to glean more through third parties, to test out the truth of what you've been told. Only you can know if that would work, it often doesn't. It seems to me that it all depends on what that something is, and how far it can coexist with your friendship and how far you can live with the shadow it casts. As I said, you could just forget it, suppress it, let it go. If it's impossible to know the truth, then I suppose we're at liberty to decide for ourselves what the truth is.'

The maritime eye regarded me differently, curiously, with perhaps a touch of suspicion, as if Muriel had not expected such pragmatism from me, we tend to assume that youth is all vehemence and intransigence, hating uncertainty and awkward compromises, as having an element of fanaticism in its search for any truth, however small and circumstantial that might be.

'It's always impossible to know the truth. One never can,' he said. 'The truth is a category –' He broke off; he was thinking about what he was saying while he was saying it, this was not a sentence he had worked out beforehand; or else he was remembering it as if it were a quotation. 'The truth is a category that remains in suspension while we're alive.' He pondered this phrase for a few seconds, gazing up at the ceiling, as though expecting to see it appear there, like the words and names that teachers of old used to write so painstakingly on the blackboard. 'While we're alive,' he repeated. 'Yes, it's illusory to go in pursuit of the truth, a waste of time and a source of conflict, sheer folly. And yet we can't not do it. Or, rather, we can't help wondering about it, knowing that it does exist and is to be found in a place and a time to which we have no access. I realize that I'll probably never know for sure if that friend did or didn't do what I've been told he did. But I also know that the truth will be one of two things, or rather three: he either did it or didn't do it or he did something in between, something not as black as I've been told and not as white as he would describe it to me. The fact that I'm doomed not to find out doesn't mean that the truth doesn't exist. The worst thing is that, by this stage, even the person concerned may not know what the truth is. When many years or even not so many years have passed, people tell the facts as it suits them to and come to believe their own version, their own distorted view of the facts. They often erase them altogether, banish them, blow them away like a piece of thistledown' – he made a gesture with his fingers as if he were holding a thistle head, but he did not blow – 'they convince themselves that nothing happened or that their role in events was quite different from what it actually was. There are cases of genuine amnesia or honest distortion, in which the person lying is not lying or at least not consciously. Sometimes not even the perpetrator of an act can dispel our doubts; he's simply incapable of telling the truth. It's all a blur, he can't remember, he muddles things up or simply doesn't know. And yet that doesn't mean there isn't a truth, there is. Something happened or didn't happen, and if it did happen, it did so in a certain way, that is how it took place. Notice that expression "to take place", which we use as a synonym of "happen" and "occur". It's curiously appropriate and exact, because that is precisely what happens with the truth, it has a place and there it stays; and it has a time and it stays there too. It remains locked up inside that time and place and there's no way we can undo that lock, we can't travel back to either time or place in order to get a glimpse of their contents. All we're left with are guesses and approximations, it becomes a matter of encircling the truth and trying to make out its shape in the distance or through veils and mists, but we never can, it's just a ridiculous waste of time . . . And yet, and yet . . .'

He coughed, a nervous cough I thought, impotent, uneasy. He sat up and leaned slightly to one side, one elbow resting on the floor, to feel for the matches in his trouser pocket so as to relight his pipe. He also took out an antique silver pillbox with a tiny compass on the lid; he used to study that compass imprisoned behind glass whenever he was plunged in thought, whenever he didn't know how to continue or if he should continue, whenever he was filled by doubts and more doubts, as if he were hoping that the compass needle would guide him, would perhaps stop pointing north. I had the feeling that not only was he uncertain as to whether or not to reveal to me his friend's supposed crime or vile deed or mean act (I knew for the moment that it wasn't a betrayal), but also whether or not he should charge me with some related task, some mission, a bit of espionage, an investigation, whether he should ask me to intervene, though who knows how, for it would be hard for me to help without knowing the facts or, indeed, even if I did know them. And yet that was the feeling I had, that the hardest thing for him was deciding whether or not to involve me in something grubby, disagreeable, foul, knowing that if he did succumb to the temptation of involving me, I would cease to be a mere listener or even confidant and instead become party to certain facts or, rather, to a suspicion and a rumour. It was as if he knew that, once he explained the situation to me, he would also have to direct or guide me, to give me an order or ask me a favour.

26

'And yet what?' I didn't know how else to encourage him to speak, apart from showing that I was interested and prepared to listen. I realize now that this was a sign of my youth, because what could be easier than drawing someone out when almost everyone is bursting to talk?

At last, Muriel got nimbly and effortlessly to his feet and began pacing up and down before me, taking long strides around the living room and the study, skirting the desk, and I had to keep craning my neck so as not to lose sight of him, his pipe in one hand and, in the other, the pillbox, which he kept rubbing against his chin, as if smoothing a fortunately non-existent goatee beard – 'fortunately' because men who wear such beards are not usually to be trusted. He would also occasionally study the compass on the box. It amused me to see his one eye scrutinizing that diminutive object, and he did so, I think, partly for comic effect, perhaps to mitigate the waves of vacillation and anxiety given off by his endless circumvolutions.

'And yet, and yet,' he repeated, or replied, 'I have no option but to try and get closer, to dispel the mist or remove the veil, to waste a little of my life on it. Sometimes, in order to justify making a decision, to, as you put it, decide what the truth is and to stick fast to that truth from then on and for ever, all it takes is the removal of a single layer, even if you only pretend to remove it. After that one attempt – however sceptical and superficial – you can, as you suggested, ignore

27

what you've been told or else believe it wholeheartedly and allow a friendship to languish, put it on hold or end it once and for all, but not immediately. You need either to have in your possession or to acquire some clue to serve as a guide, however false or erroneous. We have to find by our own means some way of orienting ourselves' – and he tapped with the stem of his pipe on the glass cover – 'some intuition that will allow us to say: "That's a downright lie" or "Oh dear, it must be true."' He suddenly stopped pacing and looked at me, a look of infinite sorrow, but I couldn't tell who he was feeling sorry for, himself or me, because I had so much still to discover, so far to go. I find myself looking at young people like that now, when I see them worried and bewildered or discouraged, and also when I see them excited and full of plans, and I cross my fingers to wish them luck, a pointless, superstitious gesture, a gesture of resignation. It's a paternalistic look that ignores the fact that we are all different and that some generations are more worldly-wise than others; I think my generation was tougher than Muriel's and, beneath our motley idealistic disguises, we certainly had fewer scruples. 'My first impulse was to believe what I was being told,' he went on, still wearing the same sorrowful expression. 'I had an initial doubt, but dismissed it out of hand because I thought no one would lie about something so important. Not important for other people, because it would be a matter of indifference to most, but important for the person telling me that lie or that truth. You assume that no one would willingly harm himself, at least you probably still do at your age. How old are you now? Twenty-three? It certainly took me a long time to learn that this was a false assumption, that one should assume nothing. People make wild calculations and are often prepared to take a risk. Most suffer from a strange overdose of optimism, convinced they'll get their own way, that they'll change things or that luck will smile on them; that

28

any harm inflicted will be compensated for in the long term by some greater benefit and that no one will ever find out what they said or did in order to gain their objective: to hold on to someone, to ruin another, to send someone else to prison or to the wall, to profit from something and grow rich, or to get into bed with some woman. And perhaps they're right, we probably never will know very much about what really happened, most of which will never see the light of day. And so on that occasion, I didn't test out what I was told, I just accepted it and acted accordingly and held to my decision and thus ruined one life or perhaps two or even three, depending on your point of view, perhaps more if you count any descendants, individuals who should never really have been born and others who were prevented from being born in their place.' After this *excursus*, he resumed his pacing, still with his pipe in one hand and the compass in the other, then added: 'Yes, I'm going to have to waste a little of my life over this friend of mine.'

I didn't understand much of what he was saying. He was circling around another story now, a story from the past, possibly the remote past, but, again, he wasn't really telling me that story either. Finally, I thought of a question that might encourage him to be more explicit. He had mentioned the possibility of bringing his friendship to a drastic end, were this justified by his tentative future inquiries or explorations or intuitions. But if what he had been told did not affect or involve him personally, almost only one thing, at that time and in our country, would be deemed so objectionable as to merit ending a friendship that had lasted half a lifetime. In those days, in those years, certain distant events were just beginning to be discussed in private, things that many Spaniards had been obliged to keep quiet about in public for decades and which had only very occasionally been talked about in whispers within the family and with ever-longer intervening silences, as if, quite apart from the forbidden nature of the subject matter, there was a desire to confine such events to the realm of nightmares, to relegate them to the bearable fog of what may or may not have happened. Such is the fate of things deemed shameful, the fate of all humiliations and impositions. None of us likes to dwell on past defeats or on the times when we or our families were the victims of injustices or acts of cruelty or were forced to surrender or to pander to the other side in order to survive, to betray our comrades in order to ingratiate ourselves with the vicious new powers that be – who are also tireless persecutors of the defeated – or to crouch in a corner so as not to attract attention, leading a cowardly, submissive life spent kowtowing to the crazy demands of the victorious regime; and – despite the damage inflicted by that regime, of which you and your parents or siblings all had personal experience – to try to embrace it, praise it, become part of it and thus prosper under its aegis. Nowadays, people tell many a tall tale of unbowed resistance fighters, whether passive or active, but the truth is that most real-life resistance fighters – of whom there were few and all of them short-lived – were shot or imprisoned during the years after the War or else went into exile or were purged and suffered reprisals and were prevented from freely exercising their professions: some were elderly or mature men who spent the rest of their days watching their widows and daughters going out to work so they could afford to buy food – because it was as if their wives were already widows – while they, ill-shaven pre-cadavers – engineers, doctors, lawyers, architects, professors, scientists, even the occasional loyal soldier who had somehow survived – gazed out of the window and tried hard not to think too much. After a while, most of the population were enthusiastically pro-Franco, or were timidly so, out of fear. Many of those who had loathed him and suffered under him gradually became convinced that things were, in fact, better, that they had been mistaken and had lived and even fought in error. Never have there been so many turncoats, such a mass display of turncoatery. The Civil War ended in 1939, and whatever people may say now, no one was eager to give their version of events, I mean those who could not have done so safely, either in the 1940s or 50s, nor, of course, in the somewhat more relaxed 60s or even in the 70s, right up until the death of the dictator in 1975. The winning side had initially repeated their version ad nauseam and continued to do so, but they larded it with so many lies, so much grandiloquence, so many obfuscations, calumnies and prejudices, that, ultimately, their version of events no longer satisfied them and wore so thin with repetition that it reached a point where, on the assumption that everyone must know the story by heart, they, too, fell almost silent and stopped harping on about it and applied themselves instead to forgetting the darker aspects of their deeds, their more superfluous crimes. In the long run, there's little to be gained by imposing your story on other people, it's almost like telling a story to yourself, which is no fun at all: if your views are only ever endorsed by your co-religionists or by mere acolytes and fearful servants, it's a bit like playing yourself at chess. And those who had lost preferred to forget the atrocities committed, either by them or the still worse ones committed by the other side – more enduring, more brutal, more gratuitous – and they certainly didn't tell their children (after all, no one would choose to describe episodes or scenes in which they appear in such a poor light), for whom their one wish was that nothing similar would ever happen to them and that they would be blessed with a boring, uneventful life, albeit a life lived with head bowed and with no real freedom, because one can live without freedom. Indeed, freedom is the first thing that fearful citizens are prepared to give up. So much so that they often ask to lose it, ask for it to be taken away, banished from their sight, which is why they not only applaud the very person intending to take it from them, they even vote for him.

'Is it something to do with the Civil War, Don Eduardo, I mean, Eduardo? Something that your friend did at the time and that you knew nothing about until someone came to you now with the story? Is that what it is?' And I even dared to be more precise and urge him to explain what he meant. 'Did he participate in a massacre? Did he carry out summary executions?' And here I used the expression *darle a uno el paseo*, literally 'take someone out for a stroll', which few young people nowadays would know, but which was still familiar to my generation, because it formed part of the normal vocabulary of both parents and grandparents, and most families had experienced such summary executions during the three years that the War lasted: *darle a uno el paseo* meant going to someone's house with a group of other men, either at night or in the early hours or even in broad daylight, bundling him into a car, driving him to the outskirts of the town, to some deserted spot or even to the cemetery walls, where he would be shot in the head or the back of the neck, and his corpse left at the gates of his future home or, more likely, kicked into the gutter; in Madrid or in Seville, in both the Republican and the *franquista* zones, there were months when not a morning went by without numerous bodies being picked up in the streets, as if they were a new kind of rubbish, too awkward for the road sweepers to deal with, too heavy and difficult to handle, and with a face. 'Was he one of those Falangists who strutted around with a pistol in his belt? Or a militiaman with a rifle over his shoulder? Did he betray someone as soon as the War was over, denounce people he knew and send them to the firing squad? Was he some kind of butcher, did he commit a lot of murders or order others to do so? What is it you've been told, what is it you find so troubling?'

32

Things had changed a little in that respect, as regards telling people things, although not very much. Adolfo Suárez was in power, the first elected Prime Minister for forty years, Franco having died four or five years before. On the one hand, Franco had been instantly discarded and was seen by most as a kind of dinosaur, and, six months on, the more thinking members of the public were astonished at how little time had passed, because it felt as if entire centuries had gone by since his disappearance. It wasn't just that one part of the population had longed and hoped and yearned for this, and that in a number of respects – insofar as this was possible – society had, for some time, begun to behave as if he had already gone; what also became clear, even to his supporters, was the extraordinary speed with which he came to be viewed as a complete anachronism, as superfluous: himself, his dictatorship and his Church, to whom he had granted unlimited powers and privileges. On the other hand, incredible though it seemed, we were aware that his regime had withdrawn almost without a murmur (people commented at the time that the regime had committed hara-kiri), obeying the will of the King, which is why we had been granted democracy. We, of course, had not imposed democracy ourselves, because it would not have been in our power to do so without further spillage of the mingled bloods of both sides, which would have ended in certain disaster, although it

33

didn't take us long to call for more and more freedoms. In those years, though, we were keenly aware that everything hung by a thread, that concessions can always be revoked, that the suicides might well have second thoughts and decide to come back to life, that they had the support of most of the army, who were still *franquista* to the core and remained in possession of the nation's only weapons.

One of the conditions for granting us democracy and for that astonishing act of hara-kiri had been an agreement that, to put it bluntly, no one would call anyone else to account. Not for the distant outrages and crimes of the Civil War committed by both sides at the front and in the rearguard, nor for the infinitely more recent crimes committed by the dictatorship, during the seemingly endless thirty-six years of punitive, vengeful rearguard actions, a boom time for their henchmen and a time of humiliation and silence for everyone else. Although it was far from equitable – the losers had been called to account time and again for both real and imaginary crimes – everyone accepted this condition, not just because it was the only way the transition from one system to another could proceed more or less peacefully, but also because those who had suffered most had no alternative and were in no position to make demands. The promise of living in a normal country – with elections every four years, the legalization of all political parties, a new constitution approved by the majority, no censorship – and, one imagined, the rapid implementation of a new divorce bill – with trade unions, freedom of expression and freedom of the press, and no bishops meddling with the law of the land – all of that was far more alluring than the old quest for an apology or the desire for reparation. Both apology and reparation had been so long postponed, and we had so little faith that they would ever appear, that they'd grown worn and frayed in the eternal, never-advancing journey of hopeless hope. The dead were

34

dead and would not return; those who had spent years unjustly imprisoned had lost those years and would never recover them; the subjugated would cease to be subjugated; political prisoners would be amnestied and released with their criminal record wiped clean; those in exile could come home to grow old and die; no one could be arrested or sentenced arbitrarily; we could punish tyrants by not voting for them, ousting them from their posts and stripping them of their privileges, or at least some of them. So tempting was this future that it was worth burying the past – both the old and the more recent – especially if that past threatened to ruin a future that was, comparatively speaking, so good. Many people nowadays have forgotten all this or know nothing about it, either because they don't remember or because they cannot even conceive of what it means to live under a dictatorship, but to us, who had experienced it at first hand, this promised horizon seemed like an almost impossible dream, and our overriding feeling was one of relief and of great good fortune: we were about to be set free from a totalitarian regime without having to live through any further carnage, and we could at last talk openly about that first time of bloodletting.

And that is what happened, people started talking about the War in broad, historical terms, rather than going into personal or individual details. We accepted the condition and carried it out to the letter, perhaps too faithfully. Under the general amnesty, no one attempted to bring anyone to justice, and this clearly saved us from endless bitter confrontations and accusations and the ever-present possibility of a return of the hara-kiri-ides, although each day that passed pushed them further and further into a ghostly territory from which, by the time they realized what was happening, it was impossible to escape. During those years, therefore, denouncing someone for what they had done during the dictatorship or during the War was unthinkable.

35

Not calling for justice implied a kind of social pact, tantamount to us saying: 'Fine, let's just let sleeping dogs lie. If the price we have to pay for a return to normality and for us not to go back to killing each other is that no one calls anyone to account, then let's just tear up the bills and start again, because, in exchange, we will have, if not the country we wanted, one that comes very close. That, at least, is what we're seeking, without violence, without prohibitions and without rising up in armed struggle against those who win an election fair and square.' They were years of optimism and generosity and hope, and I'm quite sure that, at the time, this was the best possible outcome.

However, something strange happened: the social pact became so internalized that we ended up fulfilling the condition almost too scrupulously, especially when it came to talking about the past. It made good sense for us not to get embroiled with the courts and for the courts not to get clogged up with painful lawsuits that would have made it impossible for us to continue living together and would have ended very badly. Preferring not to know and not to talk about it was another matter entirely. And yet most people chose that route, chose to remain silent, certainly in public, but often in private too. There was still a degree of stoicism and discretion then, this was before the times – which continue to this day – in which everyone saw the advantages of playing the victim and bemoaning and profiting from their personal woes, whether real or imaginary, or those of their antecedents of class or gender, ideology or region. There was a certain sense of elegance that advised against boasting about suffering and persecution, and made those most badly affected hold their tongues. This attitude only changed when a few notable individuals who had supported Franco at some point – either at the beginning, when repression was at its fiercest, or in the middle or at the end – pushed their luck and, not content with their state of impunity, which meant that they could live in peace and unreproached and with the privileges from their past careers intact, began elaborating illusory biographies, pretending that they had been democrats since the Athenian age and claiming that their anti-*franquista* attitudes dated back a long way, if not for ever. They took shelter in the ignorance of the younger citizens – and in the ignorance of the population as a whole – and in the discretion of those of their own age, who knew better. One novelist stated in a newspaper that, when the Civil War broke out, he was in Galicia, a *franquista* stronghold, and so had no alternative but to fight on their side, but that had he been in Madrid, he would have ardently defended the Republic, as had been his intention at the time. Those who knew him also knew that he had, in fact, been in Madrid at the start of the War, and had done all he could to escape from there and travel to Galicia to join the very side he was now renouncing with such aplomb. A historian boasted of his 'years of exile in Paris', when he had, in fact, spent those years working in the Spanish embassy, representing Franco, of course. Another intellectual mentioned his 'enforced exile', which had consisted of a lucrative two-year contract with an American university in the comparatively peaceful 1960s – a time when no one who had survived the worst bothered going into exile – having benefited in previous harsher years from the numerous favours bestowed on him by the regime for being a fellow Falangist and adoring supporter. And there were many more such cases.

These false declarations and denials, these inventions and presumptions, proved irritating to anyone who had genuinely opposed the regime or refused to collaborate, who had suffered for decades and had a pretty fair idea of the role played by various individuals; irritating, that is, to the few people who had the necessary knowledge and memory and so could not be deceived. Most could be and were deceived, because no letters were sent to the press or to the television stations contradicting these pompous asses who, instead of counting themselves lucky to have survived unscathed following the restoration of democracy, had absolutely no compunction about concocting these stories, presenting themselves with non-existent medals, and generally manufacturing a convenient pedigree. The people who knew the truth were accustomed to losing and to keeping quiet. The agreement, the pact of silence, weighed on them excessively, as did the general distaste for and aversion to revenge and betrayal. And so the lies of these former Franco supporters went unchallenged and no one spoke of their personal experiences in public, apart from the brazen few and their fallacious tales. However, the brazen few grew still bolder and went so far with their barefaced lies that they gradually provoked more and more of those in the know to react in private — how much restraint and patience they showed, how much they continue to show now — and to talk about what they knew, what they had done or said or written, how they had behaved during the War and during the dictatorship, behaviour that thousands or even hundreds of thousands of people were now taking great pains to hide, embellish or erase. There were so many backing each other up that the great labour of concealment and disguise was sure to succeed: I'll stand by you if you stand by me, I'll keep schtum for you if you keep schtum for me, I'll put a flattering gloss on your past if you do the same for me. And I thought that perhaps it was some such murmur, from those resisting the sham and telling the truth — toned down, discreet, mentioned only to family members or at meetings and suppers with friends or in the even greater privacy of bed — that had recently reached Muriel's ears.

While I was submitting him to my brief interrogation, Muriel had continued his pacing, every now and then glancing across at me, merely to check that I was still there, still listening, glances that led me to think that he hadn't grasped what I was getting at. He stopped when I stopped talking. Then he gave me a grave, sober look, which I didn't know how to interpret. Perhaps it bothered him to be asked so many direct questions, which might force him to tell me the story when he had not yet decided whether to tell me or not. He put away the pillbox-cum-compass and with his free hand fumbled for his tie underneath his sweater and smoothed it out – it must have got wrinkled or ridden up while he was lying on the floor. He also straightened the knot, although, having no mirror handy, it remained crooked. I pointed this out to him, gesturing with my left hand, and he again adjusted the knot, this time successfully. He went over to one of the sofas, sat down, crossed his legs and said:

'Almost everything has to do with the War, Juan, one way or another. Let's just hope that one day this will cease to be the case, but I fear I won't see that day. I doubt if even you will, despite being so much younger and even though what happened then must seem as remote to you as the Cuban or the Carlist wars or even the Napoleonic invasion. If that's what you believe, then you're quite wrong. You'll continue to hear people talking about our dreadful War for far longer than you might think. Especially those who didn't live through it, because they're the ones who need it most, in order to give meaning to their existence, to feel anger or pity, to have a mission in life, to feel they belong to the right side, to seek retrospective or abstract vengeance, what they would call justice when there can be no posthumous justice; to be moved and to move others to tears, to write books or make films and earn money, to gain prestige, to benefit sentimentally from the poor wretches who died, to imagine hardships and sufferings no one could possibly understand even if they heard about them first-hand; to set themselves up as their heirs. A war like that is a stigma that takes one or even two centuries to disappear, because it contains everything and affects and debases everything. It contains the very worst of everything. It was like removing the mask of civilization that all presentable nations wear, firmly attached like this patch' – and he tapped his own eyepatch – 'and which allows them to pretend. Pretending is essential if we are to live together, to prosper and progress, and here, where we've seen the criminals' true faces, seen what happened, pretence is impossible. It will take a very long time for us to forget what we are or what we could be, and how easily too, all it takes is a single match. There will be times when that war dwindles in importance, as is beginning to happen now, but it will be like one of those family feuds that last for generations, and you find the great-great-great-grandchildren of one family hating the great-great-great-grandchildren of another family even though they have no idea why; simply because that hatred was drummed into them from birth, enough for those two lots of great-great-great-grandchildren to have inflicted harm on each other and thus see in their respective actions proof of what they were told: "Our elders warned us about them, and they were quite right." And so it goes on. None of us can possibly comprehend the harm done by

Franco and his henchmen, by those who began that entirely unnecessary War, with such deliberate, extreme intent, as an exercise in extermination, and who enjoyed it all so much that they didn't want it ever to end. Of course those they attacked were equally extreme. But it isn't just what they did, it's the curse they placed on this country. And, unlike Hitler, the great oafs weren't even aware of that curse. They didn't consider the consequences, why would they? And, on the other hand, on the other hand, who can say how much longer those will last . . .' Muriel stopped speaking and remained sunk in thought, again looking up, perhaps at the painting by Casanova's brother. But it was as if his one eye were contemplating not the horseman in the picture (possibly a scene depicting peaceful military manoeuvres, if that isn't a contradiction in terms), but a very slow, almost motionless, future of imperceptible advances and retreats. That is precisely the effect produced by the best paintings, which, despite everything, never move, going neither forward nor back.

I didn't know if this long speech was intended as a way of avoiding giving me an answer and thus abandoning the subject, but then, I wondered, why had he chosen to bring the subject up in the first place and why ask me that question? I tried again, swearing to myself that it would be the last time, at least for that morning. He would soon be leaving for his office, where he spent most of the morning until lunchtime; at first, he didn't usually take me with him, although later on he did. Sometimes he had lunch out, with other people, and did not come back until mid-afternoon. Sometimes he wouldn't reappear all day and would return only at night when his wife, Beatriz, had gone to bed. If that occurred on several consecutive days, they would only see each other over breakfast. When, that is, he wasn't travelling or filming.

'So is this business with your friend to do with the Civil War or not? You haven't yet answered my question, Eduardo. Or, rather, I'm not sure whether what you've just told me is a Yes or a No. But if you're not more explicit with me, I still can't help you.'

He smiled his luminous smile, and his eye smiled too, sympathetically, indulgently, the look of amused indulgence with which many adults regard or speak to children.

'Don't be in such a hurry, so impatient, I was just coming to that. No, it's neither of the things you mentioned. As far as I know, he didn't kill anyone or take part in any summary executions or send anyone to their death, among other things because he wasn't old enough to do that between 1936 and 1939, or only if he'd been some prodigy of precocious evil, of which there were a few. He's not much older than me. Nor did he betray or denounce anyone. It's actually related to the fact that he apparently didn't betray or denounce anyone. Of course he's always had a reputation for having behaved very well in the post-war years, of having helped those who most needed him, I mean for political reasons. He's irreproachable in that sense, in that respect. As I say, that, at least, has been his reputation.'

I couldn't help but notice the words 'in that respect', as if his friend had been less irreproachable in other respects, which, to be fair, was not so very unusual: there are so many aspects to our lives that we are bound to be found wanting in some. Nor had I failed to notice the even stranger part of what he had said, the part I had most difficulty in grasping, and that I couldn't simply allow to pass:

'Yes, but what I don't understand is how the problem can possibly be related to the fact that your friend neither betrayed nor denounced anyone, isn't that what you said? Because surely that's a good thing. And if what you've been told doesn't imply any crime and doesn't affect you directly because it isn't a betrayal of you as such, well – I mean, you can tell me about it another day, if you like – but I really

42

can't understand what you meant when you said "something like that". Something that you can't dismiss as mere gossip and that anyone would deny to anyone who asked, "to a friend, an enemy, a mistress, a stranger, a judge, not to mention his wife or children". Those were your words. Don't go thinking I haven't been listening. I have, as you see.'

He ran his hand over his cheeks and chin, as if checking to see that he had shaved properly. Then he rubbed his forefinger several times up and down his large, straight nose, which resembled that of a TV actor from my youth, Richard Boone, who also had a slender moustache; in fact, Muriel was possibly more like him than any of the others I mentioned earlier. Then he gently drummed his fingertips on his bulbous eyepatch, doubtless preparing himself to make a decision, although perhaps only as regards me, rather than the matter in hand.

'Look,' he said. 'I'm sorry to have got you all intrigued for no reason, but just for the moment, you're going to have to wait. I still don't know what to do with this story. In fact, it's really bothering me. So much so that I daren't tell anyone else. I don't think I should. Not yet. And if I did tell someone, you or whoever, I would be spreading the story, and there's no way of catching or stopping something once you've thrown it to the winds. Later, depending on what I decide (which will be soon, don't worry, one way or another), I might have to ask you to do something for me, might need your help as my assistant or, more than that, as my bishop or even my knight, for, as you may or may not know, the knight is the most unpredictable piece on the chessboard, capable of leaping over obstacles in eight different directions. I may also simply ask you to forget this whole conversation, as if it had never happened. But I don't want to leave you completely in the dark and, besides, since it's quite likely that you'll

43

meet this friend at some point, you could, anyway, see what you think, since he's the person involved, just to see how he strikes you; one tends not to notice things so much in people one has known for ages. His name is Jorge Van Vechten and he's a doctor. Dr Van Vechten.'

I couldn't resist interrupting him, we all leap up like a coiled spring whenever we hear an unfamiliar word or name. Now I know exactly how that name is written, but when I first heard it (Muriel pronounced it 'Ban Bekten', as did Van Vechten himself and everyone who knew him, although later I was told that in Holland and Flemish-speaking Belgium, they would say 'Fan Fechten' or something like that), I couldn't catch it the first time nor imagine how it was written.

'Van what? Is he Dutch?'

'No, he's as Spanish as you and me.' And he spelled out the obscure part of the name. 'But his distant ancestors must, of course, have been Flemish, like the painter Carlos de Haes or that other artist, Van Loo, although *he* may have been French, but of Dutch descent, or Antonio Moro, who was really Anthonis Mor, they all came to Spain and stayed; or like the soldier-sailor Juan Van Halen and possibly the Marqués de Morbecq, do you know him, he has a collection of editions of *Don Quixote* that would take your breath away; Professor Rico is green with envy. So there have been quite a few in Spain. His family, Van Vechten's that is, came from Arévalo, in Ávila, if I remember rightly, he told me about it once: apparently, there are lots of fair-haired, blue-eyed people there because it's one of the places, in Castile and Andalusia, that was repopulated with Flemings and Germans and Swiss in the time of Felipe IV or Carlos III, or perhaps both, I'm not sure. Not that it matters. Now he's as Spanish as Lorca. Or as Manolete. Or as Lola Flores. Or as Professor Rico himself. Imagine that!' He smiled. He had amused himself more than he had me. I knew Professor Rico only by name. He paused and asked: 'So, can I count on your help if I need it? As an infiltrator, shall we say? Or would you rather not get involved in anything that goes beyond your strict duties? Not that we've ever defined what those are, so they can't be very strict.'

Having just about finished my degree, not only did it suit me perfectly to earn the monthly wage that Muriel paid me, but I counted myself lucky that, thanks to my parents, I had found a job so quickly, however strange and transitory it might be. Most young people then – things have changed since – subscribed to my father's view: 'There's no such thing as a bad job as long as there's no better one in sight.' Also, right from the start, Eduardo Muriel had become for me one of those people whom one admires unreservedly, whose company one finds enjoyable and illuminating and whom one very much wants to please. Or more than that, one of those people whose esteem and approval you hope to gain. As you would with a particularly good lecturer at college or university (although, with one exception, all the teachers in my faculty were absolutely dreadful) or a school teacher, or a guru if you're an ignoramus trying to be less of one, even if only by dint of staying close and being in the presence of his wisdom. At the time, I would have done almost anything Muriel asked, I was at his service and very happily so, and was filled with a growing sense of loyalty that bordered on the unconditional. He wasn't even in the habit of issuing orders, or only when it came to minor matters and practices. When, as in this case, it was something unusual, he would consult me and ask my opinion; he was always polite and never imposed his views on me. He was also very persuasive: having drawn me in, having aroused or pricked my curiosity (and he must have known that, as a great admirer of his, I would be interested in everything he did), he would doubtless know that

I would go wherever he sent me, find out whatever he asked me to, if that was within my capabilities, and would even be prepared to strike up a friendship with the most vile or unpleasant of individuals.

'I'm entirely at your disposal, Don Eduardo, I mean, Eduardo, in whatever way I can help. You just have to tell me when and where. I await your orders. If I should meet Dr Van Vechten, do you want me to give you my impressions?'

'No, if you do meet, which is highly likely, leave it to me to ask you. Don't confuse me by taking the initiative.' He fell silent again. I thought he was going to bring the conversation to a close and would leave any letters to be dictated for another occasion; that he would get up, put on his jacket and head off to his office, where he was usually alone, or so I assumed, or, at most, accompanied by a kind of telephonist-cum-accounts-clerk-cum-representative-cum-housekeeper, a woman who did not come in every day, but only when she wanted to or when Muriel expressly asked her to. Instead, he went on: 'Listen, Juan. A moment ago, when you quoted my words and boasted of your good memory, you said "to a friend, an enemy, a mistress, a stranger . . ." I'm sure I didn't mention a mistress, so where did you get that from? What made you think my friend would have a mistress? Though I did mention a wife and children.'

'I've no idea, Don Eduardo, it was just a manner of speaking. I didn't even realize you were referring to that particular friend, but rather to anyone with some deep, dark secret to conceal. Besides, doesn't everyone have a mistress? Temporary ones at least, on and off. Since there's still no divorce . . . Until they change the law, whenever that will be. Meanwhile people have mistresses, and a mistress is also someone close to you, someone on whom you want to make a favourable impression, from whom you would conceal or deny

46

anything that made you look bad. Anyway, I'm sorry if I misquoted you and for my arrogance.'

He gave an ironic or amused smile.

'So everyone has a mistress, do they? Since it seems to me that you've less experience of life than you have of books or films, what do you know about such things? Not that it really matters, I just happened to notice.' It took only a second for him to recover his air of seriousness or concern, or was it anxiety or sadness, or even perhaps a degree of suppressed or postponed anger, postponed perhaps until his fears were confirmed. And he added: 'You'll find out eventually, but this is the last thing I'm going to tell you today about this discomfiting, distasteful story, a story I wish I'd never heard; as I said, what I was told about my friend Van Vechten has nothing to do with any deaths, not at least with any actual, physical deaths, either to his credit or to his shame, I'm not sure which is the right word here. It's nothing that bad, but it is, in a way, more disappointing, more depressing, more banal and more contemptible. More incongruous.' He had searched around for another more conclusive, all-embracing adjective, but had encountered only that one, as if by chance. He himself seemed surprised by his choice. He shook his head then as though the memory of the story made him shudder. 'Any benefits and favours gained won't haunt his memory or gnaw at his conscience or have left any mark, since nothing irreparable occurred, and so he can wash his hands of it, as if it had never happened. So he won't be worried in the slightest, always assuming it did happen. What stops me simply dropping the matter, rejecting it as frankly unbelievable and not even worth considering, is that, according to what I've been told, the Doctor behaved in an indecent manner towards a woman or possibly more than one. Call me old-fashioned or whatever you like, but that, to me, is unforgivable, the lowest of the low.' He paused briefly,

47

stood up, looked at me with his marine eye as though it could see straight through me or had gobbled me up with one glance, then moved on, in search of something more resistant to his dark gaze; there was such anger in his one blue eye that I felt a flicker of fear, not for myself but just to see that eye grow suddenly so dark, so pitiless; he pointed at me with the stem of his pipe as if I were Van Vechten and his pipe were an accusatory implement or perhaps a knife with which one might cut up a piece of fruit, with no intention, as yet, of using it for any other purpose. 'Do you understand? That's as low as one can go.'

II

I was astonished by these words. Not because they jarred with the general character I attributed to Muriel, who had captivated me right from the start, ever since he put me through a brief examination before taking me on, or, rather, chatted to me and asked a few questions, just to see if he liked me. In his comments and conversations and in his attitude towards most people, he seemed to me one of the most upright, charming, fair-minded men I had ever met or have met since. There was even a kind of ingenuousness – almost innocence – about him, unusual for someone approaching his fifties, a well-travelled, restless man, who, while he'd made some really good films, had nevertheless had to lower himself, with no great fuss – that is, resignedly – to make some distinctly bad ones, at least from his point of view ('To what base occupations one is sometimes reduced: you must be prepared for that, Juan,' he said to me once); someone who had to put up with producers – all of them bandits to a greater or lesser degree – and movie actors and actresses – almost without exception, puerile and spiteful or, which comes to the same thing, cruel and hard as nails, or so he said; someone who spent long periods of time immersed in the pragmatic world of advertising in order to raise lots of money very fast and so allow him to maintain his old family fortune more or less intact; someone who devoted much of his time to seeking exotic sources of funding for the projects that really interested him, a process that involved mixing with the fairly brutal or, at best, surly and cunning people who inhabit the business world – that is, the one real, universal world – and others with whom he had little or nothing in common: he was often called on to have lunch or supper or go to nightclubs or out drinking with uncouth property developers and ignorant secretaries of state, with the loud-mouthed presidents of football clubs or dull producers of milk products, with excitable shoemakers from Elda, canners of tuna and clams from Villagarcía de Arosa or curers of ham from Salamanca, even breeders of fighting bulls – a lot of people are completely crazy about the *idea* of films in general, rather than about the actual films – all of whom he tried to persuade or, rather, cajole into investing, and he himself recognized that he had no real talent for the task, although he had, over the years, acquired a certain expertise. He also occasionally received and entertained various foreigners who were passing through Madrid and who, he had been told by someone in the know, were interested in dipping a toe in the film industry and putting money into some film or other: from semi-retired sly old foxes or hyenas, who had a whole backlist of co-productions behind them and couldn't kick the habit, to the semi-fascistic patrons of Formula 1; from German cigarette manufacturers with an artistic streak to shady Italian property developers (if those two adjectives are not surplus to requirements); from Scotch whisky distillers who didn't know what to do with their excess money and wanted to please a mythomaniac wife who, at the end of that very long and winding road, hoped to sign up or have supper with Sean Connery, to the representative of the adviser of the secretary of some uppity Arab sheikh (here, just one of the adjectives is surplus to requirements) bound for Marbella.

He usually returned from those evenings and encounters exhausted and chastened, and pretty much empty-handed, his usual complaint being: 'You have to speak to fifteen people in order for just one of them to write you a cheque or express an apparently genuine or at least half-credible interest. Then the cheques might bounce and their declared interest vanish. And if that's the case, they'll put you off with a lot of lame excuses, so it's best to assume from the start that any show of interest will lead nowhere.' Sometimes, he returned from these meetings in a state of almost comic humiliation and frustration, by which I mean that he tried to make it seem comic; once he had recovered, he could see the funny side of his frustrations and humiliations, and had both a highly developed sense of the absurd and the ability to take a few knocks. Hoping to dazzle and impress – as I said, he *was* a touch ingenuous – the shrewd, refined owner of a fashion boutique, who had deigned to receive him in her office, he decided to play the intellectual card and launch into some pedantic, historical anecdote about the Second World War, but before he had even completed the first paragraph (admittedly one with various subordinate clauses), she interrupted him with a sympathetic but firm smile: 'That's hardly relevant now and, besides, my time is not like this piece of chewing-gum.' Muriel was completely taken aback (as well as somewhat in awe of this attractive, elegant, educated woman, who was, of course, very well dressed), because there was no chewing-gum in sight, not even an empty packet on the desk or the merest whiff of mint or strawberry. True, the office was so pleasant and so highly perfumed that no other odour could possibly have survived, and at first, Muriel felt as if he were floating helplessly in the air, drunk or even drugged. 'What chewing-gum? What are you talking about?' he asked with genuine curiosity. 'This chewing-gum, although it could be any gum,' and with that, she drew a piece of gum out of her mouth between thumb and forefinger – my boss hadn't noticed that she was chewing anything, she was so distinguished

53

and cultivated, that she must have kept it glued to the roof of her mouth or to her gums while they were talking – and she stretched it out like a long tongue; it came so close that Muriel thought she was about to stick one end of it to his nose and he recoiled despite the coarse sensuality of her gesture, which, on reflection, did not displease him in the least, I think it even rather excited him and he regretted retreating instead of allowing himself to be joined to her by that pink gum or, which comes to the same thing, by her saliva. 'You see how far it will stretch,' added the owner of the boutique, Cecilia Alemany by name, who had amassed a fortune in a matter of years, and she wasn't yet thirty-five. 'Well, my time won't stretch that far. So get to the point, my dear man, and make it snappy.' And with one quick, skilful curl of her tongue, she rolled the long, flexible substance back into her mouth, she probably blew bubbles too, and it would have been a treat to see them, since she was clearly a real artist. Muriel admitted that this gummy threat had left him stammering and embarrassed, almost unable to speak, and that the rest of his spiel (with no subordinate clauses this time) had been one incoherent sentence after another, a mess. His admiration for Cecilia Alemany had only grown as a consequence, and he now considered her to be not only a terrific businesswoman who wouldn't put up with any nonsense or with any smooth-talkers, but also a demigoddess, even though he knew he would never get a single penny out of her for any of his projects, whether cheap or expensive, and that she must have thought him little more than a parasite. What he had found most humiliating – and fascinating too – wasn't her cutting short his erudite, intellectual preamble, but that she had called him 'my dear man', as if he were a labourer she had met down a lane. Whenever she appeared on television or in the newspaper, he would gaze at her enraptured, and a smile would appear on his lips as he listened to what she had to say or else read the relevant article, and he would murmur: 'Ah, Cecilia Alemany, what a remarkable woman. Who wouldn't want to be the object of her esteem rather than of her utmost scorn? Needless to say, there's almost no one alive who would deserve her esteem, myself included; I had a rare opportunity, but, like a peasant, like a fool, I failed to seize it.'

Muriel was generally good-humoured, when he wasn't in one of his dark moods, to which all of us are prey sometimes, or in one of his melancholic, misanthropic phases. He would listen discreetly (alone, although I would come and go and was always nearby, alert to what was happening) to whoever came to him with a request or problem, and there were quite a number in those uncertain times; he would listen to them, their odd appeals amused him and he took an interest in all of them, even those I would have thought he would find boring; he was curious to hear other people's stories, I suppose, even when they seemed somewhat sordid. I observed him lending or giving small or large amounts of money to friends in trouble or to technicians or actors who had worked with him on some film and were having a tough time of it – or even to one or two of their widows, whom he had never met before; but then the world produces widows at a giddying pace and, for most, no financial aid is too small. He did this almost secretly (when they said goodbye, he would slip a cheque or a few notes into their hand, or send them a banker's order the next day), but I was often a witness to those scenes too. He always assumed that any loans he made would never be repaid. One night, when we were having a drink together in Bar Chicote, he said: 'You should never lend more money than you would be prepared to give as a gift to the person asking for a loan. So it's best to gauge quantities carefully and judge how much each person wants or how much pity they inspire, so that you don't feel resentful later on. If they pay it back, so much the better; if they don't, well, that's what you were expecting anyway.'

I believe that modesty and tact led him to cover up his natural generosity (and which, contrary to what happens nowadays, one should never boast about), as well as his extreme sensitivity, which he thought was hidden away, and of which he was probably embarrassed and which, with undeniable skill and talent, but little conviction, he would sometimes try to disguise by being brusque or sarcastic; it was as if he were suddenly aware of how he should behave and had to press a button to set that behaviour in motion, as if he decided to act, but only after an almost imperceptible pause; as if any intemperate or impertinent outbursts always required a minimum of willpower – a little play-acting, a little fabrication. Perhaps the only person with whom there was no such transition – not always, but at least most of the time – the only one who regularly bore the brunt of those harsh, unpleasant, cold outbursts, was his poor wife, Beatriz Noguera, or so she seemed to me, a poor, unhappy woman, sad and affectionate. Poor soul, poor wretch.

That's why I was so astonished by those words: 'That, to me, is unforgivable, the lowest of the low. Do you understand? That's as low as one can go', the words with which he had brought the conversation – his lament – to a close for that day and for several more to come. It was the idea that Van Vechten had behaved in an indecent manner towards a woman, 'or possibly more than one', that had provoked these drastically negative statements and prevented Muriel from choosing to forget the troubling thing he had been told about Van Vechten. Knowing Muriel's ideas and having observed his habits and seen some of his films – especially those he had made in the days of censorship, with one version intended for the home market and another for abroad, or made solely for the foreign market – it seemed to me impossible that he would use the word 'indecent' when applied to sexual behaviour, to disapprove of or condemn any such activity from a moral or religious perspective (the latter was quite simply unimaginable). Despite the intrinsically ambiguous nature of the term, when I heard him say it, I understood him to mean 'vile', 'despicable' or 'base', and certainly not 'sinful' or 'obscene'. And it struck me as both paradoxical and shocking that he should find such behaviour so execrable – I noticed that he laid special emphasis on the fact that the victim was a woman, possibly more than one – when he, who could often be utterly charming and indeed was so with almost everyone, as long as he didn't instantly judge them to be either pompous or imbecilic, made one exception, his own wife, Beatriz Noguera, the person who was and had been closest to him for much of his life, regardless of how much time he spent, and always had spent, filming and on location, on occasional pilgrimages in search of funds, and on visits to actors and actresses whom he had to flatter into taking a role in his films, although there was a time when they were the ones to flatter him and were eager to be involved in his projects, at least among Spaniards and the occasional other European national, and even among certain Americans, nonconformist or arty types (everything that came out of Europe at the time was considered to be arty). This period had lasted for only five or six years, because the period during which a film-maker is deemed fashionable can be very brief, a gentle breeze that almost never returns.

By the time I got to know him and his wife, he was no longer going away quite so often and was working less than he had in the past. He still enjoyed a certain prestige, and the fact that he'd made a couple of feature films in the States, with American money and some fairly big names, conferred on him an almost mythical aura in a country as easily impressed as ours. He capitalized on this as best he could – as well as on his image as a slightly mysterious, elusive figure – but he had no illusions about his position. 'I'm a bit like Sara Montiel,' he would say, 'she dined out for years on her three or four Hollywood appearances, one of which meant sharing the screen with Gary Cooper and Burt Lancaster. She wasn't so lucky with the others: Rod Steiger, despite his Oscar and all that, wasn't much help to her, because he was too unpleasant, too histrionic and unpopular, and poor Mario Lanza was no use at all, because he died soon afterwards and who now has heard of him or remembers him? You don't even hear his famous voice any more. So I depend in large measure not only on what I do from now on, like anyone else, but also on the future careers, stretching far ahead, of the people who worked for me, no, more than that, on how long they survive in filmgoers' fickle memories. In my world, and, indeed, in all worlds, you never know who will be remembered, not just in five or ten years' time, but the day after tomorrow, or even tomorrow. Or who will leave not the slightest trace, however glittering their career, as they say on TV and in the magazines. In a few years' time, the stars that shine brightest now might as well never have existed. And any real hate-objects are guaranteed oblivion, unless they truly were evil and people enjoy hating them retrospectively, even after they've left the stage or died.'

With Beatriz Noguera, he was often sharp and malicious, even cruel and hateful, verbally that is. He could be really foul. I had known bickering couples – who hasn't? – who often traded wounding comments, almost casually, as though they couldn't help themselves. People who stay together out of sheer habit, because they're as much a part of each other's existence as the air they breathe, or at least as the city they live in and which, however unbearable, they would never dream of leaving. Each spouse has about the same value as the view from the living room or bedroom of their apartment: they are neither good nor bad, loathsome nor pleasant, depressing nor stimulating, beneficial nor harmful. They are simply what's there – the envelope, the setting, the day's normal grey pallor – we never question them or consider the possibility of dispensing with their breathing or with their permanent nearby murmurings, never consider making them change or improving the terms of our relationship. We take them for granted, they seem to be an utterly natural part of our existence, and we continue in their company, but not because we have decided to, nor do we even consider ceasing or reversing or suppressing our relationship, as if this were quite impossible, as if it were fate, just as we happened to be born in a particular country or in the bosom of a particular family or ended up with those particular parents or siblings. Such couples completely forget that they ever made a choice, albeit only partial or apparent and tinged with resignation, they forget that the presence of the other could be eliminated quite easily, unless, of course, they chose to use violence, and then the ensuing complications would be either infinite or non-existent, depending on the skill with which they rid themselves of the obstacle, or sometimes they have merely grown bored with looking at the same scenery. Otherwise, there are complications, but not that many, especially if divorce is legal, as it is in Spain today and has been for more than thirty years. Nevertheless, a few melodramatic scenes are pretty much inevitable.

This was not the case with Eduardo Muriel and Beatriz Noguera, his was not, to put it in pedantic terms, a quotidian or perfunctory aggression. There was on his part a deep-seated antagonism, vital and pulsating and far from ordinary, and a kind of strangely inconstant desire to inflict frequent punishments. It was as if he had to force himself to remember (once the right ice-cold button had been pressed) that he must behave towards her with a complete lack of consideration, with revulsion and scorn, to make it clear to her what a curse and a burden it was to endure her presence; to mistreat and even abuse her, and certainly to undermine her and make her feel insecure and even hopeless about her personality, her work, her body, and he was doubtless successful; after all, anyone can do that, even the most stupid of us, it's the easiest thing in the world to destroy and wound, you don't have to be especially wily or astute, still less intelligent, a fool can easily crush someone cleverer, and Muriel was a clever man. You just have to be ill-natured, ill-intentioned, ill-disposed, qualities to be found in abundance among the brutish and the dim. I sometimes had the feeling that, at some point in his married life, Muriel had decided to embark on a revenge that would never end, never be sated, and I wondered about his possible motives, what unforgivable offence Beatriz Noguera might have committed. Not that I was convinced she had. I was already aware that the cruellest of individuals depend a great deal on the puzzlement of others, trusting that their assaults will seem so disproportionate that other people, rather than judging the assailant severely and trying to placate him or get him to stop, will merely shrug and wonder what terrible crime the object of his cruelty could have committed, and conclude, even though they have no idea if they're right or wrong, that 'it must have been something really bad, otherwise how explain such venom; whatever it is must justify such extreme behaviour'. And the cruel beast does his best to ensure that no one uncovers the truth, that nothing leaks out about that 'whatever it is', the mysterious alibi, which, up to a point, protects the perpetrator and, odd though it may seem, even saves him.

So I was greatly alarmed by what I saw and heard, because it made me think that, when no witnesses were around, his irritation would only increase, his wounding words would become still more cutting, and he might even use foul language, which he rarely did in my presence or even when we were with his friends. I trusted that it never went beyond words, that he never raised his hand to her (I was less alarmed by the thought that she might slap his face, for she had more than enough reason to), and I didn't believe he would ever do that. My belief, however, was also my wish, which meant that my belief was necessarily a qualified one, and this did not entirely reassure me. At first, I didn't dare ask Muriel what lay behind the sharp, sullen, scornful way in which he treated his wife, he had already warned me once that he wasn't paying me to ask questions about matters that were none of my business, and on that occasion I'd been asking him about something far less delicate than his wretchedly unhappy relationship with his wife, namely, the silencing of his now silent eye. And in those early days, I rarely or almost never saw Beatriz on her own; she viewed me from afar as a mere appendage of her husband, which I suppose I was. And yet, doubtless because of my youth, she looked on me kindly. Besides, I was always solicitous and attentive, which is how I was brought up to treat all women (initially), and I was in no way infected – as would have been equally inappropriate – by my boss's rough ways. On the contrary, I tried to oppose them, insofar as I could, without stepping out of line or butting in where I wasn't wanted. I mean that I would always, without fail, stand up whenever Beatriz entered the room, although Muriel never followed my example, but then, between a married couple, that might have been a touch excessive; I would greet her with a slight nod, as if we were still living in the nineteenth century, and with a broad, spontaneous smile, making it clear by my amiable attitude that, should she ever need me, I would always be glad to help. She was, after all, the wife of my employer, a man whom I admired. As such, she deserved my utmost respect and all I could do was to demonstrate this to her, regardless of what great rifts lay between them. And Muriel would doubtless have ticked me off had he noticed the slightest negligence in my treatment of his wife. I should add that there were also times when he spoke or listened to her with deference, interest and even affection. As I said, I found it very easy to be nice to her. In fact, I liked Beatriz Noguera right from the start.

I didn't like her any less than I did her husband, which says a lot; her life, albeit in a different way, was also being ground down by the weak wheel of the world, and I imagined that the indifferent sentinel observing all our lives would be more than usually bored by hers. But who knows, that same moon, just as we writers do (even if we only write private memoirs or diaries or letters, not intending them to be read by anyone or perhaps by just one person), may occasionally take a long hard look at those who will never go beyond their own bounds, those who one knows early on will leave no trace or track and will barely be remembered once they disappear (they will be like falling snow that does not settle, like a lizard climbing up a sunny wall in summer, like the words, all those years ago, that a teacher painstakingly wrote on the blackboard only to erase them herself at the end of the class, or leave them to be erased by the next teacher to occupy the room) and about whom not even their nearest and dearest will have any anecdotes to recount. That sentinel has doubtless grown weary of watching with half an eye the battles and travails of those whose foolish fate and future it can already foresee, weary of hearing their shouts and embarrassed by their bragging, of being present at the usually avoidable tragedies most such creatures bring upon themselves, and to which, from time immemorial, it has sworn to be a silent witness, impartial and useless, as darkness falls and throughout the night. Yes, just to pass the time – to vary and escape the tedium imposed on it by the monotonous masses – it might notice those beings who seem to tiptoe through life and to be just passing through or on temporary loan even while they're alive, knowing that some of them might well harbour stories that are far odder and more intriguing, clearer and more personal, than the stories of the shrill exhibitionists who fill most of the globe with their racket and exhaust it with their wild gesticulations.

For a time, I assumed that this night sentinel would pay closest attention to what Shakespeare called 'a woeful bed', like that of the young widowed princess, whose husband had been murdered in Tewkesbury, stabbed in a conveniently 'angry mood' by the person who had most to gain. Except that Muriel was still alive and, when he was in Madrid, he shared an apartment with Beatriz. They did not, however, share a bedroom, they each had their own, and I soon realized that she was banned from entering his room, its door kept firmly shut day and night, night after night and day after day.

It was after a week or more of intense work, involving the feverish preparation and translation of a hastily cobbled-together script to be presented to Harry Alan Towers (I was, by then, an English graduate), when Muriel decided that I should spend the night there so that I could work until late and start again, without delay, the following morning. It was the first time I'd stayed over in his spacious apartment (although there were other occasions later on), in a big house near the top of Calle Velázquez, with, from the balconies, a view to one side of the Parque del Retiro; an old house that had not yet been divided up into several smaller apartments, as has become the norm in Madrid and in other cities since the well-to-do or merely bourgeois families ceased to be quite so large and dispensed with any live-in servants; the Muriels still employed a maid, who had been the children's nanny when they were small. The very long corridor was in the shape of a U, although it seemed more like a J if you stopped in the kitchen, where you felt it came to a complete halt, just where the curve of a J would end. The maid's room was immediately before that, and she took efficient care of all the housekeeping, a stoical or possibly merely puzzled woman – or maybe these were simply the disguises adopted by her discretion – who had probably been of an indefinable age ever since she was in the first flower of youth (it was odd to think of her like that, even retrospectively and speculatively) and who bore the unlikely name of Flavia, as if she were a Roman. Anyway, a white door at the far end of the kitchen gave unexpected access to the rest of the apartment, and once you got past a tiny bedroom and a minuscule bathroom with a shower over one of those once fashionable hip baths (an idiotic, uncomfortable invention) and an area of apparently redundant space reached through a low, arched doorway, seemingly made for children or dwarves, you returned once more to the corridor and the remaining part of the U. And that *chambre de bonne* with barely enough space for a bed and a chair – it had probably belonged to the maid in bygone days, and the room Flavia now occupied would have been the cook's room, for cooks traditionally had more authority – was where I stayed for those few nights, as though I were living in a diminutive, separate apartment, almost cut off from the rest of the house, given that the only access was through the kitchen. However, this wasn't quite true because, as I said, if you went through that gnome-sized door, theoretically unusable – it had no external handle or knob, only an internal one, so while you could open it from the inside, from the corridor it appeared to be blocked, and there was no lighting in that forgotten area either – you then found yourself at the end of the U and, although you were some considerable distance from the apartment proper and from the main bedrooms, all or most of those rooms opened out on to that corridor.

It was only on my second night that I noticed the empty area adjacent to my bolt-hole, from which it was separated by another small but less pygmyish door, which I had been too exhausted even to notice on the first night. On the second night, however, my brain was perhaps overexcited by the frenetic pace of work and the slap-dash, improvised nature of that script being written at breakneck speed, and I was so wide awake that I sat down on the bed fully clothed, intending to smoke and read and while away the hours. And for a long time, I looked around me without noticing anything, until I realized that what I had mistakenly assumed to be a built-in, white lacquer wardrobe was no such thing. Its door opened on to a very narrow space that had probably once been used as a small lumber room, but which was now clean and empty, and just beyond was that other tiny door which I automatically assumed would bring me out into the corridor. I opened it and, as soon as I did, saw that it could only be opened from the inside and that if I wanted to return by the same route, without having to go via the kitchen, I would have to take care not to close it behind me. I was just about to crouch down and peer through – I was still half-sitting on the bed – when I saw a dim light in the distance and the figure of Beatriz Noguera in a night-dress taking short steps back and forth in the corridor outside her husband's bedroom – or, rather, her steps were not particularly short, it was just that the area she was pacing up and down in was very small – she was not so much pacing as prowling. My first impulse was to withdraw into my room, but instead I assumed a squatting position and stayed there watching, realizing at once that it would be virtually impossible for her to see me: I was crouched down at a distance and in darkness, and no one would expect that door, which must have been closed for ages, to open. Beatriz did not once glance over to where I was hiding, not just because it didn't occur to her that, most unusually, someone was occupying that abandoned spot, but because every one of her five senses was focused on what she was doing, even though she was merely smoking – she had a cigarette in one hand and, in the other, the cigarette packet and an ashtray – and walking back and forth outside the closed door, as if waiting for someone who was late for an appointment.

She wasn't wearing a dressing gown, just a brief, thigh-length nightdress that revealed her strong legs, and at first I thought she was barefoot, because her steps made no sound or so little that you could almost blame any noise she made on the disquiets of the somewhat elderly wooden floorboards, which, like all old floorboards, occasionally seemed to be bemoaning all the things they had seen, after the manner perhaps of old ships, although far less so, given that they are never called on to be pitched and tossed by the waves. Her nightdress was made of white or cream-coloured silk, and was either slightly transparent or, because of the way the light fell – from a discreet wall lamp in the corridor – merely seemed more than usually transparent, allowing me to see her as almost naked but clothed, which is perhaps the most attractive way of seeing an attractive naked body, involving as it does an element of guesswork, surreptitiousness or theft. (I say 'more than usually' because, as it turned out, there was a witness, but she couldn't have known there would be, or rather the only likely witness would be one for whom her attire, alas, would seem neither revealing nor novel.) I should say that this was my main reason for staying there studying her, for I was still at an age when a glimpse of any forbidden image seemed like a trophy to be stored away on the retina for days or weeks or months, if not, in some mysterious way, for ever. I still have the Beatriz Noguera of that night: I could sense – or more than sense – that she had nothing on beneath her nightdress, not even the tiny undergarment that many women wear in bed, perhaps as a kind of superstitious protection, perhaps so as not to risk staining the sheets with any involuntary secretions. I saw her mainly from the back, because she would occasionally stop her pacing and stand motionless outside Muriel's door as if she were tempted to rap on it with her knuckles and either could not bring herself to do so or did not dare. She must have been about twenty years older than me, and up until then, I had viewed her with a kind of distant esteem, with growing pity and – how can I put it without being misunderstood? – a vague sexual admiration so muted and latent as to be purely theoretical, as though belonging to another hypothetical life, to another me that would never exist, not even in my imagination (real life is so all-absorbing that it doesn't leave us time to create an imaginary, parallel life). We know the kind of glances we must avoid, and also those that are inappropriate because of age, position or hierarchy, and it's easy enough to give them up, to dismiss rather than repress them, no, 'repress' would be the wrong word. With the wife of a brother or a superior or a friend we adopt a veiled or neutral gaze and do so effortlessly and as if under orders, except in very unusual and extremely rare cases, when the lust aroused is unstoppable, explosive, a whirlwind. If, in addition, the wife in question is much older, the task is made easier by habit: when you're twenty-three, you tend to notice women of the same age, or at most ten years older or five years younger – although there are exceptions – and to ignore all the others as one might ignore trees or bits of furniture, or perhaps paintings. Until that night, that is how I had viewed Beatriz Noguera, like a picture that arouses a feeble, ephemeral flicker of desire, quite impossible to satisfy: the woman you're looking at is on one plane, silent, motionless and imprisoned for all eternity; she has only one gesture, one angle and one expression, however challenging the look in her eyes, and her unchanging flesh has no texture, no pulse; she lacks volume and what we are attracted to is pure illusion and, if the portrait is an old one, the woman is probably dead. You study her for a few moments, think fleetingly about what might have been had you shared the same time and space, then, with no regrets, move on and forget her.

The vague sexual admiration I had felt for Beatriz was of that same almost unconscious order. Given that she was Muriel's wife and many years older than me, I considered her, as an object of desire, someone with whom I no longer shared the same time and space, as though I lived in the real and present dimension and she only in long-past, inanimate representations. And all the thoughts I had – which were not even thoughts, more like mental flashes bereft of the words I give them now from the distance of my maturity – were of a conditional or chimerical nature, if, indeed, they existed at all: 'If I were Muriel, I wouldn't treat her like that, I would respond to her occasional, intended caresses, which he rejects so forcefully, and move closer' or 'She must have been very alluring when she was young, I can understand why Muriel would have wanted her at his side day and night, I'm sure I would have too. Even if only for her sheer carnality, which counts for a lot in a marriage. But I wasn't Muriel then, nor am I now.'

And that night, Beatriz Noguera seemed to me neither long-past nor inanimate, nor, indeed, a representation, even though, to my hidden, watching eyes, there was something theatrical about her pacing up and down and her waiting and her hesitations, it was like spying on some minor display of voluptuosity (that revealing nightdress) or a painful monologue without words. Until, that is, there *were* some words. After smoking two cigarettes, Beatriz finally decided to knock timidly at her husband's bedroom door with the knuckle of her middle finger. It was a very quiet knock, like that of a fearful child who has already gone too many times to her parents' room and is afraid she won't be welcome, but could be seen as too easily frightened, importunate and annoying, or might even be told off.

'Eduardo.' Her voice was almost inaudible. There was no reply, and it occurred to me that Beatriz had chosen a bad night to approach him; Muriel would be tired after all his work, possibly already asleep, or else absorbed by thoughts of that urgent script about which he had his doubts. 'Eduardo,' she said again, a little louder this time, and she bent down slightly to look at the crack under the door, to see if the light was on in his room. (When she bent down – this lasted only five seconds, which I counted, the better to enjoy them: one, two, three, four; and five – I had an even clearer view of her bottom, which I had noticed before when she was walking around the apartment fully clothed and erect: round or curvaceous, pert and shapely – or 'firm', to use the adjective so often used to describe tempting flesh – contrary to what Muriel thought, or said he thought, in order to undermine and humiliate her, I had heard him call her 'fat' and a few other more offensive things; and when she bent down, her already brief nightdress rode up another centimetre, revealing more of her sturdy thighs – this time unclothed – although not enough to show her actual buttocks, she would have had to bend further, as if to pick something up from the floor.) Muriel immediately turned off the light, but it was too late for him to pretend to be asleep or to have abandoned wakefulness, this much was clear from what his wife said next: 'Eduardo, I saw the light under the door, I know you're awake. Please open the door. It will only take a second, I promise.' And she knocked again with that one knuckle, more boldly this time. Then she pressed her ear to the door, as if to make sure her husband really was awake, sometimes we need to confirm what we know perfectly well, or to have someone else do so, it's typical of people who no longer entirely trust their own five senses; perhaps, I thought, because this has been going on for years, night after night, and neither of them is capable now of distinguishing the day before yesterday from yesterday or today or tomorrow. I thought this, I really did, just before there came an unexpected response (I was expecting a continued state of imperviousness, although that is a very slow form of dissuasion), which led me to believe that this was the case, that Beatriz's possibly frustrated visit was something she repeated each *conticinium*, as the Romans called the night hour when everything was still and silent, something that no longer exists in our cities, which is perhaps why the word has died out or lies languishing in dictionaries.

'Don't you get bored making the same scene over and over? How many more nights are you going to keep it up? I have to sleep, I'm really tired. Juan and I are working against the clock, you know.' Through the door, Muriel's voice sounded patient rather than irritated. Although he had spoken quite loudly, I was sure that neither of them wanted this exchange to be heard by anyone else in the house, at least in principle. It could also be that this scene had become so customary that everyone knew about it anyway and paid no attention. Even though there was nothing remarkable about him mentioning my name, it still made me jump. I was, after all, spying, and if the spied-upon refer to the spy, this makes him feel more exposed, a somewhat irrational reflex reaction and, fortunately, short-lived.

'I don't want to talk or anything, Eduardo. I won't go on at you. I won't take up much time, I promise. I just want to embrace you, it's been ages since I did. That would soothe me, and then I could go to sleep. Please, open the door.' She said this meekly, sweetly.

'It's a trick,' I thought. 'He doesn't know she's out here with no dressing gown on, nothing, nothing to cover her nightdress, nothing underneath. Or maybe he does and doesn't care, maybe it no longer affects him.' It occurred to me that it would be hard to embrace that voluptuous body and do nothing more, not linger or run your hands over it. 'But then I'm not Muriel,' I said again. 'He's seen it all before, whereas it's all new to me. The touch of her flesh will be a matter of indifference to him, possibly even tedious or unpleasant, I mustn't even think about it.'

There was no immediate reply. I thought Muriel must be considering whether to give in to her request, even if only as a quick way of putting an end to the siege. After a few seconds, he spoke and, from what I heard, his tone of voice had a mocking edge to it.

'No, I've already given myself an embrace, thank you. Consider your embrace duly delivered and go back to bed, off you go.'

He wasn't angry or at least not yet, it was just one of his witty comments. And those last words, 'off you go', had sounded kind, almost affectionate, the words of a long-suffering father to an overly anxious, nervous daughter. After all, he was six or seven or eight years her senior, which was, I would say, a normal age difference between couples at the time, or indeed now, but ultimately, all these things count in how couples treat each other, including who has more experience of the world, who has been in the world longest (and this inevitably strikes a paternalistic note), and the nature of the relationship.

'Don't be silly, Eduardo. Just one embrace. I'm so on edge tonight, I can't sleep.' And when she said this (the first part), Beatriz Noguera gave a little laugh; even though her husband was mocking her, she still found his joke funny. Perhaps that was her curse, her main problem, and one of the reasons why she still loved him so much: he made her laugh and always had. It's very hard not to stay in love with or be captivated by someone who makes us laugh and does so even though he often mistreats us; the hardest thing to give up is that companionable laughter, once you've met someone and decided to stay with them. (When you have a clear memory of that shared laughter and it occasionally recurs, even if only very infrequently and even though the intervals between are long and bitter.) It's the tie that binds most tightly, apart from sex when that's still an urgent need and more than sex as that need grows less.

'No, really, I gave myself a very warm and tender embrace,' retorted Muriel, still in joking mode. 'Yours would be quite unnecessary.' Then his voice changed suddenly, as if, from one moment to the next, he had grown tired of being humorous or had suddenly recalled some injury or source of resentment, and he added sharply: 'Look, go away and leave me in peace, will you? Aren't Roy, Rico and all the others enough for you? You're not exactly in need of more diversions, so why keep pestering me every night? You've known for years what I'm going to say. You've known for years what my terms are. I made them quite clear. God, you're a pain. Unbearable. Just listen to yourself, begging and pleading, how do you stand it? And you're getting a bit long in the tooth to be permanently on heat.'

Beatriz Noguera clearly lacked all dignity and pride, she must have left them behind long ago, and probably had no use for them during the many years Muriel kept referring to. She neither missed them nor had any plans to recover them, they were absent from her life, at least from her married life. For she gave no sharp retort, did not move or leave, she took not a step, nor did she go back to her own room, as would anyone else after receiving such a cruel, emphatic rejection.

'You're so certain, aren't you? And your certainty is so convenient too,' she answered, 'that way you can feel free of all responsibilities and all doubts. You know perfectly well that there is no Rico, no Roy or anyone else for that matter, I just go out with them occasionally, and it's lucky for you I have them to distract me, because I can hardly count on you to do as much, or only when you want to put a good face on things and not turn up with one of your actresses, or whatever they are, at some place where they shouldn't be seen.' She did not say this bitterly or reproachfully, it was, rather, an attempt to be persuasive, and she returned at once to her previous line of attack: 'You're the only one I'm interested in, you're the only one I love, surely I don't need to tell you that, however hard you try to drive me away. And I don't do this every night, don't exaggerate. Why shouldn't I try or at least make an attempt? It costs me nothing. It wasn't like this before. I didn't bore you then, and our relationship wasn't exactly languishing. You suddenly broke it all off, over some stupid thing that happened ages ago. However determined they might be, people don't just stop desiring or loving each other from one day to the next, it just doesn't happen. If it did, it would save everyone a lot of problems and dramas. If you could see me now . . . Go on, just open the door for a moment and look at me. Put your arms around me. And then go back in, if you can.'

Her tone was still cautious, even in those final, slightly challenging words, although they were spoken modestly, more in order to encourage herself than with any real expectation that Muriel would respond. I was nonetheless struck by the fact that she had summoned up the necessary courage and vanity to say them, bearing in mind how disagreeable he could be in his comments, or insults, about her physical appearance: 'Isn't it time you lost some weight? Your backside's the size of a bus!' he would say for no reason. Or 'You're looking more and more like Shelley Winters, not facially, which is something, but otherwise, you're the spitting image; put a short, blonde wig on you and in a three-quarter shot or from behind, you could get a part as her double.' He often made cinematographic comparisons, holding his hands as if he were framing a shot, doubtless an occupational habit. She took these very sportingly sometimes – at others, she was almost reduced to tears – and was undaunted, knowing as she did all his references: 'She can't have been that ugly, after all, she married two good-looking actors, Vittorio Gassman and Tony Franciosa,' she would say. Beatriz bore no resemblance at all either to a bus or to the poor, clumsy, albeit excellent actress Shelley Winters, who, broad in the beam as a young woman, and heavy-set in her mature years, almost always played touching characters worthy of our pity. To start with, Beatriz was very tall, almost as tall as her husband and, with heels on, even taller. She was also strongly built and large-boned, which meant that she aroused neither female solidarity nor male compassion, for it was hard to imagine that someone so strong and healthy would ever need any kind of protection or consolation. As for her supposed fatness and her figure, in this – give or take some obvious differences, and bearing in mind that Beatriz had had children – she was more like Senta Berger, an Austrian actress who had been at the peak of her fame in the decade just drawing to a close and in the preceding one, perhaps more because of her green eyes and her prominent bust than because of her talent as an actress, although she hadn't actually ruined any films either. Perhaps that figure and those breasts would be considered excessive by today's more parsimonious young men, but, at the time, she was merely regarded as buxom and considered to be a real stunner by most male filmgoers, including me and my friends, who, when she was in her heyday, were young men or boys. For a woman like that, however (almost bursting out, shall we say, not from her clothes, of course, but from her own flesh that completely fills her skin, leaving not a fold or wrinkle), it's hard to be sure that she isn't somehow excessive and to accept, fully and unselfconsciously, the way she looks, especially if the person closest to her, the person she most wants to please, is constantly bombarding her with denigratory and sometimes almost ingenious comparisons – there's no defending oneself against the latter without appearing ridiculous – or with out-and-out insults. (The praise and flattery of other men count for nothing, they neither counteract the insults nor help, vanishing as soon as they are spoken.) I assumed that to have said what she said ('If you could see me now . . . Go on, look at me. And then go back in, if you can.'), Beatriz must have spent a long time studying herself in the mirror in her skimpy nightdress, from every angle; she must have persuaded and convinced herself of her own desirability, emboldened perhaps by a couple of drinks; she must have dredged up sufficient pride and self-approval.

That takes a lot of willpower or, in her case, a lot of passion or neediness, both of which distort our perceptions and our understanding, and tend to lead to errors when calculating probabilities. I would have said that, in theory, everything was in her favour. I was still not so very far from my boyhood, and as I crouched there, enjoying her figure, I remembered the childish, slightly coarse word we used to describe any beautiful woman, *macizo*, which means both 'gorgeous' and 'solid' or 'well built' (it's considered old-fashioned now and rather frowned upon), but it seemed to me then that it fitted her exactly.

Muriel did not speak again for a while. I wondered if he was perhaps considering opening the door. As a spectator, I would have preferred him to appear and thus add to the spectacle, because once you begin to look and listen, you always want the performance to continue. It's an instantaneous addiction if your curiosity is aroused, a stronger and more irresistible poison than acting and taking part. If you do take part, you have to make decisions and invent, which is hard work and depends on you ending a conversation or a scene, it brings with it responsibilities; if you merely look, everything is done for you, as in a novel or a film, you simply wait to be shown or told about events that haven't actually happened, and sometimes you get so caught up in them that no one can shift you from your sofa or armchair and you would curse the first person to try. Except that the events *were* happening that night, and despite the unreality of the dark corridor, a little light was coming in from the street, the pale, indirect light from the street lamps or from the sentinel moon was slipping into the rooms and was reflected more palely still on the waxed floorboards, on which stood the apparently bare feet of a tall, anxious, well-built woman of about forty or perhaps a little more by then, who, having knocked on her husband's door, was humbly waiting, begging him for a little sex or a little affection, I couldn't be sure, or perhaps she wanted both things, or to her they were indistinguishable, I couldn't be sure of that either; at any moment, I thought, she might lose her initial fearlessness and feel ashamed, ugly, pathetic and fat, if he did open the door, it was, I thought, possible that Beatriz would suddenly feel too skimpily dressed, too exposed, with her voluptuous figure covered only by the brief nightdress she had chosen after trying on all her other night attire, that she might see herself as a shameless beggar and cover herself with her arms in a sudden fit of modesty, when she was at last given her opportunity, when she was at last seen as she had wanted to be seen. She would certainly have done so had she noticed my presence and my admiring eyes drinking in every detail – they did not, I think, dare to be covetous, insofar as one can control such things. What I had seen and heard was enough for me to hope the scene would not end, not yet, I at least wanted to find out if Muriel would soften or would keep his door as blank and shut as a wall, as if there were no door, only a wall, however flimsy, because I had been able to hear his voice through the door's constraining thickness. I saw Beatriz lean forward again to study the crack under the door – a clearer view of buttocks and thighs, my gaze sharper – and heard her utter an expectant or triumphant or relieved 'Ah'. I deduced from this that the light in Muriel's room had been turned on and then I thought I heard his footsteps, or perhaps I was merely anticipating, as one does in the cinema. Or perhaps he had got up and was going over to the door, to look at his wife as she had asked, and then go back in or not, if he could.

This did not happen as quickly as I expected. He must have made some minimal preparations, or perhaps more than that, put on his long, dark navy-blue dressing gown and rinsed out his mouth or, who knows, had a pee – both he and Beatriz had small private bathrooms in their respective bedrooms. Perhaps he had already removed his patch in order to go to sleep and had to put it on again and adjust it in front of a mirror, because when he did finally emerge, he was wearing it as usual, which slightly disappointed me, because I was hoping to see what was hidden underneath, even though I could only do so in very dim lighting and from a distance, after all, there was no reason why he should cover his eye in his wife's presence, she must often have seen it or what remained of his eye, at least before he suddenly broke off their relationship, before he had begun to find her presence boring and before their relationship had languished, according to what Beatriz had said, and there was no reason why this should not be true, there had been no witnesses and, normally, where there are no witnesses, the two interlocutors are unlikely to lie about the facts, not in principle, unless one of them does so without really knowing what they're doing, because they've told themselves the only version of events they find bearable, for example: 'I can't believe you've stopped wanting to have sex with me. It must have been a decision taken against your own instincts, self-imposed, and now

79

you're sticking to it blindly because you feel a hostage to your own words. One day or one night of frustration and yearning, you'll forget them, you'll rebel and believe you never spoke them. Perhaps tonight or else tomorrow or the day after, and I'll be here to help you erase them.'

Muriel flung open the door, although without making any noise, you might say he did so with mute, measured violence so that everything continued to happen soundlessly and nothing shattered the silence of the house, the city, the universe, as if he didn't want the scene he was making, or that domestic quarrel, to trouble them in the least, house, city or universe. Perhaps it was true what he had said and what she had called exaggerated, that she came to his door every night from her woeful bed, and thus both were skilled at holding their conversations almost in a whisper and tempering their anger so as not to disturb or wake anyone else. Perhaps, too, so that their story would remain a tenuous, never-told tale, as tends to be the case with such deeply personal matters, and would be seen only by the moon's somnolent, half-open eye. On that night, however, the moon's eye had been joined by my eyes, somnolent certainly, but wide open and far from cold.

Muriel appeared at his door, lit by the light that he had finally turned on, weary of listening to her spiel. His dark dressing gown contrasted with his white pyjamas, of which I could see only the collar and part of the legs, for his dressing gown hung elegantly halfway down his calves. His hair had not had time to become tousled by the pillow and, apart from being in his nightclothes, he looked his usual self. He folded his arms sternly and, with his one eye, fixed Beatriz with the piercing gaze of a teacher who has caught a pupil telling a lie so grave that all her virtues – in this case her exuberant flesh – were cancelled out by his condemnation; as if his indignation had, in a

second, transformed his inevitable feelings of pleasure into pure dis-
pleasure. (Because seeing her there in that nightdress, such pleasure
did seem to me inevitable.) Insofar as I could discern such subtleties,
I thought I saw in his eye annoyance, scorn and anger, and perhaps,
too, the kind of embarrassment one might feel on behalf of someone
close to you and which tends to provoke rage rather than pity. His
voice, even in a whisper, sounded ice-cold, metallic.

'Some stupid thing that happened ages ago?' he said, repeating her
words. 'Some stupid thing? How dare you describe it like that, even
now, after all the pain it's caused and continues to cause us. A prank,
eh? A little game, is that right? And all's fair in love and war? How very
witty, how very astute.' He placed his hands on her shoulders as if he
were about to shake her, and I was afraid he would give her a shove
and send her flying, and if she did fall, she might hit the back of her
head on the wall or the floor, just one sharp blow and she could be
dead, anyone can die at any time. Muriel was clearly in a violent
mood, and I feared that things might get out of hand, that he might
lose control. 'You just don't get it, do you? You never will. You'll
never understand what it was that you did, it's of no importance to
you, it wasn't then and it never will be for as long as you live, which
I hope won't be much longer, yes, let's hope you die soon. How stupid
of me to love you during all those years, love you with all my heart,
as long, that is, as I knew nothing. It's as if I'd loved a lemon, a
melon, an artichoke.' The comparison surprised me and made me
hope that Muriel had perhaps recovered his sense of humour, even if
it was the kind of abusive humour he sometimes used with her. While
a lemon can sometimes mean a fool or a dupe, the same could not be
said of a melon or an artichoke: he had, I thought, been unable to
resist adding further jokey references to other fruits, or however you
choose to classify an artichoke. But I was alarmed to see him shift his

hands from her shoulders to her neck (the long neck of a tall woman, unlined and still firm), where it's so easy to start pressing and, in a matter of two or three minutes, it's all over, the irritating or hated person no longer exists and there's nothing to be done, the tongue that speaks and wounds has fallen silent and is perhaps now protruding from the mouth, motionless and bloated and purple, that's how films sometimes depict the victim of a strangling. I don't know if it has any basis in reality or is merely intended to terrify the viewer, who will think that, as well as kicking the bucket, he might end up looking like a complete grotesque, with wide, bulging eyes that resemble painted porcelain or eggs. 'What is it you want me to look at? That nightdress? Did you buy it or did someone give it to you? Don't be ridiculous, I've seen more than enough of you, keep it for your lovers, who clearly have no taste anyway, keep it for those two horny bastards, and don't waste it on me. All right, I'm looking at you, so what? Lard, pure lard, that's all you are to me.' And he ran his fingertips up the fine cloth, from hem to neck, a scornful gesture, as if he found it repugnant to touch both the cloth and her. 'How can he say that?' I thought. 'He's either mad or lying through his teeth. And how can he persuade her that he means it, if he can persuade her? "Lard" is the last word you would use to describe her.' Fortunately, that last gesture led his hands elsewhere, removed them from her neck, so that I no longer feared they would close around it and squeeze, and, unexpectedly after that initial gesture of disgust, he placed his hands on her breasts and began groping them clumsily, roughly, with not a hint of a caress, not a suggestion of eroticism, or so it seemed to me, but who knows what a touch or a contact might mean to someone else, it's often unpredictable, and you can make strange discoveries when touching or when touched, when you accidently brush against someone's thigh (the woman's skirt having

82

slightly ridden up) and notice that the thigh is not withdrawn, does not move away, that's often all it takes to prompt you to touch the thigh again and not by accident this time but just to make sure, out of curiosity and a sudden desire you hadn't expected, the unpremeditated desire which finds so many beauties hooked up with horrible men or men they had, at first sight, detested, the skin is a very treacherous thing, the flesh disconcerting. Muriel almost crushed Beatriz Noguera's doubtless firm breasts, he brazenly pawed them, yes, just as an impatient, unimpugnable groper on the metro might do, the kind who waits until the train is coming into the station to unleash his talons for a few interminable seconds, then shoots off as soon as the doors open. His attitude was vengeful, inconsiderate, loutish, and I wondered what it would have cost him simply to embrace her, which was all she had so far asked of him. 'But no one touches the thing that repels him,' I thought, 'not even in that disdainful, mechanical way, as if the body being touched were of no significance. You don't put your hands on someone's breasts if you don't expect to get some pleasure from it, however minimal. And yet I'm sure that, afterwards, he's going to reject her and send her away, he won't accept that she is even the tiniest bit in the right, even if she is. He'll go against his own lascivious feelings, which he pretends are of no significance merely in order to repress them more easily. He couldn't help giving in to those feelings for a moment (her nightdress that both conceals and reveals), but he has to disguise it with indifference and contempt, as if all it provoked in him was this insulting, brutish, boorish behaviour.' Then he slid one hand, his left hand, further down and grabbed her crotch through her nightdress (I had already seen that she had nothing on underneath), he didn't stroke or rub nor, of course, introduce one finger or two, no, he merely grabbed it like someone picking up a handful of earth or a clump of grass or catching

83

a thistle head in the air or grasping one of the handles in table football or the handle of a frying pan, something trivial like that, unimportant, inconsequential, that one forgets a moment later. 'See,' said Muriel, still grabbing her, holding her. 'You wanted me to look at you, and I am. I'm touching you too, as you may have noticed. So what? I don't fancy you one bit, you can dress how you like, it makes no difference, and that's how it's always going to be. I might as well be touching a pillow, you might as well be an elephant, for all I care. A bag of flour, a bag of flesh.' He couldn't bear to miss an opportunity to be offensive. She allowed herself to be grabbed in that brusque, indelicate manner, she didn't attempt to resist or detach herself from his grasp or take a step back. It seemed to me that, despite the rough way he was groping her, her impulse was to throw herself into his arms, to encircle his neck with her own arms; but if that were so, she either lacked the necessary courage or he didn't give her time, it was all very quick and grubby. 'Go on, go back to bed. Clear off, there's nothing for you here, this is no place for you. How many more times do I have to tell you? When the hell are you going to understand that this is serious and for good, until you die or I do? I just hope I'm the one who'll carry your coffin, because I could never be sure you wouldn't rub yourself up against my still warm or already cold corpse, because warm or cold it would be all the same to you. God, you don't seem to register anything, it's as though, for years now, you haven't even been able to remember what happened yesterday, and each night wiped your memory clean of whatever happened the day before. Will you never give up?'

He suddenly withdrew his hands with what was doubtless an exaggerated shudder, holding them up like a surgeon and then shaking them as if they were dripping wet and urgently in need of drying. He withdrew them like someone who has just completed an unpleasant task, like someone who has touched something sticky, like someone removing a sword from a body after plunging it in up to the hilt, much to his regret, because he had been challenged, because he had become drawn into a duel and had no alternative but to fight. And after making these gestures, he put his hands into the pockets of his dressing gown, puffed out his chest and drew himself up. He resembled a high priest or a Dracula or a Fu Manchu, in his tunic or his dark cape reaching almost down to his feet, with the eye covered by the black patch seeming to look even more sternly and with even more distaste than the one that was the colour of the sea at evening or at night and which *was* capable of seeing, as if both eyes were piercing Beatriz with a mixture of ferocity and embarrassment. And when he released her, she went limp and I suddenly saw her – just for a moment – as he saw her or claimed to see her: a plain, cowed, charmless woman, ashamed now perhaps of her skimpy attire, as though all her voluptuous curves had collapsed and flattened out, had suddenly deflated, and all her firmness grown slack; a poor wretch brought low by disappointment and undermined by humiliation, almost a piece of debris, a crumpled, defeated woman who could not even cover herself with her arms – that would have been too pathetic, too much of a surrender, after she had managed to dredge up from somewhere her one remaining scrap of defiance, only a scrap, and display herself to him – but who probably now longed to retreat and run back to her room, to escape and disappear.

'How changed we are by someone's adverse reaction,' I thought, or I think I thought, remembering it now from another age, although probably not in those precise words. 'How cast down we are by rejection, and how much power accrues to the person to whom we gave that power, for no one can take power unless it is first given or conferred, unless you're prepared to adore and fear that person, unless you aspire to being loved by him or to enjoy his unswerving approval, any such ambition is a sign of conceit and that conceit is what weakens and leaves us defenceless: once that ambition remains unsatisfied or unfulfilled, it marks the beginning of our downfall and we apply ourselves to it day after day, hour after hour, and it's perfectly natural then that dissatisfaction should predominate and prevail from the start, from the very first steps we take, either sooner or later . . . Why should we be loved by the person we have chosen with our tremulous finger? Why that one person, as if he were obliged to obey us? Why should the person who troubles or arouses us and for whose flesh and bones we yearn, why should he desire us? Why should we believe in such coincidences? And when they do happen, why should they last? Yes, why should it last, this rarest of conjunctions, something so fragile, so held together with pins? Reciprocal love, reciprocal lust, mutual fever, eyes and mouths in simultaneous pursuit and necks that crane to see the chosen one among the multitude, bodies that seek to join together time and time again, taking a strange delight in that repetition, returning and returning to the same body, then coming back for more . . . Normally, almost no one coincides, and the existence of so many supposedly loving couples is, in part, a matter of imitation, but largely a matter of convention, or else because the one who first pointed a finger, a man let's say, has imposed his will, has persuaded, led, propelled, obliged the other to do what she isn't even sure she wants to do and to follow a path she would never have taken without the urgency or insistence or guidance of the other, and the flattered and courted one – the one who stepped on to the other person's cloud – has simply allowed herself to be dragged along. That's why the seducer doesn't need to persist, the charm and the misty penumbra vanish, the seduced party grows weary or wakes up, and then it's the turn of the seducer to despair and panic and live on tenterhooks, to resume his labours if he still has the strength, to mount guard on the door and to beg and implore night after night and to be at the mercy of the other. Nothing is so exposing or so enslaving as trying to hold on to the person we chose or who, extraordinarily, came when summoned by our tremulous, beckoning finger, as if by a miracle or as though our word were law, something that would never normally happen.'

Beatriz soon recovered, it did not take long; she again took on her proper size and shape, having apparently, for a few seconds, inexplicably lost or been deserted by both. She straightened up, lifted her head, regained her striking corporeality, and looked straight at Muriel. I couldn't see her face clearly, but I thought it would have been very hard for her not to shed tears when she heard her husband's words – 'I hope to be the one to bury you, the one to see your lifeless body, your deathly pallor' – but if she had, she neither sobbed nor groaned, perhaps she had a better memory than Muriel thought and nothing could now hurt her very much, perhaps her nocturnal prowlings were due not to her instantly forgetting what had happened yesterday or the day before, but to her unshakable belief that she could demolish all resistance, wear down all reluctance, as long as she kept trying, and did not retreat or abandon the field, did not faint away. However, those were not the words that haunted her, the words she had retained, the words to which she responded and that had, I assume, wounded her most deeply:

'No, it wasn't stupid of you. On the contrary, you were quite right to love me during all those years, all those past years . . . You've probably never done anything better.'

Then I felt sure that her eyes must have filled with tears, because we men are easily moved by a woman's silent weeping, even if it's false, feigned, forced, even if provoked by some thought to which we have no access and which may have nothing whatever to do with us, but with another man, a rival, someone she lost some time before or who, unbeknown to us, she has only just lost. Even if we sense that we're not the direct cause of her tears, her weeping melts our heart and fills us with pity and we feel obliged to make it stop. That is the only explanation I can find for Muriel's reaction.

'I'll grant you that,' he said. 'All the more reason for me to feel I've thrown away my life. A part of my life. That's why I can't forgive you.' He said this in a gentle, almost regretful voice, nothing like the bitter, insulting tone he had used up until then, as if this were the first time he was giving her these sorrowful explanations. 'If only you'd never told me,' he went on, 'if only you'd kept me in the dark. When you embark on a deception, you should maintain it right until the end. What is the point of setting the record straight, of suddenly telling the truth? That's even worse, because it invalidates or gives the lie to everything that went before, it obliges the deceived person to look at their whole life in a new light, or else deny it. And yet that *was* your life, and you can't unlive what you've lived. So, as the now undeceived person, what do you do? Strike out your whole existence, retrospectively cancel everything you felt or believed? That's impossible, but neither can you preserve it intact, as if it had all been true, when you know it wasn't. You can't ignore it, but neither can you simply discard all those years, which were what they were and can be no other way, and of which there will always be a remnant, a memory, even if it smacks of the phantasmagorical, something that both happened and didn't happen. And what do you do with something that both happened and didn't happen? Ah, what a fool you were, Beatriz. Not just once, but twice.'

Yes, the tone was one of lamentation now, not scornful or aggressive, although there was still perhaps a hint of rancour. Beatriz

88

Noguera immediately adopted that same tone, perhaps knowingly, perhaps sincerely.

'I'm so sorry, my love, I'm so sorry I hurt you. I wish I could turn back the clock,' she said, not making it clear whether she would like to turn it back to the moment before she deceived him, in whatever way that was, or to the moment before she had undeceived him. Whether she wished not to have done the former or the latter. And after all the barbarous things he had said to her, she still had courage enough to call him 'my love', that's what she said, I heard her.

Then Muriel, doubtless seeing the slow tears that I could not see, leaned forward very slightly and embraced her, gave her the embrace she had asked for and which he had denied her. I imagine she could not then contain herself, for she flung herself into his arms and pressed him to her tempting bosom; and not only that, she pressed her belly against his, her thighs against his, her whole, firm, abundant body wrapped around him, she clung to him with her whole self, as if desperate to relive something from the remote past she had almost given up for lost. I felt almost envious of him, even though there was nothing sexual about his embrace, whereas, despite the circumstances, there *had* been something sexual about his earlier gropings. On the other hand, I saw instantly that her embrace was overtly sexual, which is doubtless why it was so short-lived, with him firmly pushing her away, he must have noticed too, only far more viscerally; and it seemed to him outrageous and he couldn't allow her that or perhaps he feared contagion, that she might transmit to him her sensuality, her lust, her unfettered adoration. Muriel again placed one hand on her shoulder and thus kept her at a distance, an authoritarian gesture worthy of Fu Manchu.

'Go on, clear off. I need to sleep and so do you. And don't forget, Juan is sleeping here night, he might have heard us.'

I again jumped at the mention of my name, especially given my role at the time, that of gossip and spy. I had been crouching for a while now and longed to get up, although when I did, my legs and feet would probably have gone to sleep. However, sheer dread of being discovered helped me not to move a millimetre, to remain inaudible and undetected in the dark, to avoid making the floorboards creak by any movement of mine.

'Eduardo, Eduardo,' she said, and she placed one hand on that distancing arm, squeezing and rubbing it with a mixture of boundless affection and fear. It was a clumsy, untimely gesture. That was all she said, but it came across as importunate and would not, therefore, be well received. And it was not.

'Look, I've told you already, you fat cow, just leave me in peace.' It wasn't just that the term 'fat cow' was in bad taste, inappropriate, hurtful and humiliating. His tone was once again harsh, insulting, bordering on the irascible. 'I opened the door to you and I embraced you, but, no, you always want more. You don't know when to stop. You simply can't tell when enough is enough. Just piss off, will you, and don't come back.'

He took a step back and closed the door, calmly but quickly. I heard him slide the bolt across. Beatriz stood for a few moments staring at the door, as she had at the start. She had left her pack of cigarettes and her ashtray on the floor. She picked them up and, this time, when her nightdress rode up higher, I did see the beginning of her buttocks. Or perhaps I imagined it – wishful thinking – and I didn't actually see anything. She took out another cigarette and lit it. She remained there smoking for a while longer, recovering, waiting until her breathing had calmed. She took a few steps back and forth, I couldn't tell if she was simply bewildered or if she was resuming her prowling, reluctant to abandon her post as sentinel. I could see her face more clearly. She had, as I thought, shed a few tears, but she seemed not so much disconsolate as relieved, almost serene, I'm not sure. Perhaps resigned, as if she were thinking that ever-comforting thought: 'We'll see.' Then she walked unhurriedly back to her room, her half-smoked cigarette in one hand and the packet and the ashtray in the other, leaving not a trace of her incursion. She returned to her woeful bed as she did every night, but this time, unlike on other nights, she was taking with her a small trophy, a sensation. Sensations are unstable things, they become transformed in memory, they shift and dance, they can prevail over what was said and heard, over rejection or acceptance. Sometimes, sensations can make us give up and, at others, encourage us to try again.

III

The Muriels, as people knew and referred to them, gave suppers and small parties, and this was presumably part of the diurnal pact by which they had agreed to live. These occasions were not that common, but nor were they a rarity. The suppers were less frequent and required more organization, that is, when they were arranged ahead of time rather than being impromptu affairs, as happened when a good friend – or several – stayed longer than expected and ended up sharing a meal with them. Every now and then, however, Muriel would invite a professional or amateur producer – plus his wife or mistress – who needed to be feted, or an impresario – and his wife – whom Muriel was trying to persuade to invest in a project, or an ambassador or cultural attaché – and their wives – to whom he had to cosy up, indulging in that Spanish mania for mixing business deals with a semblance of incipient friendship; Muriel had to explore every possible source of finance, and he knew from experience that when foreigners promised to lend a hand or to intercede, they proved far more trustworthy than our fellow Spaniards, who were much given to putting on airs, yapping on gratuitously and incomprehensibly, then disappearing without handing over any money at all and without explanation. This was why he had made a number of his films abroad or as co-productions, the good, the average and the feeble, the ones that were all his own work and those that weren't, and, of course, the bits of nonsense he'd been commissioned to make in the late 1960s and early 70s by the prolific Harry Alan Towers, although most of those were directed by Jesús Franco, aka Jess Frank, Towers's favourite Spanish director, with whom Muriel enjoyed an intermittent and superficial friendship. He had, you might say, inherited or been bequeathed any film – only two or three – that Frank or Franco had been too busy to make, which was hard to imagine since the latter usually made time for everything that was thrown at him, indeed, according to legend, that ubiquitous, tireless, supernatural creature sometimes worked on three films at once, using the same actors on two of them, but without the actors realizing they were doing double the work for a single fee, and using an entirely different cast and location for the third.

Muriel met these people (although not Towers or Franco) at receptions and suppers, at premieres, gala dinners and cocktail dos, at poker evenings, at parties and even at the occasional literary gathering, where he also met some of the inexperienced politicians of the day, one of whom – a fairly prominent figure – he once managed to inveigle into having supper at his apartment. On first meeting, Muriel made an instantly good impression, he could be friendly and pleasant and slightly enigmatic – playing down his bitter, melancholic or misanthropic side as best he could and instead bringing to the fore his natural joviality – and not only was he good at social chit-chat, he had a reputation for being able to banish boredom from any soirée, for, in those days, people still had a taste for social occasions where relatively theoretical or abstract topics were raised, inviting serious discussion, even if it was only around the dinner table. He also had a way of being impertinent without causing any real offence, or only to pompous fools; and he was aware that his presence was sought after at meetings and parties by people eager to hear his good-humoured jibes or to watch him pulling the leg of some vain, puffed-up individual — well, we all have our wares to sell, a contribution to make to the general gaiety, and it's best to know this and accept that everyone who goes into society has a role to play as jester, even a banker or the King, who, as well as playing the fool like everyone else, has to pay for the feast, where everyone is everyone else's jester, including those who believe they were the ones who hired the entertainment. The other almost equally undignified reason for these invitations was his fast-fading prestige, but he was happy to take advantage of this, knowing that people still liked to say: 'We had Muriel over to supper the other night' or 'Muriel has invited us to one of his private parties'; and in his more pessimistic moments, he wondered how much longer this would last, given that his films hadn't met with any real critical or public success for five or six years, which is an eternity in the world of cinema. When someone becomes known merely by his surname, he usually considers this a triumph — especially in France, where it's proof of one's uniqueness — but, in actual fact, it's an act of depersonalization, reification, commercialization, a cheap medal that others can pin on themselves in exchange for almost nothing: a little flattery, a small investment of money or a few vague promises. In Spain, oddly enough, it's considered far more prestigious to be known by one's first name, and this applies to only four or five or six people: 'Federico' is always García Lorca, just as 'Rubén' is Rubén Darío, 'Juan Ramón' is the Nobel Laureate Jiménez, 'Ramón' is Gómez de la Serna, 'Mossèn Cinto' is Verdaguer and, five centuries on, 'Garcilaso' is Garcilaso de la Vega, and this list has remained unchanged for ages, perhaps because in order to join it, you need to have a surname that is either too long or too commonplace or might lead to confusion (the existence of Lope de Vega must have helped all three, 'Garcilaso', 'Lope' and 'El Inca

Garcilaso', the latter owing his absurd designation to the need to differentiate him from his more important namesake), as well, perhaps, as a touch of pseudo-popular affection that encourages familiarity.

These 'private parties' – which took place on Muriel's birthday and saint's day, or were impromptu affairs put on to entertain a visitor or celebrate some promising bit of news when it was still little more than a promise – usually had a fairly fixed guest list, with others being added as and when. Regulars on that list were Rico and Roy, whom Muriel, on my first night as a spy, had accused of having carnal relations with his despised wife, an accusation she had brushed aside. Rico was Professor Francisco Rico, who, although far more famous now than he was then, was nevertheless pretty well known; he was not yet forty, but already had a veritable library behind him (by which I mean books that he himself had written or created), and enjoyed a brilliant career as scholar, expert, righter of literary wrongs, luminary, highbrow, perfect pedant (for he made of his pedantry an art), professional schemer and, of course, eminent and much-feared teacher (he was probably already a professor when I met him; in fact, given his astonishing precociousness in all things, he had probably been a professor since puberty). He lived and taught in Barcelona and its environs, but travelled widely within Europe in order to scheme and plot (the Americas did not attract him, because it was a continent with no Middle Ages and no Renaissance) and he often came to Madrid to engage in murky and disastrous dealings (God had not called him to the path he insisted on travelling), to establish diplomatic relations with the various circles he had access to, including the world of politics, and to work on his candidature to the Real Academia Española, a body he probably despised deep down, but which he nonetheless wished to enter. He was clearly only prepared to remain outside those bodies where membership depended not on others, but solely on himself, just as he could happily leave behind him those places where the doors had already been flung wide to him and where, if possible, he was being begged to cross the threshold. Needless to say, he also came for his own amusement, and there was no doubting the affection bordering on adoration that he felt for Muriel. He clearly enjoyed Muriel's company enormously and admired him too, perhaps not so much for his films – Rico did not care for the cinema, an art invented far too late and in what, for him, was a hideously decadent century – but for his personality and because of an affinity of character that meant they sparked each other off and generally got on like a house on fire: they both, each in his own way, tended to be arrogant and disrespectful and had a sharp sense of humour that not everyone understood. Such was the Professor's veneration for Muriel that he pretty much extended it to everyone who surrounded him, as if their nearness to and acceptance of the maestro in itself gave them value, and it seemed to me that it was for this reason – at least in principle – that he acted as *chevalier servant* to Beatriz Noguera and, whenever he was in Madrid, often accompanied her to the theatre, to a museum, a concert or even shopping. He was a salacious fellow, as was clear from the overeager look on his face, although he was oblivious both to this and to the fact that women find such eagerness either a complete turn-off or rather attractive – there's no halfway house – but I nevertheless believe that, regardless of the state of the Muriel marriage, the enormous respect and affection he felt for Muriel would have prevented him from getting close to his wife in any capacity other than that of companion, friend and helpmate, as an extreme gesture of deference towards Muriel with Beatriz as intermediary. It was quite likely that Rico and Beatriz also got on well and had developed their own

99

estimable friendship; it was equally possible that the Professor's eyes did occasionally linger on her opulent figure (he was a man who, like me and despite the difference in our ages, appreciated flesh and detested bone), or that their fingers might accidentally have touched when she was trying on a dress in a shop and invited him to feel the fabric, or that he had placed a hand on her shoulder, arm or waist to protect her from the speeding cars as she was about to cross the street, but nothing more than that, at least in my opinion. And Beatriz was three or four years older than him, enough for her to treat any suggestion or advance on his part with a certain irony, if she preferred not to take him up on them, but play them down and let them pass.

Rico's salacious nature – or, perhaps, his strong sexuality – was evident in his soft, flexible mouth permanently occupied by a cigarette, in his oblique gaze hidden behind rather large spectacles that made him seem diligent and innocuous – but only when you first met him – it was there even in his prematurely bald head, which he carried with a poise and an aplomb unusual in those who go bald before their time, and which can often be a cause of complexes or even a kind of universal resentment, whereas he was all loquacity, good cheer and remarkable *sans-façon*, as if he were a Don Juan or a handsome, dashing fellow adorned with a fascinating toupee that women find magnetically attractive (his bald head was, in fact, like a battering ram, make of that what you will). Once, at Muriel's apartment, he had the temerity to flirt in my presence with a girl I was going out with at the time – well, I was going out with several girls, and they, of course, as was normal among people our age, were going out with several other men – and who had come to pick me up at the end of my working day. His main method of attack always consisted in trying to impress whoever it was with his encyclopaedic knowledge, and this sometimes led him to misjudge his audience: to most twenty-one-year-old women – apart from a few rare exceptions brimming with curiosity – his excessive display of learning, in this case on the origin of my surname, would have seemed either boring or alarming or quite frankly bewildering.

'Come over here, young De Vere.' That's how I was sometimes addressed both by Muriel and his followers, although the latter did so merely by imitation or perhaps impregnation. Professor Rico always treated me kindly and benevolently because of my closeness to Muriel, but also somewhat dismissively because of my youth, he was, after all, fifteen years older than me and I was more or less the same age as his students, whom he took great pleasure in humorously despising, humiliating and terrorizing, although his victims seemed not to notice, thus demonstrating, according to him, their sad lack of little grey cells or nous (he loved to mix high-flown language with slang or sometimes even genuinely crude expressions, just so that we wouldn't think he lived entirely in the limbo of centuries past). It was the same, indeed, with his teaching assistants, with most of his colleagues or supposed peers and almost every other being under the sun; generally speaking, any contemporary of his merited little respect and was, by definition, deemed to be defective. I imagine that he himself regretted being his own contemporary as well as that of all the many ignoramuses and idiots who criss-crossed the world, happily bellowing forth their blatant idiocy, as he once put it. I still see him from time to time, and, as is only natural, his distaste has only increased with the passing decades. 'Sit down for a moment, young De Vere, I need to question you. And bring your friend too, or were you hoping to smuggle her past me? Introduce us.' She was called or called herself Bettina and worked nights in a bar, which is where I had met her; she was a cheerful, quick-witted girl and wore short skirts, well, not so very short, but they did prove pretty spectacular when she sat down, a fact doubtless anticipated by the Professor as soon as his swift eye saw her standing there. 'De Vere, now what kind of a surname is that?' And he pulled a sceptical face. 'It's not hard to pronounce nor does it look particularly odd when written down, but it is very un-Spanish, if it is Spanish at all. No, no, it's French in origin.' And he said my name with a French accent and repeated it, stressing the guttural 'r'. 'But the most famous De Veres are to be found in England, as far as I know, and I do, of course, know all there is to know, where the name is pronounced De Viah, De Viah.' He liked the sound of his own voice, and he pronounced my name this time very affectedly and with a more or less English accent; he was admirable really, he never had the slightest fear of making a fool of himself, indeed, he never did, however close to the edge he trod; he didn't care who he was talking to or who was listening, whether addressing a congregation of international luminaries or a young woman he didn't even know, he always felt he was the dominant, superior party (except when he was with Muriel). 'It's the family name of the earls of Oxford, and dates back to the reign of William the Conqueror – in the eleventh century, just in case you didn't know, nowadays, one can never assume that people know even the most basic of facts.' I did know, as it happened, having studied English history at university, but I wasn't going to interrupt him. 'Not so long ago, I had a student who was convinced that the French Revolution was a rebellion against Napoleon. I mean, for fuck's sake, *ça suffit*,' he added in French. Sometimes, by way of a preamble or conclusion, Rico would utter strange, unintelligible onomatopoeia

103

(if one can call them that) of his own invention, perhaps as a way of avoiding the usual filler words like 'Well', 'So' and 'Anyway', which he must have thought vulgar. '*Svástire*,' he said, or I think he did, then went on: 'The oldest recorded De Vere, I seem to recall – and if I seem to recall it, it must be true – was named Aubrey, which is neither more nor less than a distorted version of Albericus (how's that for a bit of unexpected Latin), a Christian name that has recurred several times throughout the family history. There has also been a Robert, a Francis, a Horace and a few Johns, which means that you share the same name as – or have copied it from – a couple of far nobler subjects from an earlier age.' He was speaking to me, but was sitting half-turned towards Bettina and kept shooting sideways glances at her thighs or perhaps higher up than that; she had not crossed her legs, and so her brief, tight skirt allowed one to discern something in between them; the crotch of her knickers, I suppose, although she, like so many of her contemporaries, did not always wear knickers: it was all part and parcel of that liberated age and of a consequent desire to provoke. She noticed these myopic glances and allowed herself to be looked at; she appeared to be listening to Rico with close attention, although it could equally well have been amazement. 'More than that, I have an Anglo-Saxon colleague who is just beginning to maintain, secretly until he has published his study (it won't be worth a button, but that's his lookout), that the corpus of texts we believe to have been written by William Shakespeare' – that's what he said, 'corpus of texts' – 'was in fact written by a De Vere.' Pleased with his phonetic skills, he again pronounced this as 'De Viah', with great delight and exaggeration, it sounded almost like an insult or as if he were retching. 'Edward, the seventeenth Earl of Oxford, Lord Great Chamberlain, ambassador, a wild, quarrelsome individual, not without talent: soldier, duellist, poet, failed plotter against Sidney and the person responsible for introducing into Elizabeth I's court the perfumed, embroidered glove. You probably haven't a clue who Sidney was, but never mind, now you do,' and he paused for a second. This was entirely untrue, because how could we know who Sidney was from the mere mention of his name? I was also confused by that mention of a glove, but perhaps he hadn't just slipped it in by chance, maybe it was a way of drawing us in.

'Perfumed gloves? I've never heard of those before,' commented Bettina, who probably wasn't much interested, but whom the Professor appeared to have entranced with his torrent of useless knowledge (useless to most of humanity, but not to him). 'How do they make sure they stay perfumed?'

'You mean how *did* they, because no one wastes their time nowadays on such folderols. I'll explain later, *rica*,' replied the Professor. I was taken aback to hear him address her as *rica* – or sweetheart – given that his name was Rico, unless it was intended as a prophetic appellation, as if he were summoning her to a subsequent secret meeting. He was in his stride now and wanted to tell us everything he knew about that particular De Vere. He again turned to me, although still looking at Bettina out of the corner of his eye. 'As you know, there are numerous theories about the non-existence of Shakespeare, each one stranger than the last; to be honest, it's developing into a real industry. Or, I should say, theories about whether his name was used as a pseudonym or perhaps as a front for that incomparable literary treasure for which some cretinous critics can see no human explanation, which is understandable really when measured by the standard of their own sterility. Some say that Marlowe wasn't stabbed in a tavern brawl when he was twenty-nine, but staged and faked his own death in order to escape his enemies and then continue writing as Shakespeare; some claim that the real author of the plays was

Bacon, while others say it was Heywood or Fletcher, or several of them all together; others opt for Kyd or Middleton, others Webster or Beaumont or even Rowley, Chettle, Lord Brooke, even Florio or Fludd, all utterly absurd, ridiculous.' I had heard a couple of those names in my lectures, but most were new to me. I was impressed by his knowledge, he was like a walking biographical dictionary, although it also occurred to me that they might be invented names, because, in the face of ignorance, one is always free to invent. '*Frushta*,' he said, using one of his original onomatopoeia to fill the brief pause. 'And now there's this arrogant sod who thinks he can prove that Shakespeare was a front for Edward de Vere; he vouch-safed this information to me at a conference – in utmost confidence, of course – urging me to keep his secret safe. For several years! Can you imagine? I had no qualms, however, about spilling the beans, hoping either that someone would refute his theory before he finally gave birth to his Big Book or that someone would get in first and ruin his discovery, my colleagues have no scruples whatsoever and are constantly stealing other people's ideas and, besides, I don't like the fellow.' ('OK, we get the picture,' I thought, scandalized.) 'He dared to challenge something I had written about *Lazarillo de Tormes*. True, there weren't many people present, but still he had the nerve to chal-lenge *me*. An Anglo-Saxon challenging *me* on *Lazarillo*,' he said again. 'They'll invite any ragamuffin to these symposia nowadays and allow them to hold forth on whatever they bloody well like. Yes, any rapscallion is welcome.'

'What's a rapscallion?' asked Bettina. It was a fairly antiquated word that she might never have heard or read.

'I'll tell you that later too, *rica*.' Rico, again rather suspiciously, repeated that assimilatory or bamboozling appellation. You had to watch that bald-headed man, he was quite capable of stealing a girl from under your nose. And yet I still couldn't believe that he would take advantage of his closeness to Beatriz, however much she enjoyed his company. He could hold your attention whatever the subject and even if you didn't understand half of what he said, he was doubtless a magnetic teacher, a mesmerizer of students (whether blockheads or geniuses, it didn't matter). In fact, I noticed that Muriel and Beatriz, who had been elsewhere in the apartment, had come to the living-room door when they heard him speechifying and were smiling as they listened, and they rarely smiled at the same time. They each raised a finger to their lips almost simultaneously, as if they were well matched to the point of synchronicity, warning me to say nothing and not to interrupt. However, it was Rico himself who suddenly stopped talking, surprised and bewildered: 'But why the fuck am I talking about this?' he asked. 'How did I get on to the subject of that impostor in the first place?'

'It was because of my surname, Professor,' I said.

'Ah, yes. Now then, can you explain to me the sham of your being called De Vere?' and he again pronounced this as 'De Viah', to which he had obviously taken a great liking and which emerged from his mouth like an explosion.

'There's no mystery about it, Professor, and you're right, it really is a complete sham, although a fairly ancient one. Apparently, our original surname was the much more common Vera. My family clearly has a long history of delusions of grandeur or perhaps originality. On a whim, some great-grandfather or great-great-grandfather of mine changed it to Vere, thinking that changing one letter would lend it a certain distinction. And I believe it was my grandfather who added the "de". My father likes it and has kept it, he obviously has his own delusions of grandeur and must think it suits his profession, where high-sounding surnames are par for the course. He'll be thrilled when he finds out that there was a De Vere hiding behind Shakespeare'– and I pronounced it Spanish fashion, it was, after all, my surname – 'even though we're not related to those genuine De Viahs.' I couldn't help myself this time and the name came out like a roar, even more exaggerated than his own pronunciation; Rico realized I was making fun of him and looked at me somewhat askance. 'He'll boast about it, he'll tell everyone and will contribute more than anyone else to spreading the word. That Anglo-Saxon colleague of yours is well and truly finished. Soon, half the world will know about it.'

This, however, seemed to vex the Professor.

'Your father's profession? He's a diplomat, isn't he?'

'Yes, a career diplomat, not a political one.'

'He must know people all over the world.'

'Quite a few, yes. He's travelled around a lot.'

'And where has he been posted to now? Algeria, I hope.'

I didn't understand why he said this.

'He's Consul in Frankfurt,' I replied. 'Why?'

The Professor pondered deeply and, while he did so, kept up a rapid muttering like a man possessed, although none of his comments seemed addressed to me.

'Far too civilized. Airport hub. Business deals by the shedload. No, I don't like it, I don't like it all. Tons of visitors. The annual *Buchmesse*. Money calling to money. A lot of very cultivated people. *Buchmesse*,' he repeated, as if it were one of his onomatopoeia. Then he uttered a real one, which sounded like an interjection. '*Áfguebar*. No, best not. He'll send a circular. To all the delegations in the world. And the world's a big place. National and foreign delegations. Multiplication. Too many countries. Telegrams. Best not. No, I'd rather be hanged first.' And then he spoke to me again: 'Listen, young De

Vere or De Vera, be very careful. Something that's merely a tall story could be taken for the truth. That fellow will never be able to prove it, for all his research and rummaging around in archives and however much he twists and distorts the facts to fit his theory. He'll never get away with it. So I ask you to be discreet, best not say anything to anyone, I wouldn't want things to backfire on me because of that gossipy father of yours. We certainly don't want it to become a generally held idea that Shakespeare was just an actor and didn't write a single line and that it was all the work of Edward de Vere. If he ever does publish his book, maybe fifty experts will know about it, of which forty-five will ignore it and the other five, having flipped through a couple of pages, will gladly lay into him, out of sheer spite (that's what it's like in the groves of academe). If the press picked it up, then a lot more people would find out, although, it would doubtless be forgotten again within a month. Rumour on the other hand is what lasts, it's unstoppable, undying, the one thing that endures. I certainly don't want to give that imbecile the gift of a rumour. Like the man said . . .' And here the Professor began reciting from memory, in a loud, passionate voice, his arm raised (not, fortunately, in the Roman or the Fascist manner, he was merely trying to be theatrical and eloquent, but his arm remained rigid): 'Open your ears; for which of you will stop the vent of hearing when loud Rumour speaks? I, from the orient to the drooping west, making the wind my post-horse, still unfold the acts commenced on this ball of earth. Upon my tongues continual slanders ride, the which in every language I pronounce, stuffing the ears of men with false reports.' Rico had the bit between his teeth now and didn't look as if he were about to stop, this was no parenthesis, no mere footnote. Absorbed, perhaps enthused, he continued to declaim as if only that ancient text existed in the room or in the universe, and it was doubtless a very

long text. 'And who but Rumour, who but only I, make fearful mus-
ters and prepared defence, whiles the big year, swoln with some other
grief, is thought with child by the stern tyrant war . . . ?' I looked at
Bettina, who was listening open-mouthed to these barely compre-
hensible words. I touched her thigh, the thigh that Rico had so
coveted (although not now, for poetry drives out or suspends lust),
and she emerged from her trance and, in turn, looked at me as if she
had suddenly woken up. She realized that it was time for us to leave,
she had, after all, come to pick me up on her way to a couple of parties. I glanced across at Muriel and Beatriz, who were watching Rico
with affection and amusement, it was clear that they were both very
fond of him and that they occasionally still enjoyed a certain compli-
city, a shared sense of humour, perhaps dating back to their youth.
They gestured to us, letting us know that the way was clear and that
the reciter would not miss us if we left. And so we very quietly got up
and left the room, without the Professor even noticing, sequestered
in his mind by his invasive memory, his arm still held stiffly aloft, as
if it were mummified. He probably often had such attacks of oral literature. When I opened the front door, I could still hear his vibrant
voice in the distance, addressing his words now only to himself and
his two watching friends. 'The posts come tiring on, and not a man
of them brings other news than they have learn'd of me . . .'

The reason I can remember and reproduce these lines is that, a few days later, Muriel dispatched me to Bourguignon the florist's to choose and order some flowers to be sent to an actress, and when I set off to perform this errand, I felt a sudden twinge of curiosity and went into the library of the British Institute in Calle Almagro, which is right next to the florist's, and there I tracked them down in English. Just as I thought, they were Shakespeare's (or Edward de Vere's) words and it was easy enough to find out in which play he had assumed the voice of noisy Rumour. What I couldn't find, later on, was a Spanish translation that corresponded to the one the Professor had unleashed on us, and so I wondered if it was perhaps his own work, even though English was not the foreign language in which he was most fluent. It had sounded pretty good. In none of the existing translations (there were various then and there are even more now) did I come across the expressions *el año grávido* and *el encorvado oeste* ('the pregnant year' and 'the stoop-backed west') to translate 'the big year' and 'the drooping west', two images that had particularly struck me. Next time I see him, I'll have to ask Paco about it, he's insisted I call him 'Paco' for years now, much against my will, and he insists on calling me 'Juan' and not 'young De Vere'. His arguments for this are indisputable: a long time has passed, I'm no longer young, Muriel and Beatriz are both dead, and they were the ones who gave us our respective appellations, and what binds us together is that 'before' (which means we should not be ironic or overly formal with each other), having met in an age that is beginning to seem as remote as the Second World War seemed to us then, with the added complication that while we hadn't personally experienced that War and it had been swallowed up by fiction, 1980 was still for us a recent date and entirely real. Yes, we're bound together by something troubling, sad and, at the same time, comforting: being survivors, that is, having outlived far too many friends, of whom we become the intermittent wake or the brief memory which is, for a while, transmitted in ever-quieter whispers.

In honour of Professor Rico, I should mention a couple of things. One morning, about three months after that occasion, when I'd stopped seeing Bettina (nothing lasted very long in those effervescent days), I saw them together at the Academia de Bellas Artes de San Fernando, towards the top of Calle de Alcalá, standing before a painting by Mengs, which, if I remember rightly, is a full-length portrait of an eighteenth-century lady wearing a beret, holding a mask and with a parakeet perched on her shoulder. Muriel had sent me there to the Reproductions Department to buy a print of an etching by Fortuny ('Don't forget,' he said, 'it's called *Meditation*'), which he wanted as inspiration for some shots in his latest film: a man in a frock coat, breeches and stockings, leaning against a wall, his chin in one hand and his head bowed so low that his elongated bicorn hat covers his face completely, invisible then and forever more. After buying the print, I went for a wander round that small, discreet and somewhat unfrequented museum (*The Knight's Dream* is the best thing there), and I saw them some way off, but chose not to approach or to wave; he, I think, would have felt triumphant rather than embarrassed, but she might have felt a little awkward. Rico was giving her a (doubtless prolix) explanation, and Bettina, her lovely eyes fixed on the painting, was listening devotedly, which was surprising in a girl who, when we were going out together, used to jump rapidly from one subject to the next, never focusing on anything for very long. This was probably all down to the magnetic qualities of the Professor, who, while he was speaking, kept running his hand up and down her spine and waist (I imagine this was intended as a fond caress, but there was, too, an element of satisfied or possibly newly reawakened lust), and his hand even ventured as far as the incipient curve of her bottom (possibly covered by nothing but her flimsy skirt), and as she made not the slightest gesture or movement to avoid that hand, it was also clear that the Professor had already explored that territory without the hindrance of any intervening fabric; I didn't even rule out the possibility that they had woken up together in a hotel room and that Rico, not wishing to get rid of her too abruptly or brusquely, and unable to think of any better way of distracting her, had decided to educate and enlighten her solely because, whoever he was with and whatever the circumstances, he found it hard not to slip into pedantic, didactic mode. He probably continued to lecture even between the sheets or in his bathrobe. I wondered half-heartedly quite when he had managed to obtain her phone number or how he had got in touch with her. I was astonished to see how much could be achieved with a few oblique, appreciative glances and a few lines quoted from memory. I always was impressed by his ability to get his own way.

However, I had to wait ten or twelve years for proof of the accuracy or truth of what he had told us. It was in 1991, I think, while browsing in a couple of shops, either Miessner or Buchholz, that I came across a volume whose title I've since forgotten, but which included the name of Edward de Vere, and whose subtitle described him as 'Lord Great Chamberlain, seventeenth Earl of Oxford and poet and dramatist William Shakespeare', taking it for granted that they were one and the same. And as if that were not enough, the blurb declared: 'A fascinating biographical account of the man who was Shakespeare.' I leafed through a few pages, and since it seemed to me to be a work of pure fiction, I didn't buy it; novels are such arbitrary, impure things and that book, I felt, was merely a pretentious albeit erudite pastiche. I don't know if it was the book Rico had referred to years before (although the author was a British university lecturer), but I was pleased anyway to discover that the identification of those two Elizabethan celebrities by some mad scholar in search of notoriety had not been pure invention or fantasy on the part of the Professor. Between him and my father, who proclaimed it to the four winds, they had, of course, given the idea if not to one then to ten scholars. But let it be set down here in fairness to the Professor.

I found out a little more about Edward de Vere, because I took advantage of that visit to the British Institute library to track down Rumour's boastful words and the *Oxford Dictionary of National Biography* in search of that unruly, scheming nobleman, who had died nearly four hundred years before and who, oddly enough, shared both my surname (because it *was* still mine, even if it began as a fabrication or adulteration) and Muriel's first name. I read the whole of the long entry to see if he had at least known Shakespeare and, if memory serves me right, there was no mention of their having known each other or of any possible connection. However, one particular sentence caught my eye, and I wrote it down in my notebook, which I still have; and I did this not because it had any relevance to myself, but because I saw a slight parallelism with the strange situation that existed between Muriel and Beatriz. According to the long biographical note, De Vere married Anne, the oldest daughter of Elizabeth I's Treasurer, Lord Burghley, and the Queen herself attended the ceremony, 'celebrated with great pomp', when the bride was only fifteen and the Earl six years older. According to the article, on his return from his travels in Italy, he was temporarily estranged from his wife. On 29 March 1576, five years after the wedding, his father-in-law, Lord Burghley, wrote this about De Vere in his Diary: 'He was enticed by certain lewd persons to be a stranger to his wife.' The biography did not go into detail and chastely concluded: 'Although the quarrel was resolved, their domestic relations were never very cordial thereafter.' That wife, Anne, died several years later, after a reconciliation that resulted in the birth of three daughters (there had been a first child, born before the estrangement) and after he'd had an affair with another Anne, Anne Vavasour, who gave birth to an illegitimate son; he subsequently married again, a certain Elizabeth Trentham. It occurred to me that perhaps this was Muriel's problem, that Beatriz Noguera had not died when she should have done or when it would have suited him. The legalization of divorce was expected very soon in Spain, indeed, the law was passed in mid-1981, but it still did not exist when I began working for Muriel and had not existed during the whole of his marriage. And over the centuries, in an anomalous country like ours, many couples who had grown indifferent to or even come to loathe each other had long yearned silently for their spouse to die or had even procured or induced or sought that death, usually even more silently or, rather, in utter secrecy.

I can't remember all the facts and names from that hasty reading years ago, but I've now consulted the entry on the seventeenth Earl of Oxford in the online version of the *Dictionary of National Biography* only to discover that it's not exactly the same as in the old print versions. The current entry is shorter and more superficial, less chaste, more gossipy and more explicit. It mentions something that does not appear in the older version, something that had crossed my mind, not when I was reading about De Vere, about whom I cared nothing (mere momentary curiosity aroused by Rico the trouble-maker), but when I was thinking about Muriel and the possible reasons for his stark rejection of Beatriz. One of the classic reasons for a husband to bar from his bed a wife he once desired and to insult her, convinced that no punishment will ever suffice and convinced, too, that he's totally right and justified, is for that woman to have passed off as his a child engendered by another man. Many bastard children have, throughout history, been handed over for adoption or sent far away or simply made to disappear, thus most cruelly punishing the adulterous woman, who, once she has had the child (and sometimes even before it is born) no longer cares who the father was; all she wants is to sit beside the cradle of a child she often loves more than herself, and nothing else matters: it is then that a woman becomes utterly fearless. The night I saw Beatriz Noguera standing outside Muriel's bedroom begging him to open the door, he had said to her: 'Some stupid thing that happened ages ago? Some stupid thing? How dare you describe it like that, even now, after all the pain it's caused and continues to cause us. A prank, eh? A little game, is that right? And all's fair in love and war? How very witty, how very astute.' His voice had taken on a metallic edge, an icy whisper of indignation. And later, he had said reproachfully: 'If only you'd never told me, if only you'd kept me in the dark. When you embark on a deception, you should maintain it right until the end. What is the point of setting the record straight, of suddenly telling the truth? That's even worse . . .' I thought he might have been referring to something like this, to the fact that one of his children was not actually his and that he hadn't found out until it was too late to withdraw all the affection he had showered on the child over the years, still less get rid of him or her. Worse still was Beatriz having revealed this to him, put him right, unnecessarily and inopportunely, because that 'invalidates or

116

gives the lie to everything that went before, it obliges the deceived person to look at their whole life in a new light, or else deny it,' he had said, adding: 'And yet that *was* your life, and you can't unlive what you've lived. So, as the now undeceived person, what do you do? Strike out your whole existence, retrospectively cancel everything you felt or believed? That's impossible, but neither can you preserve it intact, as if it had all been true, when you know it wasn't.' And he had concluded this lament or reprimand by saying: 'Ah, what a fool you were, Beatriz. Not just once, but twice.' The first time was the deception, the second her confession. It was possible.

The new biographical note on Edward de Vere explained how, while he was travelling on the Continent in 1575 (Paris, Strasbourg, Siena, Milan, Padua, Venice), his wife gave birth to a daughter, their firstborn, whom he refused to acknowledge as his. (A strange idea, because he had left England in February and the child was born in July; unless he hadn't had sex with his wife for some time before his departure, just as Muriel had not had sex with Beatriz since who knows when.) That, however, does not appear to have been the cause of the estrangement, or not, at least, the only one: having been way-laid by pirates on crossing the Channel, he returned to London on a river-wherry to avoid meeting his wife at Gravesend. Perhaps this was because of the birth in his absence of his supposed daughter and his subsequent anger or annoyance or perhaps the rather odd and eccentric company he brought with him, which included, according to the *Dictionary* now turned gossip: 'a Venetian choirboy named Orazio Cogno' (for any Spanish speaker, his surname was a bad joke, coarse and accusatory, since *coño* means 'cunt'), 'and memories of a Venetian courtesan named Virginia Padoana' (whose name also seems to be a joke, perhaps patronymic, toponymic or metonymic, or none of the above). These must be the 'lewd persons' to whom his astonished father-in-law and mentor, Lord Burghley, refers in his Diary, 'apparently unable to conceive that his son-in-law preferred the company of the choirboy, whom he kept in his London lodgings for eleven months, giving rise to suspicions of pedarasty'. Suspicions, it must be said (unless the boy merely sang to him when they were alone), that seem more than credible. In this regard, there was no parallel at all with Muriel, who, from what I saw and knew, drifted from woman to grown-up woman, and I say 'drifted' because I never saw him make the slightest attempt to conquer any of them, he seemed merely to consent distractedly, inconsequentially, to being seduced now and then by the more determined, capricious or utilitarian of those women, as if he were reluctant or indifferent or oblivious. A famous actress once complained to me sadly, in a fit of humiliated sincerity: 'Can you believe it,' she said, 'after we'd been to bed together one night, he continued to treat me as if nothing had ever happened? In the end, I had to put him straight. "Oh really?" he said. "We had carnal relations? Are you sure? You and me? Well, it's the first I've heard of it." True, he'd had quite a lot to drink, but, really, to remember nothing at all about our little roll in the hay . . . I've never been so insulted in my life. What a slap in the face for a woman as coveted as I am!' That's what she said, 'coveted', a word rarely used in that context then and even less so now.

The new entry in the *DNB* provided me with another piece of useless information: it mentioned the attempts by a few scholars to attribute Shakespeare's plays to De Vere and dismissed them scornfully as being 'without merit'. The most striking thing is that the earliest of these attempts was dated 1920 and written by one Thomas Looney (another accusatory surname). So Rico's hated colleague wasn't even a pioneer, or even original. I imagine the Professor would be pleased to hear that, although he may remember nothing about it.

Eduardo Muriel and Beatriz Noguera had three children, two girls and a boy, the latter being their youngest child, and once the idea of a possible false paternity had crossed my mind, I began studying their faces, their gestures, their behaviour with an extemporaneous detective's eye, trying to discover in them clear traces of Muriel or, indeed, a complete absence of any resemblance or reminiscence or affinity. This was a somewhat vain endeavour, since I hardly saw them: they were at school most of the time or else in their bedrooms, for Beatriz and Flavia ensured that they made few if any incursions into the areas occupied by their father, who treated them with undoubted but absent-minded affection, as if they were guests or permanent residents in the same hotel. Besides, all three were so like their mother that it was as if she had conceived them entirely alone without any help from a man. The oldest, Susana, who was fifteen when I met her, was the very image of the youthful Beatriz I had seen in photos: there were a couple of framed photographs on full view, one of her wedding day with Muriel, when she must have been about twenty-two or twenty-three, and which was probably kept on display at her request or insistence (for him, that bond would be a bitter memory), and another – I wasn't sure whether it was earlier or later – which showed her wearing a small brimless hat, in the style of the late 1950s or early 60s, and holding in her arms a little child whose identity I did not, at first, know: a very sweet two-year-old boy with fine features, his bright eyes looking to his left (Beatriz was to his right), and wearing a little fur coat, something of an exaggeration even for the cold of a Madrid winter, and a kind of white balaclava topped with a pompom, which covered most of his hair, ears and neck, but not his oval face, which stood out clearly. She wasn't looking at the child either, but wore a vaguely distracted expression, as if she were thinking some pleasant thought quite unrelated to that particular occasion, which, despite the dark background that offered no clues, seemed to me to be some church ceremony, a christening or another wedding perhaps. Beatriz was slimmer, but, contrary to her husband's jibes, perfectly recognizable, she hadn't changed much at all; the same bold eyebrows, the very thick eyelashes, which were neither turned back on themselves nor curled, the straight nose so charmingly retroussé, the full, wide mouth that revealed – in a dreamy half-smile – the slightly widely spaced teeth that unwittingly lent her a vaguely salacious air, in marked contrast to her otherwise childish face, both in photos and in reality. (It was one of those mouths that would instantly lead many men to imagine unexpected and inappropriate scenes, often quite against their perfectly respectful efforts to suppress such scenes entirely.) Her features (or what they conveyed of her spirit, on the occasions when that spirit grew animated and sloughed off its usual languor or prostration) were not in keeping with her curvaceous body, they seemed to demand a less powerful, more moderate trunk, abdomen and legs, and her insolent curves a less innocent or ingenuous face. In the wedding photo, in which she was looking directly at the camera and smiling unreservedly, with a look of evident euphoria or possible triumphalism, her features were decidedly childlike, as if she were a mere girl disguised as a bride, albeit prematurely well developed. Muriel, on the other hand, already wearing his eyepatch, even all those years ago, appeared not sombre or grave exactly, but solemn, like a man convinced he is taking on an enormous responsibility. He looked young, but, in comparison with her, seemed a veteran of adulthood. She was still playing at contracting marriage, whereas he was utterly serious and conscious of the appropriateness of that verb 'contract', which could equally be applied to obligations, debts, responsibilities and diseases. And this wasn't only because he was a few years older than her, it wasn't that simple. He was someone who already knew what it means to renounce something, or who was aware that love always arrives late for its appointment with people, as he once gloomily told me, a phrase he had read somewhere.

In their firstborn, Susana, one could already clearly see (although it was more of a manifestation really) the mother's candid expression, which both daughters would retain intermittently into their old age (no life is without its intermittencies, and no character is exempt from, on occasions, betraying itself), along with the intimidating, explosive body, which, if I can put it like this, was already beginning to blossom, whether precociously or not I didn't know nor was I even prepared to think about it: if I refused to take any pleasure in looking at Beatriz, I strictly forbade myself from doing so when in the presence of her promising adolescent daughter, of whom, besides, I only ever caught fleeting glimpses. As for any sexual attraction, Susana and I coincided even less in time and space; she was more like a painting, an inanimate representation, not past but future, as yet unfinished. With their second daughter, there was no danger of my eyes straying: Alicia was twelve when I first went to their apartment, although her resemblance to her mother and her sister would doubtless increase with age. As for the boy, Tomás, who was eight years old, his face was another perfect copy of Beatriz's. All three were like miniature versions of her, in different sizes. It was therefore impossible to find in them any trace of Muriel, nor, of course, of anyone else, if, that is, another man had participated in the engendering of one of them.

I imagine that neither her unhappiness nor her occupations prevented Beatriz Noguera from being a good mother. Although she did not live solely for them and delegated quite a lot of work to Flavia, she was always available to attend to them, listen to them and console them when necessary, insofar as a woman contemplating suicide, as I later found out, could. She was extremely affectionate and, seeing her embrace and caress her children, one could imagine the kind of affection, at once warm and delicate, that she would have bestowed on Muriel had he allowed her to, or that she had perhaps bestowed on him at another time, a time still invoked by her and not forgotten. However, perhaps as a reflex response – that of the beaten dog – perhaps influenced and inhibited by her husband's continued rejection of her, she did not go out of her way to lavish affection on her children unless they asked her to. It was as though her whole existence, or her passage through the world, had become tainted with timidity or restraint; perhaps that is how it had been right from the start or perhaps it began at one particular moment. When you're rejected by the main object of your love, it's easy to become filled with a general feeling of being surplus to requirements, to feel that any display of affection could be deemed bothersome or undesirable, that the quality of your love has somehow been downgraded and so should never be imposed on others without your first being invited to do so. It saddened me a little to see her waiting for some sign from her children before she dared to pet or pamper them. Fortunately for her, the two younger children still naturally and regularly sought such petting and pampering, and she seized on and enjoyed those occasions, her face bright with contentment, but, at the same time, with a slightly distant, apprehensive look in her eyes, as if she could already see on the horizon an end to such effusions – children grow up and move away and, for far too many years, sink into surliness, and when they do come back, they're no longer the same – and as if, with some uncontrollably fatalistic part of her mind, she were already saying goodbye to them. Her eldest daughter no longer sought such displays of affection and was more reserved, although her trusting, ingenuous temperament led her to develop a certain sense of camaraderie with her mother, I would occasionally hear the murmur of their talk and their laughter, although these conversations were, nevertheless, short-lived, superficial and the laughter brief, to do with some recent incident or practical everyday matter. It seemed to me sometimes that Beatriz walked about the apartment putting herself in the firing line, if I can put it like that, waiting for someone to summon or approach her and demand her company, her advice, her mediation or help, or as though asking permission with her wary eyes to kiss or embrace them.

She was not, however, an idle woman, as might be inferred from my description of her, and she earned a modest salary, compared, that is, with what Muriel brought in (as well as being modest, it was probably unnecessary as a contribution to their household expenses and she spent it on other things). She taught English at a school three mornings a week and, on a couple of afternoons, gave a few private lessons at her students' homes, or at least that is the version she gave. I don't think she had ever studied English systematically, but, born in Madrid towards the end of the Civil War, she had been taken, when still very young, to the United States and had spent part of her childhood, adolescence and early youth there, alternating periods spent in America with time spent in Spain, under the guardianship of an aunt and uncle (who were on good terms with the regime), and in close fraternity with her cousins. She was, out of laziness really, not completely bilingual, but very nearly. Her father, who had not been active during the Civil War and was not initially pursued by the *franquistas* (although in the 1930s and 40s and even in the 50s, this could change from one day to the next, all it took was some neighbourhood enmity, some old insult or affront to one of the victors, some arbitrary, false accusation, or people desperate to curry favour with the authorities), had succeeded in leaving the country a few months before Madrid was taken by Franco's troops. A man of moderately Republican, secular views, aware of what the country could become in the hands of the rebels (who would now have a free, unfettered hand), he had been filled with distaste and fear, if not horror and panic, and had made the most of his sudden solitude to leave for France, taking his young daughter with him, despite all the difficulties this would involve and the potential risk to such a small child. From there Ernesto had managed to travel to Mexico with the support of the Foreign Office of that generous country (they cushioned the fall of many who fell at the time), where he stayed for almost a year, until – possibly thanks to the poet Salinas or the poet Guillén, both of whom he had known and admired in Madrid, or directly through Justina Ruiz de Conde – he was given the post of Spanish teacher at Wellesley College in Massachusetts or at Smith or Tufts or Lesley or some other institution near Boston (or perhaps he did the rounds of them all, but who knows in which order), which was considerably steadier and better paid than the sporadic work he found in the insecure world of publishing in a Mexico plagued with compatriot competitors. He had graduated in Philosophy and Literature shortly before the War broke out and, in Spain, had taught at a language school and translated books from German and English, works by Joseph Roth and

Arthur Schnitzler, H. G. Wells, Bernard Shaw and Bertrand Russell, among others. He had an excellent grasp of English, although he had never spoken it much and, according to his daughter, even after all his years in America, he never lost his Spanish accent.

She had never quite understood what I described earlier as his 'sudden solitude'. According to the version she was given as a child, her mother had died shortly after giving birth to her in the midst of a bombardment or when a shell had fallen on the house, leaving a huge hole in the next-door apartment, so they had, all things considered, been very lucky. Her father never went into detail when she asked him about it, sometimes changing the story or contradicting himself, as if he had invented the whole thing as well as the circumstances surrounding it and had never bothered to fix the lie in his imagination or his memory. He rarely spoke about his wife and when he did, his tone was rather cool and indifferent; he wasn't one of those young widowers who are devastated by their loss and find it terribly hard to recover. On weekends, he would hire a babysitter and go off to Boston, returning late at night. He clearly adored his daughter and cared for her, but with a kind of inherent negligence, after all, he was a man on his own, fairly young and inexperienced, doubtless distracted by his own youth. And so he found it relatively easy to send her off to her aunt and uncle, who often paid for her fare: Beatriz spent nearly every summer and sometimes a whole school year in Spain and, during those stays, she picked up certain comments and insinuations, which escaped – either deliberately or by chance – the lips of those relatives on her father's side, the only ones she knew or had seen, and who seemed vexed with their brother or brother-in-law, and this had led her to think that perhaps her mother hadn't died, but had either left her husband shortly after she was born and chosen not to keep the child of a man she bitterly resented or found repulsive or, because of political differences that proved insuperable at the time, had refused to accompany him on his journey into exile and allowed the child to go with him instead of demanding that she remain in her care in Spain. In short, she had either given up her child or the child had been snatched or stolen by her father. It wasn't until much later that Beatriz dared to ask openly what had happened, in fact, it wasn't until shortly before her wedding, she was never in much of a hurry to find out. There are some things about which it's best just to have your suspicions, as long as these are not pressing or unbearable, rather than pursue some disappointing or painful certainty that, as Muriel had more or less said, would oblige you to go on living, meanwhile having to tell yourself a different story from the one you had lived with up until then, always supposing it was possible to cancel out or replace what you had already lived. Or even cancel out or replace what you had believed, if you had believed it for a long time.

Needless to say, I gleaned most of these facts from Muriel or Beatriz or from third parties later on, and some facts (for example, the translations Beatriz's father had published) I learned more recently thanks to the Internet and its boundless but not always accurate information. Anyway, Beatriz spoke English almost like a native, and although many years of barely leaving Spain had made her accent a little rusty and corrupted her syntax (she sometimes made mistakes), this nevertheless meant she could be something more than a mere housewife and earn a little money. Not that she was entirely inactive or idle when she wasn't teaching; she appeared to do her best to fend off her underlying unhappiness by filling her days, at least in fits and starts. On her free mornings or afternoons she would leave the apartment without saying where she was going and without Muriel asking her — well, why would he, given how estranged they were from one another? Sometimes Rico would come and pick her up when he was in Madrid, and sometimes it was Roy or a female friend, of which she had several, but two of whom were particular favourites, although I liked neither very much. However, she would always try to be back in time for the children's supper, if not before, just in case they needed help with their homework or to tell her their troubles, especially the two younger ones (troubles at school, I mean, the kind that can still be talked about openly).

When she was at her lowest ebb, however, she would take refuge in her part of the apartment and could be heard playing the piano badly, practising so very lazily or reluctantly that what we mainly heard was the metronome, which ticked away for long periods without a single note or chord being played, as if it were a perpetual threat or a representation of the tempo of her thoughts or the insistent beat of her sufferings, perhaps it was a way of telling Muriel that her life was passing by without his company and without her regaining his affection, of making him notice her absence second by second, or at the very least, I would think, forty times a minute. It used to make me nervous, and I would sometimes wonder if Beatriz had lost consciousness and was lying on the floor beside the piano – or if she were dead – so prolonged were the intervals without any music or something at least resembling music, while the needle beat back and forth, indifferent to the fate of the person who had set it in motion. I've no idea how long those machines can keep going, but I had the impression that, as soon as it wound down, Beatriz would immediately reactivate it, and there were some mornings or afternoons when its tick-tock seemed to me eternal, as though Beatriz were insisting to us that she was there, just a short distance away, thus imposing her invisible presence on us, so that we would not forget her for a single moment, however busy or distracted we were. Muriel was so used to it that he never succumbed to the disquiet provoked by that rhythmic, tireless, monotonous sound, but for me there was something ominous about it, an element of pent-up waiting or warning. Sometimes, I felt I could almost see Beatriz interminably drumming her fingers, about to explode or attack someone or destroy the piano or do something foolish, to use the classic euphemism that avoids actually saying the word 'suicide'. He, however, immune to that obsessive reminder, would continue talking or speechifying or dictating, as if the noise didn't exist. On those occasions, I thought he had managed to erase her from the face of the earth, even though she was there every day, so close, and even though he occasionally exchanged with her a few almost friendly domestic words and even unwittingly smiled at her now and then, like an automatic reflex reaction from a past, long-past, affection, or like the palest of ghosts of a defunct desire; it's hard to keep a permanent frown on your face in anyone's company.

One day, when the metronome had been beating away for more than half an hour, untempered by a single note from the piano, I dared to express my fears.

'Excuse me, Eduardo,' I said, 'I don't know if you've noticed, but there hasn't been any music for quite a while and yet the metronome hasn't stopped. Do you think your wife's all right? She may be ill or have fainted. It just seems very odd.'

'No,' he answered. 'She takes her time, then gets distracted and falls asleep at the piano. As long as she's there, she's fine. It's quite another matter when she goes out and about on her own.'

'Do you mean we should be worried about her when she goes out, then?'

'Not necessarily,' he said and changed the subject or picked up whatever we had been doing before. He was clearly not going to explain or add anything more. And so I didn't insist and accepted the convention that as long as we could hear the tick-tock of the metronome, everything was fine, more or less, and Beatriz was safe and sound, which was not the same thing as her being at peace and in her right mind.

Fortunately, she was usually very active. I don't know why – perhaps it was that remark of her husband's, or, if I do know why, I'd rather not say, or not yet, perhaps later – but when Muriel was out, looking for locations or travelling around in search of financial backing or shooting the one film he made during the time I was working for him, a strictly bread-and-butter project for the British producer Harry Alan Towers, when the latter returned to Spain to try his luck again after the 1960s and 70s, when he had made films about or based on Fu Manchu, Dracula, Sumuru and the Marquis de Sade, usually with Jesús Franco aka Jess Frank as director and with Muriel himself occasionally deputizing (although he would always become as involved in the project as if the original idea had been his alone, convinced that, thanks to his finer hand and eye, he would produce something that would be both personal and rather artistic); anyway, while he was away for a week here and there, and I had nothing much to do but draw up exhaustive chronological lists of authors, in an attempt to impose some order on his vast library, and other such tasks (I have known few men who were so well read), as I say, when he was absent, I took to following his wife whenever she went out alone. Not, of course, when she was escorted from the apartment by Rico or Roy or one of her meddlesome female friends. I knew then that they would be going to the theatre or shopping or to a concert or a museum, or even to the occasional lecture or some old-fashioned literary gathering (Beatriz adored the writer Juan Benet, a friend of Rico's, and whom she also found extremely attractive); sometimes, on her return, she would tell me what she had been up to and even relate the odd anecdote. Rico always complained about being dragged off to the cinema, but he pleased her in order to please Muriel. Roy was far more docile, and just as the Professor couldn't be totally ruled out as anybody's lover, even, in theory, Beatriz's (he was a dangerous fellow, despite his deceptively scholarly air and his dissuasively off-hand manner, which he extended even to the women he was wooing or pretending to woo, I think he enjoyed seeing how far he could go, often simply dropping the whole business once he'd proved to himself that he could, if he'd wanted, have gone all the way), Roy, however, appeared inoffensive, a genuine *cicisbeo*, to use the old Italian name given to the merely obliging and, in principle, non-carnivorous escorts of neglected married ladies, widows with a social position to keep up and even a few spinsters nervous of going into society alone.

He owned an agency, inherited from his father, which practically ran itself and to which he devoted almost no time at all, apart from spending a few hours there in the morning to greet some particularly demanding client, supervise the work of his employees and pretend to give them orders. His real passion was the cinema, and his admiration for Muriel infinite. He had invested modest sums in Muriel's productions (entirely non-recoverable, but he liked to feel he was participating in what, for him, would always be a grand enterprise) and had written a couple of brief monographs on Muriel's work, which were taken up by publishers with limited distribution, and which provided him with an excuse to meet the maestro, as he often called Muriel when addressing or referring to him, as if Muriel were the conductor of an orchestra or a matador, the only people in Spain to merit such a form of address without it sounding either adulatory or phoney. Muriel had welcomed him and opened his doors to him (there were a few regular visitors to the apartment who would turn up unannounced or at short notice, and who were often to be found there, almost part of the furniture, and whom one could, without causing offence, either put off or simply dismiss if they arrived at an awkward moment) and he did so largely because he liked him, but partly out of fellow feeling and pity: Roy clearly led a very empty life and was such a devoted fan that the maestro allowed him to fill up that emptiness a little with the leavings from his own life, which Roy greedily gobbled up. For him, every visit to our household was an event (and I say 'our household' because I ended up becoming part of the furniture too, often opening the door to visitors and either ushering them in or barring the way), especially when he, being rather star-struck, met the occasional semi-famous director, actor or actress. He would sit apart from everyone else, never joining in the conversation, discreet, invisible, a mere shape, so that some people thought he was a kind of silent attorney literally lurking in the shadows, as a witness to certain meetings and encounters, indeed, Muriel didn't even always introduce him. Roy savoured every moment, every fleeting contact with anyone (even me), but especially with the famous, and one day, he was struck dumb and rigid (although he did subsequently begin to shake) when he entered the living room and saw Jack Palance, the bad guy in *Shane* and in so many other unforgettable films, and with whom Muriel had become friends when Palance appeared in a completely insane adaptation of de Sade's *Justine* in Spain, under the baton (if I may put it like that) of that crazy and prolific duo Towers and Franco. Palance had studied at Stanford University, recorded an album of country music, painted, written poetry, and was filled by far more artistic impulses than one would ever have imagined when seeing him play Attila, a cruel gladiator or a hot- or cold-blooded murderer; he considered Muriel to be an intellectual and that was the aspect of his personality he most respected and found most interesting. When Roy came in, Palance, being a gentleman, stood up and, since he was extremely tall and Roy was on the short side, had to bend so low to shake his hand that it looked almost as if he were bowing to him. He slightly lost his balance and, to steady himself, placed his other large hand on the shoulder of the diminutive Roy. When this failed, he had no option but to turn that gesture into a clumsy embrace, but then, fearing perhaps that he might crush Roy beneath his weight, he nimbly recovered himself and instead lifted Roy into the air as though he were a doll. For a few seconds he offered Muriel and me an image that we would often recall later on: Roy in Jack Palance's arms, his feet off the ground and his face pressed to Palance's breast. Palance gave a loud laugh and gracefully returned Roy to earth, like a dancer lightly depositing a ballerina he had been holding aloft. 'I'm sorry,' he said, 'my fault entirely. I really should make myself shorter when I visit southern Europe.' And he laughed again, revealing his small teeth. Roy did not understand and could only stammer out something supposedly English and which ended in 'meet you', then he smoothed down his jacket and his hair and withdrew to his usual corner to observe Palance avidly, if not rapturously, not daring to utter another word for as long as he remained there, eclipsed and trembling with excitement, like a filmgoer sitting in a darkened cinema. I'm sure he wrote a very long entry in his diary that night (like many unhappy, lonely people, he kept a diary) in which, as well as setting down the little he could have understood of the English conversation, he would doubtless write, accompanied by many exclamation marks, some such puerile words as: 'The very hand now wielding this pen was tonight shaken by Jack Palance!!! The great gunman even lifted me up in his arms!!!' In the late 1990s, by the way, I found a book written and illustrated by Palance and entitled: *The Forest of Love: A Love Story in Blank Verse.* As with his album of country music, which has some nice songs sung in a pleasant, unusual voice (one song begins rather comically with the words: 'I'm the meanest guy that ever lived, I spit when others cry'), in memory of that evening and out of my unconditional, completely star-struck admiration for the actor, I prefer not to pass comment on his blank verse.

And so, for Alberto Augusto Roy, it was a pleasure and an honour to make himself available to the maestro's wife, and she would, I imagine, turn to him when there was no more fascinating or enjoyable company on offer. As I said, Roy was quite short (strikingly so when Beatriz wore high heels, which she usually did), but by no means weedy, indeed, he was well built and in proportion to his height, and he had a nice face too when he took off the large, pale tortoise-shell spectacles that made his greenish eyes seem smaller and covered most of his face and made it seem more uniform and more seriously myopic; they also gave him a slightly professorial air, which did not fit well with his very tanned complexion, the same colour as his thick, almost brown lips, as though both complexion and lips were part of a continuum of tones and had both, since birth, been left exposed to a powerful, perpetual sun. Sometimes – in an attack of ill-judged coquetry – he would let his hair grow very long and comb it back so that it lay plastered to his head and coiled over his collar in a few brazen curls, whether deliberately or naturally I couldn't tell; this quite ruined that professorial air and made him look instead half like an aspiring, ageing, greasy rich kid and half like a strange, bespectacled flamenco singer. Until, that is, Muriel called him to order, holding his fingers as if they were the barrel of a gun and wagging them at the offending area: 'Alberto Augusto, that curly endive of yours has sprouted again, making you resemble nothing so much as a swarthy, small-time crook or an ex-*franquista* nostalgic for the good old days. What will people think if we're seen together?' Alarmed, Roy would raise one hand to the back of his neck; he would stroke the curls in a farewell gesture and head straight to the barber's to have them cut off and his hair unplastered from his head. Anything to avoid getting told off by Muriel.

He always seemed contented, or else he was one of those people who, precisely because their lives are so empty, have no difficulty in finding reasons to be happy, I mean, they pass lightly from one day to the next, buoyed up by the most modest of promises, which they transform into thrilling prospects (although basically that's what we all do, however few or many demands we have on our time), from the premiere of some particularly appetizing film – in his case – to an imminent supper with an old, often seen friend or – in his case – a cousin from Málaga, who visited every four to six weeks – oddly enough, Roy always referred to his cousin by his two family names, Baringo Roy – and whom Roy admired for his busy sex life and his prowess in that field, about which he would occasionally tell us (Rico would sometimes mischievously pump him for details) and while these tales always sounded to us like pure invention, he believed every word; dazzled and deliciously scandalized, he wasn't going to give up a titillating pleasure like that, far less a fantasy. And, of course, equally vital to his happiness was being part of Muriel's circle, if it could be called that, even though it wasn't a circle at all, but a random amalgam. There was a very kind, generous, magnanimous side to Muriel, for he never prevented or inhibited the people around him from forming friendships among themselves or establishing ties other than with him. He had no sense of ownership or precedence, nor did he fear what others might be plotting when he wasn't looking.

He was not one of those agglutinative individuals who wants to control and supervise all contact between those closest to him and who happen to have met through his mediation, and to be kept abreast of any alliance or rapprochement or encounter that might occur, no, he was very hands-off in that respect and even took pleasure in seeing his friends get on well together and develop their own friendships. And in keeping with that, he had no objections to each of his friends forming whatever kind of relationship with Beatriz they chose and to which she was agreeable; on the contrary, this was, I think, a boon and a relief to him. And so Rico and Roy, for example, despite being so different and even opposite, were also fond of each other, amused each other, chatted and joked together, as, to a greater or lesser extent and with the occasional inevitable exception, they did with the other regulars.

I was among those regulars, as were Dr Van Vechten and Beatriz's two troubling female friends, but not the others so much or not at all. I even suspected some promiscuity – real or purely hypothetical or merely hanging in the air – between one or other of them and some of our habitual visitors, perhaps not behind Beatriz's back (it seemed to me that the three women told each other everything, even too much), but probably behind Muriel's back, although he initially gave the impression that he knew nothing, more out of choice than because he couldn't or hadn't noticed, as if he had long ago decided that he really didn't care about other people's entanglements and the passions that provoked them, their infatuations and suspicions and susceptibilities; as if he'd decided that he had quite enough of such feelings to deal with in his own past, feelings that don't always vanish when they cease, but continue to accumulate and to weigh on one.

One of those female friends was related to Muriel by marriage, being the widow of an older brother, who had died in a car crash near

Ávila, on a snowy day in deepest winter and in circumstances that were not at all flattering to her: the police found two bodies, his and that of a pretty, blonde Frenchwoman, much younger than him and unknown to the family – Muriel included – or so they all said. However, she didn't look like a professional prostitute, given the quality of the clothes she was wearing (unless she was a very high-class whore with excellent taste) and which barely covered her: her elegant jacket was unbuttoned – revealing a skimpy bra – and her skirt was up to her navel, despite the low temperatures; this could have been caused by the impact when they hit a truck coming towards them in the opposite lane, into which the couple had strayed while making a foolish, reckless attempt to overtake, but it was rather too much of a coincidence that the brother had his flies open – a buttoned fly as it happened not a zip. One could not help thinking that the laborious business of unbuttoning had been the main cause of the crash, especially if they had each been responsible for undoing the other's buttons, which would inevitably be highly distracting and might well create the illusion – the pressing prospect of future pleasure – of invulnerability. Muriel told me all this later on, when we were chatting one day – he revealed various details of his life unthinkingly and liberally, as if he didn't care or it didn't matter, and yet, on the other hand, was very reserved and guarded when asked a direct question, as happened when I inquired about his eyepatch – to explain why his sister-in-law Gloria disliked him so much.

She had remained calm during the period of mourning, then carried out her own investigation, doubtless with the help of an under-employed detective, and discovered that the Frenchwoman had played a few minor roles in films made in France, in *99 Women* by the omnipresent Franco and Towers (they can't have been very fussy about who they picked, assuming the content matched the title) as well as in a few Spaghetti Westerns shot in Spain, and had auditioned for a larger part in one of Muriel's projects. And although the woman hadn't been chosen, Gloria insisted on suspecting that her brother-in-law, contrary to what he said, knew who she was and, not only that, had probably introduced her to his brother, or perhaps offered or leased her to him. Or, at the very least, had told him where and when the auditions for attractive young supporting actresses would be taking place, so that he could cast an eye over all the candidates and then make his own arrangements. Muriel swore he had no memory of the woman ('How can I possibly remember the faces of all the women who audition for a part and are rejected?') nor if, by ill luck, his brother Roberto had come to see him at the studio on that particular day and met the poor and now deceased and almost bare-breasted actress. The fact is that Gloria blamed him totally for both misfortunes (and it wasn't at all clear which she most regretted or which most tormented her), for her husband's infidelity – fleeting or permanent, there was no way of knowing – as well as for the accident and her loss. 'You and your films and your actresses,' she had said reproachfully to him on more than one occasion. 'Roberto was so envious, he would have thought he'd died and gone to heaven if he'd had your job, and now, of course, he has died, and died making a complete fool of himself.' Muriel did not respond, so as not to get drawn in, however irritating he found her accusations. He was just grateful that Gloria refrained from giving expression, at least in his presence, to the tormenting sense of her own absurdity that must have assailed her on many nights, for, like so many elegant, frivolous, fairly cultivated ladies, behind her undeniably worldly appearance lay a woman of basic religious beliefs, because even now in Spain one continues to come across such surprises; she made no public display of her beliefs, aware that they belonged in the most private of domains, but she probably thought with horror that, as well as making a complete fool of himself, Roberto had died in mortal sin (or almost). Muriel was convinced that she must often wonder how far the couple had got before the crash, and it must have comforted her to know that he would not have had time to ejaculate while still at the wheel. Or so Muriel would say with a bitter laugh. Or perhaps someone had informed him of his sister-in-law's casuistic-cum-spiritual preoccupations.

There was something else that only increased her resentment: his treatment of Beatriz – which had been going on for who knows how long: 'I didn't bore you then, and our relationship wasn't exactly languishing' – Gloria probably saw in this a prolongation or repetition or variant of what her husband had perhaps dished out to her in the latter years of his life. This led her to feel or, rather, display an ostentatious, delighted solidarity with her sister-in-law and friend – although this was possibly more lip-service than anything, because, as I said, Beatriz's curvaceous, vigorous appearance elicited little solidarity from her own sex or compassion from the opposite sex – and to take every jibe or repudiation from Muriel – about which she was doubtless instantly informed – or every suspected or rumoured flirtation on his part, as a personal insult and betrayal; and even to see the evil or cruelty of those two brothers as genetic. That is how Muriel interpreted it, and the truth is that when I overheard snippets of conversation between the two women (or three if her other great friend, Marcela, was there), while my boss was out and I was working on those chronological lists of authors, searching out and filling in dates of birth and death, or on the English translation of a script or a synopsis, or checking facts or whatever, what I heard were seditious, provocative words and phrases, intended to incite Beatriz to revolt, things like 'I don't know how you let him get away with it',

'All that sarcasm is just intended to humiliate and denigrate you', 'I can't understand why you didn't just slap him there and then' or 'Threaten him with divorce, because it's sure to be made legal soon, although they're certainly taking their time.' I remember once hearing Beatriz's response to that last remark and, feeling curious and in order to hear better, I looked up from my work. I was in my or Muriel's area, and they were in Beatriz's, with the doors open as if I didn't exist or didn't count, the sound of the typewriter a guarantee of my indifference, I suppose. I sometimes felt like an old-fashioned servant, the kind who would see everything and say nothing, as though they were statues in the trusting imaginations of their masters, who got some very nasty surprises later on, when they discovered that the statues had tongues.

'Yes, it's been about to be made legal since 1977, but it never happens, thanks to those priests of yours and their political allies determined to keep it off the statute book. Besides, what kind of threat would that be, when it's clearly what he most wants. As soon as it does become law, I'll be preparing myself to be left alone with the children and to lose him for ever. That's what will happen. And then there'll be no hope.'

It was very difficult to incite Beatriz or rouse her to rebellion. She always seemed more sad than angry, more afflicted than indignant, at least when she was with him, but also when he was the main topic of conversation. She was calm and long-suffering, not so much because she hoped her patience would make him change his attitude towards her as because she was sure that any show of impatience would only make matters worse, that shouting, raging, rebelling, returning his insults and making a scene would only strengthen his case and make him more splenetic, thus ensuring that he would be forever incapable of uttering a momentarily gentle, grieving, almost mournful word, like the words I'd heard him say: 'I'll grant you that.' I don't know, but it was as if Beatriz loved Muriel so much and felt so deeply in his debt that she found it as hard to face up to him as to tear him to pieces behind his back, but that she found relief in talking about him and complaining, without the need to spit venom or get overly worked up. Yet when she wasn't with him and wasn't talking about him, Beatriz didn't just lie doggo like some pitiful victim. She led a separate, independent life, as if she didn't care about her husband or had formally renounced him.

'I wouldn't be so sure,' Gloria responded, 'it could cost him an arm and a leg, so he'd think long and hard before asking for a divorce. We don't know what the terms of the law will be, but the spouse with the least money is sure to come out well. Especially if the children stay with her.' She took it for granted that all wives would earn less than their husbands and that the children would automatically stay with them, which is how it usually was in 1980, and as it still is now with a few exceptions, nothing much has changed really. 'As far as we know, he has no other stable relationship. No woman pressurizing him to marry her. Besides, do you really see him marrying again? I don't. He couldn't stand being close to anyone else, and new wives tend to be jealous and clinging, and he couldn't bear having someone asking him all the time where he was off to and keeping a note of his various trips. Basically, he's very comfortable with the way things are, however much he spurns you and hates the sight of you. Threatening him with the new divorce bill will scare the pants off him. He'll moderate his behaviour then and stop all the insults, well, the worst ones. Sometimes I find it hard to believe the things he says to you, but I'm sure you're not inventing it. You shouldn't have to put up with it, no one should. And you'll soon find someone else to take you in.'

I sensed a certain malicious edge to those words 'take you in', as if, when Beatriz divorced, she would inevitably fall into the void or be cast out into the wilderness, and would need another man to protect her from the nothingness or the cold. Beatriz ignored her comments and did not respond, probably inured to her friends' smiling sideswipes.

'I don't know how you, a dyed-in-the-wool Catholic, can advise me to get a divorce, and as soon as possible too, the moment the bill is passed.'

'Yes,' said Gloria, 'but I'm perhaps not as dyed-in-the-wool as all that, besides you don't want to be the only one to lose out. If divorce is made legal, you can bet your boots it won't be only agnostics and atheists taking advantage of it. Do you really think that the people who are so fiercely opposed to it now won't end up embracing it too? They fight it because they have to, but we all know how open to interpretation God is and that he'll understand if we just explain properly and provide him with some solid arguments. They'll each make their peace with him, don't you worry. After all, that's what we've been doing all our lives: pacts and compromises, bargains and pay-offs. God is more than used to that, at least with the people he knows best, namely, religious folk.'

'That makes him sound like some stallholder desperate to sell his wares,' said Beatriz with a little laugh. 'Don't tell me you would have divorced Roberto, because I don't believe you.'

'Sadly, I haven't had to consider it, I only wish he were still alive. But yes, if he had carried on as he was, I would have felt justified in doing so. It would have been his fault, not mine. And his initiative too, which is what really matters. I might have been the one to start divorce proceedings, but he would have sown the seed. Oh, I'd have given him a second chance, I'd have waited. But that Ávila business, assuming it had been a serious affair, would have provided me with sufficient grounds. But I'll never know for sure now, and not knowing is a real curse, believe me. Not knowing if your husband died because he was seriously in love, the kind of love that would have left you sidelined, or because of some mad, insignificant fling. He would probably never have seen her again. Or even thought about her. What a waste!' 'That Ávila business' was how she used to refer to her husband's death and its circumstances. And she added: 'Just as in your case, the fault lies with Eduardo, not with you. Whatever you did afterwards is another matter, you could hardly be expected to sit on your hands for ever.'

There was a long silence, as if Beatriz were thinking or hesitating. I hadn't typed anything for a while, and I was afraid they had noticed and prudently fallen silent, imagining that if I was typing I wouldn't hear their voices clearly. I typed a few more lines to inspire them with confidence, even if only at a subconscious level, as people used to say then. Not that it mattered, they had clearly forgotten I was even there.

'It's odd,' Beatriz said at last. 'It's odd that for me, a non-believer, the bond is stronger than it is for you, a believer, albeit a rather flexible, rather lax one, luckily for you. I could never get divorced or even separated, not on *my* initiative; blaming him for it wouldn't help at all, because I would be the one starting the proceedings and setting it all in motion. It would be quite different if Eduardo began proceedings, then I would just have to lump it. I don't care what he does or doesn't do to me, what he says, I don't care that he avoids me like the plague, that the mere sight of me, at best, irritates him and, at worst, fills him with despair and rage, because there was a time when it wasn't like that, and as long as I hang on to that memory, I can also hang on to the hope that things will go back to the way they once were, and permanently too. Of *course* I care how he treats me, it's dreadful, I can feel myself shrivelling up, and every night I go to bed in such a state of anxiety I can barely sleep; but I still won't leave. You can't just erase memories at will, and as long as those memories last, the person you shared the good times with continues to be the person closest to them, the person who best embodies them. He's both their representative and their witness, if you see what I mean, as well as being the only person capable of bringing those good times back, the only person who can possibly restore them to me. I wouldn't want a new life with another man. I want the life I had for quite a number of years and with the same man. I don't want to forget or get over it or move on, as they say, but to carry on in exactly the same way, like a prolongation of what was. I was never dissatisfied, I never longed for change, I was never one of those women who gets bored and requires movement, variety, arguments and reconciliations, moments of euphoria and terrible shocks. I would have been happy for everything to have stayed eternally the same. Some people are content and satisfied, and hope only for each day to be the same as the previous day and the next. I was one of those people. Until everything went wrong. If I distanced myself from him now, if I left or threw him out, then I really would be giving up what I most want, and that would be the end of me, the final sentence.'

'But as you well know, Beatriz, that man no longer exists. It's just absurd for you to go on suffering like this day after day with no end in sight, hoping for the return of someone who will never come back. Why would he? The return of someone who has vanished, is dead, as dead as my husband, even though he's still moving about in the world and we can see and hear him. The man living with you today is a ghost, a usurper, a bodysnatcher like in the films. At least as regards you. He may live on for others, but that's no consolation to you, it may even highlight his desertion of you, as if he'd decided to die or kill himself as far as you're concerned, but not perhaps as regards the others, and that makes it all the worse. What's the point of remaining by his side? It's like living with the reverse or the negative of that person, his double, if you like. Despite what you say, I can imagine no greater torment.'

Gloria probably didn't use those exact words, but that is how I remember the gist of what she said now, after all this time.

Beatriz again remained silent, as if she were pondering what her friend had said. She was a good listener, unlike most people, who, while the other person is talking, usually remain impatiently silent merely out of politeness (those who aspire to such heights), waiting only to say their piece. She wasn't like that, she really did pay attention and concentrate, thinking about what she was hearing. Then she would answer or not.

'Yes, you're right, that is how it is, superficially, apparently,' she said after a few seconds. 'But that's precisely why you must bear this in mind: the person most like the man who, according to you, is dead, continues to be him, or his usurper or ghost. Unlike what happened with Roberto, who can no longer remember anything, the memory of that protective, affectionate, happy man must still be there in the man who, for years now, has treated me so vilely. In the man who comes and goes, who gets up and goes to bed in this apartment when he's not off travelling or endlessly out partying or whatever. In the man who makes cutting remarks to me and cannot even bear me to touch him, and who never comes to my bed or allows me to go to his. It makes no difference. If the man I yearn for is somewhere, he's there and nowhere else. It would make no sense for me to leave him, even if he is only a ghost of himself. What do I care about other men?

I prefer the pallor of that walking dead man to all the colours of the whole world. I prefer to linger and die in the dim glow of his deathly pallor than live in the bright light of the living.'

She probably didn't use those exact words either, but that was definitely the gist of what she said, as I sat, head raised, like a listening animal, looking up from my work.

IV

I didn't follow Beatriz Noguera when she went out with these people, nor, of course, when she took Muriel's motorbike and headed off who knows where, she once said that she simply liked to leave Madrid behind and imagine (that's what she said, 'imagine', as if she knew it was an illusion) that she could go anywhere she wanted and feel the strong wind in her face on those little-frequented B-roads flanked by trees. Twice she said that she'd been to El Escorial (fifty or so kilometres away), and I know that, on the odd Sunday, with her binoculars in her pocket, she went to the race course (only eight kilometres away) and spent the afternoon there, watching all six races or only the four main ones. I found it odd that she should take no one else with her to that sociable place, or perhaps she found company in those old stands, built in 1941 by the engineer Eduardo Torroja and only belatedly declared a monument of historic and artistic interest in 1980: on a couple of occasions, she returned with tales about the philosopher Savater, a great fan of horse-racing, indeed, a connoisseur, whom she knew and who advised her, successfully it seems, on which horses she should place her meagre bets, thus helping her to return contented with her modest winnings. Apparently, unless he was away travelling, he never missed the Sunday races and went there with his little boy and one of his brothers. Or perhaps she picked up a companion en route – another motorcyclist for example, with whom, unbeknown to me, she would set off to the races. On Sundays, I would often go to the Muriels' apartment and get on with my work, his library being a mine of information on any period or subject that might be required for a script or for some vague project-in-the-making; I ended up coming and going as I pleased, almost as if I were another resident (they even gave me a key); but I lacked the means to follow her on her Harley-Davidson.

Muriel had bought the bike for himself a few years before, a classic or, who knows, an ultra-classic Electra Glide, as he told me proudly the first time he showed it to me: 'What power,' he said. The film *Easy Rider* was already a bit old hat by then, but he had enjoyed a later and less famous film: *Electra Glide in Blue*, blue being the colour of the model used by American motorcycle patrolmen, and on which, I believe, they got up to all kinds of nasty things. Muriel, by the way, went to see all sorts of films, the good, the average and the bad, and he learned from all of them: 'Good films make you want to emulate them, but that's inhibiting; bad films give you good ideas and the cheek to put them into practice.' He seemed to me such a reckless motorcyclist (it was perhaps not the best mode of transport for a man with only one eye), that, after riding pillion with him once and being driven like the clappers through the streets, I decided never to repeat the experience. He didn't use it much, though, once the fever of novelty and excitement had worn off, and Beatriz was the one who used it most, although again not that much, just for her sporadic and apparently solitary excursions, for I had no way of knowing if she met someone else in El Escorial or in other places, like her brother-in-law Roberto, who had driven off to die near Ávila with a woman who was a stranger to his family. (None of us can ever know for sure who we are going to die with.) She would pull on some jeans and don a helmet, get the bike out of the garage and, from the balcony, I would watch her speed away, her large body looking smaller on the back of that vast mount which, to me, seemed a mass of tubes, but, at the same time, she looked somehow more confident and less fragile, an image, I thought, that any man would find attractive, something she would surely be aware of – a sturdy woman astride a fast, powerful machine, it's an erotic cliché really, and I did notice heads turn as she rode off down the street – but Muriel was not there to see her.

Anyway, I took to following her when she went out on her own and on foot, on afternoons when she wasn't giving one of those theoretical private lessons at the home of a student. I would hear her getting ready, humming to herself without realizing that she was, an unusual sound, because when she was alone, she tended to be serious, not to say sad, my presence almost invisible to her – until, that is, it ceased to be – and she viewed me in a kindly, friendly fashion, but otherwise ignored me. When I could hear the click-clack of the slenderest of her high heels (she put these on last, and every shoe sounds different to the discerning ear), I knew she was about to leave. I would wait for a minute after she had closed the front door, then cautiously go after her and, spotting her just a short way from the street door, I would begin my pursuit; she cut such a tall, striking figure that I never lost her among the other passers-by. She would stop now and then to look in a shop window or pause at the traffic lights, but otherwise, she walked at a brisk pace, determined and even jaunty despite her height, and during these walks, I noticed that, despite her sometimes three-inch heels, she could walk without wobbling or stumbling and without them distorting her legs, which remained straight and erect; I was also able to contemplate at my leisure the sway of her skirt, a rare sight these days, most women having forgotten how to walk gracefully, which is not the same as swinging your

151

hips, or not necessarily. Her flesh was so abundant and firm when seen from behind – the only view available to the persistent pursuer – that no fabric could entirely conceal or suppress it, I had the sense that I was admiring not only her visible, vigorous calves, but also her naked thighs and pert buttocks, even though they were covered. This is why Muriel considered her fat. Or perhaps he only called her that.

The first time I followed her, she went to a strange place near the top of Calle de Serrano, where there are plenty of old mansions and a few shops, and I saw her vanish through the doorway of one of the former. When I went closer, after prudently waiting for a few minutes, I saw that it was not a private house owned by the wealthy, but a kind of sanctuary called Our Lady of Darmstadt, or so it said on a sign made of ceramic tiles. I peered in, and even from the street I could see a small, well-kept courtyard and a brief flight of double stairs leading up to a large, raised garden and a couple of low, two-storey buildings, which looked rather cosy, with their white wood lattice windows, like foreign windows from more northerly climes; both garden and buildings were visible from down below; it had the air of being a posh private school, but there was not a voice or a sound to be heard. To the right, in the entrance, was a lodge with a sign saying 'Information', so this was presumably a place open to the public; to the left was another identical lodge with a sign bearing the words 'The Father Gustavo Hörbiger Room', the sign consisting of blue lettering on white tiles, like the sign in the middle of the courtyard, which greeted visitors with: 'Come and you will see'; I don't know why religions always address even complete strangers in such familiar terms. Despite this open invitation, however, I did not at first dare to go any further, just in case Beatriz saw me from wherever it was she had gone. There was no movement or activity, no sign of life; even the information lodge, I discovered, was empty, and so I was obliged to remain uninformed, at least just then. I was getting bored standing outside on the pavement and so I decided to risk it and enter, gingerly, almost stealthily, even though I could easily be spotted in that open space. When no one came out to meet me, I carried on up the short stairs and took a stroll around the very kempt garden, at the far end of which stood an ugly cream-painted chapel with an exaggeratedly pointed slate roof and, near the very plain belfry, one tiny window very high up, it certainly wouldn't let in much light, and the chapel itself resembled a bunker, but one with a vaguely fairy-tale, vaguely German look about it, as suggested by the name of the place – Darmstadt is in the state of Hesse, near Frankfurt and not far from Heidelberg – and of that Father, whose first name had been Hispanized to Gustavo. The chapel was firmly locked, and on the door was a notice protected by glass, which read: 'Our Lady of Darmstadt Sanctuary, Madrid. Open every day from 08.00 to 22.00', which was wrong for a start, given that it was then about five o'clock in the afternoon. There followed a list of communion services and, after that, some special mass for the 'renewal of vows', which took place 'on the 18th of every month' at 20.30, a time at which, depending on the season, it would either be getting dark or already night. 'Something extraordinary must have happened to these people on the eighteenth day of some month in some year,' I thought somewhat lamely. 'Perhaps the Virgin made a mass appearance to every single one of Darmstadt's inhabitants.' What I found strangest of all was that, in the garden, along with the plant pots and the flower beds, there were, in the shade of the various tall trees, benches and small round tables and comfortable chairs, all in white, some already set out and others piled up as they are on café terraces at closing time, as if drinks or snacks or aperitifs might be served there or as if it were a

153

venue for festive gatherings. 'Perhaps when there's a christening or a wedding in the "bunker",' I thought, again rather pointlessly.

I don't quite know why – perhaps it was the ivy-clad walls and the immaculate lawn – but I was reminded vaguely of the house in which Cary Grant both was and wasn't kidnapped and held in *North by Northwest* and, at the same time, although very different and set in a different country – but then directors with real style leave their mark on everything and bring together apparent opposites – of the garden in the part of London where James Stewart went looking for Ambrose Chappell in *The Man Who Knew Too Much*, I had just seen both films at a Hitchcock season at the Filmoteca, to which Muriel had insisted on taking me – and to which I more than happily went – saying that you had to see his films over and over, because with each viewing you discovered and learned something new, something you hadn't noticed before. I had a sudden feeling that the exquisite James Mason or the ominous Martin Landau might suddenly appear in the garden, or that a group of angry taxidermists or the slightly cross-eyed actress Brenda de Banzie would emerge from the sanctuary, Muriel knew all the supporting actors ('You never know when you might need them') and pointed out their names to me and taught me to recognize them. It occurred to me that, just like Brenda the Strabismic, who, in the film, was hiding in the Ambrose Chapel – hence the confusion with Ambrose Chappell – Beatriz might have slipped in there, alone or accompanied, and bolted the door from the inside. And so, very cautiously, I approached from one side, where there was a much larger and lower window than the one on the chapel's façade, and peered in as best I could, trying to ensure that I would not be seen, even in silhouette. But there was no one there, the place was deserted and rather too Germanically dark and unadorned, too much so for a Catholic chapel in southern Europe.

154

I became intensely curious, and curiosity makes us lose all caution. Especially when you begin to become accustomed to observing and eavesdropping without being seen, which anyone living or working in someone else's house inevitably does. Plus, you're unlikely to be found out, because you always have the excuse of chance, accident or coincidence, you're always around and the other inhabitants forget that you're there. However, I was also becoming aware that I was actively developing this habit and beginning to enjoy it, the habit of espionage or voyeurism, whatever you choose to call it, the latter being only a pretentious term to describe the former. Muriel was partly to blame, I told myself on the rare occasions when my con- science pricked me, although only very lightly: in a sense, he had encouraged me to take up spying, urging me to keep a close eye on Dr Van Vechten and see what I thought of him and store away my impressions – or hoard them – until he inquired about them; and as I said, I would, at the time, have done almost anything he asked, keen to do whatever I could to please him. Up until then, I had carried out his instructions to the letter: I had, of course, met Dr Van Vechten, as Muriel had foreseen, and paid close attention, keeping the strictest silence ('Don't confuse me by taking the initiative,' he had warned), and he had so far asked me nothing, whether I liked the man or what I thought, nor had he told me to forget the whole conversation, 'as if it had never happened'. The only reason I haven't as yet spoken about Jorge Van Vechten, who was almost as much of a regular as Rico and Roy, Gloria and Marcela and others, is that my boss had not yet indicated which path I should take, but I will speak about him soon.

I couldn't understand how Beatriz could have vanished so quickly, without trace, not that there was any sign of anyone else either. The Sanctuary was clearly inhabited, cared for and venerated, but, at that precise moment, it seemed to have been abandoned even by Our Lady's most devout, not to say fanatical followers. 'Maybe they all just happened to have errands to run or are having tea together somewhere,' I thought somewhat irrelevantly, as if I were in England, while I strolled about the garden ever-more nonchalantly, keeping close to the two-storey buildings, hoping to see something through the ground-floor windows, which were on my level, keeping half an eye out, so to speak. I still saw no one, and I walked round nearly the whole area, until I came to a protecting boundary wall, where the garden ended on that side. So I turned back and stood beside the chapel to get a better view of the upper floor. At first, even by craning my neck, I still saw no one. Until suddenly, someone's back appeared at a window or was propelled towards it and, for a moment, appeared in my field of vision. I craned my neck still more, wishing I was taller, I stood on tiptoe, thinking if only I had a ladder, I looked around me, but there was none to be seen, I considered climbing on to a chair or one of the tables, but it would make little difference and I'd have to pick it up and carry it over to where I was standing, I hesitated, didn't move, glued to the spot, paralysed perhaps.

The first time lasted only a moment, the back appeared and disappeared, but I already felt, in that flash, that it was Beatriz, not for nothing had I contemplated that back during my long pursuit. I kept my eyes fixed on that point, on that frame, and the back soon reappeared, and it really was as if the person to whom it belonged had been hurled against the glass with a touch of aggression or violence. If so, I definitely couldn't see who was doing the pushing and hurling. I felt alarmed, afraid that someone might be mistreating her, harming her, I even had the wild idea that someone was trying to push her through the lattice window, those wooden struts could easily give way, could break and shatter, a body can easily pass through glass if pushed hard enough, and those struts were quite slender. 'A tree,' I thought, 'I'll climb a tree,' they were there beside me, far closer than the tables and chairs. I was very agile then and perfectly capable of scaling the trunk, grabbing a low branch and, from there, scrambling up to the very top. However, I was afraid I might miss something while I climbed, I realized that I couldn't take my eyes off the window for a second, I saw Beatriz's back thud again and again into the window, remain pressed against it for a moment, then move away, and this was happening continuously, as if they wouldn't leave her alone or even allow her to take two steps. 'Perhaps they're hitting her,' I thought, 'or shoving her around, so that she keeps hitting the window, they've got her corralled, cornered like a boxer.' I was about to call out and thus reveal my presence, although I don't know if I would have been heard. Another possibility would have been to go upstairs to help her or save her from whatever was happening, but I didn't know which door to go through (there were several) or if it would be open.

I was the victim of my own ingenuousness, you have to be much older than I was at the time to lose that quality, always assuming we more trusting souls ever do lose it entirely. I suddenly understood what was happening: someone – a man – was fucking her or pressing himself on her or gripping her hard in readiness to begin, standing up, with no preliminaries and fully clothed, without removing a single item of clothing, hurriedly or perhaps on the spur of the moment, as they say, they probably had very little time before the custodians of the temple returned and were making the most of that moment when they knew that, for whatever reason, the place would be empty, perhaps it always was at that hour. I could only see Beatriz's back from the waist up or not even that, just the upper part of her torso and the old-fashioned nape of her neck – she was wearing her hair up that day. Obviously, the man who was pressing or pounding her – I don't much like that verb, but it might be the most appropriate – was further away from the window, and, besides, she filled the whole space with her large body, for she had fairly broad shoulders, although her hips, fortunately, were less so. He was invisible to me, a ghost, I could see nothing of him, not so much as a hair. And I had no further doubts about what was happening when Beatriz brusquely turned round – or was made to – and leaned forward, and it seemed to me then that her hands must be resting on or gripping the lower part of the window frame or perhaps the sill. Instead of her back and the nape of her neck, I could now see her face, only her face and throat, not her body at all, and this really scared me: if I could see her from below, then she would be able to see me from above. In two strides I was behind a tree, from where I continued to watch. This proved to be an unnecessary precaution, because Beatriz had her eyes tight shut, she wasn't looking outside or anywhere, she was absorbed in herself, I assumed, and in her sensations. I imagined that the man, when he spun her round, would have hoisted up her skirt – there would be no comings and goings now or only of a very different kind – and he would have yanked down her tights and knickers to mid-thigh level so that he could penetrate her with the necessary ease, given the relative discomfort of their vertical position, especially his, because she would have to bend over.

I felt embarrassed, even though I was fairly well hidden behind the tree, peering out just enough – again with half an eye. Now it wasn't only that I was afraid of being caught out, but all that espionage and seeing what I was seeing filled me with guilt: Beatriz's face during what I supposed to be an orgasm, or more than one, or maybe a pre-orgasm, I've never really been able to tell the difference, women tend to string these things together and it's not always easy to tell them apart, people also say that they're brilliant at faking it, and all I could see now was her face pressed against the glass like an odd portrait with eyes tight shut, there are hardly any such portraits in the history of painting – when an artist paints or draws someone asleep or dead, the eyelids are soft or at peace – I couldn't see the possible quickening of her movements or the trembling of her limbs, nor, of course, could I hear anything, no moan, no heavy breathing, no word, if, that is, she uttered any – it didn't look as if she did – in such circumstances, some women talk and urge the man on, or even shout barely credible obscenities, at the risk of making utter fools of themselves or turning their lover off completely, as if they were performing for the benefit of their one witness or for themselves alone, a few even make jokes, while some concentrate hard and say nothing. There are still others who close their eyes tight so that they can imagine they're with someone other than the person embracing or clasping or penetrating them, and I wondered if this would be the case here, if Beatriz would be imagining that she was with the elusive Muriel or if she would be quite clear about the identity and presence of the man she was coupling or copulating with, all barriers down, no precautions taken, I don't think we had heard about AIDS in Spain then, nor perhaps had the rest of the world.

Yes, I felt ashamed and embarrassed, but still I looked and looked at that face in the window, almost squashed against it sometimes – a hint of breath on the glass – sometimes it's hard to interpret the expression on the face of a woman you're screwing, you assume it's pleasure she's feeling, but it can look very like pain (you stop and scrutinize her face and ask: 'Are you OK? Am I hurting you?') or even like despair or profound grief or bitterness, I have occasionally suspected a woman of being with me in that most intimate of situations in order to deaden her sadness or to have her revenge on someone else without his knowledge (thinking somewhat irrelevantly, 'If he only knew' instead of 'When he finds out': as if she were never going to tell him), so as to alleviate for a while the loneliness of her woeful bed, or even to degrade herself in her own imagination and feel sticky and dirty and treacherous, a fleeting illusion, because that muddy feeling soon dissolves, and the following day there's not a trace of mud and you're as clean as you were before – cleanliness is more persistent than dirt, and almost anything can be washed away. I have sometimes suspected that I was just a mechanism, a tool, an instrument. The expression on Beatriz's face could mean anything, and I wasn't there with her, I couldn't stop and ask: 'Are you OK? Am I hurting you?' Because I wasn't the one doing the hurting, if anyone was.

'But what if she's being raped? What if she's being threatened by whoever's with her? And what if she's being forced to submit to him, what if she's being blackmailed?' I thought these thoughts without really believing them, as if I were merely playing at thinking them. But they helped me overcome my desire to discover the man's identity, to see his known or unknown face. I didn't for a moment think it would be Roy the *cicisbeo*, although on the night of Beatriz's patient, pleading wait outside his bedroom door, Muriel – doubtless to humiliate her or as a joke – had accused him of being her lover, and no idea should be rejected out of hand under the distracted sun, still less under the vigilant moon; he had named Rico as well, and it could be him, unlikely but not impossible, for in certain situations he would behave with utter scrupulousness and in others not, like a lot of men, utterly scrupulous when it comes to friendships, but not when it comes to women, and they would get their scruples well and truly singed when presented with an opportunity to go to bed with the wife of a friend, although they can't usually stand the heat for very long. In this case, though, I assumed his loyalty to Muriel would prevail – a possibly unwanted loyalty, since Muriel might prefer it if Beatriz were out enjoying herself so that she would then stop pestering him – as I said, Rico worshipped Muriel. Besides, he was in love with his own wife, who never accompanied him to Madrid, so perhaps he wasn't an adulterer at all, except as an enjoyable hypothesis, another fantasy, like going for a stroll and a chat with Petrarch.

'Why here, in this strange and inappropriate place, in a sanctuary devoted to worship?' I wondered. 'They're not in the chapel, of course; that would, I imagine, have been profanation or sacrilege, or both. Why the rush and why fully clothed, at least in her case? Not that I can imagine that he, whoever he is, would remain completely naked while she kept all her clothes on, it would be too much of a contrast, because I don't think she's actually taken off anything, just pulled down her tights and knickers, but not removed them. And why at this anodyne time of day when nothing really tempts one and everything seems a bit of an effort? Why don't they meet at his place or pay for a hotel room, why risk being discovered by a gardener, a guard, an employee of some kind or, even worse, by a priest or a nun or a devout parishioner? There must be quite a few of them around when Our Lady isn't left here all on her own.' The place had a strong whiff of the far right about it, and the far right, at the time, was very active, not to say rabid, having been in power for thirty-seven years up until only five years before; we all knew the stench well, it was unmistakable and still is now, three decades on, for those of us who had been choked by it: we can pick the scent up instantly, in an office, a room or a building, whether on an ordinary civilian, male or female, a bishop, or a politician pretending to be a democrat and proud of having been elected, some part of Spain will always smell like that. 'Beatriz isn't religious, so what on earth is she doing here? She obviously hasn't come to light a candle, although someone might be dipping his wick.' I was surprised by this coarse thought, this bad play on words, it's not my style and it wasn't then, but we do sometimes succumb to such facile crudity and our mind runs away with us even more than our tongue. It's not so bad if we stop ourselves, or even if we don't; after all, no one's listening to our mental associations, our meandering thoughts, our scornful comments and our curses. I was surprised, too, by this lack of respect on my part: perhaps there was an element of disappointment – so much love for her husband and now this; how could there be any possible connection between the two things? – perhaps an element of unconscious platonic spite; or perhaps it's impossible to feel respect for anyone we observe engaged in such activities. 'I must climb this tree,' I thought, moving swiftly on to the practical, 'before they finish and leave, or she leaves, because she's the visitor, the one who came when called. If I don't, I'll never know who the man is, I'll never see him.'

And so I began to climb and had no difficulty reaching one of the lower branches, from where I moved on to a higher branch and then to a higher one still, until I was on the same level as the window or even just above, I didn't even have to climb to the very top, in those days, I was pretty good at acrobatics and semi-acrobatics, and it only took me a minute, if that. I crouched on my chosen branch, making sure I was concealed by the foliage. But I still couldn't see the man, he must have bent over too, hidden behind Beatriz's face that was still pressed against or very close to the glass, she hadn't opened her eyes for an instant. Now, being directly opposite, I could interpret her expression more easily, if the face of a woman in that situation can ever be interpreted, it's all pure conjecture really. Her face was more attractive than usual, her skin firmer and more youthful, her lips fuller or fleshier, as if this were unknown territory for them, and they had grown more porous, softer, redder, and slightly parted to allow her panting breath to escape, as well, possibly, as the occasional discreet groan (certainly no screams), her eyelashes longer or more visible because her lids remained firmly shut, it was remarkable that not once did she open her eyes, as though she didn't want to know

163

where she was. I've known rather plain women become really pretty in that moment of semi-oblivion, although, to be blunt, it lasts only as long as the sex does. But it seemed to me that she didn't much care about the man she was with, that it was all very routine, or not even that, perhaps purely functional, which, as I've said, is something I myself have noticed, probably we all have, men and women alike, and anyone who says he hasn't is heading for a disappointment, it's no big deal and, depending on the circumstances, might even have its advantages. 'The man's certainly got stamina,' I thought, 'he's been going at it for a while now,' and I felt a little envious, I was still too young always to be able to show sufficient restraint, to contain myself. I learned this somewhat later, with practice and distance and by dint of conjuring up various random images.

And no sooner had I thought this than he stopped or finished, and then, as he pulled away from Beatriz, took a couple of steps back and drew himself up to his full height, I finally saw him and his large, smiling teeth and his satisfied blue eyes, not filled with sexual satisfaction, as would have been logical, but mental satisfaction, thinking 'Take that' or 'Job done' or – even more puerile – 'I certainly gave her a good seeing-to' or perhaps something more comprehensive, 'I can still wreak havoc when I want to and the list continues to grow'; as if he wasn't so much pleased with the physical pleasure he had felt as with his awareness of having experienced it in an unseemly place and at an untimely hour, and with a married woman, the wife of a friend, even if that friend didn't even want to touch her, let alone venture into the very place he had just poked and penetrated. He was wearing a doctor's white coat, as befitted his title; naturally, I had never seen him in this before. He wore it unbuttoned over his ordinary clothes, a tie and a cream-coloured shirt, although no jacket, which he had clearly removed beforehand. Dr Van Vechten's fair hair had become quite dishevelled, quite unkempt, with all that rhythmic pumping away, and had almost toppled forward to form a fringe, because when he wore it, as he usually did, with a neat side parting, it stood out, high and compact, so that from a distance, he looked as though he were balancing a baguette on his head rather than hair, his hair being the same colour as a lightly baked crust. He smoothed it down a little with one hand, while Beatriz stepped back from the window and finally opened her eyes – but she can't have seen me, not just because I was camouflaged among the branches, but because she probably couldn't see anything, her gaze cloudy and confused as if she were emerging from a daydream or from deep thought or an involuntary nap – and she walked hesitantly and slowly to the back of the room, her thighs perhaps numb after standing in that fixed position, she was doubtless going to the bathroom, which he would allow her to do first so that she could compose herself. Of Van Vechten all I could see was his torso, from the waist up, I assumed he had put everything below that back in his trousers, although he wouldn't have been able to wash himself, unless he had made do with a bit of gauze; that whole area was outside my field of vision. I saw him half-sit, half-lean on a table and light a cigarette. He maintained his perennial smile – his teeth as dazzling as those of some foreign film star – which he knew to be one of his main assets, and he was probably now incapable of not smiling even when alone, he would have grown so accustomed to wearing that smile for the benefit of others, that it had, I guessed, become frozen there and, contrary to my original belief – for I had taken him to be an exaggeratedly cordial, overfamiliar fellow – it doubtless meant nothing at all. I even thought he was smiling out of sheer vanity, pleased as punch with what had happened a moment before. Some men chalk up every sexual encounter as if it were a medal or a victory, even grown-up, mature men. It's a young man's response really, from a time when they won't have had many such encounters, but some males preserve that trophy-hunting spirit throughout their life.

After a couple of minutes, Beatriz returned – well, since she hadn't got undressed, she wouldn't have had much to do in the bathroom. He then went in after her, while she straightened her skirt as best she could, smoothed her hair with her fingers and picked up her handbag, as if there were no further reason to hang around and she was ready to leave without delay. I realized that this was one of those wham-bam-thank-you-ma'am situations: not much to talk about before and nothing at all afterwards. He must have shouted 'Wait!' from the bathroom because she put her bag down on the table again and leaned heavily on the back of a chair in a slight gesture of impatience. When he reappeared with hair combed – his usual baguette crowning his cranium – he moved very close to her and said something, almost in her ear. Beatriz, seriously and emphatically, shook her head. She certainly didn't look like a happy lover, neither affectionate nor even content, I wondered how long they had been seeing each other like that, or if it was the first time – which is always a somewhat awkward and prickly situation, haunted by instant regret; on the theory of probabilities, I judged this to be completely impossible: it would have been an incredible coincidence that the very first time I had decided to follow Beatriz should also be the first of such encounters for her, and with Dr Van Vechten of all people, the man Muriel suspected of committing foul deeds in the past and whom he had charged me with observing. The Doctor stroked her cheek and she drew back. 'No, no caresses,' she might have said as she dodged the kindly gesture of that huge hand. (And at that very moment, the French equivalent of those words came into my head, as if I had read it somewhere: *Non, pas de caresses*.) But I heard nothing.

'What are you doing up there, my child? You could crack your head open.'

This I did hear, a disagreeable voice coming from below, I hadn't heard anyone talk about cracking their head open in ages, it was something only the old would say, and it was an old nun who had spoken. She was there at my feet, so to speak, at the foot of the tree, and I realized then the full absurdity of my situation and my behaviour: what was I doing crouched up there, it was hard to justify apart from saying that young people do sometimes do eccentric, inexplicable things, but that was a very poor excuse. The nun was wearing a blue habit and one of those floaty, winged headdresses or helmets or whatever they're called, resembling an origami bird or a light sailing boat, though you don't often see them in Spain, perhaps more in France and Italy. Anyway, my spying was at an end, and it occurred to me then that it would be best to make a swift getaway, before Beatriz said her goodbyes and came downstairs, I didn't want to meet her in the garden or the little courtyard at the entrance, I needed to get out into the street as quickly as possible and vanish. As I made my descent, I was trying to think of a way of preventing the nun from delaying me with questions about who I was, why I had come in, and what I was doing perched on that fairly high branch. When I reached the ground, I decided to pretend to be offended, to divert attention from my entirely anomalous presence and position there:

'Be so kind as not to address me as "my child", Mother,' I said in a rather blunt, pompous tone, 'because I'm not your child, is that clear? You shouldn't be so familiar with a complete stranger.' How ridiculous to tell her off for calling me 'my child' and then address her as 'Mother'. However, I knew this was a sure-fire way of pleasing elderly nuns (who may well be mothers superior) and softening them up, just as priests come over all sentimental when you call them 'Father', as they would like you to; a somewhat vain ambition in both cases.

She looked slightly put out and eyed me curiously. She had very arched eyebrows.

'Now, now, my child,' she said, ignoring my comment entirely. 'There's no need to get upset, that's how I address all the other young people who come here, and it doesn't seem to bother them. Come to think of it, I haven't seen you before. But whatever were you doing up there? You could have taken a real tumble.'

I found it odd that she should speak so colloquially, it had been a long time too since I'd heard the expression 'take a tumble'. She must be from a village originally or a small town.

I hesitated for a moment, I needed to get going. I said the first idiotic thing that came into my head:

'I wanted to go up really high to see if Our Lady would appear to me, Our Lady of Darmstadt,' I explained unnecessarily. 'I know she often does appear to people.'

I had no idea if this was true or not, but I assumed it was: any Virgin with a sanctuary named after her was sure to have appeared several times suspended in mid-air or over the sea or on a rock or even at the top of a tree (which, after all, is where I had been – or almost). That's their way of indicating where a church should be built in their honour, or so they say. And they show themselves in various places in order to get a basilica here, a shrine there, a niche over there – they're never satisfied.

'She doesn't just appear like that, at the beck and call of the believer. That would be too theatrical. And if she did keep appearing, then where would we be? In a right pickle.' I didn't even know that last expression. It sounded very old-fashioned, although I could guess what it meant. That nun had definitely come from some hidden-away place or, possibly, the Middle Ages.

'Ah, I see. You mean she's shy. Well, yes, that makes sense. And if she did keep making those theatrical appearances, we would, as you say, be in a right pickle.' I repeated her words as if this were an expression I used all the time. I glanced over at the double staircase, down which Beatriz, I assumed, would have to come on her way out. From where I was, I could see only one flight of stairs, the other remained hidden; I trusted that Beatriz would choose those stairs and would, therefore, not see me, just as I could not see them. Or that Van Vechten had detained her for a while longer. At any rate, I needed to get away as quickly as possible. 'Well, I have to rush off now, Mother. Forgive my reaction, my ignorance, and for having startled or bothered you in any way. It was a pleasure to meet you.'

I kissed her hand as if she were a cardinal or a bishop, I had little experience of ecclesiasticals, but had observed that with some of them, you were expected to plant a kiss on the big purple ring they wore – and if that isn't theatrical, I don't know what is – and besides, that nun from some remote time or place deserved no less: she had been very kind, despite her grating voice. In a few strides I had reached the street door. I looked left and right, but luckily saw no one else and only hoped that neither Beatriz nor Van Vechten had come over to the window during the few minutes I had stood talking to the nun at the foot of the tree. I strode rapidly off down the street, but stopped short when I had gone barely twenty paces, because I spotted Beatriz in the distance, the sway of her skirt was unmistakable, although now it swayed with rather less ease, since it had, needless to say, become somewhat creased. She had been very quick and had clearly allowed Van Vechten neither caresses nor words (*Non, pas de mots*, she might have said, had she been in a novel), she had obviously departed unnoticed while I was still talking to the old lady. She was about to go into the nearby Museo Lázaro Galdiano, on the opposite side of a broad street. This time, I did not go after her, doubting that yet another lover would be waiting for her inside.

And yet when I followed Beatriz again a few days later, during that same period when Muriel was away from Madrid, I did think there might be a second lover. On that occasion, Beatriz had again gone out for a walk and at a similar hour. She walked for a while along Calle Velázquez where she lived, or where we (in a sense) lived, for I was spending more and more time at the apartment, whether intentionally or by chance, I'm not sure; when she reached Lista – the name we *madrileños* gave, and still give, to what is officially Calle de Ortega y Gasset, as it appears on maps and in guides – she turned right and walked the short distance to Plaza del Marqués de Salamanca. I saw her go in through the high doorway of one of the houses in the square. I allowed a few minutes to pass before going over to read the small metal plaques – there were a few of them, mostly brass – screwed into the wall beside the door, so that they could easily be seen from the street, perhaps as a discreet advertisement for companies that had their headquarters in the building in question or for professionals with a certain prestige or reputation or for those aspiring to that and trying their luck and making their way. There were seven plaques beside that particular door: three were rather cryptic, 'Meridianos', '221B BS' and 'Gekoski', but I presumed they were the names of companies. The same would be true of 'Marius Kociejowski. Middle Eastern Travel', but at least it told you what he did (broad, but specific; he was not, I presumed, a mere travel agent). I was struck by the fact that there were two more or less Polish surnames on the plaques, or so they seemed to me, there weren't as many Poles in Madrid then as there would be a decade or more later, after the fall of the Iron Curtain, and the Poles who arrived then tended not to be businessmen. I knew 'Deverne Films', a very influential and successful film distributor, which also owned various cinemas, and, after all, who didn't know the vast logo that regularly filled cinema screens, announcing: 'Deverne Films presents . . .'? Muriel, I recall, had dealings with the family, as, no doubt, did all directors. In fact, a few months before, I had accompanied Muriel to a meeting in a café with the company's founder and one of his sons, who although not yet thirty, was already very much part of the firm. The distributors were involved in film production, advancing initial funding so that a film could be made and, assuming they liked the finished product, reserving the distribution rights or else making money by selling it off to another distributor. The two remaining plaques were more run of the mill: 'Juan Mollá. Lawyer', said one, and the last was equally terse: 'Dr Carlos Arranz. Medical Consultant'.

I crossed Calle Príncipe de Vergara and waited outside a shop called La Continental, which sold all kinds of things for the home: furniture, crockery, artefacts, all in excellent taste. (At least I think that was the shop: I'm not sure now if it existed then, and it certainly doesn't now; and yet that is the shop that has remained lodged in my memory, perhaps because, later on, I spent a lot of time there with my wife, choosing items for our apartment, with me occasionally glancing across at No. 2 and thinking back to that day.) I could go inside to pass the time, while keeping a close eye on the doorway for when Beatriz re-emerged, I wanted at least to know how long she would spend in there, not that any activity requires a great deal of time, how long a meeting lasts doesn't really tell you anything. I couldn't help but speculate while I waited: I didn't think she would have gone to see the lawyer or the doctor, although that couldn't be discounted. The name '221B BS' made me suspect that it was a detective agency; I couldn't help associating that strange name with 221B Baker Street, where Sherlock Holmes and Dr Watson lived and received their various intriguing commissions. It seemed more likely to me that Beatriz would be visiting them: unhappy people often insist on trying to uncover the full magnitude of their unhappiness, or choose to investigate other people's lives as a distraction from their own. She could have been visiting Gekoski or Meridianos, whatever they were, or Marius K and his journeys to the Middle East, or someone else, who had no plaque. However, I inclined towards Deverne Films, after all, they were in the same line of work as her husband and she would probably know them. I hadn't paid much attention to that conversation in the café, but I did notice the founder's handsome son, Miguel Deverne, a young man not much older than me, but who was dressed with surprising aplomb in suit and tie and even wearing cufflinks, which I thought very old-fashioned. He was a friendly man, with a warm, ready laugh, any woman would have found him attractive, even a woman in her forties, especially if she had spent painful, frustrating years being rejected by her husband.

The sight of Beatriz and Van Vechten a few days before had revealed a new active aspect of her personality, or had perhaps shrouded or contaminated my view of her, if I can put it like that (the truth is that I had seen nothing, only her face and her closed eyes), and now I imagined her in that same pose all the time, which was both inappropriate and unfair, since at home she always behaved discreetly and even timidly sometimes – especially in Muriel's presence, as if she were apologizing for her very existence – he had managed to cow her, to diminish her, despite her robust build and stature, to make her feel she was in the way, as if she were something imposed by custom or by a commitment made long ago, which, precisely because it was now old, could no longer be questioned; she even seemed somewhat apologetic with me too, and for months hardly dared to speak to me because I so clearly belonged to her husband's world, and he was someone she dreaded, possibly even feared. And so it seemed to me that regardless of who she was seeing in Plaza del Marqués de Salamanca, the meeting was sure to be of a sexual nature, however much I kept telling myself that this wasn't necessarily the case, that she might well have an appointment with the lawyer, Mollá, to discuss a possible divorce when divorce eventually became legal; or with Dr Arranz about some problem or symptom or out of pure hypochondria, and that the doctor could well be a psychiatrist or psychologist – the plaque didn't specify what field he was in – and it would have come as no surprise to discover that Beatriz was going to a therapist to unburden herself or to learn to cope better with her sorrow; she could be hiring a private investigator to look into some incident or individual from the past or present (she might want to probe into the origin of her misfortune), or be planning a trip to Egypt or Syria; she could be interceding on Muriel's behalf, trying to get the distributors to take on a project of his that was otherwise hanging by a thread; she could be doing business with Gekoski, which sounded to me like the name of a dodgy auctioneer or an upmarket pawnbroker, if such things still exist. And yet despite all this hypothesizing, I still kept imagining a repetition of the scene with Van Vechten. It even occurred to me, in my meanderings, that she might be prostituting herself to help her husband – unconditional love does not exclude paradox and, as the word 'unconditional' indicates, such love is capable of anything – and she had gone there to offer her body to the founder of the company, Deverne, who would be in his sixties or older and would be unlikely to turn his nose up at the chance.

'Hers is such a woeful bed,' I thought, 'that she has to visit other beds, or dispense with beds altogether, so that she doesn't risk feeling the contrast with her own cold, solitary bed, to which she returns each night. She can't bear to be still and simply accept her fate, so she seeks out these forays, these adventures. She would far rather be with Muriel, but since he won't have her, she refuses simply to languish or waste away at home, and in her more animated moments, she looks for substitutes, as almost everyone does, very few of us ever find what we yearn for, or if we do, we don't hang on to it for very long, and who knows how long she managed to hang on to her happiness.' We strive to conquer things, never thinking, in our eagerness, that they will never definitely be ours, that they rarely last and are always susceptible to loss, nothing is ever for ever, we often fight battles or hatch plots or tell lies, commit vile deeds or acts of treachery or foment crimes always forgetting that the thing we obtain might not last (it's a very ancient fault in all of us, to see the present as final and forget that it's inevitably and infuriatingly transitory), and that once their effect fades or expires, all the battles and plots, the lies and vile deeds, the betrayals and crimes will seem utterly futile to us, or worse, superfluous: such a waste of verve, such a squandering of energy, we might as well have saved ourselves the bother, since nothing much has changed. We are led on by wicked haste and easily surrender ourselves to poisonous impatience, as I once heard Muriel describe it, although whether he was quoting someone else I have no idea. We see no further than tomorrow and see it as the end of time, just as if we were little children believing that our mother's momentary absence will be definitive and irreversible, that she has abandoned us completely; that if our hunger or thirst is not immediately satisfied, we will remain hungry and thirsty for ever; that if we suffer even the tiniest of scratches, the pain will never end, we don't even foresee the scab forming; that if we feel safe and protected now, we will feel so for the rest of our life, which we can only conceive of from day to day or hour to hour or five minutes to five minutes. In that respect, we don't change very much when we're adults, not even when we're old and what remains to us of life is so much shorter. The past doesn't count, it's time expired and negated, a time of error or ingenuousness and ignorance, which we end up perceiving as merely pathetic, and what ultimately invalidates and overwhelms it is this idea: 'How little we knew, how stupid we were, how innocent, we had no idea what awaited us and now we do.' And in that state of present knowledge, we are incapable of bearing in mind that tomorrow we will know something else and today will seem as stupid to us as yesterday or the day before or the day on which we were first thrust into the world, or perhaps this happened in the middle of the night beneath the bored and scornful moon. We go from deceit to deceit and know that, in that respect, we are not deceived, and yet we always take the latest deceit for the truth.

I waited and waited and felt as if I had been waiting a long time. I went into the shop and left again over and over, I browsed around inside without buying anything, avoiding the solicitous assistants as best I could ('No, thank you, I'm just looking, I'll come back when I've made a decision'). I gazed up at the windows of the building opposite, but saw no one, and it was impossible to know which floor Beatriz had gone to. I was tempted to peer in and ask the porter, but that would have been inappropriate and he would have answered in rude, patronizing tones: 'What's it got to do with you, young man, why do you want to know? It's no business of yours who the lady is visiting. Who sent you, anyway? I'm going to tell Señor Gekoski, Dr

Arranz, Señor Mollá, Mr Holmes, Señor Kociejowski, and the Devernes, so that they can take action and know all about your meddling.' Of course, by threatening me with a name, he would have answered my question. I continued to wait, and the more time passed, the more likely it seemed to me that Beatriz's meeting was a carnal one; then, a few seconds later, I thought exactly the opposite, it takes longer to talk than it does to have a prearranged fuck, forgive the vulgarity, but it's best to call a spade a spade.

She did not reappear for nearly an hour, but which of those men had she been with and what had she done? At first, I noticed no change in her attitude or her appearance, although there was perhaps a change in her expression, which seemed to me – how can I put it? – disjointed or blurred, as if one part of her face expressed pleasurable intensity and the other disgust, as if she had just had a thrilling but somehow distasteful experience. She began walking back the way she came. I followed her at a distance, to see where she was going, until she went into a very classy clothes shop on Calle de Ortega y Gasset, or, rather, Lista. And it was while she was walking that I noticed the enormous ladder in her tights, almost a tear, and her skirt, obviously disarranged in the fray, was slightly caught up at the back, despite her efforts to smooth it into place while she walked. I know now and knew then how very easily tights ladder, you only have to brush against something, but it confirmed my suppositions: whoever she had just gone to bed with – well, not bed, of course, but there are always ledges and walls and tables on which to lean – the man had not been as careful as Van Vechten; if you keep your clothes on, they can easily become dirty or torn. When she left the shop, she had changed her tights and her skirt swung freely, any obstacle removed. She must have bought them there and then, and gone into the shop for that purpose.

No one had sent me, contrary to what the porter would have thought had I inquired who Beatriz Noguera was visiting, asked the name of her visitee. No, no one had ordered me to follow her when she went out alone, and at the time, I myself didn't really know why I was doing it, or felt no need to explain to myself or preferred not to recognize the real reason, despite my naturally reflective nature. That is one of the advantages of youth: you allow yourself to act far more impulsively and obliquely, it makes you feel terribly original somehow – even though this turns out not to be the case at all, and what you're doing is actually supremely banal – because you're prepared to take rash, instantaneous decisions, thinking you can get away with a certain degree of eccentricity or irresponsibility or even a touch of feigned madness, or, rather, you're of an age that allows for that – only a little sporadic madness, because flirting with insanity is never risk-free – without incurring any real consequences, and you rarely do slide into a more serious, more enduring madness; and you are still very close to childhood and adolescence, when you see yourself as a character out of a novel or a comic or a film and try to emulate them; perhaps I was imitating Hitchcock's creations, suggested by that season of films to which Muriel had taken me, unresisting, and in which there are often long sequences during which no one says a word, no dialogue at all, just people coming and going from one place to another, and yet you sit, eyes glued to the screen, feeling increasingly intrigued and anxious, even when sometimes there's no objective reason to feel that. The mere act of watching creates that feeling of anxiety, that sense of intrigue. We just have to lay eyes on someone for us to begin to ask questions and fear for their fate.

That is how I explained my own behaviour: pure curiosity, I *was* intrigued and I *did* feel somewhat anxious about Beatriz's fate and the company she was keeping; or perhaps, despite my youth and the general freedom of the times, I found her visits quite frankly exciting, visits of which Muriel would know nothing. Not that he would have cared, he might even have been pleased had he known. She was much older than me, and yet my attitude towards her was tinged with a strange, respectful desire to protect her, even if only as an unseen companion and invisible witness, tinged too with an incongruous paternalism, as if she were a fictional character, for when a character captures our imagination, we observe her with unease and fear, indeed, in the field of fiction, it's not unusual for a child to watch out for an adult, from his seat in the dark or from his startled eyes as he turns the pages with bated breath. In the land of fiction, there are no adults and children, there are no ages. We worry about those who are stronger, wiser, cleverer, older and more experienced than us, and the child, who, in his elemental state, can still not see this clearly, aches or struggles to warn someone that he's being tricked or is in grave danger, even though that someone cannot hear; he can see what's happening, because he is the chosen witness (absorbed in contemplation or in reading, the child really believes he is the sole witness). And Beatriz did seem disoriented and helpless, although not in any obvious or self-pitying way, as I said, I liked her and felt sorry for her – 'poor unhappy woman, sad and affectionate; poor soul, poor wretch' – not that she intentionally sought my pity. Had

I thought this was her way of getting through life, a tactic intended to attract kindness and gain advantages, I would never have worried about her in that passive, distant, silent manner – although 'worried' is not perhaps the right verb – it would, instead, have provoked a certain irritation and suspicion in me. I don't like victims who are too keenly aware of their victimhood.

It was only days after Muriel's return from that absence that he finally gave me my orders. One morning, when there was no one else in the apartment, we went into the living room next to the office and he closed the door, something he didn't normally do. Then he lay down full length on the floor, as he had on other occasions, with his forearm cushioning his head: I came to think this was his way of avoiding looking directly at me, of keeping his lost eye trained on the ceiling, or on the highest shelf in the library, or on the painting by Casanova's brother, a way of saying things without really saying them, of seeming to be talking to himself or of allowing me to pluck his words – his indications, digressions, confidences, his mildly spoken orders – out of the air and not directly from his one eye or from his lips. It seemed to me that he was directing his gaze at the oil painting, which depicted an exotic horseman with a drooping moustache and an unusual plumed cap or hat, who was half-turning, so that his right eye, and only that eye, was fixed for ever on Catherine the Great of Russia or on some other viewer, the left almost hidden or perhaps sightless – from what one could see, it appeared to be defective, half-closed or perhaps simply clumsily painted – he could have been one-eyed like Muriel, having lost his eye in battle, for, unlike Muriel, he was a soldier. I sometimes suspected that Muriel wore his patch so as to resemble John Ford, Raoul Walsh, André de Toth, Nicholas Ray or possibly Fritz Lang, a strange plague among individuals whose work depended in large measure on their sight.

But in the background could be seen another six horsemen, all riding away on their horses, all with their backs to us and wearing less unusual hats with broad brims – they looked vaguely Velázquezian – whereas the red figure in the foreground had paused, looking over his shoulder, as if wishing to retain, before he rode off, the image of the deaths he had caused, as if he were the only one listening to the dumb plea of the dead, who, in all wars, seem to send out a murmur from their bodies that lie as still as figures in a painting: 'Remember us. Or at least, remember *me*.'

Muriel took out his compass-pillbox and studied the north-pointing needle.

'Do you remember what I told you about Dr Van Vechten?' he asked.

I think I blushed – although only very briefly, just for a moment, he wouldn't have noticed – when I heard him mention that name which, only months before, I hadn't even understood. Now it was different. I not only knew Van Vechten and had spoken to him at meetings and suppers and over card games, with other people present, I had also found out something about his personal life which, to put it more delicately this time, deeply affected Beatriz. Ever since that partially seen episode in the Darmstadt Sanctuary, I had been dreading Muriel mentioning the Doctor again. I didn't know whether I should tell him about what I had witnessed while up a tree or if I should keep silent; it depended on what he asked or requested, I would decide then, I told myself, all the while hoping not to have to decide anything.

'Yes, I do. Well, you didn't really tell me anything, you were, you remember, reluctant. You announced it rather than telling me. You explained your doubts. And you also warned me that you might ask me to forget the conversation entirely, or forget what you had skirted round or announced. And that, more or less, is what I've done up until now.' I reminded him of this possibility in the hope that he would choose that option, although he clearly wasn't going to. Ever since that afternoon, I found everything to do with Van Vechten troubling, and thought that when I next saw him, I would try to avoid him. 'But yes, of course, I remember. One can't simply forget at will.'

'Well, Juan, I told you that I might want you to do something for me,' he went on, still staring up at the ceiling or at the painting. 'And what I want you to do is to make friends with Van Vechten. More than that, I want you to make him one of your drinking companions, to involve him as much as you can in your nocturnal excursions and sorties. You often go out at night, don't you? To discos, concerts, bars, the celebrated Madrid *movida*. Invite him to join you. He may be a lot older, but I can assure you, he'll jump at the chance. He'll be pleased to have a guide. Introduce him to your girlfriends or to your female acquaintances, to women young and old, I don't care what age they are, and observe how he behaves with them, with women in general. Gain his confidence. Talk to him about your sex life. Tell him all about your promiscuity, your conquests (you've had a few, haven't you?), and any other adventures in that field, and if they're nothing to write home about, then invent some. Show off. Boast. Make him green with envy. Things were far more difficult when he was young, there were far fewer opportunities. When he sees how easy things are now, he'll wish he'd been born two decades later. Don't worry about seeming vulgar or even disrespectful when talk-ing about women, be as vulgar and disrespectful as you like, exaggerate. Draw him out and, above all, observe him. I want you to encourage him to confide in you, about what he gets up to now and about his past exploits, his glory days. He always was a womanizer and, as you've probably noticed, still is. And he's had quite a few

183

successes too. But in his day, women played hard to get, here more than in most countries. Most were so armour-plated and bulletproof you had to resort to promises and tricks. See if you can get him talking about the past, because that's what interests me most. There's nothing like boasting about your own exploits to get others to tell you theirs, however ancient; it never fails. Make a note of any chat-up lines, watch him in action, see if he tries to get off with anyone, and he'll try often, believe you me. Things will be more difficult for him now, but see how far he gets. Reveal yourself as vile and unscrupulous and watch his response, whether he approves or is of a like mind, whether he urges you on or censures you. Let me know what he tells you and what impression he makes on you. Let me know what you find out.'

'But find out what, Eduardo? I don't understand. It's as plain as day that he's the sort who'll try it on with anyone, with the slightest encouragement and even without. He's always looking to see how the land lies, with any woman worth pursuing that is, because he never gives the ugly or the asexual a second glance, which is not to say that he isn't open to offers. Anyone can tell he's a man with his eye on the main chance, and if there were no witnesses about, he'd be quite likely to overstep the mark. Compared to him, Professor Rico – to mention another friend of yours with very keen antennae – is a respectful, delicate herbivore. A contemplative. But you must know this better than I, given that you've known the Doctor most of your life. What is it that you want me to discover or coax from him? It's hard to draw someone out if you don't know what he's got to tell you. Could you give me a bit more guidance, tell me more precisely what it is you're looking for?'

Muriel drummed his nails on his bulky Bakelite or whatever eyepatch, cric cric cric, a pleasant sound, which I longed to imitate

184

with my own fingers. Then he suddenly turned his one intense, dark blue eye on me with all the intimidating penetration of which he was sometimes capable, as if he were compensating for the immutable opacity of the other eye. He hadn't looked at me until then. He seemed to ponder his answer for a few seconds, tempted to grant my wish. In the end, he let out a long sigh, perhaps frustrated that he must deny me any further information or help, or perhaps irritated by my faulty memory.

'No, I mustn't. As I said before, if I start voicing my suspicions, if I start revealing the story I've been told and which might or might not be true, I could be doing him an irreparable injustice. The Doctor is a great friend of mine, remember, whom I wouldn't wish to harm without good reason. Or at least without a hint of certainty, if that isn't a contradiction in terms; without more proof. As I explained, he would never tell me about something so very shameful; he's told me other things, that is, I know a few things that he definitely wouldn't want to be proclaimed to the four winds, but not this. Because he'd be ashamed if I knew. He knows me well and knows that I'm the very opposite of a puritan and not at all strait-laced, but that there are certain indecencies I cannot tolerate.' (I remembered he had used the corresponding adjective when he had spoken more explicitly before: 'According to what I've been told,' he had said, 'the Doctor behaved in an indecent manner towards a woman or possibly more than one.' And he had, to my astonishment, concluded: 'That, to me, is unforgivable, the lowest of the low. Do you understand? That's as low as one can go.') 'With you it would be different, if you gave him the chance. He could tell you, because he hardly knows you.' He fell silent. He looked at me still more intensely and with something bordering on curiosity, as if he were suddenly seeing me for the first time, or had just realized the truth of what he went on to say: 'Even

I don't really know you.' Then he averted his eye and fixed it once more on the ceiling or on the painting, and, still lying flat on the floor, started stroking his chin with that silver pillbox. What he said next was spoken in an indolent tone, as though it were almost too obvious to be put into words. 'But then neither do you. You're not quite fully formed.'

To him this was an obvious thing to say, but to me it was a surprise and even rather troubling. Probably no one ever is quite fully formed, still less the young, and that's how we adults tend to see them, incomplete, indecisive, confused, like an unfinished painting or a half-written or half-read novel – there's not a great deal of difference – in which anything could happen, well, not perhaps anything – but too many things – one or more characters could die or none at all; and one of them might kill someone and then he would be both formed and finished, or so it would seem in the eyes of a stern author or reader; what we are told in a book could be totally gripping or not at all, in which case the passage from page to page becomes a torment and the finger turning the page grows weary and stops, it doesn't wait until the final page, after which there is nothing, even if, on the contrary, the finger wants to remain indefinitely in that world and with those invented people. It's the same with people's lives; some, however filled with troubles and vicissitudes, arouse in us so little curiosity that we can barely stand to hear about them, yet other lives, for some reason, prove hypnotic, even though there appears to be nothing very special about them, or the best part remains hidden and is mere supposition.

But each individual believes he is fully formed in each and every phase of his existence, that he has a specific character subject only to minor variations, and considers himself to be prone to certain actions and immune to others, when the truth is that, as children or youths, most of us have not been tested, we have not yet found ourselves at a crossroads or faced with a dilemma. Maybe we never are fully formed, but begin unwittingly to configure and forge ourselves from the moment we first hove into view as a tiny dot on the ocean, one that gradually grows in size until we form a definite shape to be either avoided or approached, and as the years pass and events enfold us, we accept or reject the options offered to us or allow others to do so on our behalf (or is it just the air itself?). It doesn't matter who makes the decision, everything is horribly irreversible and, in that sense, everything evens out: the deliberate and the involuntary, the accidental and the planned, the impulsive and the premeditated, and, ultimately, who cares about the whys, still less about the wherefores?

When I look at my own daughters, they don't seem very formed to me, but, given their young age, that's only natural; on the other hand, they doubtless consider themselves to be fully formed, as almost fixed entities, just as I did when I was twenty-three and before that too, I suppose; we pay so little attention to the changes that take place in us that we forget how they happened and forget them entirely once we've been through them. I had finished my degree with good marks and without any mishaps; and even though it was entirely thanks to my parents and their long friendship with Muriel that I had instantly found employment with a remarkable person, whom I admired almost unreservedly and whose approval and trust contributed to my seeing myself in a highly favourable light, I couldn't help but feel proud as well, convinced that my boss must have seen something in me, that he had, at the very least, taken a liking to me, given that he had employed me and kept me on; I sometimes even had the flattering sense that he occasionally forgot about my family connections and about how he had come to give me the job, that I was the son of those old friends from his youth, the De Veres, of whom he remained very fond, even though they were now more often in touch by letter or only very infrequently, since my parents were usually living in some far-flung place and I was seldom with them. After all, I was very well read, had seen a lot of paintings and even more films; I had a considerable store of knowledge and was doubtless a pedantic young man, although I kept my pedantry to myself when it was inappropriate, for example, when I went out at night with my friends or with girls; I was fluent in one foreign language and spoke another reasonably well, and I knew that in my own language I had access to a wide vocabulary, far wider than that of most of my contemporaries, which meant I could comfortably take part in the conversations held by Muriel and his circle, who were older and wiser than me (at least in theory), although on those occasions I tended to listen and not intervene too much, and their talk often descended from the heights and meandered about in some very low territory, accompanied by loud guffaws; I had spent time abroad, whenever my parents included me in their prolonged and varied diplomatic postings, although they usually preferred me to stay in Madrid and to continue my education at the same school, wanting me to put down some deeper roots, at least that was the excuse they used for leaving me here in term-time, and even when there were no more terms, in the care of my aunt and uncle, Julia and Luis; they were happy for me to grow up alongside my cousins Luis and Julia, who have been like half-siblings to me, since I have no siblings of my own. No one has ever kept a very close watch on me, and for the most part – except when my parents were visiting or during the vacations, although they didn't always come even then, often taking the opportunity to travel on their own – I was left alone in the family home under the negligent eye of various nursemaids or housekeepers or whatever you might call them, who never stayed long enough to become attached to me or to wield any real authority over me. From adolescence on, I was accustomed to never really having to answer to anyone very much, to returning home at odd hours and choosing where I slept, in my parents' apartment or at my aunt and uncle's place or, on some nights, at neither: this was in my early youth, from the time, let's say, when I became an undergraduate at seventeen.

When I was twenty-three, I was still living like that, or possibly even more autonomously: alone in my parents' apartment, with a backdrop of ever-changing daily helps, who would leave me food in the fridge and do the cleaning, who saw very little of me and of whom I saw even less. My parents were not so much wealthy – although they had no financial worries, they lived pretty much from day to day – as superficial and casual. Despite my father's vague aspirations to originality or greatness, his diplomatic career had not been particularly dazzling, his main achievement being his appointment to the consulate in Frankfurt, which happened rather late; however, he retained the kind of deep-seated youthful optimism typical of the frivolously minded, an optimism he shared with my mother. I often had the feeling that I was slightly superfluous to their lives, or not superfluous exactly, more as if I were an old acquaintance over whom they watched from a distance, with no great enthusiasm or concern, but with undeniable affection; they behaved like a childless couple or as if they were my aunt and uncle or my godparents; I never had any cause for complaint, for they were charming if inconstant companions, or is it simply that we accept as normal whatever world or situation we're born into? At any rate, I couldn't rely on receiving much in the way of an inheritance (although they did own their apartment), and so, despite the privileges I'd enjoyed in childhood and adolescence, I was aware from early on that I would have to earn my own living like everyone else; that was why I was so delighted to have a job and an income, however temporary, and even though I had no idea what I would do when Muriel eventually dispensed with my services, as was bound to happen at some point. At the time, I felt no need to gain my independence, since I'd been living entirely independently for a long time, perhaps from too young an age, which is possibly why I began spending more and more hours at Muriel's apartment, where there was, at least, a family, people companionably coming and going, entering and leaving, and some nights I even slept in that isolated bedroom, beyond the kitchen, which was, up to a point, mine, for habitual use makes us tacit owners as long as that habit or use is not taken away from us or expressly forbidden; so many people arrive at some temporary stopping-place from which there's no uprooting them and where they end up spending half their lives. You should never allow anyone to stay, not even for a day, unless you're prepared for them to stay for ever.

Anyway, I believed myself to be fully formed and finished and felt that, broadly speaking, I knew my own character. I didn't know where I'd learned the rules of behaviour by which I tried to live my life (not from my parents, who had no rules at all or else kept changing them, but then maybe that's part of being a diplomat), but I never behaved in a solemn or ostentatious manner; I've always loathed pompous, bombastic individuals, or recriminatory types, who insist on imposing their guidelines on others instead of keeping them to themselves. Perhaps I'd gleaned those rules from films, novels or comic books, which is how it was, up until fairly recently, for boys and young men who lacked any clear role models in real life (and in real life nothing is ever very clear; it doesn't even tell a story), especially when those stories were troubling and ambiguous and not mere edifying nonsense. I considered myself to be fairly respectful and loyal and a man of scruples, capable of guarding any confidence entrusted to me and of keeping a secret if asked to do so; what I feared most was disappointing those I loved or admired. Muriel belonged to the latter group right from the start and gradually became one of the former — no, not gradually, quickly: unless you really take against someone, you inevitably grow fond of them over time (there isn't any happy medium, indifference barely exists, however many struggle to achieve it); and that is what happened to me with him and, of course, with Beatriz Noguera, and with their children, especially their oldest daughter, Susana, partly because of her resemblance to her mother, but also partly because of her kind heart and friendly nature; and even with Flavia and Rico and Roy, and with Gloria and Marcela, however much they irritated me and made me feel uneasy and however much I felt they were a bad influence on their friend. And even with Van Vechten before that afternoon in the sanctuary of Our Lady of Darmstadt; after that, for no objective reason, I couldn't stomach the man, although it was no business of mine what Beatriz did, let alone what he did — that was up to them. One of the rules I was trying to follow was more or less this: to judge other people as little as possible and not to meddle in their lives, still less intervene in them. My wish was to see no shape in the ocean, and not to have to come to any decision as to what it was, but that's impossible, because I, too, was a shape which others might recoil from or aim for or collide with.

And so I didn't at all like the task Muriel had set me, because of its very nature. I had withdrawn some of the superficial esteem I had felt for Van Vechten, both equally arbitrary acts, but we allow ourselves such absolute arbitrariness with those we know only slightly, whom we see as provisional or circumstantial and not of our choosing, mere ramifications of or bequests from someone else; the problem arises if that someone else is important to us, because then we feel under an obligation to accept those inherited friends and even to care for and protect them, especially if the person who bequeathed them to us is still alive and can find out if we have done as he asked, can thank or reproach us with his quick eye, can, at the very least, notice. Sometimes someone we really care for makes an explicit request ('Treat that person as you would treat me, as if he *were* me; give him whatever he asks for and help him in every way possible'), sometimes this isn't even necessary and we mentally anticipate that request ('I get the message, I understand and will ask no more questions'). If we are staunch supporters of a lover, a friend, a teacher, we tend to welcome all those who surround them, not just those people who are essential to them: idiot children, demanding or poisonous wives, boring, even despotic husbands, dubious or disagreeable friends, unscrupulous colleagues on whom they depend, people in whom we can detect not a single good quality, not the slightest attraction and who lead us to wonder about the origin of the admiration expressed by those beings whose approval we ourselves crave: what past events bind them together, what shared suffering, what common experiences, what secret knowledge or vengeful motives; what strange, invincible nostalgia. We try to appear friendly, pleasant and intelligent and gain a pat on the back – from our lover a kiss or what usually follows kisses, or at least a look that prolongs our hopes a little longer – and cannot understand why these shrill or dull or inadequate or limited people, who, in our eyes, are entirely without merit, should obtain gratis and for nothing what costs us such invention, brio and vigilance. The only possible answer is often simply that these people came before us, date back to long before we entered the life of the lover, friend or teacher and that we know nothing of what happened between them and probably never will; that they may have travelled many possibly muddy paths together, without us there as companion or witness. We always arrive late in people's lives.

For me, Van Vechten was one such individual, up to a point, though not entirely. He was clearly no fool, but he lacked Rico's depth and cleverness as well as his not always intentional absurdity, he lacked Roy's devotion and exhaustive knowledge of Muriel's work, which made my boss's patience and willingness to take him under his wing perfectly understandable, he lacked the ingenuity or kindness of other friends. At the time, Van Vechten was a highly respected paediatrician with a very successful practice in the Salamanca area of Madrid, and he also acted as occasional family or duty doctor to the Muriels and to a few other prestigious or neighbouring families (by which I mean that, since he was a good friend and close neighbour, a combination of convenience and confidence meant that they would call him out for almost any reason, even if the complaint had nothing to do with his specialism and was afflicting a grown adult; he would then advise them what to do or, if it came to it, who to go to, on the few occasions when he thought a second opinion necessary, and would refer them to a consultant at the lavish hospital that had opened to a great fanfare in 1968 and where he had been appointed Head of Paediatrics). Like many men in his profession, he enjoyed rubbing shoulders with the intelligentsia and with show-business types, who tended to belong to the Left or were, at the very least, opposed to Franco, and he was well received by them – for other reasons too, I suppose: his influence and his money being among them, I fear – because in the difficult and seemingly endless years of the dictatorship, that is, during most of Van Vechten's career, he had treated the persecuted and the victims of reprisals very well, despite having fought during the Civil War on the so-called Nationalist side and despite being on good terms with the regime, a relationship that had, in part, helped him build a successful career. His early affiliation had been watered down, if not forgotten, and later, younger generations never knew about it, as was the case with so many others who were quick to dissemble or to sever any embarrassing links, or else to sit on the fence and act with generosity and understanding towards the losers: they were sometimes quite sincere, supporters of the new harmony (which ultimately depended on them); others were equally quick to see what was likely to happen in the long term and were mere opportunists. The latter were always aware that even in a situation in which the winners ruled absolutely and completely crushed the opposition or their scattered and battered remnants, it suited them to be at least partly on good terms with everyone or to have them all partly in their debt, or at least not to be seen by anyone as their bitter enemy. They know that any such remnant will, sooner or later, regroup and recover enough to reorganize itself and reconquer those areas despised and ignored by the current tyrant, usually because he has no idea what to do with them: in Spain, for example, this applied to culture and the arts.

Van Vechten had been one of the sincere ones, at least he had that reputation. It was said that even during the 1940s and 50s, when the repression was still at its most hyperactively meticulous, and he could have been accused of being nice to the 'Reds' and thus damaged his career prospects, he had nonetheless made home visits, completely free of charge, to the sick children of individuals who had been purged and those who had been banned from exercising their professions and were thus condemned to earning nothing or only what they managed to scrape together as and when they could (an eminent botanist was reduced to working as a gardener and certain university professors became teachers at some modest language academy), obliging their wives and older daughters to offer their services as seamstresses or cleaners in the wealthy households of those who had them in their power or of the black marketeers who took advantage of everyone. Van Vechten had been conciliatory or magnanimous and compassionate, as had some of his colleagues, and he had appeared promptly to deal with cases of influenza and colic and measles, mumps and chickenpox, even meningitis and other such serious ailments afflicting those proscribed children. He had salved and saved many small lives, a service for which the parents could not have paid or only with great difficulty and by sliding into unpayable debt and bankruptcy. He had built a reputation as a good, kind man, civilized and caring, and with the passing of time – which passes particularly slowly during dictatorships, where everything becomes legend, often heavily embellished, especially if the interested party has a role in spreading that legend – democratic, cultivated people had come to consider him to be one of them, quite ignorant of how he had prospered under the regime or else attributing this to his extraordinary professional skills, his ability to get on with everyone and to move easily in all circles, and a little, too, to the luck that accompanies any success. This gave him the aura of a moderate, theoretical and almost semi-heroic left-winger, someone who, in the hardest of times, had put his shoulder to the wheel and run risks in order to help valuable, useful people who had been cast into the outer darkness to fend for themselves.

No one gave any importance to the fact that he had completed his medical degree when he was only twenty, in 1940, the first year after the victory, when the universities had been closed for the three years that the War had lasted; that when he was twenty-three (my age at the time), he had been appointed Assistant Paediatrician at the Hospital de San Carlos; or that when he was thirty-one he had been able to open his own surgery, which met with immediate success and acclaim, in the then relatively new Clínica Ruber, founded in 1942 by the very *franquista* and very clever doctors-cum-impresarios Ruiz and Bergaz, who combined the first letters of their two surnames to give the clinic its absurd title. Or maybe it was simply that no one knew, just as in the years of the Transition, people preferred to ignore or deny the past lives of many individuals opposed to the regime – whose opposition only began at some early or late moment in slow-moving time – whose trajectory was considered impeccable, especially if they were confident and distinguished, not to mention vociferous. No one bothers to trace the steps or origins of someone they admire and respect, still less if they owe them a debt of gratitude. No one noticed either that Van Vechten had always enjoyed prestige, reputation and money. It was assumed he had earned this through hard work, talent, dedication and effort.

Of course, I knew nothing of all this when Muriel charged me with that task. I knew only of Van Vechten's excellent reputation as a doctor and that he had selflessly given aid to those victims of political reprisals who lacked the means to pay him, or so people said and so anyone would tell you if asked. It was easy enough to check the facts of his biography and career, but no one bothered, even though they were there for all to see in Spanish encyclopaedias, Durban, for example, or even in the most recent edition of *Who's Who in Europe*, which I found in the British Institute library in Calle Almagro; I was surprised to see his name there, I didn't know at the time that there are various short cuts you can take in order to appear in almost any list of important people, if you're determined enough. It was because of the mission Muriel had given me that I decided to find out exactly who I was trying to entrap, hoping to find some more justification for what I was about to do. That's what I didn't like, having to drag him along with me and observe him, with the intention of informing Muriel about his behaviour, especially with women. Even though I didn't much like doing this (right from the start, I could have given my boss some very concrete facts about how, where and who Van Vechten was screwing, at least on that one afternoon, but I had decided to keep quiet about that or keep it to myself for the moment); even though Muriel had been told an ugly story from the past and now harboured grave reservations about Van Vechten that troubled him deeply and threatened their friendship; even though I soon learned that the Doctor had clearly had certain links with the regime in the remote or not so remote past (possibly merely passively or by silent consent; after all, what else could they do, the majority of those who felt unable to give up prospering or growing rich for forty years, it took real guts to abandon all hope), but what I really disliked was the idea of deceiving someone from the outset, of offering him a camaraderie based entirely on someone else's initiative – I mean, why on earth would I choose as a companion on my nights out a sixty-year-old man, even one who looked ten years younger? – and which was completely false from top to bottom. Not only because that camaraderie was feigned, but because behind it lay an ulterior motive, a desire to unmask him, the setting of bait with which to tempt him.

I realized how uncomfortable it is being a spy, however worthy the cause, and in this situation, I wasn't even sure what the cause was, I was simply following orders. There is something base, something grubby about passing yourself off as someone else, about behaving in an underhand manner, gaining the confidence of someone in order to betray him, even if that person is a villain, an enemy, a murderer. That is the job of moles and infiltrators, of the secret or double agents who inhabit every sphere of society, even the most innocuous; of the policemen who sometimes spend years working, for example, for a terrorist organization or a mafia, as if they were just another member of the gang. They must be thoroughly convinced of the ultimate nobility of their job, they must think every day, when they get up and when they go to bed, that thanks to their imposture, lives will be saved and crimes averted. And yet, I thought, I could not be one of them. Perhaps it's a matter of training and practice and habit, of feeding an already existing hatred; of developing a sense of righteous indignation, of severity and indifference and hardness of heart, a renunciation of any finer feelings for those around you, or modifying or neutralizing your conscience. I imagine I would have felt guilty when I saw the criminal or fanatic growing fond of me, gradually abandoning his suspicions and becoming ever-more confiding, when I saw that he genuinely liked me, possibly, in the long term, unconditionally, if such people have such feelings. I suspect that they do, since feelings of loyalty and friendship are within everyone's grasp, even a ruthless, malicious monster. Who doesn't have a soft spot for someone, a lover, a daughter, a colleague, a comrade?

I had no difficulty whatsoever in persuading Van Vechten ('persuade' is hardly the right word). It was child's play really and he was the child, which only added to my bad conscience. In those days of permissiveness and freedom, which had been going on for quite a while, even some years before Franco died, it was not unusual for men of previous generations to regard us youngsters with amazement and envy, imagining that we led a wild, unruly existence, something to which they had aspired in vain in their stricter, more confined youth. On one occasion, at a card game to which Muriel invited me, along with other people of his age or even slightly older (I remember there was a bullfighter and an actor there, men who, all things considered, had not exactly lacked opportunities for a certain amount of old-fashioned professional promiscuity, now long since past), their curiosity centred on me for a few minutes, because of my youth. I discovered that, because they thought me good-looking, they took it for granted, with touching ingenuousness, that I spent my nights hopping from bed to bed – that's what they said – screwing away to my heart's content. And the most ingenuous or perhaps the most lustful, the most prurient, was Van Vechten, who, in the cheerily frank tone he occasionally adopted – but only occasionally – concluded this brief interrogation or display of old men's fantasies by asking me point-blank:

'So, young De Vere.' This was the way in which Muriel introduced me and how all his friends addressed me, at least initially. 'You're a handsome lad, so tell us all, in confidence, of course: given the age we live in, with all these liberated young women around, how often do you get laid a month, more or less? In a good month, that is. I shouldn't think you ever stop.' And he awaited my response with a salacious look in his eyes, anticipatorily greedy and amazed, I could have given him any number, and he would have swallowed it down enthusiastically. They all imagined a world that did not exist or only among the more active and fortunate of huntsmen, just as in any other age, although things were certainly a lot easier then: a world with no moral restrictions or hindrances, a kind of neopaganism as portrayed in certain scandalous, pseudo-artistic films, of which there was a veritable plague in European cinemas at the time and to which those men would flock, not to Jess Franco's films, but to the more famous ones that they would find easier to justify seeing. As I said, there was no AIDS at the time or no one knew of its existence, and so there was no fear and no precautions taken. It was a privileged time in that respect, a time that has not so far returned.

I felt awkward talking about such things, still less pretending I was a womanizer, it wasn't my style. I could see that the truth – something normal, something modest, although I certainly had no complaints in that regard – would have disappointed them, especially Van Vechten, the most febrile, the most eager, the most gullible. I found his old-school fantasies depressing and rather pathetic, not so very different from those of adolescents crowding round the pioneer who claims to have already had certain sexual experiences and is prepared to describe them in detail, in the playground, to a credulous because ignorant audience, which expects and even demands lies and exaggerations, because without them no story is worth listening to. His fantasies struck me as somewhat pitiful or creepy. There were two women present, lovers or friends or rather ex-lovers of the actor or the bullfighter or of both, who were not playing cards, but were there to provide company or decoration and were keeping each other amused; every now and then, Van Vechten's eyes would swivel over to them, for they were both wearing tight skirts and showing quite a lot of leg, greatly enhanced by their high heels. I noticed that they had stopped talking to each other and were awaiting my answer, which made me feel even more embarrassed than if there had been only men present; we speak more freely and feel less absurd in exclusively male encounters. I hesitated. Then I remembered that many women don't normally mind a man or a youth having such multiple adventures. On the contrary, they admire him in an imaginary way and feel intrigued, it can even be an incentive to them to become one of those adventures, either at once or at some future date, as if they made a mental note: 'He's a sexy guy and popular with women, better bear that in mind and not discount him.' I saw that Muriel was also awaiting my response. He would never have asked such a question himself (he did not sail in those particular waters), but now that someone else had asked, he was hoping I would provide his friends with some satisfaction and amusement, as if, having brought me with him, I were his responsibility. And so when my silence grew somewhat lengthy, creating an unnecessary sense of expectation, he decided to prompt me:

'What's wrong, lad, has the cat got your tongue? You're being awfully coy. Don't let me down now, answer the Doctor, he wants to know what you young people get up to with your limitless freedom.'

I decided it would be best to lie. In order to make those grown men green with envy, which is what they wanted: to be amazed and to bemoan their having been born too soon. To arouse the imaginations of the two thirty-something women, who would see me as an indefatigable near-child, possibly a demon between the sheets. To please my employer, who had deemed me worthy of being present, along with the grown-ups. After all, we were there to have a good time, it was a jolly occasion.

'Well, in a good month, as you put it, Doctor,' I said at last (despite his protests, I addressed him as 'Doctor' at first, although not, of course, once he started accompanying me to places where he would never have gone alone), 'I'll have seven or eight, never less than that. In a slow month, three or four.' And I think I must have visibly blushed, more at my own brazen deceit than for any other reason. They probably thought I was blushing at this confession of my own greed.

There was a murmur of voices around me, the odd whistle of astonishment, I was, for a moment, the centre of attention. The bullfighter and the actor must have felt their own glorious past lives as ladykillers somewhat diminished. Muriel, I thought, looked half-surprised, half-pleased ('That many, eh?' he said paternally). The two women exchanged glances, raised their eyebrows, and then uncrossed and crossed their legs at the same time (a flash of thighs), as if this were a dance routine they had rehearsed or as if they were twins. Van Vechten's eyes almost popped out of their sockets and he repeatedly tugged at his tie and then again at the knot in order to straighten it, it was a gesture he made whenever he was agitated or excited at some interesting prospect or promise. Most striking of all was that no one showed the least scepticism, they clearly didn't know the world, however long they had been in it, or knew only the world of their youth, the only one we understand naturally and effortlessly: in life we experience a little of what will happen after our death, when time leaves us behind at such incredible speed and transforms us into the remote past and lumps us together with the antiquities. When still alive, we realize that we cannot possibly keep up, we get left behind and waste our energy and begin to grow weary of so much change and tell ourselves: 'This is where my age ends, I'm not going to bother with the next one, it doesn't belong to me; I'll pretend as best I can, but I'm fast becoming an anachronism and outstaying my welcome.' Things would have been minimally different had Professor Rico been there. Not because he knew the world any better, not at all, but because he would never have allowed himself to appear to be impressed with witnesses present and would have come out with some scornful comment: 'Ha, a mere bagatelle' or 'Is that all?' or even 'And you call that a good month, young De Vere? I thought you were more competent, more adept.' But he wasn't in Madrid that night, and so no one called my bluff, and Van Vechten, the most inclined to believe what I had said and impressed by the sheer scale of it, tried to draw me out, with the acquiescence of the others as a background rumble.

'Come on, then, tell us all,' said the Doctor, highly excited, as if this were the beginning of another party. 'Ages? Places? Settings? And where do you pick them up?' The expression 'pick them up' betrayed his view of these encounters, the old world to which he belonged. 'Do you stick with girls your own age or are you happy with anyone who isn't actually old? I imagine you have your limits. When you're spoiled for choice, you have to, at least that's how it was for me when I was your age.' He glanced across at the two women, some comment dancing on the tip of his tongue, I feared the worst, some unpleasantly vengeful remark, because they gave no response, either visual or verbal. I was afraid he might say something like: 'Those two lovely ladies over there, for example, would have seemed old to me at the time, but now I'd quite happily screw them.' Fortunately, he said nothing, but, given the context, that glance in itself seemed crude and inappropriate. They were quite attractive, those two ex-lovers of the actor or the bullfighter, one rather coarse, the other more delicate. They didn't deserve to be belittled like that, not even hypothetically or retrospectively. They had noticed Van Vechten's sidelong glance and understood its meaning. They exchanged another subtle look as if to check that they were in accord, then they uncrossed and crossed their legs again, not, this time, as a mark of their approval of me, the young man, but as a reproof to that man in the autumn of his years. The Doctor was often impertinent and expansive and not fully aware of his age because it was not as yet apparent on his still unlined face or on his still agile body; his lack of tact meant that one had to give him more than the usual amount of leeway.

I was not prepared to continue along the path he was suggesting. It was one thing to lie briefly about numbers, as a joke and so as not to disappoint, but quite another to provide detailed descriptions and accounts, continuously, inevitably, boastfully, even if it was all invented. There was something unpleasant and unsavoury about his questions, however jovial or jokey his tone; a lack of respect for women which, even though it was pretty much the norm in many areas of life, both Spanish and non-Spanish, both then and now, nonetheless troubled me. Not that I didn't occasionally slip into that mode myself (I'm not going to pretend I've always been the perfect gentleman), but he went too far, he teetered on the edge of abuse, or, rather, that was his normal mode. Having daughters cures one of that involuntary or reflex disdain that far too many of us men inherit. In the Doctor, it was deliberate; even though, as I found out later, he himself had sons and daughters, he had never moved on from that instinctive disdain.

I smiled apologetically:

'No, Doctor. I'm sure you've had far more success than me. I just catch what I can, like most people. What I didn't tell you was how many women I try it on with, and if I were to total them up, I'd definitely have far more failures than successes.'

The actor and the bullfighter and Muriel and a few other men laughed, even though what I said was also a lie, because I wasn't the kind who went around making a play for women left, right and centre. The first two must have felt slightly relieved, thinking that nothing very much had changed and that, regardless of the times, any success is always the result of skill, luck and effort. Van Vechten didn't laugh, or only belatedly, reluctantly copying the others. He looked at me as if I were wilfully concealing useful information, as if I had whisked away from him the anecdotes he had been so looking forward to hearing, perhaps hoping to learn something about the new world that lay just beyond his grasp. He once again immersed himself in the poker game, but with a look of puerile resentment on his face.

Not long after this, one of the women decided she wanted to leave, having got what she could out of the evening. Since it was nearly three o'clock in the morning (these poker evenings used to begin after supper, at around midnight, and, at the time, people of all ages tended to stay up very late and we *madrileños* have always only ever slept the bare minimum) someone needed to accompany her, but the bullfighter and the actor (she had come with one of them, if not both) were not yet ready to strike camp, preferring to recover some of their losses and return home victorious and slightly richer.

'The boy will take you in a taxi,' the bullfighter said, 'he's not playing at the moment.' And he took a note from his wallet and handed it to me, for the taxi fare, and I took it so as not to leave him with his hand poised disdainfully in mid-air. It was true, I had hardly played at all, they had merely made room for me for five or six rounds when Muriel was taking a somewhat curmudgeonly rest from a series of bad hands. I hadn't even bet any of my own money, only his, and had managed to break his run of bad luck, which had cheered him up sufficiently for him to resume his place at the table.

'Leave it to me now, clever clogs, let's see if I can hang on to some of your good luck,' he said, happily patting the back of the chair to indicate that I should give it up to him. He had recovered his good humour, and it pleased me to be called 'clever clogs', you only call someone that if you're genuinely fond of them, and it's usually a term reserved for children. Or it used to be, that's yet another term that, like so many others, has fallen into disuse; our languages are slowly shrinking. 'If it lasts, I'll give you a percentage of the booty. Does five per cent seem reasonable?' he added mockingly.

The woman and I had to walk quite a way in search of a taxi, she should have booked one over the phone, but once she had decided she was going, she wanted to leave immediately and was too impatient to wait. No taxis, either occupied or free, passed through that residential area near El Viso or thereabouts, with its detached houses, large and small, the streets unlit by a single shop or cinema, bar or restaurant, and besides, it was late, and the street lamps fewer and further between. It was a spring night verging on summer, she was wearing only a skirt and a close-fitting, low-cut top that left her arms almost bare, and no tights either, she had clearly not been expecting to have to walk anywhere, or only from a car to the house, which belonged either to the actor or the bullfighter. Her high heels meant that she had to walk fairly slowly, and I had to fall in with her rhythm, but she walked well, with a discreet wiggle. It made me think that she was not entirely indifferent to how she appeared in my eyes, that she wanted me to like her, not that this means very much, some people have a need to be liked by whoever they're with, even if it's the monster from the deep or, if they're in the countryside, a herd of pigs. She was the one I described as being more delicate, which means only that she was more so than her friend, but not necessarily delicate per se. She was too curvaceous for that (not that I minded in the least) and she was wearing very large hoop earrings and a very short skirt, short even by the brazen standards of the time, revealing most of her tanned thighs, in fact, she was tanned all over; as soon as the good weather arrived, she must have spent every spare minute at the local swimming pool or at the poolside of some wealthy friends. I asked her name (we hadn't been formally introduced) and she said it was Celia and asked me for mine, for throughout the evening, everyone had referred to me as either 'young De Vere' or 'the boy' or 'Romeo' or even 'the lad'.

'Do you know Dr Jorge well?' she asked. She perhaps couldn't remember Van Vechten's surname or didn't feel like struggling to say it.

'No, not well. I've only ever met him at gatherings like tonight's. Only with other people around.'

'He's a bit of an old lecher.' She said this confidently, without expecting any corroboration on my part. But I didn't know if she was saying this after what she had just heard, after his inquisitorial questions about my exploits, or because she'd had dealings with him herself and knew all about his manners and manias.

'Why do you say that? Because he kept asking me questions? Or have you been out with him and he's tried it on with you?'

'No, I wouldn't even go rowing on the Retiro lake with him, and there are always loads of people there. But I once went to him for a medical examination, I was getting these pains and Rafael sent me to see him for a consultation.' Rafael was the bullfighter, Maestro Rafael Viana. 'I know he mainly treats children, but since he was a friend, Rafael thought he could perhaps check me over just to see if there was anything wrong.'

'And what happened? Was there something wrong?'

'No, he said it was nothing and that it would pass, and he was right, because the pain hasn't come back. No, I mean, he must be a good doctor, he's highly respected and all that, but it seemed to me that he touched me more than was necessary, a woman notices these things straight away. He had me lie down on a couch and get

209

half-undressed, which was fine, perfectly normal. But then he kept saying, "Does it hurt you here?" "Can you feel this?" "And this?" and "What happens if I press harder?" I don't know, he spent far too long doing this and in places that were some way away from where I was getting the pain. He'd say, "Relax your stomach" and then stroke my abdomen as if his fingers were about to go where they shouldn't, if you know what I mean, and he kept brushing my breasts with the sleeve of his white coat or with his wrist, as though by accident. But almost no such contact is purely accidental, we all know that, you're almost always aware of touch, I mean, aware of what you're touching or what's being touched, and if you don't move away, that's fine. That's all I'm saying, that he kept touching me. I tried to move away, but he took no notice. It went no further than that, but the fact is I felt sort of queasy when I left. Not because of the pain, which vanished magically as soon as he told me it was nothing to worry about' – 'The hand of the doctor that calms and dispels,' I thought, 'his words like a balm' – 'but because I felt like I'd been groped. I think he probably didn't dare go any further because Rafael had sent me, and he was afraid I might tell on him and Rafael might get angry, because otherwise . . .'

'Otherwise what? Would he have gone further, forced the matter? I mean, doctors do have to touch you. And it's easy to misinterpret such things. In America, oversensitive patients are always suing their doctors for some mad reason. I think most doctors are so used to touching people that they no longer feel anything, it's as if they were touching cork. With their patients, I mean.'

'Well, I know what I felt and I'm not a prude or a hysteric. I know what I'm talking about.' – She didn't sound offended, she just wanted to be clear. – 'But no, he's not the violent type, I don't think that's his style, and I've known a few of them. He's just a pest, the kind who doesn't quite overstep the mark, but comes very close. He's a lecher, a sleazebag, someone who stores up sensations for later on, do you know what I mean? Someone who pretends not to know what he's doing, but keeps trying again and again, just to see what happens, to see if he gets anywhere. Thinking that you'll get all excited, if he touches you here, feels you up there, or that you'll just give in to avoid an embarrassing situation. Some men take advantage of women who are very timid or young or polite, women who have a horror of confrontations or of giving a straight No. You may not believe it, but there still are women like that. And they'll end up letting a man get away with a lot, just so as not to seem rude or to avoid making a scene.'

'Really? Even nowadays? That sounds like something out of a novel from the eighteenth or nineteenth century? A novel set in the country, you know, the young master of the house and the peasant girl.'

She didn't seem put out by my unwitting pedantry. She was probably more educated than I had at first thought.

'You mean Dickens and the like? I don't know about that, but I can assure you it still goes on, and it's not that uncommon either. They plead with you and you give in. They insist and you give in. Oh, they flatter you too, I don't deny it, and that counts and sometimes even convinces. Anyway, you may not much want to do it, but it's almost easier to give in than to refuse. It doesn't wash with me, mind, but it happens to a lot of women.'

'Really?' I thought of the bullfighter, who was at least twenty years older than her. 'Do you only ever go with someone you really like? With someone you liked before they made it clear that they liked you too? Sometimes you only notice someone because that someone has noticed you. Sometimes we only consider those who have already considered us. It's not unknown for the way someone looks at you to influence the way you look at them.'

She smiled and answered only my first question; she must have found the rest far too complicated.

'More or less. There's always the exception, of course. I'm sure it's happened to you too, with some overly affectionate or overly enthusiastic girl you couldn't bring yourself to reject. Come on, own up, I'm sure you have plenty of admirers.' And she nudged me with her elbow, very gently, not in a vulgar way, while we were walking shoulder to shoulder along the empty streets, just as she would occasionally grab my arm to steady herself, our footsteps made a lot of clatter, especially her high heels (such a promising sound). With each step her earrings swung gracefully back and forth, and sooner or later, I imagined, if it took us much longer to find a taxi, she would regretfully take them off, because they must have been bothering her.

I took her words as a compliment not a come-on. She was some ten years older than me, possibly more, and so could allow herself to be a kind of pretend older sister to me. She knew a lot, but not enough, or else, accustomed as she was to being with older men like the actor or the bullfighter, she had forgotten what many young men are like. She must have forgotten that for most of us any sexual relationship is still a miracle, a gift (at least it was in 1980), unless we find the girl in question repellent or creepy, someone we had discounted at first glance, someone horribly obese and flabby or an out-and-out freak. When you're young, you're not that fussy or pernickety, you're still rather coarse-minded, in that area and in others. You hardly ever turn down an acceptable opportunity, especially if you don't have to try very hard. Young men are often quite heartless when it comes to sex. Or at least unscrupulous. I was, I don't deny it, and I remained so for a few more years after that. Considerateness is something you

212

learn, as is the advisability of not gaily forging links with people. However unlikely, there is always a stronger link than you might believe, even if it springs from one night of wild partying and you eventually forget the person's name and even her existence or almost what happened. The truth is that you never forget anyone you've been with, if you ever happen to meet them again, even though, paradoxically, you have retained no images, no memory, of the occasion. It's like a mental record on which the information is stored, and which reappears the moment you see that face again or hear the name if the face has changed beyond all recognition. You know it, you know you had that experience, that you fucked that woman in another life, another you of whom there is only evidence rather than memory. It doesn't make much sense, knowing something that you can't remember, but that's how it is.

I was about to answer Celia: 'Yes, it's true, I've experienced that myself, which leads me to suspect that some girl must have experienced the same thing with me, which is not a pleasant thought. But what can you do, it's impossible to know what someone else is thinking, which is just as well really, because, otherwise, we'd never do anything, never even tentatively brush another's hand.' I was just about to say something along those lines when we spotted the green light of a taxi far off and started waving frantically like exiles or shipwreck victims; her feet must have been hurting by then, although, with great dignity, she wasn't complaining, and at no time did she appear to consider taking her shoes off, not even once inside the taxi. I let her get in first, not yet having learned that the man should always get into a car ahead of the woman, especially if the woman is wearing a skirt, and especially if that skirt is short and tight. When she sat down, it became still shorter, indeed it was almost as if she wasn't wearing one at all (but she was, that was the point), I kept casting

213

sideways glances at her smooth, firm, tanned thighs, which, all the while we were walking, I hadn't been able to see. I asked where she lived, she said in Calle Watteau and launched into a complicated explanation, I had no idea where it was nor indeed that Watteau even had a street named after him. The driver had never heard of it either and got out his *A–Z*, she spelled the name for him ('Bloody hell, the names they give streets these days,' he muttered when he had finally grasped not just the initial 'W' but all the other letters too), and she ended up giving him directions, which I ignored completely, and we finally set off. I soon found myself in completely unknown territory, as if I had been transported to another city, and with the meter ticking too. 'It's just as well Viana gave me some dosh,' I thought. 'If he hadn't, I'd be in trouble.'

We didn't continue our earlier conversation; that had got left behind. I asked where she worked.

'In a government department,' she said bluntly. 'I'm a civil servant.'

'Oh, really?' I could not, I think, avoid the note of surprise in my voice, and to make amends, I added: 'High up?'

'Hmm,' she said with a smile, then added after a pause: 'Not low down.'

I made no attempt to draw her out further, I was waiting for something else to happen, one of those things that makes you fall silent, hold your breath a little and concentrate solely on that for as long as it lasts. Celia had not sat at the furthest end of the back seat (perhaps momentary carelessness or laziness, perhaps because of her skirt), but had stopped about halfway along (or less), so that I had no alternative but to sit very close to her, with her right thigh rubbing or, rather, pressing against my left thigh. She obviously wasn't bothered by this (she could have moved along, there was plenty of space).

Perhaps she was too tired to notice or didn't care, she saw me as almost a boy, and certainly not as an indefatigable demon between the sheets. I didn't move away either. Not that I had much room for manoeuvre, but I did have a little, or I could have asked her to shift over and allow me more space. But I wasn't going to do that. Certainly not. It wasn't flesh against flesh, but flesh against fabric, not that it mattered, I could still feel it, feel her firm, warm flesh, and I preferred to go on feeling it. I wondered if she could feel my warmth too or not at all. Only a few minutes before she had spoken about precisely this with regard to Van Vechten, saying: 'But almost no such contact is purely accidental, we all know that, you're almost always aware of touch.' What more did I need? And yet I did need more: even young men whom others judge to be good-looking are insecure and even the boldest are timid. There was that qualifying 'almost', she might consider that contact in the taxi to be accidental, and it could be the exceptional occasion on which she didn't notice. She had added: 'You're aware of what you're touching or what is being touched, and if you don't move away, that's fine.' What if she was experimenting to see if I would be the one to move, or if I was perfectly fine with the insistent touch of her thigh? I, of course, didn't draw back or move away or retreat. Nor did she, but what the other person does is never clear, it's always obscure, even wives and children are opaque to us, and we can never know what someone else is thinking and sometimes the other person isn't thinking at all, but merely responding to stimuli or bypassing the brain or ignoring or avoiding it, not giving it time to express itself or to formulate a thought, I've never had the good fortune of being in that position, and it probably is fortunate rather than unfortunate.

And never having had that good fortune, not even as a young man, I decided to do something positive and half-calculated, but which would still act as a safeguard, something that would not dispel my doubts, but would at least diminish them. I offered her a cigarette, which, although she was a smoker, she declined. I lit my cigarette and, contrary to my usual habit – I always hold my cigarette in my left hand – I held it instead between the index and middle finger of my right hand and allowed my other hand, still holding my lighter, to fall on her thigh, which gleamed resplendent beneath the street lamps as they flashed past or beneath the intermittent moon. Not the palm, of course, that would have been cheeky, but the back of my hand. And not the whole of my hand either, but, initially, just the side or the edge, and then a little more, as if my hand were giving in of its own accord or being jolted into position by the occasional bumps in the road or by the driver when he accelerated through a green light. It seems absurd, a hand is just a hand, but there's an enormous difference between the back and the palm of the hand, the palm is the part that feels and caresses and speaks, usually deliberately, while the back pretends and is silent.

She didn't move her thigh, not a millimetre, she didn't avoid or evade that new contact and she could easily have done so, there was room to her left; now it was flesh against flesh, still cautious, almost motionless, still wearing the mask of chance. I took the risk of moving the back of my hand very minimally during what remained of the journey, as though impelled by the slight swaying of the car when going round bends or corners or roundabouts, of which there are many all over Madrid. We didn't speak. We didn't speak. We didn't speak. The longer you go without speaking, the harder it is to begin again, or so it seems, and yet all you have to do is open your mouth and utter one or two or three meaningful syllables: 'Yes' or 'No' or 'What' or 'How'; or 'Come here' or 'Go away' or 'More' or 'Nothing'. Or perhaps 'Do you want', and other words always follow. But neither of us said a word for the rest of the ride, we didn't even have to give directions to the driver, as he knew where he was going now. When I finished my cigarette, I stubbed it out in the ashtray next to me, but my left hand remained where it was, still gripping the lighter as if it were a talisman or a relic, and this allowed me to keep the back of my hand resting on her leg, and with every minor swerve or lurch it gently caressed her thigh as if by chance. It met with no opposition, no rebuff, Celia didn't seem bothered nor did she change her position. 'And now what?' I thought. 'What will happen when we stop? Will we just go our separate ways, with a kiss on both cheeks? That would be the most natural thing, we've only walked a few blocks together, it's just another minor nocturnal escapade – one of many – one that we probably won't even remember. I'll get out of the taxi first, so that she can get out the way she got in, it's always dangerous to do so on the left-hand side, and it would be rude not to accompany her to her door, not after travelling all this way and with all these twists and turns, after which I have no idea where we are. Until she's safe and sound, although she still wouldn't necessarily be safe even then, I've heard of women being attacked in the lift, when they thought they were already safe, by men who've been waiting for hours, if they know a woman's late-night habits, or who emerge out of the shadows and slip in behind her before the street door closes, and then she's trapped when she's so close to home, to her welcoming or woeful bed. Perhaps I should go upstairs with her, leave her outside her apartment door, play at being one of those almost non-existent gentlemen and thus get as close as I can to her sheets; absurd as it may seem, proximity facilitates and suggests, and can even tempt someone who had considered herself immune and had dismissed the possibility right from the start, but then suddenly changes her mind and succumbs to that feeblest and most decisive of

217

arguments: 'Why not?' she says to herself. 'I can always pretend it never happened.'

Calle Watteau was a short, narrow street, more of an affront to the French painter than an honour. I discovered with surprise that the road running parallel to it was called Juan de Vera, almost my name, or the one it should have been, and that seemed to me a sign and an incentive – who could he be? I wondered. The city council clearly thought him more important than Watteau at any rate, and about on a par with the Batalla de Belchite, of which Watteau was a side street. I knew none of them, but had suddenly, belatedly, recognized the area, and it occurred to me that the driver had taken us the long way round and that Celia had allowed him to or even led him to do so with her directions, so as to lengthen the journey and have more time to study me. We were a stone's throw from the Paseo de las Delicias on one side and from the Museo del Ferrocarril on the other, and not very far from the river on another. Almost directly opposite where Celia lived was a women's prison, or so the sign said, and a sad, chilling thought crossed my mind: what if she worked for the prison service, for the Ministry of the Interior? I looked at the walls and the high, dark windows. The inmates would have long since been in their beds, sleeping soundly, free from temptation, or only in dreams or, who knows, perhaps every night of those febrile years was the same to them. They would inevitably be aware of each other's smell, a strong smell perhaps, I could smell Celia and she smelled sweet, even after the trek that had left us both slightly hot and out of breath and made her largish feet ache. The taxi stopped. I deliberately (I pretended not to notice, to forget) allowed the taxi driver to stop the meter, I pretended to protest.

'Oh, you've stopped the meter,' I said. I could have told him long before that I would be continuing on, but I hadn't. He or another driver would have to take me home, that much was certain.

'Well, since you didn't say anything, I assumed . . . Shall I start the meter again or just work out a price for you?'

I didn't need to respond or hesitate or ponder or shoot Celia an interrogative glance or pine palely away or put my expectations into words. I had the feeling that I'd been saved by the bell, as people used to say then, when there were still boxing matches and before they were frowned on.

'Would you like to come up?' Celia asked. She asked this quite naturally or, rather, with unequivocal certainty. It was a simple matter of going upstairs with her, not to have a drink or because we had got on so famously, nor so as not to interrupt the animated conversation we hadn't had. Since she was, as I said, about ten years older than me, she would have seen straight through me from first to last, including now. Perhaps my false boast to Van Vechten had intrigued her, even though I had myself partly denied it immediately afterwards. There are lies and jokes that arouse our curiosity simply because we can never be absolutely sure what is a lie and what is a joke. And just in case there was any doubt as to whether her question was genuine, or that she had not meant it at all, but was merely being polite, or was testing me out, she repeated it, this time as a statement of fact: 'Yes, you would like to come up. Come on, then, let's go.' I didn't reply at once, I didn't react. She smiled at me as one might smile at someone in shock. 'Come on, what are you waiting for? Pay the man.'

She opened the door and got out on her side. That was the first time she had removed her thigh from mine, and I missed its warmth. I was still trying to work out if I would have enough money for a taxi later on or the following morning, the kind of anxieties and calculations that afflict the young, who are always short of funds. In the morning, I could get a bus or the metro, and besides what did it matter? At that age, you don't care where you end up and are quite

219

prepared to walk back home across the entire city, and will often find yourself marooned in some remote place in the early hours just on the off-chance or promise or possibility of getting a decent, memorable fuck, it's that crude, that coarse; in the majority of cases this changes with time, after about thirty-five or thereabouts you become warier, lazier, you can no longer face the prospect of waking up in someone else's bed and having to eat breakfast with an unappealing, unkempt, unpainted ghost, of getting undressed in the early hours, and, even though it isn't strictly necessary, of becoming involved and establishing a link that the other person won't forget, or not as instantly as you do. You also have a keener sense of loyalty towards the person waiting for you at home or away travelling or towards the woman's unwitting or absent partner, whom perhaps you've never even met; you learn to put yourself in someone else's shoes, even those of some imbecilic stranger (in the eyes of the lover, however fleeting or casual, almost all husbands appear imbecilic, just as all lovers are cretins in the imaginations of husbands, even if they don't know who they are and aren't even sure they exist). But none of this holds true when you're twenty-three – on the contrary. It's then that you're most capable of deceiving, of playing tricks and using sophistry to persuade, of committing treacherous acts, pretending to be hard done by and even humiliating yourself in order to get what you want, of trying to arouse a woman's pity, pretending to be tormented or ill, of lying to a woman and betraying a friend, of resorting to contemptible behaviour of which you will later feel ashamed, or which you will try not to recall so as to pretend it never happened and that the person who committed it is dead and buried: 'That's not me any more, he was just a child, and what children do doesn't count. The real countdown begins today, or possibly tomorrow.' You extend at will what you consider to be the age of irresponsibility.

I paid the driver and got out on my side. The taxi moved off, vanished in a second, leaving the two of us alone in the diminutive Calle Watteau, separated by the space previously occupied by the car. I didn't notice the building or the door or anything, I can remember nothing of that. I only had eyes for Celia, who, for the first time in a long while, I was able to study from that short distance, all of her, including her high heels, which she had not for a moment taken off. Her skirt had ridden up slightly and grown creased during the journey. She held out her hand to me, then changed her mind and linked arms instead, and together we walked over to the street door. It was probably something of an event for her too, coming home with a young man. No, I didn't really believe that, she could have made off with as many young men as she wanted, some are impatient and eager, others timid and grateful and others insatiable. I doubtless belonged a little to all three categories. I couldn't help looking at us for a moment with the eyes of a spectator or a collector, with the eyes of the imagination, which are the eyes that best remember a scene and best recall it later. I couldn't help thinking that if Dr Van Vechten had seen us, he would have added another notch to my gun and would have felt rather proud of me. And hated me too.

But I didn't know then that nothing heals over time, nothing abates, nor that we can become lazier or more cautious, that we won't necessarily pay more heed to private loyalties, which act as a filter, guide and brake, and I had plenty of examples to prove this was the case for many people, mature adults who never give up and who are always insatiable and restless, at least mentally, I mean: it's as if they had to keep going merely in order to satisfy a tyrannical mind that never rests and never stops, having grown too accustomed to its own way of being for far too many years – youth and maturity are very long and the frontiers that mark their end very vague – independent of the needs and vicissitudes and capacities of their body, which they increasingly see as an annoying tool from which they have to demand ever greater efforts; too accustomed, as well, to carrying out certain habitual calculations – how many different women have I been to bed with this year, for example; how many didn't I pay for – who will be the next man to fill this void, for example; I only need one more, then I'll stick with him and ask no more questions. (Just as there are older people who seem to soften and become inoffensive, and whose indecipherable or fickle or absent minds – it's impossible to know what someone else is thinking – are perhaps ceaselessly plotting vile deeds and accumulating ill will towards everyone around them. It is our deceived minds that never surrender, that feel the same as they always did and see no reason to change. And if they do ever look back with the advantage of distance, it is only to think: 'My guilt has passed. The years have diluted it, I've been washed clean. I can start counting again, even if I'll only be counting further guilty acts. It will be new, different, and shorter, because I don't have so much time now.')

I could see that Beatriz had not given up counting, at least that seemed to me to be the point of those afternoon visits, even though from the outside they appeared banal and routine and in no way hopeful, even though she knew that basically, for her, the next man was the one she had always and only wanted, the one she had been with for longest and whom she still did not rule out ('You're the only one I'm interested in, you're the only one I love, surely I don't need to tell you that, however hard you try to drive me away'), but who had grown bitter and vengeful. When he was in a bad mood or had met with one too many setbacks in his dealings with Towers, Muriel didn't only call her a 'fat cow' or a 'bag of flour', a 'pachyderm', 'a lump of lard' or 'a ball of flab', he didn't only compare her to the big bell at El Alamo or to the stagecoach in *Stagecoach* or suggest that she resembled Shelley Winters at her plumpest or 'Baudelaire's Giantess' (an allusion that escaped me at the time), he also compared her to obese actors ('Stick a moustache on you and you'd look just like Oliver Hardy' or 'I hope you don't start going thin on top, otherwise you could be mistaken for Zero Mostel, you remember him, don't you, he was our friend Jack Palance's sweaty sidekick'), knowing that she would know all the cinematographic references, far better than me. His insults were so unjustified and disproportionate, so ludicrous and ill-intentioned and absurd – almost comic – that perhaps, for that reason, she found them less wounding – they may even have made her laugh, somewhere deep inside – although they must also have been very hard to take, must have undermined her self-esteem and created a terrible sense of insecurity. I often wondered why she didn't just fade away and give up her nocturnal expeditions to her husband's bedroom door, perhaps what helped her recover from these rejections and to pluck up courage were her encounters with Van Vechten in that ultra-religious context and in the purely secular context of Plaza del Marqués de Salamanca with whoever it was she visited there (because both those visits were repeated), and possibly with someone else in El Escorial or wherever else she drove to on her motorbike. And perhaps she sensed what she could not know, but that I did, that while Muriel would happily throw these insults in her face, he would never refer to her in such terms in her absence, I mean, he never spoke of Beatriz in another person's presence as 'a cask of amontillado' or as Charles Laughton, but always as 'Beatriz' or 'my wife' to third parties, and as 'Mama' or 'your mother' to the children and 'Señora Beatriz' or simply 'Beatriz' to Flavia, and he took great pains to make sure there were no witnesses around when he addressed her in that distasteful manner, this included myself, in theory, although he did let slip the occasional abusive phrase in my presence (I became as invisible as the air), but I also did my own bit of spying and heard things I shouldn't have heard. Anyway, the fact that he refrained from reviling her so brutally when other people were present seemed to me a very feeble show of respect, or perhaps a feeble remnant of the affection he must have felt for her in prehistory.

Nor did I see Muriel, who was approaching or already in his fifties, relenting in his pursuit of women, if 'pursuit' is the right word. He never seemed to be urgently pursuing anyone, he appeared, rather, distracted, at least in that regard, and adopted a negligent, contemplative attitude. He appeared surprised when he discovered he was being lusted after by some beautiful young upstart or by some more upmarket seductress. On those occasions, however, he never paused to wonder if his suitors wanted something from him – a minor role in a film or the mere allure of his name – nor did he drive them away when this became obvious. He allowed himself to be led and manipulated, or so it seemed, but afterwards would appear indifferent and stoical or wouldn't even remember – indeed he sometimes said as much, and I've already mentioned one such case – having shared a bed with someone who would have liked to have made further visits to his bed – with him inside it of course – or had dared to demand a small favour. Since he had offered nothing, he felt under no obligation, it was up to them what they did, but he certainly hadn't encouraged them. I never saw him seriously 'paired up' with any woman, at most he would go out with the same woman several times if he got on well with her and liked her, usually just as a companion at premieres or cocktail parties, at superficial and usually group outings with other people, I thought he would probably get bored having supper with any of them alone, or having to engage in conversation with them after those occasional rolls in the hay, which I imagined would be rather mechanical, more medicinal than sexual and certainly not passionate. I'm sure he found tedious the young and not-so-young, be they upstarts or aristocrats, who had never heard of Zero Mostel or Andy Devine or Eugene Pallette or Sydney Greenstreet, to mention other overweight actors to whom, on his angry or overly jocular days, he might have compared Beatriz, nor would they have heard of Baudelaire, with or without his giantess. On the other hand, with those women he genuinely admired or found interesting or fascinating, like Cecilia Alemany, not only were they few and far between, he didn't usually stand much chance, for they belonged to other worlds where he was just a pauper at the gate or, at best, an intriguing artist who might bring a little sparkle or glamour to the supper table.

And perhaps he allowed himself to praise them and tell them he adored them precisely because they were mere chimera. It sometimes occurred to me that Muriel would probably have had one or two or three women in his life, to whom he would have given himself unreservedly, but who were so important and intelligent, so fine, that he found it hard to take seriously almost any other woman who approached him. I was convinced that one of those two or three – if there *had* been two or three – would have been the Beatriz of earlier days, the one who had lived in America and whom he had married, the willing, optimistic, cheerful Beatriz who was still there, the Beatriz who had not yet gone half-mad, who was not yet utterly wretched. Or, how can I put it, cast adrift.

Professor Rico was quite a lot younger than Muriel and had not yet reached the age when nothing can be healed, although it was fast approaching. Even though he was getting on for forty, he was still childishly and verbally lewd and opinionated and arrogant, and therein lay much of his wit and charm (for those who could see them, because some people couldn't stand him), and these qualities brought him quite a few conquests, theoretical or hypothetical ones at least, as I've explained. He might have been the sort to engage in the kind of masculine calculations I mentioned before ('How many women etc. etc. . . .'), except that he would have made a mental notch on his gun as soon as he saw that a seduction was a sure thing, as soon as he was certain that, as he had occasionally declared with touching glee – or, rather, complacency – 'that woman could be mine at the click of my fingers, it's obvious, indubitable', which was his reason for not always feeling it necessary to allow the seduction to reach its inevitable conclusion or 'to finish the job', although this was more Van Vechten's way of putting it than Rico's.

No, it seemed to me that almost no one around me had lost any of their eager desires – perhaps it was the unexpected, agitated nature of the times – least of all the celebrated paediatrician, the oldest member of the group – he was about ten years older than Muriel, nearly twenty years older than Beatriz or Rico and almost forty years older than me. And although, as I said, he looked more like a fifty-year-old and was still strong and agile, it still seemed incomprehensible and incongruous that I should invite him to go out with me and my friends. However, it proved easy enough to persuade him, he certainly didn't play hard to get, he didn't resist or turn up his nose; he was a pushover, fertile ground. Such was his keenness, such was his sorrow at missing out on that easy-going, permissive age, such was his desperation when he imagined what was slipping past him because of a mere incompatibility of dates (which is something that, as long as we live, we still think can be remedied, if not turned on its head), he was over the moon when I invited him to go with me, first, to bars and, later, to discotheques and live-music venues. The latter were full of people of various ages, where you could talk despite the decibels and even sit down now and then, and so he wouldn't feel so very out of place, especially since some of those venues were old haunts of his, which had come back into fashion with a new, enthusiastic clientele, generally ignorant of the past and utterly different from the clientele who had frequented them during their various antediluvian phases. This was the case, I think, with El Sol in Calle Jardines or, later on, the Cock in Calle de la Reina, or, of course, Bar Chicote, in Gran Vía, which, if I'm not mistaken, had been open since before the Civil War and is, inevitably, mentioned by Hemingway in some of his articles and his more touristy novels. Afterwards, during the post-war years, it had first been taken over by discreet, fairly classy whores, by bullfighters, actors, singers, footballers, actresses and, later, by high-ranking civil servants in Franco's government, businessmen with close links to the regime and even the occasional party-mad minister; the first group were eager to meet the second group, and the second group to meet the first, and the club provided the ideal meeting place. I wondered if Van Vechten had been a regular during those seemingly endless years, when he was officially on good terms with the victors (well, in the 1940s he was one of them, something people always forgot) and benefited from his contacts; if he had joined the rich and powerful in partaking of Bar Chicote's famous cocktails and occasionally glanced over at the stools where any women on their own used to sit, leaning on the bar, carefully seated in half-profile (so as not to offer only a monotonous view of female posteriors) and pretending to chat with each other, until they were invited to join a group at a table. Around 1980, you would still see the occasional elderly, absent-minded woman, who, perhaps seeing the place so lively again after a long period of decay, again sat down on her bar stool of yesteryear, thinking that the good old days had somehow miraculously been restored and the clocks turned back. In fact, one of those veteran ladies once came over to our table, where she stood staring at Van Vechten, then said very sweetly:

'I know you, don't I? I remember those blue, blue eyes and that blond hair. You've hardly changed at all. Not a grey hair in sight and not a hint of a bald patch.'

However, Van Vechten, who remained seated and adopted a look of genuine surprise and doubtless genuine malice, responded:

'No, Señora. You must be confusing me with my father, whom I greatly resemble. As you can see, the people who come here now' – he paused heartlessly, looking round at me and my group and smugly, arrogantly including himself – 'are all rather young.'

Dr Van Vechten was anything but inhibited, so much so that my initial fears proved not only unfounded, but ridiculous, namely, that he would find my friendly suggestion that he join me now and then on my nocturnal sorties suspicious and inappropriate. Muriel knew him well, which is why he'd had no qualms about setting me that task, sure that Van Vechten would never judge anything to be gratuitous or unmerited if it brought with it the promise of amusement and pleasure. I had put this down at first to a misjudgement on the part of my boss, to his often unworldly sense of reality. This was not entirely true, however, for I soon realized that he missed almost nothing of what really mattered about people or situations; that beneath his abstracted, even self-absorbed appearance, he noticed and saw far more than he seemed to. Whenever I failed in my attempts to decipher his thoughts, I assumed he must be making plans in his head, imagining future shots and camera moves, and this may have been true, but he still never lost track of the story he was telling or that was being told to him, or of the idea that was troubling him. He had a very distinctive style, but he wasn't a mere stylist, still less an aesthete, either in his films or in life. He liked to pretend that he knew very little about what was going on around him and preferred to say nothing about what he did notice, but I think he noticed a lot and knew about almost everything.

Van Vechten did indeed have very blue eyes and the kind of blond hair which is still memorable in a country where such hair colour is much more common than people think and admit, albeit less pure and more mixed: here, pale-coloured eyes tend to be greyish or green or reminiscent of various liqueurs or dark blue like Muriel's one seeing eye, and hair is rarely that insipid or Nordic blond. He really did look like a foreigner, as if his numerous ancestors in Arévalo must have gone more and more frequently to Holland in search of a bride. That's why he was so instantly recognizable, the veteran whore was probably quite right, although he didn't at all strike me as a classic whoremonger. His eyes had a bright, youthful glint to them – indeed, they were southern European in their intensity, an intensity that could quickly become obscene and offensive; he had regular, indeed, attractive features (he must have been handsome when young), dazzling and healthy-looking teeth – large, rectangular incisors – a very strong jaw and a rather square face; the only things that slightly spoiled his looks were his rather pointed nose and ears, like an elf's ears, and his somewhat protruding chin, though not quite a witch's chin. I once remarked to Muriel that Van Vechten resembled a minor, almost incidental American actor, who appeared in hundreds of films but whose name would be unknown to most cinema-goers: 'Robert J. Wilke,' I said with youthful, point-scoring pedantry, and he nodded and replied instantly: 'Yes, one of the three gunmen who spend almost the whole of *High Noon* waiting for the train to arrive. But you're right, well spotted. And oddly enough, I think that as well as appearing in innumerable Westerns, he also appeared on more than one occasion in a doctor's white coat.' That is how I had seen Van Vechten when he was screwing Beatriz at the Sanctuary of Darmstadt, both of them standing up and both fully clothed. But Muriel didn't know that I had that image of the Doctor in my head, his white coat unbuttoned.

Van Vechten's features suggested a triumphant, expansive nature, as did the way he behaved in public: with enormous confidence, perennial good humour, too perennial not to seem somewhat false – although perhaps suitable for a paediatrician who needed to instil confidence in mothers and children – with undeniable joviality and a constant, welcoming smile, a man who told jokes, clean or dirty depending on the company he was in, and who was always joshing, perhaps too much – as if this were his visiting card – a kind of easy humour that nevertheless seemed to me old-fashioned (but perhaps that was normal, given that we were separated by many calendar years) and which I perhaps unfairly associated with the long, fast-receding Franco era, but it might have been just the same under a completely different regime. When he was a child, someone must have told him: 'You have such beautiful teeth, Jorgito, you should always smile, whether it seems appropriate or not; that will win you good friends and goodwill; it will help smooth your path.' He was very tall, almost as tall as Muriel or possibly taller, and very solidly built. That's why, I think, he was much given to slapping people on the back, to grabbing their arm, which he would then tug or shake in jocular fashion while laughing a strangely mechanical laugh; he was very strong and could doubtless have inflicted harm had he wanted to, indeed, I was sometimes left slightly bruised whenever he gave me a friendly shove or placed one of his huge hands on my shoulder, which felt as if a great paw had fallen from a considerable height and then gripped me with what was intended to be affection, but which felt more like the paw of a lion and provoked in me an immediate urge to shrug it off and free myself from both its weight and grip.

Alongside that good humour, one sensed something voracious and troubling, as if nothing ever entirely pleased him, as if he were one of those people for whom nothing is ever enough, who always want more and who reach a point when they no longer know what more they *can* want: it's difficult for them to be more successful, earn more money, more admiration from the people surrounding them, more power or influence in the world they move in. They look around, flail vainly about in search of new goals, and don't know how to channel all the ambition and energy that continue to beset them, how to raise the siege, to strike camp. You might say that age has betrayed them, has failed to teach them its usual soothing lessons; it neither softens nor makes them slower or meeker, it has too much respect for their personality and doesn't know what to do with them or else simply doesn't bother to please, still less satisfy them. They thus become creatures who are barely aware of passing time, and instead time feels to them like a kind of unvarying eternity in which they have lived their entire life and which looks unlikely to disappear or to change in pace, to withdraw from or abandon them: they are time's hostages or its willing victims; it must be said in their defence that time acts most disloyally in partly failing to fulfil its commitment to them: it merely slowly, little by little, undermines them, but – how I can put it? – without telling them. They are individuals who, if you told them they had a fatal illness and would soon die, would react with immediate and utter incredulity or scepticism – with disdain, in fact – as if to say, more or less: 'Look, I'm awfully sorry, but it really doesn't suit me to die right now. I've got such a lot to do, and I wasn't expecting it, it wasn't part of my short-term plan. If you don't mind, could we leave it for later on?' (And that's perfectly understandable really, because, with the exception of suicides and those who are old and tired of life, who doesn't want to leave it for later on, however late in the day that 'now' presents itself?) Muriel, on the other hand, would never have said that, even though, as I mentioned at the beginning, he shared with Van Vechten a certain immunity to the passage

232

of time, and the years seemed to have little effect on his appearance or perhaps only that of a slow fall of sleet or a faint shadow. However, unlike his friend, there was no voracity or disquiet in him, no vague dissatisfactions, there was, rather, stillness and pause and calm: he merely ignored the passing of time, as if it were so familiar that it wasn't worth devoting a single minute to bemoaning or pondering it. Or as if all the really important things had happened to him in the past.

In Van Vechten's search to satisfy his permanent, albeit aimless and directionless greed, nothing could have suited him better than my suggestion, or what he perceived as my temptations, that of being introduced, with the help of a guide or an initiate, into the wild, youthful life of the day. He didn't really need me, because the times were so effervescent that suddenly everything seemed permissible and normal in contrast to the leaden decades under Franco, although those days had already died a good five years before the dictator's actual physical disappearance, or perhaps we had merely decisively turned our back on them. People of any age felt free to go anywhere, as though everyone were trying out new habits or perhaps a new youth. Those who, not long before, and because of their age, had felt they weren't 'authorized' to go out several nights a week and stay out into the small hours, now had a sense that nothing prevented them from doing so; more than that, the general buzz and excitement seemed to be urging them to venture into places that would have been deemed inappropriate for someone of their age or position, for someone who had for so many years behaved with a certain dignity and composure. Despite all these possibilities, all these stimuli, it was not the same as having a real twenty-year-old taking you to all the fashionable bars and clubs and introducing you to his friends and, so to speak, giving you permission to approach any girl in his circle as an equal and allowing you the illusion that you were part of a kind of privileged band. It was a time when almost no one slept in Madrid, because after a night on the town, with the exception of students and artists and professional layabouts, every night owl, unlikely though it may seem and at a remarkably early hour, could be found at his or her desk the following morning. I was and so was Van Vechten, who never once missed a day in his consulting rooms, and it was the same with Muriel and Rico and Roy and Beatriz and Gloria when they stayed out late, as they all did now and again; no one could entirely avoid the nocturnal ferment of those anomalous years, which, if you had a bit of money and however wretchedly unhappy you felt, were celebratory despite the political unease and the uncertainties of all kinds. It was not unusual to find traffic jams in various parts of the city in the early hours of a Wednesday or a Monday or even a dull Tuesday. On some nights, our cold, sentinel moon must have blinked its one somnolent eye in disbelief.

I get them mixed up, the bars I used to go to in 1980 and those I went to shortly before and shortly afterwards, but in addition to the places I mentioned earlier, I think I took Van Vechten to the Dickens, El Café and Rock-Ola, to certain street cafés in Recoletos and to the Universal (on second thoughts, no, that was probably later), and to various discotheques, where, of course, I spent far too many hours, whether with him or on my own, I can't for the life of me remember, places like Pachá and Joy Eslava and others whose names escape me, one near the river (La Riviera?) and another next door to Chamartín station, and another in Calle Hortaleza and yet another in Fortuny or Jenner or Marqués del Riscal (Archy perhaps?), times and people tend to get confused, alcohol doesn't exactly clear the head, although cocaine does for as long as its effects last, but not a posteriori; someone would offer you a line of coke now and then and you took it just to be able to keep going a little longer and sustain the bellowed conversations that you somehow kept up in a losing battle with the surrounding hubbub. I didn't go to all those places with the Doctor, and I only did so for a short time, getting rid of him as soon as my mission was complete. One place I definitely did take him to was an updated, refurbished nightclub called Pintor Goya (the name it was given in its antiquated origins), in the street of the same name, that is, Goya.

Just as on that earlier poker night, when his simultaneously chilling and greedy eyes had been repeatedly drawn to Celia and her friend, so now they were drawn to women of almost any age (those places were fairly 'intergenerational' at the time, within reasonable limits), and even to the transvestites who were beginning to display themselves provocatively and brazenly on the Paseo de la Castellana near Calle Hermanos Bécquer, and who gradually spread out, eventually invading all the adjacent territory too. I always found their popularity odd, and the fact that their clients were mainly heterosexuals, many of them, apparently, married men: however convincing the transvestites were as women, you would have to go through a whole mental process, a form of self-deceit, that I find hard to comprehend, to convince yourself that they really were women, and that, in the middle of a transaction, you weren't going to be put off by the sudden appearance of certain inappropriate and dissuasive genitals. Whenever we drove past the transvestites in Dr Van Vechten's flash car, he, I recall, was always adamant that they couldn't possibly be men on hormone treatment or who had undergone surgery, or perhaps half one thing and half another. He would glance at them out of the corner of his eye while he was driving and make as if to turn to me or to my friends.

'What do you mean? How can they possibly be men? They're obviously women, and I should know. Look at those breasts, those legs. You're having me on.' And he would smile his becoming smile, half-amused, half-bewildered.

'Look, Jorge, most of them are too tall. Were women ever that tall when you were young?' I would say. He had insisted I call him 'Jorge' and not 'Dr Van Vechten'. 'Their legs are too muscular. Their tits are too hard. Some of them have suspiciously large hands. And most take at least a size eight in shoes. More importantly, if you look closely, they all have an Adam's apple.'

'How can I look closely from this far away and travelling at this speed?' On the long home straight of the Castellana, late at night, you could go like a bullet, although he always slowed down slightly when he reached the transvestite zone, for they clearly aroused in him, at the very least, great curiosity. 'I can't see a single Adam's apple from here. Don't talk nonsense, they're clearly women and pretty spectacular ones at that. The race has improved over the years, that's why they're tall. Or perhaps they're foreign – for example, there was a real stunner of a mulatta back there. You're all mad, and you want to drive me mad too.' His remarks betrayed the fact that he came from a much earlier generation. And he occasionally used very dated expressions; no one of my age would have used the word 'stunner'.

'Well, spend a night with one of them, then. You just have to stop the car and pick one up. If you don't just settle for a blow-job, it won't take you long to find out. And, as I understand it, it won't cost you much either. Then come and tell me all about it, about the nasty shock you get, I mean.'

I knew they didn't charge much because a transitory friend of mine at the time, Comendador, who was five or six years older than me, had taken to paying for their services now and then. He had always been heterosexual, and he still was, and even had a girlfriend he was madly in love with. He tried to give me details of those ambiguous encounters, but I always stopped him in his tracks, preferring not to know. He saw them as very attractive women, I'm sure, but he also knew that they weren't. I found this all very odd.

Van Vechten said nothing for a few moments (this was one of several such conversations), as if hesitating. He glanced over at the pavement, at the road, then back at those apparently real women wearing skirts or very short shorts and with their breasts almost exposed, eyeing them lustfully. The strange thing is that his hesitation appeared not to be related to the problem of their uncertain or deceiving gender, but to something else.

'No, certainly not, I've never paid for sex in my life,' he said at last, dismissing the possibility. 'And I'm not going to start now.'

This was presumably true, and from what I saw he didn't seem to be the kind of man who went with prostitutes. Perhaps he had never needed to, perhaps his height and his blond hair, his captivating teeth and his pale blue eyes, which, in certain lights, took on a watery quality, had been enough to dissipate or conceal the repellent quality I saw in him – I'm not quite sure how to describe it: a combination of conceit, a kind of exaggerated, jokey warmth and sheer ruthlessness, which, however vague, was there on his face – and which, it seemed to me, could not have gone unnoticed by women, now and in the past – it was something intrinsic and nothing to do with age. Of course, I've often been wrong about this and have seen remarkable women fall in love with and give or surrender themselves to truly nauseating men, and he wasn't quite that bad. And even though he no longer looked young, he was, as I said, very well preserved. This, however, was not enough to explain why some of my female acquaintances or friends not only didn't avoid him or exclude him from their nocturnal excursions, they happily chatted to him, sometimes while sitting slightly apart from the others, I mean, it wasn't that they were all talking together and including him in the conversation – he was there, after all, and with me as his visiting card – but they ended up talking only to him. Seeing the women laugh, I would think that perhaps he was regaling them with the string of ancient jokes he sometimes trotted out, or perhaps it was his air of sophistication and his ability to flatter – the young are so sensitive to this that you often only have to administer a good dose of it to get whatever you want from them, in almost any area.

I observed Van Vechten constantly, for this was, in part, the task Muriel had set me and I wanted to be useful to him, and, on two or three occasions, I saw the Doctor and a young woman heading towards the toilets of whatever bar or club we happened to be in. I made a mental note of how long they were away, and, on each occasion, it didn't seem to me that they would have had time to do anything more than snort a line of coke or something of the sort (cocaine wasn't as commonplace as it became years later, but it was beginning to be sold and to lose its alarming image, and Van Vechten had more than enough money and could use it as bait, as flattery, to make him look like one of us), not even time for a quick blow-job. That was the expression I used when I was with him, along with other still cruder ones. They did not come naturally to me (I've always been rather polite), but that is what Muriel had ordered me to do, along with other things I found still harder to follow: 'Show off. Boast . . . Don't worry about seeming vulgar or even disrespectful when talking about women, be as vulgar and disrespectful as you like, exaggerate . . . Reveal yourself as vile and unscrupulous and watch his response, whether he's sympathetic and even of a like mind, whether he urges you on or disapproves.' All this was unknown territory to me or went against my nature, but I forced myself to do it, as if I were an actor in a film Muriel was directing blind and at a distance, an actor who – and it frustrated and pained me that he wouldn't see me play the part – would receive neither congratulations nor applause. Soon, I was blithely boasting about supposed exploits that had never happened and talking about women as if they were objects, as if they were as interchangeable as melons, artichokes, watermelons, bags of flour or parcels of meat. At first, hearing me talk so cynically, Van Vechten would look at me wide-eyed – his eyes were positively glacial then – and listen to me part-condescending and part-surprised, as though he had already sussed out my basically respectful nature and couldn't quite square my current attitude with the impression he'd had of me at Muriel's apartment, at suppers and occasional outings and poker games, when talking to Beatriz and her children and Flavia, with whom I was usually exquisitely polite, and even with the insidious Marcela and Gloria, from whom I did my best to conceal my antipathy.

But one quickly gets used to anything and one idea can easily be replaced by another. I suppose he assumed I was putting on a front when at work and that my true self was the one I displayed when out and about, and he soon became accustomed to my coarse, contemptuous language and my predatory behaviour, although the word 'behaviour' is misleading, for I continued to behave towards my women friends and girlfriends and with any new ones (one was always meeting new people in the welcoming night of that new age) as I always had – if I hadn't, my female friends old and new would have been astonished – but later, I would discuss them all with Van Vechten as if I were a callous swine and regale him with unsavoury adventures and dirty tricks that had sometimes never happened or, if they had, had not been perpetrated in such a utilitarian, exploitative manner, certainly not with the degree of lying and indifference or deceit on my part that I described. It wasn't so much my behaviour that was disdainful and vicious, as my description of it. I heeded Muriel's advice: 'There's nothing like boasting about your own exploits to get others to tell you theirs, however ancient; it never fails.' And Muriel was right, it rarely does fail.

V

Some people take pleasure in deceit and trickery and pretence and have enormous patience when it comes to weaving their web. They're capable of living through the long present with one eye fixed on a vague future, which will arrive when it arrives or only when they decide that it should at last become the present, and then, immediately afterwards, the past. Sometimes they put off or postpone the moment when they will take their revenge, if revenge is what they're after, or when they achieve their goal, assuming they had one, or when their plan finally reaches fruition, if a plan is what they've been hatching; and sometimes they wait for so long that nothing comes of it at all and the whole thing decays inside their imagination. There are those who live their whole lives in a state of continuous secrecy and concealment, and who also have the patience never to destroy their web. Curiously, they never tire of this or miss transparency, simplicity or clarity, miss being able to lay their cards on the table, look someone straight in the eye and say: 'This is what I want and that's what I'm going to do. I don't want to confuse or fool you any more. I've lied and pretended and have been lying and pretending for a long time, almost since I met you. It was necessary or I felt obliged to do it, I was obeying orders or my happiness depended on it, or so I thought. I was weak or being loyal to others, I was afraid of losing you for ever or was persuaded to behave as if I was. You were too important to me or I didn't care about you at all, I regretted having to deceive, it went against my conscience or I found it really easy, for me you were everything or you were nothing, but it doesn't matter, not now. I feel really bad and I'm exhausted. It takes endless work to silence the truth or to tell lies, maintaining them is a titanic task and remembering which are which even more so. The fear of putting my foot in it, of contradicting myself without realizing it, of being caught out, unwittingly going back on my word, or lowering my guard, it's utterly draining. My guilt has eased, it's not so great as to stop me trying, and so I'm going to tell you the truth. My lie began a long time ago, things are as they are and there's no alternative now, no going back. At this point, the truth doesn't exist and has been replaced; all that matters is what we have experienced since. Maybe that distant deceit has become the truth. Nothing is going to change very much because you know what was once the truth and no longer is. And I need to rest.'

Yes, there are some fortunate people who never feel tempted to say this, to put things right and to confess. I'm not one of them, alas, because I do have a secret that I'll never be able to tell to a living soul, still less to those who have since died. You convince yourself that it's only a small secret, that it doesn't really matter and doesn't affect your life in the least, these things happen, youthful indiscretions, things you do without thinking and that are basically insignificant, so what need is there to know them? And yet not a day passes without my remembering what I did and what happened in my youth. It isn't and wasn't anything very grave, I don't think anyone was hurt, but it's best, just in case, to keep silent, for our own sake, for mine, perhaps for the sake of my daughters and, above all, my wife. And when I tell that secret here (except that here is not reality), you will all have to keep my secret and keep silent too, you mustn't go broadcasting it from the orient to the drooping west, making the wind your post-horse, as if it had become something trivial that belonged to you and each of you were a tongue on which rumour rides. Please, say not a word if others ask to hear my story. They will do so only to amuse themselves or to accumulate useless information, which they will forget as soon as they have indifferently scattered it further afield and a little further.

It troubled me not to be straight about things, to lurk in the shadows so to speak. I wished I could tell Van Vechten what I was after – although such were Muriel's scruples, I didn't know exactly what that was – and to put an end as soon as possible to this pantomime, to rid myself of his company, his presence, all of which I already found disagreeable or soon would. It wasn't that he himself was unpleasant or didn't try his best to be agreeable, most of my friends liked him despite the great difference in age, and he was far better received than I'd expected. When I first turned up with him in tow, they all stared at him as if he were a Martian, but it didn't take him long to blend in – insofar as that was possible, of course – and not be seen as an intruder, a nuisance, a spy. He did his bit, he was cheerful and affable, he gave advice when asked, and my friends and acquaintances inevitably saw him as a man with experience of life, they also consulted him about their fears and anxieties – doctors have it easy in that respect, they're always welcome everywhere. He bought many a round of drinks and that always helps one to be accepted into a group, and at the end of the night – if he lasted that long, some of the older people understandably flagged when we younger folk could still keep going for hours – he would deliver each of us to our door in his flash car, it was as if we'd suddenly acquired a chauffeur, which was very convenient, a blessing really, saving us the expense of getting a taxi or making the long walk home under the influence of whatever excesses we had indulged in during the night. Van Vechten justified taking such pains by saying that he couldn't allow the girls to go home alone in the early hours, that one must always accompany a lady to her door, that's how he'd been brought up, and we should take advantage of his old-fashioned ways.

I noticed that he almost never took the most logical route, never dropped us off in the most convenient order, thus avoiding having to take a circuitous route or drive unnecessarily long distances, instead he always arranged things so that the last person to be dropped off would be a girl, thus ensuring that he would be left alone with her in the car once we had all been dispatched. I was on good enough terms with most of the girls to be able to ask in a jokey way: 'So, how did you get on with the Doctor the other night? He obviously wanted to be alone with you, and you didn't exactly seem to mind.' I knew that an older man would, in principle, have difficulties getting anywhere with a young woman, but I also knew that a lot of girls – at least when they're going through a phase, as so many of them do, of going out every night, night after night – are impressed by wealth or its appearance or its symbols, and by savoir faire too, so that a man of the world often finds them easy to dazzle, especially if he's good at laying the flattery on thick both before and afterwards. Some young women feel somehow honoured if a much older man shows interest, especially if they discover they can give him exceptional pleasure, or so he tells them: 'No, really, I've never experienced anything like it in my life, and I've known a fair few women in my time, you know . . .' I soon learned not to discount anything, the most unlikely combinations are possible. When one reaches maturity, it's almost embarrassing to think how easy it can be to deceive youth.

Whenever I put that or a similar question to a female friend or acquaintance or ex-girlfriend ('girlfriend' in its widest sense, including one-night stands), I would be met with an almost serious silence and a rapid change of subject, as if something had happened on the drive home which she preferred either not to talk about or to forget altogether. And so in the end I asked him:

'So how did it go the other night with Maru? It was pretty obvious that you wanted to be alone with her. You certainly went a hell of a long way round just to drop her off last.'

This was the first time I'd asked him this openly. Van Vechten smiled broadly, like someone amused to be found out or to be complimented on his technique, however banal. Or grateful for an opportunity to show off.

'Was it that obvious?'

'Well, I don't know about the others, because they were all pretty pissed, but I've been aware of it for a few nights now. Don't worry, I won't embarrass you by mentioning it when you're driving us home. I won't pull your leg about it. If I did, that would be an end to it. The girls would smell a rat and feel awkward and wouldn't let themselves be left until last. Anyway, how did it go? And on other nights too. Do you ever get anywhere with them?'

He didn't make the most of this first interrogation to boast and show off. I had not yet gained his entire confidence, the Doctor (or 'Jorge', as he insisted I call him, especially when we were with my friends) still wasn't sure to what extent I was like him or not, if, that is, he *was* like that. He was somewhat reluctant to tell me, to respond, and he answered only vaguely.

'Well, some nights I do and some nights I don't. But they're pretty good, those girls of yours, you don't know how lucky you are. Considering the age difference, I really can't complain.'

'I could give you a few tips, if you like. Not that you need it, I'm sure. You can probably tell who's likely to come across with the goods even before she does. But as in any group anywhere, some girls put it about more than others.' I would never have used such an expression to describe the conduct of any of my friends, but Muriel had advised me to be coarse and contemptuous, and thus encourage Van Vechten to do likewise, again always assuming he was that way inclined or could be. And he certainly looked as though he could. Almost all men could if given the chance. I knew this, although I myself tended not to be.

Some days later, I boasted to him about a few imaginary conquests and what's more with girls I'd only just met, which are the kind of conquests that win you most kudos and provoke most envy: I'd come on to a girl and she'd ended up sucking me off in a dark corner of La Riviera, or whatever it was called, which had a bit of a garden at the back; in Pintor Goya I'd got off with the drop-dead-gorgeous daughter of a government minister, who was known for both things, for being his daughter and for being gorgeous, anyway, I'd taken her home with me and fucked her twice. That was the kind of lexicon I used, or worse of course. None of that had actually taken place, but I told him it had happened on the nights when he hadn't come out with us, because he didn't always join us, partly because he was unable to keep up with our supposedly fast pace, but mainly because he had certain obligations, family and professional. I say 'supposedly' because, at the time, on many of the nights when I didn't take him out with me, I simply stayed home or worked until late at Muriel's apartment even if he wasn't there (he had begun shooting the only film he made during my time with him, the Harry Alan Towers production based on a script on which I'd lent a helping hand), either compiling one of those exhaustive lists of authors or working on some other such minutiae, meanwhile discreetly keeping Beatriz and the children company, listening to her play the piano, not that she ever kept this up for long, for she soon tired of it. By then, it had become clear to me that the occasional 'sacred' meetings between her and Van Vechten were purely utilitarian for both parties. In his case, and having seen what I'd seen, he was hardly likely to turn down the chance of occasionally screwing a woman almost twenty years younger, the world of women thirty-five years younger having only just opened up to him.

The Doctor immediately took the bait and, despite his age, gave me a blunt description of what had happened. He had certain traits that were inappropriately juvenile, incorrigibly immature.

'When I took her home the other night, she sucked me off in the car, right outside her parents' house. What do you think to that?'

I gave an admiring whistle, not just congratulatory, but surprised too. There was always the possibility that his conquest might be as imaginary as mine, but I thought not.

'Really? She went that far? To be honest, I would never have thought it. How did you manage that? I don't mean to underestimate you, of course, because you look great, like some American or English actor, but you are old enough to be her father, if not more, and, forgive me, but I really can't see her suggesting it. I'd imagined that, at most, she might have let you touch her tits or shown them to you without you touching them, because you asked her to. I don't mean to offend, but you must have amazing powers of persuasion. How did it happen? Tell me. Did you offer her something in return? Lifelong medical care? Did you suggest listening to her chest and then one thing just led to another?'

I tried to adopt a light tone, a mixture of jocularity and amazement. Ever since that poker evening with Celia and all his blunt questions, I had got into the habit of sometimes gently pulling his leg. Perhaps I went too far this time. I saw at once that he was not amused, as if it really riled him to see that I considered he was not in himself seductive enough. His eyes grew cold and hard, and the rectangular smile he'd

worn as he pinned on his metaphorical medal, as he told me of his triumph, vanished completely. He was one of those people who, because
they look younger than they are, end up believing that nothing at all
has changed since their youth. If they're not stupid, they only believe
this now and then and when alone, and they know it's not true; and
Van Vechten wasn't stupid. He was proud of his fine appearance and
made good use of it, but he wasn't just a conceited fool or blind to what
he could see in the mirror, or perhaps his mirror was the wife he saw
each morning, who looked much older than him and reminded him of
his real age. He was hardly ever seen out and about with her. Perhaps
they lived separate lives, like Muriel and Beatriz, or even more so,
perhaps they were just waiting for divorce finally to be made legal in
Spain. There were an awful lot of such couples waiting impatiently or
desperately, appallingly unhappy couples who had been forced to put
up with their lot for more than four decades, if not centuries, because
the brief truce of the 1930s hardly counted.

After a few seconds, his eyes softened and he recovered his smile, his
principal charm and weapon. More than that, he even laughed,
although whether this was a forced laugh or not, I couldn't tell.

'Lifelong medical care. Listening to her chest,' he repeated. 'Oh,
very funny, very witty. I could also have offered to examine her for
cysts, you forgot to mention that, although at her age, girls have
other things on their mind. But like I said, I never offer anything in
exchange. I've never paid for sex, and what you're half-jokingly suggesting would be tantamount to paying. Albeit cheap at the price.'

He had maintained his smile throughout this speech, but his tone
had been ever so slightly more serious. I was quick to correct him, so
that he wouldn't take offence.

'There was no half-joking about it, Jorge, it was a joke, pure and
simple. Anyway, how did it happen? How was it? Did it just come out

of the blue? To be honest, I'm staggered. I take my hat off to you.'
And I made a gesture as if doffing my hat.

'You're surely not expecting me to reveal my methods to you, Juan.' He was smiling unreservedly now, flattery can soften anyone and often proves to be our undoing, our downfall. It encourages us to talk too much.

'At least give me a clue. Lessons from the master.' I immediately bit my tongue, I'd gone too far and he might get annoyed again. 'Don't play hard to get. After all, I'm the one who introduced you to all those girls.'

He hesitated. No, he wasn't stupid, and couldn't possibly hope to persuade me that whatever had happened with Maru had been at her instigation or had happened spontaneously without some trick on his part, some entreaty, some trap. Maru was quite a wild young woman, who laughed loudly at the slightest thing, regardless of whether it was funny or not, she might even have creased up at one of the Doctor's ancient jokes. But there was a vast difference between that and fellating him while he was at the wheel of his car, in downtown Madrid. He shrugged and opted for an enigmatic silence, but I sensed in him a desire to crow about his methods, which he didn't yet want to reveal. I was sure he would talk more freely on the next occasion.

'It isn't only a matter of how you get something, Juan' – and he said this rather in the tones of a master, a maestro, so perhaps I hadn't gone too far – 'what matters is getting it in a way that gives you most satisfaction. And nothing gives one more satisfaction than when a girl doesn't want to do it, but can't say No. And I can assure you most of them do want to do it, once they realize they're obliged to. They want it once they've experienced it, but they're left with the memory, the knowledge, the resentment, that the very first time, they had no choice. And as I'm sure you know, it doesn't get much better than that: new desire mingled with a touch of old resentment.'

What he had said was pretty nebulous, not to say cryptic, but it seemed worth mentioning it to Muriel, informing him. Van Vechten had referred to something that could be relevant to my boss's first semi-explicit words, to the doubts possibly sown in him by 'a spiteful, devious person who harboured an implacable grudge' against Van Vechten, 'the kind of grudge that never dies'. That is the defence Muriel imagined the Doctor would use if he asked him point-blank about the troubling story someone had told him, the story that had eventually led him to send me on this mission: 'malicious lies or the product of some vile settling of accounts', mere ill-intentioned rubbish. Those first words had remained engraved on my memory, as have so many other first words spoken to me by almost everyone: 'What stops me simply dropping the matter, rejecting it as frankly unbelievable and not even worth considering, is that, according to what I've been told, the Doctor behaved in an indecent manner towards a woman or possibly more than one . . .That, to me, is unforgivable, the lowest of the low.' Now Van Vechten had stated that he found nothing more satisfying than 'when a girl doesn't want to do it, but can't say No' and he'd spoken of them feeling 'obliged' to do it and of having no choice 'the very first time' and of an 'old resentment'. I had taken pains to remember his words exactly, which is something I've always been good at, I've always had the ability to report verbatim what people say in my presence, with no summarizing, no paraphrasing, no approximations, as long as it's not a long lecture of course. However confusing I found Van Vechten's words, I was ready to repeat them to Muriel, and they would doubtless be more meaningful to him than to me, or he could perhaps throw some light on them. What I found most bewildering was this: if Van Vechten neither paid for nor offered anything in exchange, why on earth would Maru or any of my female friends say Yes when their first reaction was to say No? I didn't think the Doctor would be capable of violence or of making physical threats. And if that had been the accusation, Muriel wouldn't have used a subtle, moral term like 'indecent', which was too flimsy a word to describe any action involving force or rape.

And so I dared to interrupt my boss in the middle of making his latest film, and he arranged to meet me two mornings later, very early, taking advantage of a brief return to Madrid to shoot a few scenes in the studio, although he usually spent whole days away when he was on location, this time in Ávila, Salamanca, La Granja and El Escorial, and from there they would later have to travel to Baeza and Úbeda, and finally, to Barcelona. He was too busy to come back to the apartment and would instead be staying in a hotel with the actors. When I arrived, he was doing repeated takes of a stern speech given by the British actor Herbert Lom, who was less of a mythic figure for me than Jack Palance, but whom I had known and admired and, indeed, feared since my childhood visits to cinemas showing double bills, and had seen him in dozens of films, often playing the refined or exotic villain (he tended to appear in oriental costumes). Seeing him in person confirmed to me his fine voice and excellent English diction, although I have since found out, after his recent death at the age of ninety-five, that he was Czech by birth – or, rather,

Austro-Hungarian – and that he didn't come to England until he was twenty-one, fleeing the Nazi invasion, and with an unpronounceable surname, as long and complicated as the professional name he adopted was short and simple: he was originally called Kuchačevič ze Schluderpacheru, but I doubt that such a name would have been allowed either on screen or on a poster. He had played minor roles in some major films, for example, Napoleon in *War and Peace*, probably more because of his short stature than because of any other physical resemblance, although his broad forehead with a single lock of hair brushed forward certainly helped; he had also played Captain Nemo and the Phantom of the Opera and one of the murderers in *The Ladykillers*, and he had appeared in *Spartacus* playing a Cilician envoy; but I had found him particularly frightening in *El Cid* as the Almoravid Ben Yusuf, all dressed in black and with his face covered throughout the film (you could only see his eyes), and with his drumming hordes, who disembarked in my own country of Spain. It didn't much matter that the action took place in the eleventh century, panic travels fast in fiction or in what one experiences as fiction.

Anyway, when Muriel stopped filming in order to talk to me and hear my report, the rest of the team dispersed, apart from Lom, who, after he and I had been introduced, did not move, but stayed where he was, perhaps so as not to lose his concentration. He took a cigarette out of his cigarette case, inserted it into a holder that he removed from its own tiny box and began smoking with an elegance that seemed to belong to another age. His successful career had come to a halt towards the end of the 1960s, and he had fallen into the hands of Inspector Clouseau (bringing to life Clouseau's crazed boss in the various sequels to *The Pink Panther*), and into the hands of Towers and even those of Jess Franco (he had appeared in the latter's lesbian-prison fantasy *99 Women* and in *Count Dracula*, which no one really thinks of as being the best version). Muriel, however, considered him to be a great artist and treated him with enormous respect ('He's worked with Vidor and Huston, with Mackendrick, Kubrick and Anthony Mann, with Dassin and Carol Reed,' he would exclaim, enraptured). According to what I've heard, he was also an extremely cultivated man and had written a novel about Marlowe, to whom, as Rico had kindly informed me, some had attributed both a fake death and the entire works of Shakespeare. And so as not to be rude to the actor and leave him out of the conversation, unable to understand a word, my boss asked me to give my report in English, having first said to me in Spanish: 'After all, he won't know what we're talking about and, even if he did, it wouldn't matter, but, as long as he remains here in our company, I don't want him to feel excluded or sidelined.' 'Couldn't you ask him to leave us alone or couldn't we just go somewhere else?' I asked apprehensively. 'It's going to seem very artificial, you and me speaking in English, and I'm not that used to speaking English, you know.' Muriel had made films in America, whereas I had made only a few brief visits to England.

Despite his short stature, I found Lom's presence intimidating, even terrifying, and not just because of the fear he had provoked in me as a child in the darkness of a cinema (I remembered him in a hat in *North West Frontier* with Lauren Bacall and Kenneth More, again playing a treacherous fanatic). His eyes were as glacial as they were magnetic, so intensely cold as to be almost troubling. His very thin upper lip (completely out of proportion with his rather plump lower lip) was clearly one of the weapons he used to radiate the air of sardonic cruelty that remained intact even though he was, by then, sixty-something years old. And yet he appeared very affable and friendly, and, having given his vehement fictional peroration, he seemed relaxed and contented, with a cigarette in one hand and, in the other, an android-green silk handkerchief, with which he was playing almost as if he were a magician. 'I couldn't possibly do that, boy.' And Muriel shot me a chiding glance with his one eye. 'It's about time you learned some manners, Juan. Show some respect for the great man. Come on, we haven't got much time before shooting begins again. But don't leave out any important details. Come on, tell me.' And to give me my cue in English, he added: 'So, tell me, Juan.' He shifted easily into English, as I had seen him do before with Palance and Towers.

And I did my best to relay to him my conversation with Van Vechten. Now and then, I would turn to Lom, so as not to exclude him and as if this were also his business. What we were talking about would have been of no interest whatsoever and wouldn't even have made much sense, but I noticed that he was nevertheless paying close attention, as though he were one of those very alert individuals, incapable of not paying attention to whatever was going on around him, and interested in any story or conversation. Perhaps he was one of those actors who absorb everything, just in case it might be of use later on. When it came to reporting the Doctor's final words to Muriel, those that had seemed of possible relevance to the investigation, I translated them clumsily into English and then asked permission to repeat them in Spanish, apologizing beforehand to the eminent Mr Lom, who, to me, was still Ben Yusuf and Napoleon:

'Forgive me, Mr Lom, but at this point, what the friend we're talking about said was somewhat ambiguous and complicated, and it would be best if I gave Mr Muriel the actual Spanish.'

Herbert Lom waved his handkerchief in the air in a gesture of largesse and generosity, so extravagantly in fact that it touched my nose, making me sneeze, not once but three times.

'No, of course, go ahead,' he said, adroitly avoiding these explosions and waiting until I had stopped. 'It's all very interesting, I must say. But, please, Juan, feel free.'

He had caught my name first time. I felt very honoured and, given his cinematographic antecedents, rather troubled too. I had seen him treat people he was planning to kill with equal deference.

Muriel looked concerned, or possibly discouraged or disappointed, when he heard the words his old friend had spoken. As if he would have preferred me to come back to him empty-handed, having made no progress, or to be able to reject what I had to say, which seemed, however, to affect him quite deeply.

'Did he really say that?' he asked in a gruff voice, seeking some opening for his incredulity. 'He actually said, "Nothing gives one more satisfaction than when a girl doesn't want to do it, but can't say No"? Are you sure, Juan?' Out of respect for Lom he was still speaking in English and translated those words more precisely than I had when I gave him my version.

'Yes, I'm sure, Don Eduardo, I mean, Eduardo.' The great actor's presence prompted me to add the 'Don', which I hadn't for a long time. I didn't want him to think I was being overfamiliar with my employer. 'I have a very good memory. Give or take a word, that's exactly what he said. Does that clarify or illuminate anything as far as you're concerned?'

'Possibly. And what did you say? Did you try to draw him out? That's what I told you to do, to encourage him to talk. That was obviously the perfect opportunity.'

'Yes, of course. I told him I didn't quite understand, I asked him what he meant by "resentment". I asked him to explain.'

'And?'

'And nothing. He burst out laughing and didn't answer. And just then a niece of García Lorca's joined us – she often goes to that same disco – and the conversation took a different direction. She's half-American and has worked as a dancer in New York. She's very pretty, a few years older than me. The Doctor couldn't keep his eyes off her legs and he had a go at chatting her up, but I very much doubt he'll get anywhere. She has a partner, a painter. And, to be honest, I didn't want to return to the subject later in case it looked like I was being too nosey. Perhaps I should have persisted. But I think he'll be more prepared to talk on another occasion if I don't insist too much.'

'All right, that's enough,' said Muriel somewhat dismissively, or perhaps he was merely distracted, weighed down by his own thoughts.

Then I told him what I found most bewildering: how did Van Vechten manage to get anywhere with Maru or with my other girl-friends if he didn't pay them or offer anything in exchange? This was a mystery to me. Muriel said nothing, as if he too were asking himself that same question. Or perhaps he was thinking about the past, per-haps his thoughts were focused on that.

Seeing us both sunk in joint meditative silence, Herbert Lom intervened, with an elegant wave of his large handkerchief. This time it flicked my eye, and for a while I had to keep that eye closed, as if I had a speck of dust in it or, worse, some fierce insect. Or as if Muriel's hard eyepatch had been placed over it.

'Insofar as I have grasped the nature of the matter in hand,' he said in his fine, deep voice, his eyes as sharp as nails, just as they were on the screen, 'if this friend of yours, this Dutch doctor, neither pays for nor offers anything in exchange; if he neither promises nor tempts, then he must demand. There is, in principle, no other option.'

Muriel and I looked at each other in surprise, we had assumed he wasn't much interested in our conversation, even though we were, *contra natura*, speaking in English (my spoken English was only average at the time, though it improved subsequently). But he had, it seemed, quickly grasped the situation. A bright, intelligent man, perhaps as fearsome as his characters, who had possibly been created simply so that he would play them.

Muriel was about to speak, but I got in before him:

'What do you mean, Mr Lom? Demand what?' I don't know how I dared question him so directly. He may have been short, but I still found him quite intimidating.

'It's obvious,' replied this Lord of the B-movie, as if it went without saying. He threw his handkerchief in the air and caught it on his forearm, like a falconer receiving his returning falcon. It missed me this time, but I was beginning to grow weary of that android-green piece of cloth, or perhaps it was Nile green, which was fashionable that season, I had seen Professor Rico sporting ties and (rather smaller) handkerchiefs in that same colour, his handkerchief protruding from his top jacket pocket. 'If someone wants something that the other person denies him, and he's not prepared to offer anything or to pay for it, then he's in a position to demand it. If that doesn't work, then his one bargaining chip is silence.'

I wasn't following. Muriel, it seemed, was, because he asked:

'So what the Doctor will have given in exchange is a promise not to do or say something that could prove detrimental to those women's reputations. Is that what you mean, Herbert?'

Lom had now tucked his silk handkerchief up his sleeve. Most of it, however, remained hanging out, like a waiter's serviette, but at least he wouldn't be able to unleash it on me again. He then made a sweeping gesture meaning *Voilà*, his floating handkerchief underlining the flourish. Kuchačevič ze Schluderpacheru was clearly a man of the world. And then he did actually say *Voilà*, as if he were quoting a piece of dialogue.

'*Voilà*. If you give me what I want, I will say nothing and do nothing, and I will not harm you with what I could do or say.' It had never occurred to me that this might be Van Vechten's weapon or attitude, and I couldn't imagine what he could possibly remain silent about with any of my female friends and acquaintances. Muriel, however, could, because he nodded sadly or perhaps resignedly. But then he knew what he was trying to find out about the Doctor, and I as yet did not.

'This may, I fear, be the case here,' he muttered. He appeared not to wish to say anything more.

Herbert Lom, on the other hand, had perked up.

'Whatever it is,' he added, 'and if he is a friend, let's hope he isn't mixed up with any activities such as those that caused our dear producer so many problems with the FBI. That's all over now, of course, but, as you know,' and he turned to Muriel this time, 'it meant that he couldn't visit America for twenty years. Or, rather, he avoided doing so, I assume because he would have been sent straight to jail if he'd so much as set foot there. These matters always end badly.'

'Harry? Wanted by the FBI? I don't know what you're talking about, Herbert, nor what activities you're referring to. Although, now you mention it, Jesús Franco did once say something of the kind. But tell me, what happened?' Muriel's anxiety had evaporated. His curiosity was aroused and proved to be the stronger emotion, after all, it's always intriguing to learn that a semi-friend or false temporary friend (someone for whom you work and who pays you) is or was a fugitive from the FBI.

It was clear that Herbert Lom liked to surprise people and to tell stories. He smiled with delight, and his thin upper lip vanished. He had doubtless mentioned this episode with the sole aim of telling us all about it.

'Really? You didn't know?' And to justify his indiscretion, he added. 'Well, now that he's paid the fine and they've dropped the charges, I don't suppose he would mind you knowing. Although, just in case, don't tell him that you do. I don't *think* he would care, I mean he's often laughed about it with me, but one never knows. It's also true that he has sometimes spoken with regret about not being able to establish himself in Hollywood because of that one mistake.'

It was hardly surprising that Towers would have spoken about the affair to Jesús Franco or to Lom. He had produced eight or nine of Jesús Franco's films, some of which were extremely erotic, and had collaborated with Lom on at least five occasions, this, the sixth, was never finished and never shown and appears in no filmography, as I discovered recently on the Internet: not in that of Muriel or Towers or Lom.

'You have my word. Tell me, though, what happened?' Muriel loved gossip, as long as it was lurid and interesting. In a matter of seconds, he had forgotten all about Van Vechten and was eager to hear about his producer's criminal adventures. Towers was a very ordinary-looking man, with greying hair, a weak chin that threatened to become double, a broad, flat nose and very thick eyebrows darker than his hair. He would have been about sixty, and I had met him on a couple of occasions, but he had barely spoken to me. Not that this means anything, it's what usually happens with secretaries and subalterns.

'It is, needless to say, an incomplete, contradictory and confusing tale,' said the man who had been Napoleon, and he lit another cigarette after first carefully inserting it in his cigarette holder, clearly pleased to have our full attention. 'What I've gleaned (and not only from Harry himself) is that in 1960 or 1961, he took with him to New York a young half-Czech, half-English woman called Mariella Novotny, with whom he was having an affair. A very fleeting affair, needless to say. He had promised to help her build a career as a model in TV commercials; she was not, it would seem, a woman of high ambitions. By then, Harry was making his way in Hollywood, in Toronto and in New York, so he had plenty of American contacts. They stayed in a hotel where Mariella began to receive influential gentlemen from the world of politics and elsewhere, always at the urging of Harry and with him as intermediary, and also, later on, in the apartment that Harry shared with his mother – our producer has a most unusual mother. That at least is what Novotny told the FBI: that he had provided her with important clients, assuring her that pleasing them would help her in her modelling career; he was, in effect, acting as her procurer and keeping seventy-five per cent of what she earned from her various sexual acts, which, inevitably, included threesomes. She added that Harry was usually present, although it seems highly unlikely that any of those important *partenaires* would have agreed to that. (She resembled a slightly less voluptuous Anita Ekberg, in both face and body, and this doubtless contributed greatly to her success.) According to the FBI, when the couple were arrested, Harry was found hiding in a wardrobe, so maybe he was always a furtive presence. He, I need hardly say, denies it all.' Herbert Lom gave a short laugh, which infected Muriel and, yes, why deny it, me too, for there was something intrinsically comic about the whole situation, or perhaps it was made amusing by the reborn Ben Yusuf's comments. 'One of Hoover's undercover men used to attend some of the parties Mariella started to frequent.' My cinematographic knowledge meant that I knew Hoover had been Head of the FBI. 'True, Harry is a pathological liar, but, according to him, what alarmed Hoover was finding out that at one of these parties, Novotny had met – the first of several meetings – with Peter Lawford, President Kennedy's brother-in-law and pimp.' He used a rather more elegant term, calling him a 'go-between'. 'And things didn't end there: at another party later on, in the apartment of the singer Vic Damone, no sooner was she formally introduced to Kennedy than Mariella was led into a bedroom where she had sex with him. Harry's mythomania is quite insatiable, and he maintains that it was a case of coitus interruptus, because shortly after the two of them had disappeared into the bedroom, a tremendous ruckus broke out in the living room: Damone's Asian girlfriend had shut herself in the bathroom where she had slashed her wrists, unsuccessfully of course. But the apartment emptied instantly, and the first to vanish was Kennedy, along with his small entourage and his bodyguard.'

'Oh, I can believe that,' said Muriel. 'It's a classic female ploy – locking themselves in the bathroom and slashing their wrists. The amazing thing is that they can almost never find their veins.'

'Possibly,' Lom responded politely, 'but I wouldn't know. There doesn't seem to have been a single beautiful woman of the day who didn't end up in bed with Kennedy. Or else in a swimming pool, a boat or a lift, it didn't matter. If all those stories were true, he wouldn't have had time to govern the country. Or even travel to Dallas, in which case, he might still be with us today. Harry, on the other hand, once showed me a copy of an internal memorandum about the Profumo affair from Hoover himself. In it he mentioned Mariella Novotny, adding in parentheses "see Kennedy Brothers file". It also mentioned her "pimp Alan Towers", and he very proudly, laughingly, showed me what it said about him: "He apparently now lives permanently behind the Iron Curtain. Novotny states that Towers was a Soviet agent and that the Soviets were collecting

compromising information about certain prominent individuals."
Hmm,' added Lom with an amused if sceptical smile, 'it may be that
the memorandum is apocryphal and was forged by Harry to impress
his friends, he's perfectly capable of doing that and more. Except that
this was also exactly what Mariella told the FBI after she was arrested
for soliciting, a charge that was mysteriously and instantly withdrawn, unlike the charges made against Harry for infringing the
White Slave Traffic Act. They accused him of having brought Mariella from London to New York with the intention of prostituting her
and profiting from her earnings. It was significant, too, that there
was no mention in the press about the incident at Vic Damone's party,
despite the large number of witnesses and despite the presence of
Hoover's undercover man, who, it must be said, had a very pleasant
job and was doubtless the one who ordered a colleague from his
department to phone up (the conversation was recorded) and hire
Maria's services on the day she was arrested. This happened when
she had just finished undressing for that FBI agent-cum-client in
Harry and his mother's apartment. According to our admired producer, he knew nothing about his protégée's grubby activities and had
no idea that she was a hooker.' That was the word Captain Nemo
chose to use. 'He claims to have been quietly writing a script in the
next room when the young woman burst in, stark naked, saying that
there was a policeman in her bedroom. That is what he told the FBI
and what he told me. He called himself ingenuous and stupid, but the
FBI didn't believe him, which is why he had to escape to England
before the trial began, once he had been released on bail after spending a couple of weeks behind bars. He lost all his money and didn't
dare go back to America for years. Now, as I said, he's sorted things
out and will, at last, be able to return.'

Muriel was so enjoying this story that he'd forgotten all about the rest of the team, who were hanging about nearby. He was listening with a smile on his lips, and I saw his one eye glint as it did when he thought of a good idea for a plot or a scene.

'So he escaped, just like that? He simply decided to be a fugitive for the rest of his life?' he asked with a mixture of incredulity and hilarity. 'He took a big risk, didn't he? I know how puritanical the Americans can be, but it doesn't seem such a very serious matter. I doubt that, in the worst-case scenario, he'd have been given anything more than a symbolic sentence. In the 1960s, vices were, I believe, viewed with a certain degree of understanding.'

'No, he was quite right to leave America, it was lucky he did,' said Lom. 'He denies it now and laughs it off, but later, when he was out of the reach of American justice, he was accused of heading up a vice ring in the United Nations, and, given the political implications, that was infinitely more serious and dangerous: 1961 was a bad year for the Cold War. I'm sure you'll understand that the United Nations building was not deemed to be quite the same as the apartment he shared with his mother, in which an ex-girlfriend was allegedly taking liberties behind his back. Always supposing that the second charge was true. Harry says that it wasn't, and I believe him. And I do wonder why the FBI didn't believe him to begin with, I mean, he's always written scripts, so why wouldn't he be immersed in one while Mariella was quietly getting undressed in the next room so as to make discreet, muted love with her boyfriend, after all, isn't that what prostitutes and their lovers have always done? Knowing his incorrigible ingenuousness, I believe him, naturally.' And Herbert Lom laughed loudly. He performed a final flourish with his handkerchief, which was very crumpled by then, and, realizing this, he flung it down on the floor. 'Anyway, are we going to carry on filming today or not?'

With the existence of the Internet, where you can find snippets of information about almost everything, I felt a kind of retrospective curiosity both about crafty Harry Alan Towers and about that whole story (after all, I had worked for him indirectly and he didn't die until 2009); and I've learned that what we were told by Mr Kuchačevič ze Schluderpacheru (who will probably now have reverted to that name) was pretty close to the truth or what is known of the truth, because it still seems as incomplete, contradictory and confusing as the celebrated actor Herbert Lom warned us it would be.

I read somewhere else that Towers's interests in New York extended beyond what took place in his apartment, and that, during the time when he was supposedly aiming high and in a position to compromise influential people, his two main contacts had been, first, his mother ('our producer has a most unusual mother' Lom had commented in an enigmatic, rather casual manner), and second, 'a certain Leslie Charteris', whose identity was known to me already in 1980, again thanks to my cinematographic-televisual knowledge, as the author of the novels and stories on which several series of Simon Templar as the Saint were based. I was intrigued to learn that, for quite a long time, Charteris was denied permanent residence in America because of the Chinese Exclusion Act, which prohibited immigration by persons of 'fifty per cent or greater Oriental blood', and that the real surname of the Saint's creator was, unexpectedly, Bowyer-Yin (Bowyer being his mother, and Yin his father), and that he had been born in Singapore. This makes it perhaps still stranger that, in 1937, he translated and edited the famous book by Manuel Chaves Nogales: *Juan Belmonte, Killer of Bulls*. However, I found nothing to link Charteris with the United Nations or with any vice ring. I was also intrigued to discover that Lom's Hollywood career was also cut short when the American embassy in London refused to issue him with a visa. He may have fled from the Nazis, but he was apparently considered to be a Communist sympathizer and fellow traveller. Almost everyone seems to have had problems with the American authorities at one time or another, it's an old tradition.

The reason I mention all this is, I think, by way of being a superstitious and hollow form of compensation, because I greatly regret that Muriel will never know about it. He loved such literary-cinematographic conundrums (he would have spent hours in front of the computer). We never grow used to not speaking to the dead we once knew, to not telling them what we imagine would have amused or interested them, to not introducing them to the important new people in our lives or to any possible posthumous grandchildren, to not giving them the good or bad news that affects us and that would perhaps have affected them were they still in the world and able to know these things. There are times, too, when one is selfishly glad that they can't know: not just because they would have been upset or concerned, but because they would have been angry and would have cursed us and withdrawn their friendship, cut us dead and even tried to ruin and destroy us. 'I got away with it while they were alive,' we think, 'and now they cannot see what they would certainly have seen as a betrayal. The person who dies will be forever deceived, because he cannot know what came afterwards or, indeed, what happened while he was alive and of which he knew nothing.' In a way, it's a positive thing that our loved ones

disappear: we miss them horribly, but we also have the relief of unending impunity. There are various things that I'm glad Muriel never
found out about, especially something that happened while he was
alive and another that happened afterwards. The second was entirely
unforeseeable, the first I was careful to conceal from him.

On the other hand, I'm sure he would have enjoyed the description
of Mariella Novotny written some years later by her colleague Christine Keeler – the main cause of the Profumo scandal that erupted in
1963 – because the next time we saw each other, he was still thinking
more about Lom's story than about what I had told him regarding Van
Vechten, he was clearly dazzled by his false or transitory friend's past
adventures in the world of high politics and high-class prostitution.

'What was it about that Novotny woman,' he murmured, 'that meant
she could seduce or ensnare so many important men, always assuming
Herbert Lom was telling the truth? Imagine, Juan, she probably slept
with the two Kennedy brothers *and* their brother-in-law Peter Lawford,
as well as sundry multimillionaires and who knows how many high-up
UN officials. Getting people like that to run such risks isn't easy, not
even in the 1960s when people were less careful; it would take more than
your average, run-of-the-mill whore to do that. There must have been
something special about her, apart from her resemblance to Anita
Ekberg.' He sat thinking for a moment, then added: 'You know, I
imagine her as being like the wonderful Cecilia Alemany. Have we
heard anything of her lately, by the way? I mean in the press or on the
television, because when I'm away filming, I lose track of everything.
She would certainly never deign to phone me, I know that.'

A possible answer to those questions about Novotny is now available to everyone. In 1983, Christine Keeler wrote: 'She had a tiny
waist that exaggerated her ample figure. She was a siren, a sexual
athlete of Olympian proportions – she could do it all. I know. I saw

270

her in action. She knew all the strange pleasures that were wanted and could deliver them.' Some have identified her as Maria Capes, Maria Chapman or Stella Capes. When telling us about her, Herbert Lom had even referred to her at one point as 'Maria'. I now think he must have known her in person, since they were both of Czech origin and had been born in Prague. But I didn't know that about him at the time and wish now that we could have asked him.

Mariella Novotny was found dead in bed in February 1983, when she was forty-one, from a drug overdose according to the police. In 1978, she had announced that she was going to write her autobiography, in which she would reveal details of her work for MI5. In 1980, she went further, announcing that her book would include details of a 'plot to discredit Jack Kennedy'. She added: 'I kept a diary of all my appointments in the UN building. Believe me, it's dynamite. It's now in the hands of the CIA.' The book never appeared. Christine Keeler later wrote: 'The Westminster Coroner, Dr Paul Knapman, called it death by misadventure . . . I still think it was murder.' We need not necessarily believe Keeler, but *Lobster Magazine* said of Novotny that '. . . shortly after her death her house was burgled and all her files and large day-to-day diaries from the early 1960s to the 70s were stolen'.

As a fan of the lurid and the fantastic, Muriel would have loved all that, as well as being able to see the few shots of Mariella or Maria or Stella that are available on the Internet, and it's true, she did bear a resemblance to Anita Ekberg. The photo I like best, and which I know would have delighted him, is like a still from a film, but one made not in 1961, which is when the photo was taken, but even earlier. It's yet another demonstration of the effect passing time has on reality, turning everything into fiction, and when we ourselves are long gone, any photos of us will suffer the same fate and we, too, will look like invented people who never existed. I'm already beginning to feel that way about pictures of Beatriz and Muriel, and in his case, the black eyepatch only reinforces the impression that what we're seeing is a still from a film, or perhaps an illustration from a book, and yet I know that they did both exist and I know their tenuous history and have told it at least once.

In the photo, Mariella looks thoughtful and slightly abstracted; she's wearing a ridiculous and yet very modest hat, and her throat and neck are discreetly covered, it seems to have been taken at the moment of her arrest at Towers's apartment or perhaps when she's about to go into the police station shortly afterwards. The FBI agent with her is a heavily built man with a broad face, hard eyes and a scornful mouth. Perhaps he was the one who pretended to be a client and laid the trap for her, let's hope not: she surely wasn't that stupid, because it stands out a mile that he's either a cop or some kind of thug. Or perhaps that's what he looks like now, when time has covered them both with a large enough dose of unreality.

Muriel, however, did not entirely forget about me nor why I had insisted on seeing him while he was in the middle of shooting a film, not even on the day when Herbert Lom commandeered our conversation. Before dismissing me so that he could do another take of the scene – he didn't want any unnecessary people present, and so I never saw that great and fearsome actor give his speech – Muriel said to me in Spanish:

'Listen, young De Vere, regarding what you told me: continue along that path, keep going. Try to draw the Doctor out about the past, ask if he ever managed in the past to have his way with a woman who didn't want to but couldn't say No, isn't that what he said? I don't much care what he gets up to now, these are different times, and people take things less seriously. So go ahead and have a good time with whoever you want, those young friends of yours are no concern of mine. See if he'll tell you how he managed it back then.' And as if offering a thread of hope, he concluded: 'If it really did happen and he really did get away with it.'

In marked contrast to the dark, angry look in his eye when he first mentioned to me his friend's possibly indecent behaviour with a woman, I had been surprised to see a benevolent, rather amused glint in that same eye when he was told about Towers's clearly indecent behaviour with several women, especially if the story of the vice ring

273

at the UN proved to be true. None of this seemed to bother him in the least, not even the suspicion that those women had been used both to earn Towers money (while he, their pimp, sat back and did nothing), and to blackmail prominent individuals and celebrities, indeed, Lom's story lent an additional fascination to the character of Towers, whom Muriel saw as a worthy subject of a work of fiction. He regretted now that Towers only rarely appeared during filming and was almost always travelling abroad somewhere, for while one of his projects was underway, Towers would already be planning the next one and seeking out new sources of finance. Muriel would like to have met his employer more often, to see if he could get the full story from the horse's mouth and flesh out all the details of his shady activities in the 1960s and of his turbulent relationship with the FBI, to have him confirm or deny that his former, fleeting lover, Novotny, had screwed Kennedy and his brother Robert and their brother-in-law Lawford, to be told whether this was all true or mere fantasies and lies. One shouldn't believe everything one finds on the Internet, but I did read somewhere that Mariella and another prostitute by the name of Suzy Chang once disguised themselves as nurses to provide the Presidential 'patient' with some physical therapy; if that's true, Kennedy's tastes were not so very different from those of any ordinary male. I was surprised at my boss's reaction to Towers, but, in part, I understood it: like nearly all those in the world of cinema, including those who fancy themselves as intellectuals or artists, he was as much of a mythomaniac as anyone.

I also noticed that in Harry Alan Towers's very long and frenetic filmography, there is a gap following our failed project, as if his career had been somehow jinxed by Muriel's failure and misfortune: his next title as producer does not appear, most unusually, until 1983. By then, however, he had already disappeared from our lives and we still more from his (well, I was never really part of it), transformed perhaps into a grim memory that was best left behind. It's also possible that, by the time he had got rid of us, Towers was once again able to visit the country he had fled from and the forbidden city of New York. I suspect that the American authorities never actually allowed him to settle there, for I see that he continued filming in such out-of-the-way places as South Africa and Bulgaria, that he took Canadian nationality and moved to Toronto, where he died in 2009, at the age of eighty-eight. He certainly lasted a long time for someone who bore all the marks of having been an utter scoundrel, in the world of cinema and a few others. A scoundrel, however, who was instantly forgiven by Muriel.

Muriel had little time to probe further during what remained of the project, what with Harry's endless travelling and his own promise to Lom not to say anything about the matter unless Harry himself happened to mention those remote events; he didn't have much chance to ask. Taking advantage of a visit by Towers to Madrid to see how everything was going and to view the rushes of what had been filmed in his absence, Muriel invited him to supper one night along with his wife, the Austrian Maria Rohm, Lom, Van Vechten and Rico (the last two could get by quite well in English, much better, of course, than Roy), the witty Oxford Hispanist Peter Wheeler, who happened to be visiting Madrid, a couple from the British embassy and two of the actresses from the film: the veteran Shirley Eaton, who achieved fame after being painted with gold in the James Bond film *Goldfinger*, and the very youthful Lisa Raines. And Beatriz, of course, whose irascible husband always expected her to be there to welcome guests and organize a proper supper and flatter any producer or hypothetical source of finance. Muriel intended to steer the conversation on to the topic of the political sex scandals of the early 1960s, and

Wheeler's presence suited him perfectly: like many Oxbridge dons, he knew all about MI5's and MI6's past shenanigans, and he had known Profumo well. Muriel was hoping thus to tempt Towers to challenge the mischievous, talkative Hispanist for the limelight and to boast and tell all, even if he gave only a watered-down version that showed him in a favourable light (depending on how you looked at it: favourable in the eyes of the police or a judge, less so at a sophisticated supper party), the version in which he proclaimed himself to be completely innocent, ingenuous and stupid.

But it was entirely the hostess's fault that the supper never happened, even though all the guests arrived and I opened the door to them and helped Flavia and Susana to greet them and show them in: I was, as usual, hanging about at the apartment and had been appointed to keep Lisa Raines entertained, since I was nearest in age to her; I hadn't been invited as a guest, and so there wasn't even a place for me at the table.

VI

Beatriz had been going through a depressive phase, that at least is how I interpreted it. While he was filming, Muriel was rarely at home and often didn't come back at night to sleep, either because he was on location somewhere or preferred to stay at a hotel, and despite their poisonous relationship, his absence probably contributed to his wife's despondency or low spirits — we miss no one so much as our adversary, when we've grown accustomed to having to defend ourselves and to resist, to stand beneath the moon, persuading and imploring. Perhaps she saw in that void a warning of what the future might hold for her one day, when divorce finally became legal. She didn't neglect her morning or evening duties as an English teacher, and she spent time with her children, her mirror-images, but otherwise I rarely saw her leave the apartment: not with Rico, nor to visit Our Lady of Darmstadt nor the Plaza del Marqués de Salamanca nor to set off on her motorbike going who knew where. On the other hand, I did hear coming from her side of the apartment the metronome ticking on and on, forty times a minute if not more, occasionally accompanied by a few chords, but usually by nothing at all, not a sound, apart from the pendulum beating back and forth like a noisy, heterodox clock telling something other than the time: the music unplayed or the words thought and stored away to the beat of the metronome, the beat of boredom or of a hesitant countdown, aborted and restarted again and again, over and over. Since Muriel was not there, it was clearly no longer a reminder to him of her existence, nor a threat or a complaint or a rhythmic representation of her sufferings, nor was it a drumming of fingers as a prelude to an explosion. Despite what my boss had told me ('She takes her time, then gets distracted and falls asleep at the piano. As long as she's there, she's fine.'), I would get worried if, for a whole long hour, I heard only that ominous, unhinging tick-tock. I would stop what I was doing, go over and press my ear to the closed door that gave on to her side of the apartment, expecting to hear her moan or sigh or hum or exclaim or sob; or to perhaps hear her talking to herself or even cursing as mad people do or the lonely or those sunk in self-pity. And when I still heard only the metronome beating on, undaunted, I would at last get up the courage to knock very lightly, as Beatriz sometimes did on Muriel's bedroom door, and when she answered: 'Yes, who is it?' or even, yearningly (I thought), 'Is that you, Eduardo? Are you home?' I would feel both relieved and ridiculous and say:

'No, I'm sorry, Beatriz, it's me, Juan. I just wondered if you needed anything, if you were all right. I haven't heard you playing for quite a while, and you know how much I like to hear you play.' I addressed her automatically and informally as *tú*, as we men do with women, as if they were children, or else they themselves urge us to do so, as if they found it far harder than men to accept being addressed more formally as *usted*, which they imagine makes them seem somehow older. At the time, she was about forty-one or forty-two, the age Mariella Novotny was when she was killed or died or committed suicide; nowadays, there would be no doubt about it, she would still be considered young. However, then, and given the difference in age, she did not seem young to me. Nor did I think of her as old, that would have made a nonsense of my vague or theoretical feelings of

280

sexual admiration for her, my attraction to her fleshly beauty, a beauty that seemed to belong to another age and another place, or, as I said before, to some other dimension, some long-past, inanimate dimension.

'Don't worry, Juan, I'm fine. I leave the metronome on even when I'm not playing. It soothes me and helps me to think.' That or something similar is what she would murmur to me through the door (her voice slurred and faint, as if I had torn her from sleep or from some imagination or machination), for she never opened the door when I knocked like that. Was she perhaps not fully dressed or only in her underwear? I would wonder, and then go back to my work.

On the day of the supper party, she was too busy getting things ready to need the metronome. She had ordered the main course from a restaurant like Mallorca or Lhardy or possibly from the Palace Hotel, I'm not sure. She gave Flavia the necessary instructions and took charge of the wines and the dessert, at least I assume she did, it wasn't really my business. Muriel was filming at the studio and wasn't expected back until eight fifteen or thereabouts, along with the two actresses and Herbert Lom, for whom he would wait at the hotel until they had showered and changed, then drive them to the apartment in his car. Rico had been given orders (as a young man, he was rather more eager to please than he is now) to pick up Towers and Wheeler, and the others would arrive under their own steam. Most of the guests were foreign, Muriel had nevertheless suggested they arrive at around half past eight and then sit down to eat at about nine; it was late spring, and the sun already took a while to disappear, and it was, he said, depressing to dine in broad daylight. By six o'clock – before the children were back from school – Beatriz appeared to have everything prepared and under control, she changed her clothes, did her hair and make-up, put on her high heels and went out. She had spent so many days without going out, except to her classes – during this sad or apathetic phase – that my curiosity got the better of me and I followed her as I had on other occasions, wanting to know who it was she had suddenly felt the need to see or who had roused her from her misanthropic mood, Van Vechten or the man in Plaza del Marqués de Salamanca, or possibly neither of them. She was wearing a skirt, which made it seem unlikely, although not impossible, that she would take the motorbike, because I did once see her mounted on the bike with her skirt pulled right up – without a flicker of embarrassment and as if it were the most natural thing in the world – revealing almost as much of her strong thighs as Celia the civil servant had in the taxi.

She did not go very far. She stopped outside the Hotel Wellington, just a few metres down the street and on the same side, and I saw her look up as if expecting a signal from someone staying in one of the rooms that faced on to the street, someone who might indicate with a nod or a lift of his eyebrows: 'Come up, come up, I'm here already.' If so, this must be a third lover, I thought, otherwise why would she meet up with Van Vechten or with one of the Poles Kociejowski or Gekoski or with Deverne or Mollá or Arranz, in a different place and so close to her own apartment, just before an evening when, purely in order to please Muriel, she was expecting a load of semi-important guests? Or perhaps that was precisely her reasoning, so that she would be close by and not risk arriving late. She stood gazing up at the windows or balconies for about thirty seconds before she went in. I approached the hotel's lofty portal – a liveried doorman was on guard, they probably still have a doorman now, I haven't been past the place for a while, I tend to avoid it – and I tried to peer in, to see if she had stopped in the foyer or headed for the bar or taken the lift. I saw no sign of her, even though I waited on the pavement for three or four or five minutes, time to chain-smoke two cigarettes. Had I gone inside, the porter wouldn't have turned a hair, the hotel has always welcomed bullfighters, and I could have been a bullfighter's young apprentice or even some up-and-coming matador; however, it made more sense not to risk her finding me there, because then it would have been clear that I had followed her, given the short distance and the closeness to home. Perhaps she was going to have a drink with Gloria and Marcela at the bar, so as not to get bored at home before supper, and the prospect of that social gathering meant that she couldn't settle down alone with her metronome. While I was watching and waiting, I spotted the conductor Odón Alonso getting out of a right-hand-drive car – a Daimler or a Jaguar, I think – already in his evening clothes, as if about to give a concert. He left the keys with a valet and walked past me, humming and smiling. It was said he had a permanent suite at the Wellington, where, curiously enough, he almost always stayed with his wife. The thought crossed my mind that Beatriz might be meeting him. For some reason, I dismissed the idea.

And so I went back to the apartment to wait. There was no way I could know for sure, unless I ventured into the foyer, and that, I had decided, would be a mistake.

As arranged, Muriel arrived at eight fifteen, along with the former Phantom of the Opera, Goldfinger's mistress and victim, and Lisa Raines, the future Fanny Hill in another Towers film. From my room, I heard Muriel ask the girls and Flavia where Beatriz was, clearly puzzled not to find her there.

'She wasn't here when we got back from school,' said Susana.

'She went out,' said Flavia. 'She should be back soon.'

'What time did she go out?' he asked.

'Shortly before six.'

'Did she say where she was going?'

'No, just that she'd be back in time for supper. But don't worry, everything's ready.'

'She's probably gone to the hairdresser's or something,' Muriel said. 'And where is young De Vere?' He tended to call me 'young De Vere' rather than 'Juan', both when addressing me and when referring to me, just as he called Rico 'the Professor' and Van Vechten 'the Doctor'.

'He's in his room.'

'I'll go and fetch him. I've brought him a young beauty of his own age for him to entertain.'

The bedroom beyond the kitchen, where I had slept the first time I stayed in the apartment, had become 'my room', and it was no longer seen as unusual for me to sleep there. I preferred not to appear just at that moment, so that Muriel wouldn't ask me directly about Beatriz and so that I wouldn't have to lie to him. Not telling him what I had seen with my own eyes, for example in the Sanctuary, was not the same as saying: 'I've no idea where she's gone. She left without saying goodbye.' Even though that last part would have been true. I thought with some irritation: 'A young beauty of my own age indeed. What is Muriel talking about? Obviously all young people look the same to him.' As Lisa Raines was about sixteen or seventeen, she really was an apprentice; for me, at twenty-three, she was almost as much of a baby as Susana.

Since Muriel had to look after the guests he had brought with him, he didn't come to demand my presence immediately. However, after four or five minutes, the doorbell rang and he strode over to my room and, without looking in, called:

'Young De Vere, would you mind opening the front door? Flavia's got things to do and Beatriz isn't back yet. And the young Raines girl may already be getting bored. Come and keep her company and stop sulking. Just because you haven't got a place at the table doesn't exempt you from being helpful. And you never know, we may end up making room for you, but that will depend on whether the young prodigy approves of you or not.'

I left my room at once, and saw him walk down the corridor and into the living room, while I went to the front door. The bell rang impertinently several more times, Rico had arrived with Towers and Wheeler (now that I think of it, Rico wasn't very eager to please them either, although he made an exception for Muriel and Beatriz, whenever he got the chance to enjoy their company: I think the only reason he had agreed to play the part of chauffeur was because he wanted to meet the illustrious Oxford Hispanist, to whom he was chatting away in Spanish, completely ignoring the producer and his wife). I ushered them all into the living room and, shortly afterwards, the couple from the British embassy arrived too, all the foreigners observing relative punctuality. I repeated the same operation and, six or seven minutes later, the person ringing the bell was Van Vechten with his inevitable rectangular smile, and I wondered if Lom would notice his resemblance to Robert J. Wilke, with whom he had appeared in *Spartacus*. When Van Vechten came in and saw everyone there, he remarked in smug, stiff, mediocre English, like a Spanish TV presenter:

'Oh dear, I must be the last. So sorry to keep the distinguished guests waiting.' He gave an anachronistic click of his heels and introduced himself to the assembled company. 'Dr George Van Vechten,' he said, absurdly translating his own name from 'Jorge' to 'George'.

The truth is that no one was waiting for him, none of the foreigners had even heard of him, and the only guest who did know him, Rico, had seen him dozens of times before, and, as far as he was concerned, Van Vechten was just another shape coming and going in Muriel's motley apartment.

'No, you're not the last, Doctor,' my boss said in Spanish, then as an aside: 'Beatriz is missing. It's really very odd that she shouldn't be here.' And he looked at his watch. 'Have you by any chance heard from her today?'

Van Vechten responded defensively, although only I would have noticed:

'No, why would I?'

Then Muriel turned to me. With all the comings and goings of people and languages, I had escaped being interrogated on the subject until then. It was gone nine o'clock and the motley English contingent and their companions were beginning to flag.

'And what about you, young De Vere, do you know anything?'

No, I couldn't tell Muriel a lie, I could, at most, tell him a half-lie, enough to cover myself.

'I'm not sure. I popped out earlier to run a couple of errands and happened to see her going into the Wellington. I was on the opposite side of the street. But that was quite some time ago, at around six.'

Muriel's one eye rested with a look of alarm and incredulity on my two eyes, as if I had just acted a scene only he could understand, perhaps because he already knew it, perhaps because he had a more penetrating visual imagination than most. For a fraction of a second, he closed his eye, as if with tedium or weariness, anticipating the labour involved in some future task or in his vision of events. Or as if gathering all his strength and patience and allowing himself time to think before taking action: 'I'm going to have to deal with it all over again. Or maybe I'll never have to deal with it ever again.'

'At the Wellington? The Hotel Wellington? But why didn't you so say before?'

He said this so loudly and in such a tremulous voice that the guests' murmured conversations ceased at once and they all looked at him, concerned or uncomprehending. Professor Peter Wheeler was the only one of the foreigners present who knew Spanish perfectly, but the couple from the embassy understood too, even though they had not long been in Madrid.

'I don't know, Eduardo, you didn't ask me. What's wrong? What does it matter? That was hours ago. It never occurred to me to mention it,' I stammered, already feeling guilty of some grave fault, although I had no idea what.

But Muriel hadn't really expected an answer to his question: I don't even know if he heard what I said.

'Quick, Jorge,' he said to Van Vechten. 'You come too, Juan.' Then he turned to Rico and said: 'Paco, please, keep our guests entertained, will you, and invent some explanation. We may have to cancel supper, I'm not sure. I'll let you know as soon as possible, or else I'll send Juan.'

This time, he called all three of us by our proper names, which meant that there was no room for so much as a hint of a joke, as there normally was when he was surrounded by his usual spectators and accomplices, of whom I was now one. He only had room in his mind now for anxiety and a deadly seriousness.

I had never seen Muriel run any distance at all. 'Running is undignified, young De Vere,' he had said to me once, telling me off after seeing me race for a taxi when the lights were about to change, or when he saw other people, either painfully struggling or brimming with health, as they engaged in what at the time we Spaniards called *footing* – as a nation, we are as useless at languages in general as we are eager to adopt foreign terms we can neither understand nor pronounce. As I say, I had never before seen him run and I don't think I've ever seen anyone run as swiftly and desperately as he did, covering the few metres between his house and the Hotel Wellington in no time at all, so at least the indignity lasted only briefly, and besides, in such an extreme situation, that would have been the last thing on his mind. He ran so fast for a man of fifty – jacket flapping open, its tails and his tie flying like flags – that even I, at half his age, would have been unable to keep up with him for another two hundred metres, and Dr Van Vechten certainly wouldn't, for despite all those hours spent working out in gyms, he was still a good ten years older than Muriel. However, the distance between house and hotel was so short that all three of us arrived pretty much at the same time, with Muriel at the head, of course, not only because he was running as if the devil himself were after him – an expression used and understood by everyone, even though no one has ever actually seen the devil – but because he knew why he was running and what he had to do. During that brief race, I also guessed what had happened, as doubtless Dr Van Vechten had, if he hadn't done so earlier: Muriel wasn't afraid that Beatriz had forgotten the time or that supper had completely slipped her mind because she was too consumed by her needs or her passions or her sexual appetites – a regular lover, the manager perhaps; a guest, maybe Baringo Roy, our friend Roy's extraordinary Andalusian cousin; a bellboy or a casual waiter, or whoever – I don't think he even imagined such a scene; what he imagined was what I had entirely failed to notice when I was trying to peer into the hotel foyer: Beatriz must already have reserved a room, perhaps that very morning or even the previous night, which is why she hadn't had to go to reception to pick up her key or fill in a form; they would have handed her the key as soon as she appeared or she would have had it with her, depending on the hotel rules; she would have gone up to the room whose window she had stopped to gaze up at from the street, already imagining herself inside it, like someone contemplating her own coffin; she would have ordered something to drink or plundered the minibar and begun swallowing pills, lying on the bed, barefoot, possibly in her underwear so as to be more comfortable and with the television on so as to feel less alone, to see faces that would not see her or be able to intervene, to hear voices in the background to make more bearable the transition from being in the world to ceasing to be in the world – that irreversible transformation – just as children fall asleep more easily to the distant murmur of conversation between their parents and a guest, if there is one: as if they were lingering for a while in the waking, adult world they are reluctant to leave, not yet, not yet. The moon would not have been present, or perhaps Beatriz would have waited to see it rise – still very pale, still intimidated by the late-setting sun – so as to die in the dim glow of its deathly pallor.

Or perhaps she would have calmly and slowly filled the bathtub and then climbed in before slitting her veins – if you cut them before, the blood will start to flow at once and stain the towels and the hotel's immaculate bathrobe, very few suicides are entirely indifferent to the mess they make or the image they leave behind – and what happened once she was in the water would depend on various factors: the number, length and depth of the cuts, whether on one wrist or on both; whether the water was really hot or not hot enough, because the cold would make the incisions close up, thus delaying death, not yet, not yet, although the cold is sure to come sooner or later; and two other things would determine the speed or otherwise of that death: if the person lost consciousness and her head slipped beneath the water, then she would drown, unless her body became wedged in the tub, her nose and mouth unsubmerged; in that case, if she didn't drown, she would lie there unconscious until her heart stopped, incapable of pumping the little remaining blood around the body. It would, therefore, be a question of when she had sliced into her veins with the razor and how often and how deeply, whether she had done this at just gone six, shortly after going up to the room, or had waited and amused herself anticipating and savouring what would happen at home when the guests had all arrived and she had still not appeared; or if she had hesitated for a long time, knowing there would be no turning back, no possible postponement, once the skin was cut and the flesh opened, now, yes, now, it's not easy to remain calm enough to staunch your own blood once it has started to flow; or if she had wanted to wait and see which complete stranger would win the latest TV quiz show – sometimes the most insignificant of things can detain us – and the minutes would have passed without her noticing, or she'd be thinking all the time that it wouldn't be much longer until the dimmest contestant was eliminated or else declared the winner. It would be the same if she had taken pills, it would be crucial to know when she had started swallowing them and how quickly – the throat rebels and you have to stop now and then – and how much alcohol she had drunk. And depending on all these things, we three would arrive in time or too late, although the presence of the Doctor meant there would be not a moment's vacillation or horror, he would know precisely what to do in any circumstance, Beatriz's life would probably be in his hands, assuming there was still life in Beatriz. There was also a third possibility that could not be ruled out, for the fact that she had not, up until then, jumped off the balcony didn't mean that even as we were still running, still on our way, she might not be climbing on to the balustrade and jumping – I didn't look up as I was running, if I had, I might have seen her crouched on the ledge, ready to let herself fall – or even as we were asking at reception for her room number or persuading the staff that, given the imminence or actual occurrence of a tragedy, they would have to break down the door or use the master key, the staff would have resisted at first and called the hotel manager so that he could take charge and authorize such an intrusion, thus wasting possibly vital minutes. There was also a chance that Beatriz had hanged herself by using strips torn from the sheets, then climbing on to a chair that she herself would have kicked away, in which case, there would be no delay, no margin, nothing to be done, she would be dead when we finally entered the room as daylight was fading, or as night had already fallen, or so it would appear from inside the room, where all the lights would be on so that she wouldn't have to kill herself without being able to see properly or perhaps so as not to have to die in the dark: it's impossible not to imagine that, afterwards, there will be only blackness and so why torment yourself with the idea beforehand, unless you prefer to become accustomed to it with your eyes wide open, with your failing, fading consciousness, clinging on to life's last threads.

Time must be very strange for a would-be suicide, because it's in her hands alone to end it, and she is the one who will decide precisely when, the actual moment, which could be just before or just afterwards, and it can't be easy to decide or to know why now and not a few seconds ago or a few seconds later, or even why today and not yesterday or tomorrow or the day before yesterday or the day after tomorrow, why today when I'm still only halfway through a book and when they're about to show a new season of a TV series I've been following for years, why decide now that I'm not going to continue and will never find out what happens at the end of either book or TV series; or why stop distractedly watching a film being shown on a channel we happened upon in this hotel room – the transient place chosen for our solitary, unwitnessed death – something is sure to arouse our curiosity when we're just about to take our leave of all curiosity, along with everything else: our memories and our patiently accumulated knowledge, the anxieties and the hard work that seem now utterly pointless or of little importance; the infinite number of images that passed before our eyes and the words our ears heard, passively or by chance; the carefree laughter and the feelings of elation, the moments of fulfilment and anxiety, of desolation and optimism, as well as the tick-tock that has accompanied us since our birth; it's in our power to silence that ticking and say to it: 'Thus far and no further. There have been times when I've ignored you completely and others when I could hear nothing else, always hoping that some other noise would be loud enough to block you out and allow me to forget you, a few longed-for words or the sound of passionate, panting, amorous fury, the muttered obscenities that simultaneously repel and attract and hold us hypnotized during the time it takes to say them. Today, I will stop you dead and put an end to your imperturbability, at least as regards myself. I know that nothing will really stop you, that you will continue to exist, but only for other people, not for me; from this moment on, I will have escaped and be beyond your reach, and you will have ceased to measure out my time.' No, it can't be easy to decide precisely when our ancient survival instinct will lead us to think: 'Not yet, not yet, what harm can there be in my lingering for a few more minutes in the world, to watch the rising of the cold, sentinel moon, who, having seen so many leave, will not even blink its somnolent, half-open eye, bored with the unending spectacle of these strange, speaking beings who weep into their pillow before saying goodbye; at least I will be able to see it.' And our weariness and suffering will lead us to think: 'Right, this is it, why delay any longer, what's the point of staying for a few minutes more, or a few days, days that will seem arduous and identical as we unwittingly draw them out and continue to live with our consciousness still fully active, a consciousness that has so often caused us pain; to wonder yet again what will become of our children, who we will not see grow up into adulthood, they will have to get by without me like so many who came before, besides, Eduardo will be there to help them, for in my eyes, he will live eternally, given that he will still be alive when my time is over and who's to say that he won't be there for ever, when, as far as I'm concerned, he will never die; on the other hand, it's asking too much to expect me to help and guide the children indefinitely, I lack the will to live, the pain is too great, and they're not enough to keep me here. I can't stand it any more, nothing else matters. I will numb myself so that I can simply drift off as if I wasn't really dying, and when I'm no longer here and am part of the past, then let others come with their accusations of egotism, with condemnations and reproaches and harsh judgements, because I won't hear any of them. Then, then, I'll be beyond caring.'

It was only a short distance, although it seemed longer, as distances always do when you're afraid you won't arrive in time for something, to catch a train, to clear up a misunderstanding, to stop someone passing on a piece of information or to hasten a letter on its way, to withdraw an ultimatum or a threat, or, as was the case then, to avoid a death. The hotel staff were very understanding: since it wasn't just a young lad and a one-eyed man talking to them, but a renowned doctor, they decided not to consult their superiors or, rather, to take immediate action and then inform the manager, whom one of them rushed off to find, while another came with us to the room and rapped vigorously on the door, Beatriz having signed in under her own name. He knocked three times, pausing in between, three apparently being the obligatory or minimum number of times he could knock before opening the door without permission, while Muriel urged him to make immediate use of the master key or spare key or whatever. The door remained locked, nor was there any reassuring response (although that could have been deceptive, the sound of someone about to kick away a chair and remain hanging in the air) – 'Just coming' or 'Who is it? I can't answer the door right now. Come back later' – and so he decided to use his key to open the door; he hadn't noticed the lady go out, although she might be in the café or in one of the hotel lounges or, indeed, in her room, in which case it looked very bad indeed. Muriel was the first to enter, followed by Van Vechten, both of them at a run, then the member of staff who had accompanied us, infected by the rapid pace of events, with me last of all, afraid of what I might see, especially if she'd hanged herself or if there was a lot of blood, but neither did I want to miss anything once I'd got there, never having seen anyone dead. Before crossing the threshold, I noticed someone hurrying down the long corridor, a man too fat actually to run, but who must have been the manager summoned by the receptionist. I also noticed a smartly dressed couple coming out of their room, and when they saw so many agitated people, they stopped to look.

It was a large room, a junior suite they'd call it now, although perhaps not then, Beatriz probably wasn't bothered about the expense if she wasn't going to leave under her own steam or have to pay the bill. There was no one there, she hadn't hanged herself nor was she sprawled or curled up on the bed having taken too many pills, but there was still the bathroom, the door of which remained stubbornly shut, bolted from the inside, and no one responded from within or protested at all the noise and fuss.

'Do you have some way of opening this?' Muriel asked the receptionist, almost at the same time as he hurled himself against the door. His face was contorted with anxiety, although this was perhaps less obvious because of his eyepatch.

'No, not with me. And I'm not sure there is a way of opening bathroom doors.' By this time, the fat man had arrived, jacket all awry and his very long, wide tie hanging over his waistband, doubtless a feeble attempt to disguise his belly, one that proved totally counterproductive, since one's eye was inevitably drawn to that dangling bit of cloth. The receptionist said: 'Is there some way of opening bathroom doors, Don Hernán?' adding an incongruous introduction: 'This is the manager, Don Hernán Gómez-Antigüedad.' I couldn't help noting that unusual, somewhat pretentious name, although I subsequently learned that it's not actually that rare. The well-dressed couple, who appeared to be French, were now peering in through the door, and suddenly, absurdly enough, there were seven of us in the room.

Gómez-Antigüedad made as if to shake someone's hand and said: 'I've no idea, we'd have to ask the maintenance people,' but no one took his proffered hand because Muriel and Van Vechten were already trying to kick in the door, while the rest of us looked on, our hearts in our mouths; it looked as though it would take a lot of kicking, but, fortunately, the door wasn't that sturdy and a crack soon appeared.

'Perhaps we should fit bathroom doors with locks not bolts,' said Gómez-Antigüedad in his role as hotel manager, observing the mess being made. 'But changing all of them would mean an awful lot of work. And this sort of thing's hardly likely to happen that often.' He was talking rather breathlessly to himself, having still not recovered from his haste.

The door finally gave way and we all rushed to look inside, but Muriel held us back with a commanding gesture, as if he didn't want us to see Beatriz in her underwear or the water stained red, which is what I did manage to glimpse before obeying his command and withdrawing, urging the assembled multitude to do likewise, for other guests, attracted by the raised voices and the sound of banging, had also now gathered – well, no one can resist the chance of having some weird and wonderful tale to tell. Knowing that she would probably be discovered by the hotel staff, Beatriz had not got fully undressed before getting into the bath, on a modest impulse she had kept on her bra and pants, or so I assumed, although I didn't see the latter, only the upper part of her torso veiled in reddish foam, she must have washed first in order to smell clean, forgetting that blood has its own odour, and that peculiar metallic effluvia had already reached my nostrils, like the smell of iron. Fortunately, she had one elbow resting on the edge of the bath and so had not sunk beneath the water, had not drowned, perhaps the idea of drowning had filled her with a particular dread or revulsion, which would explain that supporting arm. Or she might already have bled to death, and I retreated before I could know if this was so.

'Let the Doctor deal with it, let him take charge,' I murmured as I pushed the crowd back into the room. Gómez-Antigüedad was happy to help and left the room along with the intruders and remained outside with them, looking dreadful, pasty-faced and faint, and leaving the receptionist in the room as the hotel's representative or in case he was needed. It was going to be hard to stop the news spreading like wild-fire round the hotel.

So it *had* been her veins. I didn't see him do this, but I assume Van Vechten tried to bind up the cuts with bits of cloth or rags (he told Muriel to bring him a sheet, and with a single violent tug, Muriel pulled the sheet off the rumpled bed – so Beatriz must at some point have been lying down), and if the bleeding continued, I again assume that he would have improvised a tourniquet. I remained stationed at the now closed bedroom door, watching Muriel going in and out of the bathroom and hearing the orders given by Van Vechten, who did not reappear for several minutes, hidden from view, so that I had no idea what his expression would be or his degree of anxiety, or perhaps he felt no anxiety, he would be the only one with any idea as to whether she would survive or not and, besides, he was too busy. I also heard the water drain out of the bath, from which he would have removed the plug, making things easier to manage without all that liquid in the way, apart from the denser, less controllable stuff.

'Eduardo, phone the clinic, the Ruber, which is the closest. Tell them from me to send an ambulance urgently. Ask for Dr Troyano or, if he's not there, Dr Enciso, and if she's not there either, it really doesn't matter, just tell whoever picks up the phone; they all know me. Tell them not to log your call, say it's a non-residential, they'll understand what I mean. Tell them to send an ambulance immediately, I'll go with the patient and give any further instructions when I get there.' And he gave Muriel a number, which Muriel remembered at once, without noting it down, his memory made keener by the sheer uncertainty of the situation.

I saw my boss emerge from the bathroom and grab the receiver of the phone on the bedside table. He was already spattered with blood, with numerous watery drops on his shirt along with other darker drops, pure and undiluted. The Doctor would be even more soiled and sodden, and both men were dressed for a quiet supper party. I was glad they hadn't let me into the bathroom, to have been spared that, I would very likely have had to throw away my clothes afterwards.

'How do I get an outside line?'

'Press zero, wait for the tone and then dial,' said the sympathetic receptionist.

After a while, I assumed that the haemorrhaging must have stopped or at least diminished, because Muriel came back out of the bathroom, looking calmer now and said:

'Look, there's nothing for you to do here, young De Vere.' The fact that he was once more calling me 'young De Vere' meant that he had recovered from his shock and that Beatriz's life was probably not in danger. 'Go back to the apartment and send our guests home, those who haven't already got fed up with waiting, that is.' He looked at his watch, then briefly tapped the face with his middle finger – a gesture of grim resignation. 'Yes, tell them all to go home. Send them my apologies and say that I'll phone them as soon as I can tomorrow.'

'And what if they want to know what happened?'

'Don't even wait for them to ask, just tell them the truth straight away. As soon as you explain, they'll see it was an emergency, they'll understand, they'll be fine. The world of cinema is accustomed to suicide attempts, even successful ones; no one will be shocked. But don't go into detail or describe the scene in all its gory drama.' And he gestured with his head to where Beatriz would still be lying, and where she must have been getting cold unless Van Vechten had covered her with a dressing gown or some towels. 'If they ask how, just say you don't know.'

I remembered that, not long before, when Lom had told us about the events in 1961 at the home of the singer Vic Damone, which had supposedly provoked a failed suicide attempt and caused Kennedy to bolt, Muriel had even made fun of the women Beatriz had just imitated. 'Oh, I can believe that,' he had said disdainfully. 'It's a classic female ploy – locking themselves in the bathroom and slashing their wrists. The amazing thing is that they can almost never find their veins.' He probably didn't even remember saying that. Or perhaps he did – bitterly reproaching himself for being so ingenuous – if Beatriz *had* missed her veins; after all, you only have to graze your skin to make it bleed.

'OK, but what if the children are there? Do I still say what happened?'

'Take the little one out of the room, if he isn't already in bed. The girls can hear what you have to say, I mean, they won't be that surprised.'

'Really? Why not?'

I immediately thought that I had again asked too much for my boss's taste. But it was done now, I couldn't un-ask the question, that was impossible, and I felt I had a right to know, since Muriel had involved me in something that was beyond my capabilities, if anything was for someone of my age; you're so pliable then, so biddable, prepared to do whatever you can to please, and there comes a point when anyone can ask or order you to do anything, even commit a crime. Besides, it was high time Muriel answered a few of my questions. Not at that precise moment, of course, but soon. He looked me up and down for a moment with his maritime eye, as if registering my tacit demand and accepting it.

'Well,' he said, as if what he were about to say was of no importance, 'with a mother like theirs, they'd better get used to the idea that one day they might lose her. The girls already know this, I'm sure. But off you go now. Towers will be confused if not furious. Not to mention his wife.'

'How is Beatriz?' I asked before I left. And mimicking him, I gestured with my head towards the bathroom, the interior of which was outside my field of vision. I had seen very little of Beatriz's calamitous state, only that initial flash when I first entered the room. Nor did I manage to see her only in her underwear (her bra straps slipping off her shoulders) and, to my shame, I realized that I would like to have seen that, even in those dramatic circumstances, or now that the greatest danger seemed to have passed. Seeing a dead woman is not the same as seeing one unconscious or badly injured, or perhaps it's not so very different if the woman has only just died and remains unchanged, by which I mean that there hasn't been time for her to lose her attraction. I did what I could to drive away these thoughts or imaginings or whatever, for while I may have been young, I wasn't completely heartless. Although most young men's hearts are, so to speak, on hold.

Then Van Vechten emerged from the bathroom for the first time since we had arrived; he was heavily stained with blood and his sleeves were soaked up to his shoulders, doctors quite often get totally filthy, they must need a very large wardrobe of clothes, that suit, for example, would have to be thrown away, even though he'd removed his jacket early on. It was he who answered my question, being more au fait with the situation:

'Fortunately, there aren't that many cuts and they're not very deep, the pain must have been enough to frighten her, not enough for her to regret doing it, you understand, but to pull her up short, instinctively, involuntarily. And the water wasn't particularly hot either. I think she probably did it about an hour ago. She's not in any danger or won't be once that damned ambulance finally gets here and we can give her a transfusion.'

'It's probably stuck in the damned traffic,' I said – swear words are infectious.

No sooner had I said this than we heard the siren, and the ambulance must have been travelling very fast for, an instant later, it was there outside the hotel. Van Vechten went over to the balcony to check that it was ours.

'They're here,' he said.

'Did Beatriz manage to find her veins? Did she actually cut them?' I asked, one foot already out in the corridor, which I saw was still full of guests and commotion, held in check by the fat, hesitant, awkward manager. Yes, I was leaving, preferring not to have to see the stretcher-bearers and all that, and, besides, Muriel had urged me to go back to the apartment.

'Of course she did,' answered the Doctor, frowning. 'What kind of a question is that?'

It's always a bad thing to have sudden gratitude thrust upon us, it makes us forget all previous affronts or abandon our plan of revenge, it numbs our rancour and blunts our desire for justice; we overlook offences and are prepared to ignore suspicions or to renounce curiosity and suspend our investigations, to shrug our shoulders and appease our feelings by resorting to false justifications for giving up: 'What does it matter if I forget all about it, so many crimes go unpunished that no one's going to notice one more, the world won't be any different. What does it matter if no one remembers?' It's always a bad thing to feel indebted to someone who has hurt us or hurt others either close to us or unrelated, sometimes it makes no difference, someone who has behaved in an indecent manner or committed the unspeakable and the unforgivable, the lowest of the low, because that can all be abruptly cancelled out by the feeling that we owe them something really crucial, really important. Offenders sometimes resort to this consciously and deliberately and even calculatingly: 'I can't fight on every front, so I'm going to neutralize this particular person who loathes me and has a grievance against me by doing him an unexpected favour, getting him out of a real mess, flattering him and thus confusing him, lending him money when he most needs it, or sending it to him through a third party if he won't take it from me (that third party will be sure to blab once the money's spent and it's too late to reject my gift, and then it's in my power to increase the beneficiary's gratitude still further by not asking for the money back), by ensuring that he keeps his job, which is hanging by a thread, by helping one of his children who has got himself into trouble and for whom he cares more than anything else in the world, or by saving the life of a suicidal wife.'

This wasn't the case with Van Vechten of course, because he didn't even know about the resentment and suspicions harboured by his friend of so many years, still less that his friend had embarked on a secret and potentially hazardous investigation into possible facts about his past – as secret as it was erratic, as befits an amateur – using a young employee who had no idea what he was looking for and was, therefore, very much working in the dark. That night, he had helped spontaneously and disinterestedly, as would any doctor, and he would doubtless have done the same for anyone, even a complete stranger who had locked herself in a bathroom with a razor –Vic Damone's Asian girlfriend, for example, had Van Vechten been at that party in 1961 – and, it goes without saying, the wife of a great friend of his, a wife whom he occasionally fucked, because, given what I'd seen at the Sanctuary of Darmstadt, that was the only correct verb to use, there was no lying with, no making love to, they weren't even lovers, or so it seemed to me, or only technically speaking. Muriel knew nothing of all that, because, among other reasons, he didn't care what Beatriz got up to, but what seemed so extraordinary was that he should care so much about losing her or saving her, for he had seemed genuinely anguished, distraught, at times looking as deathly pale or even more so than the hotel manager, Señor Gómez-Antigüedad, as if he couldn't live without that woman who so infuriated him and whom he made so very unhappy, even haring like a mad thing down Calle Velázquez, he who never ran anywhere. And because of these new or renewed feelings of gratitude towards Van Vechten, he halted my investigation: the result of the Doctor's perfectly routine intervention at the Hotel Wellington was that, two days later, when Beatriz was in hospital, still under observation and medical care, and during one of the brief periods when Muriel was not at her bedside and had come home to rest a little, his reward to the Doctor was to cancel all his previous orders to me, to cancel my mission, if that isn't too grand a term for it.

'Listen, young De Vere, I have something to say to you.' He was once again lying full-length on the floor in the living room, and whenever he did this, I was more and more convinced that it was his way of avoiding having to look me straight in the eye, a way of preventing me from accurately reading the expression on his face, which is difficult when someone is not on the same level as you, that's why kings always insist on having an elevated throne and why the same effect is still sought by the rich and powerful, many of whom wear lifts in their shoes or a wig. And although he opted to descend to a lower level, it provided him with a similar degree of opacity. 'You saw how well the Doctor behaved a couple of nights ago. And that isn't the first favour I owe him either, he's done me a number of favours over the years; and although he couldn't save the child, he did everything in his power to do so. He did save Beatriz, and it isn't right that I should repay him with suspicions and machinations, by asking someone to spy on him. It doesn't matter if what I was told is true. Even if it were, other things are more important, namely, our friendship and what he has done for me and my family in the past. I would be an ingrate, an avenger, a fanatic, if I were to withdraw my friendship over something that doesn't even concern me, when he has done so many good things for the people who do concern me.' – 'Perhaps one of those good things is that he distracts you and occasionally rids you of Beatriz's presence,' I thought suddenly, 'and you know all about it, Muriel, and may even have encouraged it'; in my thoughts I addressed him as *tú*, for the mind tends to be less formal than the tongue. – 'What happened the night before last has forced me to remember and reflect. So just leave it be, forget all about it, ignore my orders, there's no need for you to take him to any more nightclubs, still less to draw him out and observe him, just drop the whole thing. If he did once do something vile, that's a matter for those he harmed, it's not up to me to investigate or make some decision. It's not even my business. I allowed myself to be carried away by a mere rumour.' I had wanted to interrupt him several sentences ago, but realized this was not yet the right moment, that he had paused only in order to continue or to finish what he had to say. He again fixed his eye on the Casanova painting (on that possibly one-eyed horseman listening to his possible victims outside the painting, where the viewer was standing, all of them pleading: 'Remember us'), although determining its exact trajectory belonged in the realm of divination. And he added: 'In fact, anything you're told, anything you didn't personally witness, is pure rumour, however wrapped up in oaths it comes, all swearing the story to be true. And we can't spend our lives listening to rumours, still less acting in accordance with their many fluctuations. When you give that up, when you give up trying to know what you cannot know, perhaps, to paraphrase Shakespeare, perhaps that is when bad begins, but, on the other hand, worse remains behind.'

It seemed to me now that he was about to fall silent and that I could finally ask him the question that was plaguing me. However, the mention of Shakespeare brought to mind one of the lines Rico had recited so theatrically, one arm outstretched: 'Upon my tongues continual slanders ride, the which in every language I pronounce, stuffing the ears of men with false reports . . .' Perhaps Muriel really had been listening to what the Professor was saying and had started there and then to ponder the injustice of believing what he had been told about the Doctor. If so, it hadn't been enough to put a brake on his suspicions and his unease, for he had nevertheless decided to investigate or, rather, sound out the situation.

'You said, "Although he couldn't save the child"? What child? I don't know what you're talking about, Eduardo.' That was the question that had been burning inside me ever since I heard Muriel's passing comment, made as if he assumed I would know all about whatever it was. Then suddenly I twigged, almost at the same time as he – with a look of genuine surprise, not to say astonishment – pointed at the photo, on full view, of the young Beatriz holding a child of about two in her arms and looking not at him, but to her right: the boy in the little fur coat and the white balaclava with a large pompom on top, the boy with the delicate features who was also looking intently away, but to his left. There was the photo framed and on display and about which I had never asked. I'd asked very little in fact (despite my tendency to spy, I was basically a reasonably discreet young man), ever since Muriel had abruptly brushed aside my inquiry about the origin and reason for his eyepatch.

'Who do you think? Javier, of course, our firstborn, the one who died. There he is. I thought you knew, indeed, how could you possibly not know? How long have you been working here now?'

'I don't know if I realized or not, Eduardo, but you hardly ever tell me anything. You told me off when I asked about your missing eye. And since you were determined not to tell me your suspicions about the Doctor, I'm completely in the dark about that too. I also have no idea what your wife did to cause you to be so unpleasant to her, because, you know, you don't always hide your feelings in my presence. I'm not asking that question now, certainly not, it's none of my business, but I don't see why it should surprise you that I don't know about everything else. No one has ever told me anything, and I only ask what is strictly necessary. Because of that, I still don't even know why Beatriz tried to kill herself, and I was, after all, the one who saw her go into the hotel. I'm also aware that there might be no easy answer to that.'

Muriel sat up a little and looked at me more directly, although he was still not on my level, propping himself up on his elbows.

'You're right, Juan. Sometimes I take it for granted that all the friends who come here know the basic facts of my life, those that are verifiable and public knowledge, I mean, that you've all been witness to them or that you discuss me among yourselves. Not, of course, that there's any reason why you should talk about me, even though I am the common link. I'm sure the others know about the death of our child, some of them were there at the time, that is, they attended the funeral and tried to console us in the days that followed. I forget that you're a recent addition and much younger too.'

'What happened?'

Muriel tucked his thumb under his armpit as he did sometimes, as if it were a tiny riding crop or a ridiculous little crutch, as if in search of a symbolic support on which to rest his whole body. Perhaps he did this whenever he was in low spirits, a state of mind that afflicts stomach and limbs and torso and head.

'Well, I don't much like to talk about it.' And he said this somewhat haltingly, as if he were about to lose his voice or had a sudden need to clear his throat, a need that had not been there a second before. 'We don't really know. Jorge wasn't sure, and there was no question of performing an autopsy on that poor little body. What would have been the point? He had died and, given the magnitude of that fact, it didn't really matter why. And it wasn't like it is now, when

307

people are always looking for someone to blame, to see if they can squeeze some money out of their misfortunes. He fell ill one afternoon with a high fever. We didn't think it was anything serious, a sore throat perhaps, children often run a temperature, but we called the Doctor anyway and he came rushing over, as he always did, always so ready to help. As I said, he did everything he could, none of us left Javier's side for a moment and we saw how, that same night, he suddenly got worse. No, not suddenly. It was gradual, but somehow horribly fast. The truth is that at no point did it occur to us to fear for his life, and then he died and there was nothing we could do about it. As you can imagine, it was utterly incomprehensible. Beyond our understanding, I mean. I don't think Beatriz has ever really taken it in. I'm not sure I have either.'

'But did no one have even the vaguest idea of what caused his death?'

'Jorge mentioned the possibility that it was meningococcal meningitis, which destroys the adrenal glands. It's very rare apparently and, at the time, there was no treatment for it. It was impossible to diagnose quickly enough and impossible to treat. He assured us that no one could have saved him. Nothing and no one. I don't know. We didn't really try to find out and, in all these years, we never have. Why go delving any deeper, it would only have upset us even more. It happened, and now it can't be undone.' He had referred to the Doctor as 'Jorge' and called me 'Juan', as he had on the night of the suicide attempt; any truly serious matter restores our real names to us, it cannot tolerate affectionate or ironic nicknames. He again pointed at the photograph. 'Beatriz insists on having him there on show, as if she were afraid we might forget. Or so that his brother and sisters are aware of his existence, even though they never knew him. Or perhaps she likes to see him whenever she passes by. It's the most recent one we have of him, at Susana's christening, Susana being almost two years his junior. As you can see, he was absolutely fine. He was until that final afternoon, and there was no warning of any kind.' He stayed liked that for a few seconds, leaning on one elbow, thinking or remembering, his finger still pointing. 'Fortunately, I was here in Madrid. If I'd been away, I would never have believed it. But I was, and I saw what happened.' Yes, he had been there, it wasn't something someone had told him about, it wasn't just a rumour, that's what I understood him to mean. I repeated to myself the words he had said a little earlier. 'Perhaps that is when bad begins, but, on the other hand, worse remains behind.'

'Beatriz was there too,' I said after a few seconds had passed, and once he was no longer pointing at the photo and had lowered his arm and was lying down again; before he did, though, he took the compass out of the back pocket of his trousers and began slowly rubbing it against his cheek (the little box, I mean), as if smoothing a non-existent but always incipient beard, which, one day, he would allow to grow. 'And for women, for mothers, it tends to be an even greater tragedy. It's much harder for them to recover, if they ever do. The child developed inside their womb and so they've known it for months before it's even born, isn't that right?' I uttered these banalities because I didn't really know what to say.

'Yes, unless the mothers are completely stoical,' he said. 'Because such mothers do exist, you know, no legend is without its exceptions. But, yes, Javier's death made her more fragile in a way, left her still more unbalanced. Although not more fragile or more fearful as regards the other children, not at all, rather the reverse: the worst that could happen had already happened and wouldn't happen again. It almost had the effect of an inoculation, she was much more relaxed about the other children than she'd ever been about Javier. Perhaps because he was the first, perhaps because he was a boy and because we men are said to run more risks, and so she feared for him far more than for any other child. I sometimes wonder if it wasn't those bad presentiments of hers that brought it all about. Panic attracts misfortune and catastrophe. We do sometimes bring about what we most fear because the only way of freeing ourselves from that fear is for the bad thing actually to have happened, for it to be in the past and not in the future or in the realm of possibilities.' – 'For it to remain behind,' I said to myself, those words from Shakespeare had made me think. – 'However terrible and appalling the past may be, it always seems more innocuous than the future, or at least we're better able to deal with it. I don't know, maybe it was that or the realization of how defenceless we are, that there's no point in taking precautions or protecting ourselves or anyone else, and that it's therefore absurd to make yourself suffer beforehand; that, regardless of what preventative measures you take, the worst can still happen. It happens and it's too late. It happens and that's that. As you've seen, she takes her children pretty much for granted now, to the point of suddenly leaving them orphaned.'

'Yes,' I said, 'but I don't believe Beatriz's fears could have made her son catch what you say is a very rare illness.'

He didn't even bother responding, his comment had clearly been literary, not literal, a superstitious explanation for the inexplicable, which is what literature does really, most of the time, more or less. He changed tack:

'Anyway, now I've told you. Let's see: what other complaints do you have, my poor "no-one-has-ever-told-me-anything" ' – and he imitated my voice – 'what else would you like to know? Ah, yes, about my eye. Well, there's no great mystery, it's just that I prefer not to talk about or remember it – it makes me sad and makes me seem older too. It was when I was a child, at the beginning of the Civil War. My brother and I were playing on the roof terrace of my parents' house. A bullet fired by a *paco* ricocheted off a wall and hit me.

I lost an eye, which, at the time, was a real drama. Anyway, I've been like this since 1936, and that's what makes me seem older than I am, I mean, fancy having a war wound at my young age. But, then, saying that I lost an eye during the War does make it sound as if I was old enough to fight, doesn't it? Anything else?'

I couldn't help myself and so I missed the opportunity. Few of us can resist the need for an immediate explanation of something someone says to us.

'What's a *paco*?' I asked, instead of seizing the moment and asking to know more about the Doctor or about Beatriz. Had I been more patient, I could have looked it up in a dictionary later on. According to him, the word was first used to describe the Moroccan snipers during the war in Africa and the word then spread, although it obviously didn't last very long.

'That's what they called the snipers, there were quite a lot during the first weeks and months of the Civil War and they caused a lot of injuries in Madrid, and I'm not saying that just because of my own experience. The word comes from the sound made when they fired, which happened in two stages, the second was either the impact or the echo, I'm not sure: *pa-co* or, rather, *pa-có*. There was even a verb *paquear*. But, of course, there's no reason why you should know that.'

'What I don't understand is what you and your brother were doing up on the roof if there were snipers about.'

Muriel looked up, and his non-*paco*ed eye regarded me scornfully:

'Why? Because good little boys never disobey their parents? What kind of a boy were you? We were actually playing at being *pacos*, with a couple of sticks for rifles. Children always play at being the most dangerous thing they see or hear about. I've often wondered if the man who hit me didn't realize we were children and mistook us for *pacos* like him and shot to kill. Or perhaps he did realize and fired anyway. People could be real swines then, so who knows? *I'll* certainly never know. But we've rather strayed off the subject, young De Vere. Let the Doctor go. Abandon your investigations and leave him in peace.' He was using our nicknames again, the time for seriousness having passed.

I wasn't best pleased to receive this counter-order. Having obeyed the original order with great reluctance, I was now the one who felt curious; it's always upsetting not to be able to bring to a successful conclusion some project requiring patience and skill. I suppose that's why some hitmen warn their clients that there can be no going back. Even though they'll get paid anyway, they don't want to feel they've wasted valuable time studying the victim's habits and itineraries, seeing how the land lies and painstakingly preparing the ground. It's annoying to have all your efforts come to nothing.

'I can't just drop him like that, Eduardo,' I said. 'He loves coming out and about with me, discovering the new nightlife and meeting young people. As I said before, never in his wildest dreams could he have imagined having access to the girls he's met thanks to me. Do you really expect me to suddenly stop taking him out, just like that, to tell him he's no longer welcome? He'd protest, he'd insist, he'd make an almighty scene.'

'You don't have to be abrupt about it, you can always make excuses,' said Muriel. 'Space things out. Tell him you're really busy helping me, that the filming has got bogged down what with this Beatriz business, and we're not at all sure what's going to happen. Unfortunately, that's true. I don't know how much longer Towers will allow me to be absent, he's practically climbing the walls as it is, and each day that passes is money down the drain. The director on the second unit is going ahead with some action shots in the mountains, but, as you know, there aren't that many of those; actors hate sitting around doing nothing, they get bored, so something's got to give. Or tell him you've got a steady girlfriend now and that you see each other every night, which means you can't go hanging around in clubs any more. You could also, for the moment, tell him another truth: tomorrow, or the day after, Beatriz will be coming home and I'm not going to be around very much if I start filming again. I need to go straight to Barcelona, for the scenes in Parque Güell and in a few other locations. I can't really count on the girls, and Flavia being Flavia, well, she does what she can. Oh, and best to ration any visits from Marcela and Gloria, and ideally, in the circumstances, keep them away altogether – you can imagine the poison and the hysteria they'll spread. I want you to move in, at least for the first week when I'm away, to watch her, to sleep with one eye open. It's not that I'm afraid she'll try it again soon, she usually allows some years to pass between attempts, but you never know. Keep her company, talk to her, amuse her, take her out. Don't let her get depressed, or as little as possible. I'm not sure if the Professor's going to be around at all, but he certainly won't be sleeping here. And as for Roy, well, youth makes for better company than middle age. Tell the Doctor you're looking after Beatriz, he'll accept that. He'll be sure to visit, though, but I beg you, please, not to ask him about the past, don't probe him at all.' Despite that 'please', the tone remained imperative. 'That's the last thing he deserves, after what happened a couple of days ago. Don't even, as I suggested, boast to him about your own lack of scruples; don't tempt him further. If he did show a lack of scruples on one occasion or on various, I wasn't there, and I don't want to know about it. I'm sorry, but when I asked you to do that, I allowed myself to be carried away, to be influenced by others. We should only be concerned with what we have seen with our own eyes, with what directly affects us. We can't go around handing out punishments, even if the punishment consists only in behaving coldly or withdrawing our friendship from someone who may once have done something bad. It would be never-ending, we'd never have time for anything else.' He paused for a moment, then concluded: 'We need to remember that we have all done something bad at some point. Even you, and if you haven't, you've got all the time in the world, far too many years, in fact; that's the downside of being young. So one day you, too, will do something bad.'

Again I was burning to ask a question and again I waited until Muriel had finished or reached the end of a paragraph, so to speak, just as we do with a silent book that couldn't possibly take offence, before we stop reading and go out or go to bed.

'Did you say "attempts"? How many have there been, then?'

Muriel raised his little finger, his ring finger and his middle finger.

'This was the third.'

'And always the same method?'

'No, each time has been slightly different, what happened before doesn't serve to warn or to raise one's suspicions. But the fact that I've told you a little doesn't give you the right to know everything, so don't ask what she did, I don't like talking about that either. Let's leave it there. I think you've found out quite enough for today.'

Muriel was making an effort now to put on his usual prickly self, but he had either softened or was tired, perhaps the shock of what had happened two nights before had temporarily tamed him, dulled his sharpness and his vigour. I sensed that I could push my luck a little further.

'At least tell me who came to you with that story about the Doctor. What if, one day, he tells me of some vile deed he did, without my

315

trying to wheedle it out of him? How will I know if that was the one we were after?' I deliberately used the first-person plural, in order to remind him of his disquiet and anger, now extinguished or banished or kept at bay by gratitude. 'That's how you described it, wasn't it, a vile deed? That he had behaved indecently with a woman. I assume the person who told you was the victim of that deed, a woman.'

Muriel got up from the floor and sat down at his desk, and I moved my chair so that I was facing him. He rested his cheek on one hand, rather than the other way round. As if his face had grown very heavy or as if he'd felt dizzy when he stood up, for he had done so far too suddenly, with no intermediate stage. However much you might want to limit or mete out what you say, it isn't easy to apply the brakes once you've started, you always end up saying more than you intended, more than you wanted to. He spoke without looking at me, his head bent, his eye fixed on the correspondence on the desk, and which I had left for him to read when he felt like it or had time – none of it was urgent; if he was reading one of the letters now, he was doing so purely involuntarily, without taking in what was written or without caring.

'Yes, a woman first, and then a few others,' he said, perhaps not even quite aware that he was answering my question, that there was someone there listening and making a mental note. 'A woman who deserves my complete confidence. A former friend, a former actress, although she wasn't an actress when I met her, that came later –' He paused, broke off, but sometimes the tongue gets swept along by its own wretched velocity. 'A former love.' He paused again, but this time succumbed even more easily to his tongue's speed. 'The love of my life, as people say. Or so I believed for a long time and, during that time, I always felt indebted to her. Which is why, now, when she reappeared, I felt obliged to take what she said seriously, not to doubt her word, but to believe her version of events. Holding back slightly, of course, trying to temper the shock she felt on learning of my friendship. What possible interest could she have in lying to me about the Doctor? To deprive me of an old friend? That wouldn't have been much of a revenge, if she'd wanted to have her revenge for something that happened a long, long time ago and to which she gave her consent or that she at least understood, or so she said. "Do what you think you ought to do," she said. "Do what will cause you least pain, what you'll find easiest to live with. But never think of us, of you and me. Never think of us together if you don't want to be filled with regret day after day and, still more, night after night. Never even think of us apart either, because, by remembering that, you'll bring us together again," that's what she said, what she advised. And I took her advice, while I could. The other debt, the debt owed to Beatriz, would have weighed on me far more. At the time, I did all I could to do my duty: another of youth's downsides, quite a few of which one leaves behind as one grows older. The trouble is that once you've taken those steps, there's no going back when you finally discover what a fool you've been. The film has been shot and edited, the actors have dispersed along with the rest of the team, there's no way of adding scenes or changing the plot or the ending: it is what it is and will be for ever. Far too many lives are shaped by deceit or error, it's probably always been like that, so why should I be any different, why shouldn't my life be the same? That thought gives me some consolation, convinces me that I'm not the only one – on the contrary, I'm just one more on an endless list of those who tried to act correctly, to keep their promises, those who prided themselves on being able to say something that sounds more and more like a piece of antiquated foolishness: "My word on it", when almost no one honours their word any more, or considers it a virtue to do so . . .' He fell silent, looked up from his papers and, seeing me, fixed his sharp eye on me. He had strayed from my question, had started remembering out loud. Not that he wasn't aware of my presence or had forgotten I was there or had been pretending I wasn't. It was more that he had momentarily lapsed into a soliloquy and didn't care who was listening, like a character in a play when he's on stage talking to himself, knowing that there's no point in doing this unless the rest of us are listening. Now he did care and perhaps regretted what he'd said. He managed to use a prolonged silence to rein in that wretched, racing tongue of his. He looked at his watch. He tapped its face. And finally added: 'I have to go to the hospital to relieve Susana. She spent all last night there. But let's settle this once and for all, Juan: I find it highly unlikely that the Doctor would tell you of any vile deed he committed, unless you were to ignore my orders and continue to try to draw him out for your own satisfaction. I can't stop you doing that. But if it happened, I don't want you to tell me about it, to test my curiosity. Keep it to yourself, say nothing. It was hard for me to decide not to know, but after what happened two nights ago, that decision is now unshakable. Don't tell anyone else either. A lot of vile deeds were committed here over many years, but we've managed to live with those who committed them, and some even did us favours too. We will have to live with them until we all die, and then everything will begin to even out and no one will bother trying to track down the perpetrators. It will be about as relevant to us as the Napoleonic era, which none of us experienced personally. It will be as if it had never happened or will sound to us like fiction. I'm only including myself in that "we" rhetorically, because I, too, will have to die. It's still early days, I know and, as I say, many vile deeds were committed over many years, but in what age and in what country has that not been the case?'

318

VII

It would be an exaggeration to describe what happened shortly afterwards as a vile deed. Of course, this all depends on one's point of
view, and, needless to say, the point of view of the person listening to
or reading the story – which is, after all, the viewpoint of someone
hearing a rumour, even if the teller of the tale swears he's speaking
from personal experience and that he either committed or participated in the act himself – never coincides with that of the person who
experienced or created it. When we hear or read something, it always
seems disappointing and trivial ('Big deal'), just another story ('So
what else is new?'), an occurrence similar to so many others, almost
predictable given that we've been inundated with stories ever since
the first person spoke the first word to us; there are far too many stories in the world, and we're rarely surprised or shocked by them or
even interested, it's as if everything had already happened in life or,
if not, in the imagination, disseminated by innumerable printed pages
and multiplying screens, the old screens of cinemas and televisions
and the new ones of computers and even those of the ridiculous
mobile phones that everyone now gazes into as if they were crystal
balls, which, in a way, they are: they may not predict the future, but
they do inform us about what didn't exist and hadn't even happened
only a second before, about the new-born coming into existence all
over the world, and sometimes they're in such a hurry that they tell

us things that haven't happened, a fallacy, a calumny, a false rumour that proves hard to deny or to shake off; our level of credulity has reverted to what it was in the Middle Ages, with rumour still stuffing our ears with false reports – from the orient to the drooping west – and we refuse to ask for proof, accepting everything as credible because everything has already happened, or so we believe.

We become more and more like that ancient sentinel of our existence, the moon, for whom what came later and of which I was co-creator could never be considered a vile deed, merely another banal, hackneyed episode, incapable of rousing it from the tedium in which it has been condemned to live, night after night, since before the world was peopled; perhaps, who knows, the first men and women at least provided it with some novelty and amusement, until, inevitably, they began to repeat themselves. As I said earlier, though, perhaps the moon takes less notice of the battles and travails of the monotonous masses, the strutting and the shouting, and focuses more on those beings who seem to tiptoe through life, to be just passing through or on temporary loan even while they're alive, those who will never go beyond their own bounds, those who one knows early on will leave no trace or track and will barely be remembered once they disappear (they will be like falling snow that does not settle, like a lizard climbing up a sunny wall in summer that pauses for a moment beneath the indolent eye that will not even notice it, like the words, all those years ago, that a teacher painstakingly wrote on the blackboard only to erase them herself at the end of the class, or leave them to be erased by the next teacher to occupy the room) and about whom not even their nearest and dearest will have any anecdotes to recount, for the moon knows that some of them might well harbour stories that are far odder and more intriguing, clearer and more personal than the stories of the shrill exhibitionists who fill most of the globe with their racket and exhaust it with their wild gesticulations.

But although we may more and more come to resemble that moon in our indifference and saturation, we who are still alive and active tend to endow our lives and acts with some special significance, even though, when measured against the accumulation of events, they have none and, in any case, they lose all significance – alas, even for us – as soon as we decide to talk about them to others, and they join the over-flowing ranks of stories already told. 'Ah,' thinks the person hearing or reading or watching, 'that story reminds me of another story, and now that I know it, seems almost predictable; it didn't happen to me, and so it doesn't surprise me and I only half-listen to it; what happens to others seems always so diffuse and rather unimportant and perhaps not even worth talking about.' And the person telling the story feels something similar when he passes it on, as if putting it into words or images and in order were tantamount to cheapening and trivializing it, as if only the unrevealed or the unspoken preserved its prestige and uniqueness and mystery. 'What to me was a grave and important fact – perhaps some vile deed I committed – becomes instead merely another story, nebulous and interchangeable, an original tale intended to amuse.' Having told it, whether orally or in writing or in images, it doesn't matter, you think: 'What was remarkable for me as long as it remained secret and unknown becomes commonplace once revealed and tossed into the bag along with all the other stories heard and mixed up and forgotten and that can be reported and mangled by any-one passing, by whoever hears them, because once told, they're present in the air and there's no way you can stop them floating or flying if they get caught up in the mist or the wind pushes them along, and they travel through space and time disfigured by all the many echoes, worn thin by repetition.'

323

Beatriz returned home, and Muriel set off to Barcelona with Towers, who was still alarmed, suspicious and fearful for his project – with Lom and the other actors, troubled by what had happened to their director, but more than anything bewildered, wondering if he would be in a fit state to continue filming when his suicidal wife was some six hundred kilometres away, for they knew nothing about his normal treatment of her, about the constant rebuffs and occasional insults. 'Lard, pure lard, that's all you are to me,' 'I don't think I can stand her any longer, I've got to close the door on her, I must,' and the door had been kept firmly shut for a long time, after he had made the mistake of loving her all those years, with all his heart, as long, that is, as he had known nothing, and despite her not being the love of his life, 'as people say'; or, according to her, having done the right thing: 'You've probably never done anything better.' To which he had responded oddly, gently, regretfully: 'I'll grant you that.' He had, of course, added: 'All the more reason for me to feel I've thrown away my life. A part of my life. That's why I can't forgive you.' But perhaps that old love during all those years partially explained Muriel's terrified reaction when he thought Beatriz might have been successful in her third attempt, carried out, deliberately one assumes, so close to home in the Hotel Wellington and on a night when they had invited guests to supper. It's also frightening to lose the witness to the good things one has done, even if you've long since ceased to do good and have instead done things, which, to that same witness, have seemed evil and harmful.

Or perhaps they had been brought much closer when their first-born died, because such events have one of two results: either one partner irrationally blames the other for not sensing the danger and failing to protect and save the child, with husband and wife becoming increasingly isolated, cut off, to the point where they can hardly bear to speak to or look at one another, or else they stand by each other and serve as both mirror and support: seeing their partner's grief, the wife, say, takes pity on her husband and often takes his hand or suddenly caresses or embraces him when they pass in the gloomy corridor along which small, quick steps no longer run, children only being capable of moving from one place to another hurriedly, precipitately, because the child they were left with, Susana, could not yet walk. If she was fifteen or more now, that was how long it had been since the disappearance of the brother with whom she had coincided only briefly in the world and whom she never knew.

I had always felt sympathetic towards Beatriz Noguera, had always liked her; when I found out about the death of her child, I inevitably felt even more sympathy as well as something approaching respect; it's impossible not to feel both things for someone who has suffered the loss of a child, who, however small, was already walking and babbling and asking a few elementary questions because he understood so little of the world around him. We also view with more interest someone who we know has had to overcome terrible grief and who never talks about it, mentions it or uses it to gain our pity. And so when Beatriz came home, looking thinner, but otherwise very well, with barely any visible signs that she had attempted to end her own life, she found me even more disposed to help and watch over her, to distract her and keep her company, as Muriel had instructed. He had, in effect, given me a reason to get closer to her, to talk to her, which I had always held back from doing before, out of a mixture of distance and shyness, fearing she might notice my theoretical feelings of embarrassment, of vague sexual admiration, something like the illusory desire aroused by a painting that I described earlier, but nothing more than that.

Rather than being released from hospital, it was as though she had returned from a sleep cure, her skin smooth and firm, her eyes bright, albeit quiet and slightly dreamy, even walking more lightly, more delicately, less determinedly, and nearly always wearing her high heels as if wanting to appear as attractive as possible for as long as possible or as if she were about to set off to one of her rendez-vous, except that, during that time, she didn't go out at all, apart from with Rico, who claimed he had stayed in Madrid in order to help, but was probably there in order to carry out some worldly manoeuvrings of vital importance to him alone, and who would turn up at the apartment to persuade her to go shopping or to a lecture or to a late-afternoon screening, even making impertinent jokes about her recent desperate action and about which she may have preferred not to talk.

'When are you going to show me those cuts of yours, Beatriz? Don't let them heal up without giving me a look at them while they're still red raw,' he would say tactlessly, being of the school that believes there is no better therapy than shock therapy, no better cure than making a mockery or a parody of any deep mental wound; and he would point at the bandages she had on her wrists, the only obvious sign of her recent hotel mishap or adventure. 'I want to know how you did it, whether vertically or horizontally, methodically or just any old how, in the form of an X or a cross, with minimal artistic intent or like a barber suffering from Parkinson's; in your place, I think I might have idled away the time playing noughts and crosses with the razor. *Urfe, tirsto, érbadasʒ.*' He had days when he was more than usually given to uttering his unintelligible semi-onomatopoeia and would sometimes come out with three on the trot. Fortunately, he wasn't living in the Middle Ages that he so worshipped or in his beloved Renaissance, because people then would have taken these for some diabolical language or oaths addressed to Beelzebub, and the Professor would have ended up being burned; I couldn't resist imagining him tied to the stake, with his glasses on and (naturally) a cigarette between his lips, proudly declaiming exquisite speeches before being devoured by the flames.

Beatriz didn't seem to mind, she may even have been grateful for his frank, frivolous humour. She laughed enough to make one think that the Professor was perhaps right to treat the whole episode with such healthy disrespect, and she promised him she would show him her wounds one day, before they had completely blended in with her natural skin colour.

'But that will take a long time, Professor. Besides, I'll always have the scars, so your curiosity is sure to be satisfied sooner or later.'

'Don't lie to me, Beatriz. These days, plastic surgery can erase anything. I know what you women are like. If you don't resort to surgery, then you'll cover your wrists with bracelets as big as hitching rings and there'll be nothing to see. Don't underestimate your future embarrassment, because it will come.'

'I'm not lying to you, Professor. The next time they change my bandages, I'll give you a call. Just don't expect any artistry,' said Beatriz, more seriously this time, as if she had just succumbed to an early attack of that predicted embarrassment or were reliving the moment when one liquid invaded another, the first drops of blood clouding the water, the signal for her to begin dying, to pine palely away. In fact, her voice faltered slightly when she spoke her next words. Rico was busy meticulously refilling his cigarette case, but even he noticed, looked up and listened with understanding and sorrow, a sorrow I shared. I felt a youthful desire to get up and embrace Beatriz and whisper softly: 'There, there, it's all right.' I did not, however, give in to that inappropriate impulse. 'It's hard enough to get up the courage to cut yourself, and I preferred not to look. The foam from the bubble bath helped though.'

Something similar to an embrace happened shortly afterwards.

Dr Van Vechten used to drop by later in the morning to see how the wounds were healing and to change the bandages. He didn't linger, it was more of a professional visit than a social one, and in my presence there was never any indication that what I knew to have happened between them ever did actually happen and perhaps it no longer did (in other people's relationships, you never know when something begins or ends), they were both well practised at pretending; or perhaps, if they shared no strong feelings, no grand passions, they didn't need to pretend. One day, I accompanied him to the front door ('You stay where you are, Beatriz, I'll see the Doctor out'), and on the landing, with the front door closed so that we couldn't be heard, I seized the opportunity and asked:

'Why doesn't she go to a psychiatrist or a psychologist?' And I gestured with my head towards the apartment. 'I thought that was obligatory after any suicide attempt. Or at least advisable.'

He arched his eyebrows and took a deep breath in, his nostrils dilated. Then, breathing out again like someone summoning up all his patience, he said:

'She has in the past. This time, we managed to keep her name out of the records at the clinic, so the psychiatric staff haven't intervened, and it's better like that. I don't think she wants to go through all that again, having to repeat herself and listen to long silences and the occasional platitude. I'm afraid it would be of no benefit, no help to her. In her case, there's really very little to know or find out. She's not a happy woman, as I'm sure you're aware by now, given how many hours you spend here. Sometimes she copes and sometimes she doesn't. Let's just hope many more years pass before she stops coping again.' This must have struck him as too simplistic, because he immediately added: 'Or, if you prefer, most of the time she lacks the necessary determination and only very occasionally doesn't. We can only hope those few occasions take a long time to recur.' He had basically said the same thing twice, but perhaps thought this second explanation more complex.

I presumed he didn't know about Beatriz's nocturnal incursions. The fact that she made these meant that she occasionally still had hopes, however vain, of changing Muriel's mind, and so it wasn't just that she lacked the determination to put an end to her life.

'Eduardo hinted that there had been other attempts.' Out of a kind of discretion, I didn't want to admit that he had told me this openly and graphically.

'Yes, and unless she accepts her situation or grows tired of trying or unless fear gets the better of her, then the normal thing would be for her to try again, sooner or later, and on one of those occasions, we won't arrive in time.'

'But knowing that, what can we do?'

'Not much. Nothing really. If someone wants to kill herself, there's no way you can stop her. It's the same when someone decides to murder another person and isn't concerned about eluding punishment or saving his own skin. If he really wants to do it, then he will, an opportunity will always present itself, even with the most protected and most alert of victims. How else explain the assassination of

330

prominent figures? There's no escape: if someone gets it into his head to kill you, he'll do it regardless of what precautions you take. Doubt and a lack of resolve are the only reasons a murderer or a suicide, however inept or clumsy, will fail. With Beatriz, we were lucky, that's all. Until the next time. If she keeps trying, then one day she'll succeed.'

'Do you think she lost her resolve on this last occasion?'

'Maybe, maybe not. The cuts weren't very deep, but that doesn't mean much. It isn't easy to cut your own flesh with a razor, the hand instinctively withdraws, stiffens, shrinks back. It's nothing to do with willpower. The head may want to kill itself, but the hand resists inflicting harm. The truth is that if you hadn't seen her going into the hotel, it would have taken a while, but even with those few cuts, she would have ended up bleeding to death. It was just luck. I'm sure she didn't count on you seeing her go into the hotel and reporting back.'

'But I saw her hours before supper. She would have had plenty of time to die if she'd been more diligent.' I came out with that cold adjective, infected by Van Vechten's use of language. I added: 'If you know what I mean.'

The Doctor pulled a bored face, as if he were weary of telling me what to him was obvious, with his far greater experience of such matters.

'These things take time when they're premeditated, when they're not a response to an impulse or a moment of blind emotion; and it's perfectly normal that the person should keep putting it off, you know, just a little longer. Or perhaps she was afraid that if she got into the water too soon, she might get stomach cramps or something. It may seem ridiculous, but that's how it is. Someone prepared to kill herself may, on the other hand, worry about suffering stomach cramps. I've known individuals decide not to jump from a window when they

331

noticed how cold it was outside or how hard it was raining. They were more bothered about getting cold or wet as they fell than about hitting the ground. Who knows what might turn someone off at that point, what they might tell themselves or what might go through their mind.' He did not include himself, even hypothetically, as most of us would; he could never imagine himself in such a situation. 'Anyway, I have things to do.'

Yes, I had bored him with my questions. He didn't seem deeply affected by Beatriz's suicide attempt. It was more as if he'd decided that it was none of his business and that, if she tried again, we had no option but to let her, to wait and see. He had raced down Calle Velázquez and, at the hotel, had worked furiously, done everything he could; he had probably saved her life, which was why Muriel was so grateful to him. He was a responsible doctor, who would do his duty whenever anyone was in danger or sick. However, it was not up to him to take precautions or to stop someone doing what they wanted to do. Or else he simply knew it was pointless, or so he said. And yet I found his resignation, no, his bland acceptance, chilling. It seemed to me that no one was utterly devoted to Beatriz, that she wasn't vital to anyone's existence and was doubtless one of the many people about whom no one thinks passionately: 'She doesn't deserve to die. Ever.'

As I said, Rico would come by in the afternoons – on those first afternoons when we were all treading very carefully – and would take her out or chat to her, cheer her up and make her laugh with his calculatedly condescending or fatuous remarks, and Roy came too to keep her company or simply to be there, more timidly and less enjoyably perhaps, but nonetheless eager to help. Flavia kept silent watch from her domain, and Beatriz's daughters, who tried to be around more than usual and not shut themselves away in their rooms as much, seemed slightly saddened or anxious about their mother – especially the older girl – although not exaggeratedly so, more as if they already knew about those occasional suicide attempts or about the appalling risks she took, and had assimilated them, insofar as such things can be assimilated. The boy knew nothing, he was still too young. Beatriz was left alone as little as possible, and Muriel phoned from Barcelona every day, once or twice, depending on how busy he was, as if he were a caring husband. (If he had really cared, he would have cancelled everything and not gone away at all; but given his usual rough treatment of her, it was enough that he should take an apparently sincere interest from a distance. It was as though, this time, he felt that Beatriz had come perilously close to dying. Even though this wasn't a new experience, it must have frightened him each time it happened. He doubtless preferred her as a muted, almost obscure presence in his life, but he certainly didn't want her to disappear entirely; indeed, he would probably have found that unbearable.) If I picked up the phone, he would ask: 'How is she?' and I would say: 'She seems quite normal, her usual self.' Then I would pass the phone to her, and they would talk for a while, not long (it wasn't easy to find things to say), and I would leave them alone, but I did once hear Beatriz's side of the conversation: 'No, don't worry, I'm fine . . . Hmm . . . No, Jorge says the cuts are healing nicely . . . Yes, there'll be scarring, but what does that matter now . . . I'll worry about that later . . . No, I don't feel weak at all. It's as if I'd never lost a drop of blood . . . Everyone says how well I look and I don't think they're just saying that either, because even I think I look pretty healthy, and I've never been one for admiring myself in the mirror, on the contrary . . . Thank you.' At that point, I wondered if Muriel had actually paid her a compliment, but rejected the idea as unlikely, I'd heard him make too many cruel insults about her physical appearance, but who knows, perhaps he had offered her a kind or encouraging compliment. 'Yes, they're being very good and attentive, they think I don't notice, but they're so transparent . . . It amuses me to see them trying to pretend that they're not . . . No, really, you get on with things there, work comes first . . . Has Towers calmed down now? . . . Anyway, I'm sorry to have caused you so much upset, you don't think at the time, you only think later, and I'm thinking more clearly now . . . Right, and the trouble is, he's lost confidence in you . . . Jesús? No, certainly not; he's too busy, no, *you* have to finish the film . . .' I guessed that Muriel was having trouble focusing on the job in hand and had got badly behind, that Towers was getting impatient and even considering the possibility of replacing him with that whirlwind of activity, Jess Frank. 'Tell him it will be all right, convince him . . . Me? You mean he's worried about me? No, tell him from me there's no need to worry, that I have no intention of interrupting your filming ever again . . . Of course I won't, I haven't the slightest intention . . . Eduardo, what happens happens when it happens, but that doesn't mean it will go on happening. Like I say, what happened happened . . .' After they had exchanged a few more words, this time of farewell, I heard her replace the receiver and I then went back into the living room. Oddly, once she had hung up, she stood there for a while, her hand still on the phone, gazing at it with a kind of dreamy fixity, as if, in that visual, tactile way, she wanted to prolong her contact with Muriel or to hold on for a moment to some of the words she had heard, perhaps that possible compliment. Or as if she had lied about something and was waiting to be found out and for him to call back and voice his suspicions, before she could lay down the instrument of her deception. Like someone waiting for the gun she has just used to stop smoking and grow cold in her hand.

At night, though, no one came, and it was up to me to take the initiative, to be on hand if she needed me, to distract her or talk to her or sit down with her to watch a film or a series on T V, so that she would feel less keenly her customary nocturnal solitude; my orders now were to tread carefully, but the situation wouldn't last, only as long as it took her to convalesce, the few weeks it would take for us all to recover from the shock and regain our mutual trust, no state of alarm can be maintained indefinitely. I think I talked to Beatriz more during the ten days that Muriel was away filming in Barcelona than during the whole of the rest of the time I worked for him. We tended to avoid any very personal subjects, any thorny or delicate issues, but, as always, in situations of unexpected closeness, a false, provisional camaraderie soon sprang up, and a feeling of daily normality quickly took root; you only have to condemn two reasonably nice people to spending time in each other's company for it to come to seem perfectly normal, especially if, for some reason, those exceptional circumstances become permanent; it takes only a couple of days for routines to be established, to the extent of each person always sitting in the same place, in the same armchair if they play chess or cards, on the same side of the sofa if they're watching T V, and, if they sleep in the same bed for two consecutive nights, that's quite long enough for each to choose which side he or she will sleep on.

When she went to her room, I would stay up for another hour or so, not feeling tired enough to go to bed myself, and when I did finally go to my own room, I remained, not perhaps with one eye open, as Muriel had ordered, but with some corner of my consciousness watching, in perhaps the same way that the parents of young children have to remain constantly alert, not, of course, that Beatriz was as important to me as that. Nevertheless, I would hear her whenever she left her room, as she briefly did each night, if she went into the living room or the kitchen for a few minutes, doubtless the time it took to smoke one or two cigarettes, before returning to her side of the apartment and closing her bedroom door, then I would go back to sleep, feeling easier, as if she were safer in her room, although probably quite the opposite was true: if she had tried to kill herself again, she would have avoided doing so in any communal areas, where there was a danger that her children or Flavia might find her, where there was more likelihood that someone would stop her or frustrate her in her wish to die by once again arriving just in time.

One night, I heard her clattering around in the kitchen for longer than usual, while she waited for exhaustion or sleep to get the better of her, and this was so close to where I was sleeping that I found it impossible not to listen to and interpret her every movement. She opened and closed the fridge three or four times, lit cigarettes – the repeated sound of a faulty lighter; she poured herself a cold drink – liquid falling into a glass, the clink of ice cubes – a chair or stool scraping on the floor, she would sit down only to stand up a few seconds later, then sit down again, what I couldn't hear were her footsteps, and I imagined she must be barefoot or wearing the silent slippers that allowed her to pace back and forth outside her husband's bedroom door without him hearing her, until she decided to announce her presence by rapping on the door with one knuckle. She took no such pains now, perhaps she had forgotten that I was sleeping next door or perhaps she wasn't bothered about waking me, probably too absorbed in her own thoughts and able to think only of them – insomnia is very selfish. The persistent scraping of a stool or chair – probably only restlessness and nerves, the kitchen being furnished with both stools and chairs – made me imagine a possible danger. 'I hope she's not going to climb on to one,' I thought, 'then kick it away and hang herself; I hope that's not what she's preparing to do,' and I tried fruitlessly to remember if there was anything on the ceiling to which she could attach a rope or a strip of fabric. This idea had only to cross my mind for me to listen more acutely, to struggle to decipher every sound and to worry whenever there was a longer than usual pause or silence. In the middle of the night everything seems plausible and real.

I realized that as long as Beatriz stayed in the kitchen, I wouldn't be able to relax, and so I got out of bed. It was already hot in Madrid and I was wearing only a pair of boxer shorts, the kind I've worn since I was a young man, having always found so-called Y-fronts unpleasantly macho and even faintly distasteful. I couldn't and shouldn't appear dressed like that, I thought – although I would have been justified in doing so, since this was, in a way, my territory – and since I didn't have a dressing gown, I put on my jeans and a shirt, although without bothering to button the latter up or to tuck it in. I cautiously opened the door of my cubbyhole – I didn't want to startle her – which Flavia had smartened up a bit since the first time I stayed overnight, making it a little more welcoming, a little less bare; and I saw Beatriz with her back to me, sitting, just as I had thought, on one of the stools in the kitchen, which is where we used to have breakfast, individually and at an hour of our choosing, the only ones who ate together being the children and then only on school days, no one person acted as a kind of agglutinative hub, the family tending to disperse.

The lights were already on in the kitchen, and so the light from my door when I opened it didn't warn Beatriz of my presence, locked as she was inside her own head. She wasn't wearing a dressing gown either, even though Muriel was away and there was no one she could tempt with her rather short nightdress, when she was standing it came only to mid-thigh and was identical to the one I'd seen on that now distant night, except that it wasn't white or cream, but a very pale blue – perhaps she had bought two or three, thinking it was a flattering style. I assumed that the heat had made her leave her room so very lightly dressed, that and her self-absorbed state and her sense of being alone even in an apartment where five other people were sleeping, employees and children, but perhaps we counted for little in her insomnia. Seated as she was, I couldn't tell whether, as on that night of prowling and pleading, she was wearing any knickers, although obviously, and as is only natural, she wasn't wearing a bra, well, who would go to sleep in a piece of clothing that controls and constricts; I've never in my life met a woman who kept her bra on in bed. I was surprised that the first thing my eyes noticed or tried to discover was whether she had anything on underneath her silk night-dress; or, rather, it didn't surprise me, but I silently reproached myself for a second, after all, you can't control your own gaze, it lives a quite separate existence to our instructions and our vetos, or that's the excuse we use to allow it to disobey us. I realized, moreover – and this was immediate – that I didn't care that my gaze should have become so uninhibited, as if Muriel's absence had given me – however irresponsibly, however inappropriately – the freedom to look at anything I wanted, including his wife. That sudden visual

338

incontinence of mine didn't make much sense really, given how little he cared about Beatriz physically and how violently he rejected her. But we feel more in charge of a place when the owner isn't there, as if we had temporarily replaced or usurped him. That's why every servant who has ever lived immediately lounges on the sofas, rolls around on the beds, uncorks the wine bottles and dives into the swimming pool as soon as he sees his employer vanish, or at least he secretly fantasizes about doing such things without being noticed, especially since it would be his job to erase all trace of rebellion. And I was, after all, a kind of servant, albeit in disguised form. I was aware that my brazenness also had something to do with the fact that Beatriz had recently tried to commit suicide; we take strange liberties with someone who might have killed herself: 'Well,' we say to ourselves, 'she's escaped the worst, fate has smiled on her; this period of time is a gift, and she can't really complain; she tried to make whatever happens from now on not happen, decided not even to expect it to happen, never to experience it.' And what I thought there in the kitchen, or what flashed through my mind, although certainly not in such a clearly formulated way, was this: 'If it weren't for me, that body would be rotting in a grave, beneath the earth, or reduced to a mere heap of unrecognizable ash, never to be looked at by anyone again; in a way her survival, or part of it – a few minutes or a few hours – belongs to me and I've earned the right to enjoy looking at her as much as I want.' Some cultures believe that if you save someone's life, you become responsible for whatever happens to them afterwards, for ensuring that the extra time you've granted them is neither tragic nor a torment; other cultures believe that you become not that person's owner exactly, but something like a usufructuary, and the saved person places herself at the disposal of her saviour, entrusts or surrenders herself to him. All of a sudden, I had the

339

conceited thought that if Beatriz was glad to be still alive, then she was in my debt; if she regretted it, though, she would consider herself my creditor. She was holding a glass of whisky in one hand and, in the other, an unlit cigarette, and there were already two cigarette ends in the nearby ashtray. Her bandaged wrists contrasted with the bare arms revealed by her sleeveless nightdress, because her skin was quite dark, which is why it was so worrying when she did occasionally turn terribly pale.

'Can't you sleep?' I asked, after first clearing my throat, so as to warn her of my presence in two stages, one following on from the other.

She turned and gave a faint, wan smile. She didn't just turn her head, but her whole body, thus revealing much of her strong thighs, since she was sitting with her legs crossed. (Which is also why I didn't manage to see anything more than that.) Not as much thigh as the civil servant Celia had revealed in the taxi, but quite a lot. She indicated the glass of whisky, as if to excuse herself, for she was not a heavy drinker.

'Yes, I'm just seeing if this will do the trick,' she said. 'But I'm not very used to drinking whisky.' Then she added: 'I'm sorry I woke you up. I sometimes forget you're here at night too, now that you've been appointed my sentinel. Although you've stayed over on other nights too. You don't seem very happy at home.'

It had not escaped her notice that I spent more time than necessary in the apartment, but the remark was a neutral one, it didn't come across as a hint or a complaint about my too frequent presence. She also knew what my role there was in Muriel's absence, while he was six hundred kilometres away filming his bizarre scenes.

'No, I'm fine,' I said, 'but I do sometimes miss a little company, and there's plenty of that here. I hope I'm not making a nuisance of myself, not bothering you. Do tell me if I am.'

She shook her head as if to say: 'Of course not, don't be silly.' As if my concern were a bit of nonsense not even worth trying to dissipate with words.

'Now that I've woken you up, come and sit here with me for a while, until I get sleepy.' And she pulled over another stool and placed it next to hers. I sat down to her left and, from that angle, had a partial view of her décolletage, that is, a partial view of her right breast and, of course, her cleavage, I no longer felt ashamed that my eyes should give priority to such things, but I still only looked out of the corner of one eye, it's best not to be too impertinent initially, a certain degree of dissembling is required on all occasions, even when you know how things will end or why you have come, why two people have come together. Not that this was the case then, not at all. I had no idea (I was merely accumulating elemental desires, if such a thing is necessary when one is young), and at that point, nothing of the sort would have occurred to her either, she was merely fighting against her insomnia and perhaps thinking about nothing; and ignoring everything else and barely noticing the outside world is enough of an occupation in itself. She was forty-one or forty-two, and very few women then bothered to undergo absurd, counter-productive surgical operations, and what I could see of her décolletage was natural, it moved, rose and fell with every breath, was simultaneously firm and soft, still firm and abundant, tremulous and apparently soft, and yet Muriel found this repellent, or perhaps not; after all, on that other night, he had groped her breasts, although his intention then had been to humiliate and belittle. I would never have touched her like that, certainly not, not on that night or this night or any other. The

341

tips of my fingers were itching to touch her just then, no, they weren't, that's just a manner of speaking. She remained silent for a few seconds, busy lighting her cigarette, then she inhaled deeply and her breast rose visibly, that is, both breasts rose, but I had to make do with imagining her left breast under her nightdress; and then she referred for the first time to my intervention: 'So, you saved my life. You were the one who stole me from death.'

The verb 'stole' seemed a strange one to use (but, then, insomnia does have a strange effect on the mind and the vocabulary that passes through it) and it made me wonder if she intended her words as a reproach or as an expression of gratitude or neither; perhaps she was merely stating a fact. At least she hadn't said 'who snatched me from the jaws of death', which would have sounded both affected and accusatory.

'Well, only indirectly. It was pure chance that I happened to see you go into the hotel.' Chance had nothing to do with it, but no one knew that I had taken to following her on some afternoons, and had it not been for that habit of mine, she would have moved towards her end without witnesses. 'But I wasn't the one who realized what that meant, it would never have occurred to me. It was lucky, I suppose, at least for us. Whether it was lucky for you, I'm not sure. But I hope it was.'

'Yes, let's hope it was. I'll let you know,' she replied with a touch of irony. 'And who is "us", may I ask? Who do you include in that "us"?'

I don't know why I had used the third-person plural, probably so as not to single myself out or draw attention to myself and have to explain. At that moment, on that dark night, I felt lucky to have her there alive and present, even if only because the sexual admiration I felt for her was now neither vague nor damped down, but real and palpable and growing, my gaze had cast aside all thoughts of age,

343

position or hierarchy, leaving only a remnant of courtesy, which is to say, pretence. Desire is a selfish thing too and will do almost anything to achieve satisfaction – lie, flatter, take risks, inveigle, make false promises, all to ensure that the person stays long enough in this world for us to enjoy her. What follows is another matter; afterwards, everything returns to normal and it seems to us absurd to have risked so much of real value merely in order to achieve something that immediately seems empty and meaningless and is sometimes forgotten almost as soon as it's over.

'I don't know, everyone, I suppose,' I said. 'I don't think any of us would have felt indifferent to your death. For Susana, Alicia and Tomás it would have been disastrous. For Flavia too. For your friends, for Eduardo. For me, for Rico and Roy. For Van Vechten. For everyone. And I imagine for other people as well, people I don't know.' I thought of the man, whoever he was, who lived in Plaza del Marqués de Salamanca.

'Don't exaggerate, Juan. It might have saddened you, I don't say it wouldn't, but for you, it would hardly have been a disaster, you barely know me and, besides, you're very young. It wouldn't have been a disaster for Eduardo either.'

'You should have seen him run, should have seen his distress, when we came to find you.'

'Yes, Jorge told me that too. It must be all those films he's made.' She got up and went over to the fridge. She opened it, peered in, not knowing quite what she was looking for, took out a can of coke and poured half into her glass of whisky. I saw then that she was wearing knickers, I could see them through her silk nightdress when she had her back to me, she certainly didn't have a small bottom, but it formed a pleasingly prominent curve and would have been the envy of any real fatso, any bag of flour or flesh, any ball of lard, any fat cow or El

Alamo bell; Muriel was mad to call her those names, or not mad exactly, it was more the cold, calculated punishment of years, or perhaps, in his resentment, that really was how he saw her, because when you decide to dislike someone, nothing can save them, even what we liked yesterday now seems plagued with defects and problems, and nothing and no one can resist someone's dislike. Perhaps I myself would see Beatriz differently, more negatively, were I to satisfy my desire, I mean, once that desire had been appeased, complaint and regret often follow on the achievement of an objective. But I wasn't thinking of that desire as a real thing, it was still in the realm of the purely visual, any intended or conscious contact seemed to me an impossibility. The idea hadn't so much as occurred to her, she hadn't even noticed the covetous nature of my looks, not even the most furtive, and all my glances were becoming steadily less and less furtive. She probably included me in the world of minors, the world occupied by her own children, rather than the world of the real adults like Muriel, Rico and Van Vechten; after all, far fewer years separated me from the former than from the latter, and I was far closer in age to Susana than I was to Beatriz. Perhaps that's why she didn't bother to cover herself, although it's also true to say that, at the time, the whole of society had instantly shaken off the modesty imposed by the dictatorship and its Church: it was a time of ease and unconcern as regards the way people behaved, a time of defiance. 'There's a very good reason why I don't usually drink,' she said, to justify that mixture. 'I don't actually like the taste. Do help yourself if you'd like something, though.'

'Yes, in a moment.' And almost without pause, I went on to ask: 'What was that about? Why did you do it? I mean what happened at the Hotel Wellington. I suppose that, yes, I did save you, but I could easily not have seen you going into the hotel.'

345

She hadn't yet sat down again and I was aware of her standing by my side, her large, exuberant body very close to mine, I thought I could feel her nightdress brushing against my shoulder or my arm, but I might have been imagining that, desire tends to have such imaginings. I again looked at her out of the corner of my eye, up and down, I didn't have to raise my eyes very far: her bra-less breasts rose and fell as if her breathing had grown somewhat agitated in response to my question.

'Why do you think, Juan?' she said gently, without any of the bitterness those words, that question might suggest; without implying that she thought me utterly obtuse; it was more as though she had no option but to take that as read, because it was so obvious. 'You've been here long enough to have realized that Eduardo and me . . . that I have nothing to do with Eduardo. And that sours my whole existence, I can't bear it. Each day, I find it harder and harder to get up and get going. If I had my choice, I wouldn't wake up at all, and this has been going on for years now. On some days, I just can't carry on, and that's what happened the other day. It's happened on other occasions too. On some days, it's because I don't feel quite right,' she said, then immediately corrected this to: 'I mean, I don't feel quite right in the head. You may not know it, but for years I went to a psychiatrist for intensive therapy. And when the two things come together . . . Well, even I don't know how such a day will end. When I have one of those days, I simply can't predict the outcome.'

I didn't know what to say, not straight away. She again sat down beside me and rested her forehead on her hand, her palm open, all-embracing, the same gesture we make if we're sick in the night, a memory of what our mothers did when we were children, they would hold our head in between spasms, and when they are no longer there, we, rather pathetically, as if we were them or were at least someone

346

else, do exactly the same, just as someone dying alone clasps his own hand to pretend that someone is there with him in death.

'Do you take any kind of medication?'

'I have in the past. And now, of course,' she showed me the bandage on her left wrist, 'they've started giving it to me again. It does help. It helps me to function, but it doesn't alter the basic problem, doesn't take away the pain.'

'Why don't you separate? Why don't you leave? Divorce will be made legal soon. Perhaps you would be better off putting some distance between you, just turning the page.' There was no reason why she should know that I already knew the answer to this, more or less, having heard the explanation she gave to her malevolent female friends.

She removed her hand from her forehead and turned to me. As she did, her knees met my right leg, I felt a slight pressure, which she did not withdraw; she probably didn't even notice, although I'm of the opinion that everyone always notices any contact; or perhaps she thought it unimportant. I seized the chance to glance down at her thighs, which were there before me now. They were perhaps a little plump, but I found them very attractive; so bare and sturdy, pressed tightly together.

'That's something you'd have to ask him, why he didn't leave, I mean, why he doesn't leave. As for me, it's a lot to ask of someone, to ask her to leave the person she most loves. If he left me, I would have to accept it, and he probably will, he'll probably leave me as soon as divorce becomes legal. But he can't expect me to make things easier for him, to take the initiative, when I don't want to. Besides, he would probably object if I did. People react strangely. And we've come a long way together. Perhaps that's why he doesn't leave, despite everything, perhaps that has some influence on him.'

'Yes, it's true,' I thought, 'we don't know what bonds were forged between the people who came before, and we probably never will, because we always arrive late in people's lives.'

'I don't know,' I said. 'It's hard to understand how you can still love someone who abuses you like that, verbally, that is.' I couldn't say 'physically' because that might have betrayed my nocturnal spying. 'I'm sorry, but sometimes I couldn't help but overhear. Never in your absence, mind, he's never said anything negative about you when you're not there, not when I've been present at least. But I have heard him talking to you. Well, you know how it is.'

She smiled, resumed her initial position and took a sip of her drink. She wasn't touching me now. I needed to get her to notice my desire, which was still on the increase (that's always the first and most necessary step, to get the other person to notice, and sometimes it's also the last step, the trigger), to the point where I was beginning not to feel contented with the purely visual phase, with imagining possibilities, and was now paying less attention to what she was saying, like someone who has crossed a line. In such situations, a moment always comes when all you care about are the waves of your own emotions.

'Of course you'll have heard him, and if only he *would* hold off when others are present. With some he's more careful because he knows they like and respect me. With Jorge, with Paco, with my female friends. Less so with Alberto Augusto. And not with you, with you he feels too relaxed, too comfortable, too at ease; right from the start, he made you a kind of extension of himself, which is both good and bad. But what you don't know is that it wasn't always like that, on the contrary. This began a long time ago, shortly after Tomás was born, imagine that. But for many years it was quite different, and for me it's those years that count. I lived through them, and

Eduardo . . .' She stopped as if afraid of what she was about to say, but then she said it anyway: 'Eduardo is the kindest, most upright man you could ever meet. The loathsome way he's been treating me all this time goes completely against his nature, he has to make himself do it. You'll think I'm deluding myself, but I still believe that the day will come when he can't bear it any more, going against himself and against his nature. And then he'll stop and will want to make amends.'

'The kindest and most upright man,' I thought. It was possible. As well as admiring him, I myself held him in high regard. As I said before, my loyalty bordered on the unconditional. And yet it was strange to hear such praise on the lips of the one person to whom I had seen and heard him be so cruel. Not malicious or insolent or scornful – he was capable of being all those things sometimes, and with considerable wit and relative impunity. No, with her he was wounding and vicious (although not all the time, not even with her). I remembered some of what Beatriz had said to her friends: 'I wouldn't want a new life with another man,' she had told them, had explained. 'I want the life I had for quite a number of years and with the same man. I don't want to forget or get over it or move on, as they say, but to carry on in exactly the same way, like a prolongation of what was. I was never dissatisfied, I never longed for change, I was never one of those women who gets bored and requires movement, variety, arguments and reconciliations, moments of euphoria and terrible shocks. I would have been happy for everything to have stayed eternally the same. Some people are content and satisfied, and hope only for each day to be the same as the previous day and the next. I was one of those people. Until everything went wrong.'

Then I got up and went over to the fridge. Like her, I had no idea what I wanted. I picked up a glass, put some ice in it, peered vaguely inside the fridge and then round about me, saw the bottle of whisky on the table and decided to try that, adding a little Coca-Cola too, imitating her in everything, and while I was standing, I was able to take a proper look at her from above, to gain a wider vision of her décolletage, looking down inside it, I mean, especially during the few seconds when I stood just behind her, and then I felt like reaching out a hand or placing both hands on her shoulders and from there moving them downwards, not suddenly, but gradually, distractedly, waiting for her to interrupt me, for her to shout, 'Hey, what do you think you're doing?' and for me to take fright and blush and apologize and retreat, or for her to say nothing and allow me to carry on, knowing perfectly well what I was doing, but pretending she didn't or not until later, when it would be impossible not to make some verbal acknowledgement of that contact, when it became clear that it meant more than just sympathy, although it's also true that such acknowledgement need never be articulated, there's no need for anyone to speak or say anything, or only with their breathing, and even that can be suppressed, every moan silenced, many such sounds have had to be hidden away and to remain as mute as if they'd never existed, indeed, it's impossible to lay down any strict rules for the way two people come together.

And so I lingered there, behind her – longer than a few seconds now – and decided I could make the first move without Beatriz seeing it as in any way suspicious or improper, placing my hands on her shoulders in a friendly or comforting manner; besides, many things are permissible during a sleepless night, as if that state of wakefulness were contaminated by the sleep that should replace it, but that refuses to come when called, and as if, up to a point, everything were happening under its dominion, in some borrowed life, nebulous, hypothetical and parallel. And so I did delicately place my hands on her shoulders and, at the same time, to disguise my boldness, I spoke to her too, so that she would have more than one thing to attend to.

'So what happened? Why did it all go wrong? Why did Eduardo become so unpleasant and so brusque?'

She shrugged her shoulders, but only very slightly. She could have taken the opportunity to move away from me, to free herself. However feebly she had done this, I would have understood that she was rejecting that contact and would have removed my hands at once. The movement she made was so slight, though, that I experienced it more like a response, as if her grateful shoulders were exerting a slight pressure in order to move closer and mould themselves better to the palms of my hands. That, at least, is how I chose to interpret it, doubtless pushing my luck.

'It was something really stupid,' she said. 'Because he found out that, once, years ago, I'd lied to him. An old lie that should have made him laugh, not take it to heart. So many other things had happened in between, so much had happened between us, that any importance it had at the time should have dissipated, should, how can I put it, have expired, been cancelled out by the sheer weight of our lives spent together; we had even lost a child, and nothing brings a couple closer than that, if, of course, it doesn't destroy them. In fact,

351

he wasn't even the one to discover the lie, I got angry with him one day and blurted it out.' She said nothing for a few seconds. 'I never imagined he would react the way he did. If only I had.'

This reminded me again of what I'd heard Muriel say on the night he appeared at his bedroom door, wearing his long, dark Fu Manchu or Dracula dressing gown: 'How stupid of me to love you during all those years, love you with all my heart, as long, that is, as I knew nothing.' Later, he had said: 'If only you'd never told me, if only you'd kept me in the dark . . . What is the point of setting the record straight, of suddenly telling the truth?' And he had concluded his string of reproaches, saying: 'Ah, what a fool you were, Beatriz. Not just once, but twice.' He must have been referring to the same thing Beatriz was talking about now.

'What was the lie?' I asked.

She thought for a few moments, perhaps not wanting to go into detail. She drank her glass of adulterated whisky, still without detaching herself from my hands, which were so cautious, so respectful that they hadn't shifted so much as a millimetre, as if with that initial brazen move they had exhausted all their boldness for quite a while. When she did not respond at once, I added, so as to encourage her to reply: 'Or would you rather not say?'

'Let him tell you if he wants to, young De Vere, and then you can judge for yourself.' She didn't often call me by that name, only when she was in a good mood (only very erratically) and chose to join in the household tradition of giving people jokey nicknames. 'It's so ridiculous that I'm embarrassed to tell you, that such a childish thing should have ruined my life, something so silly.' She paused again, then went on: 'The most important aspect of that lie (important to me, you understand) was that it proved to me how kind and upright Eduardo was, without him ever knowing just how well I knew this.

352

Men are very easy to deceive, however intelligent and wary and astute.' She hadn't said 'you men', and so I wasn't sure whether she was referring just to men or to mankind generally, or if she didn't yet consider me to be a proper man. 'But Eduardo was an extreme case. He was so kind and upright that he couldn't really exist in the world without being deceived by someone. So it was best if I was the one to deceive him, in our marriage at least, because I loved him so much and didn't wish him any harm. On the contrary, I thought that other people, in other fields, would find it harder to deceive him with me by his side.'

I realized then that I was finding all this slightly tedious, or that it didn't interest me in the way it would have in almost any other circumstance, or as it did interest and intrigue me a posteriori, when I thought about it on my own in the days that followed. At the time, in the middle of the night, in the kitchen, it felt to me like a toll I had to pay for a remote hope, a fantasy even, because I still didn't dare to assume that anything unforeseen or extraordinary was about to happen, but impatience and desire are, at once, both uncontrollable and all-absorbing. Actions and movements are, of course, controllable; we civilized people have learned to put a brake on them and store them away in our imaginations and postpone them, to toss them into the bag of imaginings and make do with that, at least temporarily; this, however, is not the case with feelings, and they always do, I think, end up being communicated to others and betraying us, and that is where those with very strong feelings have the advantage. The desire you give off, especially if you're young and untutored in the art of dissembling, condenses in the air and impregnates it, like a spreading mist; it reaches the object of desire and then she has to do something about it; she must either leave, remove herself, disappear and thus dissipate the feeling, or accept it and take it up and become entangled. In either case, she finds herself having to deal with something that is nothing to do with her, not of her own creation, which is often both unfair and awkward. The greatest danger (if that's the right word) is that, in noticing the other person's desire, you might come up with or conceive of the possibility of actually responding, when it would never have occurred to you to take such an initiative spontaneously. Noticing that someone wants to connect with us sexually obliges us to consider the possibility, even in the most fleeting and rudimentary way; and if you don't instantly reject or dismiss the idea, if you don't immediately flee from that mist, then it becomes very difficult not to feel those emanations, which tend not to abate, but to persist, they don't even succumb to weariness or to the knowledge that they're useless or unworkable: they exist because they exist, independent of whether they are or aren't of any use. And so that other person inoculates us with the idea or plants it in our mind, he gives it to us and infects us, and its attractiveness grows with every second that it's there floating in the air and no one punctures, deflates or bursts it. Sometimes all it takes is a little vehemence to achieve something that seemed unreachable only moments before its release, before it floated upon the air, before we liberated or unleashed it or before it escaped without our consent. Possibly much to our regret.

That is probably more or less what happened. The most probable explanation. My involuntary or voluntary emanations, or both alternately, had their effect, for there were moments when I didn't care whether she noticed or not and others when I was filled with shame and self-reproach, judging my intentions to be a betrayal of Muriel, even though he had long since abandoned that particular field. Or that's what I was thinking when I noticed that my paralysed, almost numb hands resting on Beatriz's shoulders were being drawn slowly down by hers, over her nightdress, not inside. I couldn't see her face, she was still sitting with her back to me, and I was still standing and could see only the top of her head, I had no idea what her expression might be, whether her eyes were open or closed, if she was fully aware that it was me touching her or if she was imagining the caresses or the pressure of someone else, doubtless her longed-for husband. My position was rather like that of Van Vechten at the Sanctuary, except that I was not yet thrusting away, nor was I at the right height to do so, the most I could do would be to press my belly against her shoulder, so that she could feel it, but I didn't even have the courage to establish that too explicit contact, I held back – not yet – even though she had guided my hands down towards her breasts, which were almost too large for me to encompass. When I was perched in the tree at the Sanctuary, I'd been able to see her face clearly, pressed

355

against the window, in fact, that was all I could see once the Doctor had turned her round; before that, I had, with some alarm, been staring at the back of her neck as it almost beat against the panes. And that is how I imagined her while I was touching her – yes, I was actually touching her – with her eyes tight shut as if she were some strange, unwonted portrait, her skin firmer and more youthful, her lips fuller or fleshier, as if this were unknown territory for them, more porous, softer, redder, and slightly parted, her eyelashes longer or more visible; but all that was appropriate to the moment of orgasm or to a series of orgasms or a pre-orgasm, and it was far too soon for that.

Then things accelerated and it all happened very fast. She stood up, pushed aside the stool, turned towards me and, in one movement, had pressed her whole body against mine, as she had with Muriel on that other night, when he, at last, unexpectedly granted her wish. I felt the embrace of her chest and belly and limbs, if chest, belly and limbs can be said to embrace: her breast crushed against my breast, her pelvis against mine, her thighs against mine, her arms encircling me with an iron grip, and even her feet on my feet, as if she had stood on them in order to be the same height as me, except that she was tall enough not to need to do that – in fact, in heels, she was taller than me. For a moment, I had a sense of being bound to some supernatural creature, possibly a giantess, not because of her size, for although she was well built, she was of perfectly normal stature, but because of that absolute fusion of bodies, her body coupled with mine, glued to mine, and all in a matter of seconds, with no preamble. Her mouth was the only thing she did not press to mine, though, and when I tried to kiss her, she turned away and offered me her throat or her cheek: 'No, no kisses,' I thought, as Beatriz had perhaps said to Van Vechten, 'No, no caresses', at the end of their sacred and profane fuck, from my branch I hadn't been able to hear what they said. *Non, pas de baisers, pas de caresses*, I must have read something of the sort in some French novel for these imaginary prohibitions to come into my mind in that other language. And neither she nor I said anything during that strange, perfect juxtaposition, standing in the kitchen near the fridge. And so no words either: *Non, pas de mots*.

I became impatient, in a hurry for what seemed about to happen to actually happen. I was afraid she might draw back, separate, or that I might push her away, suddenly keeping her at a distance by placing one hand on her shoulder, as Muriel had done, with that single authoritative gesture, after suffering her overwhelming response to his unexpected and doubtless commiserative embrace. There was nothing commiserative about my embrace, not at all, it was youthfully lustful or elementally lascivious; as I said, when you're young, it's hard to turn down any opportunity, you feel you should seize all opportunities or certainly the great majority of them, the only exceptions being when you feel a clear, unmistakable distaste or those occasions that don't even seem likely to be worth calling up later as a memory, as a treasured image for the mature or old man we will one day become and whom we can't even imagine then, can't even glimpse on the horizon, but who, mysteriously, is already there in our unconscious mind like a ghost of the future. It is that older man who sometimes whispers to our youthful self: 'Remember this experience and note every detail, experience it with me in mind and as if you knew it would never happen again except in your memory, which is my memory; engrave it on your retina as if these were the most memorable sequences and shots from a film; you won't be able to preserve the excitement or relive it, but you will recall the sense of triumph and, more especially, the knowledge: you will *know* that this happened and you always will; grasp it firmly, take a long look at this woman and keep that image safe, because later on, I will ask you for it and you will have to offer it to me as consolation.'

I knew very clearly that this was one of those instances. There was no distaste, quite the contrary, but if there was a risk that I might retreat (a very minor risk as I recognized at once), this was because I was troubled by the idea that I was perhaps committing a vile deed. Not just because of the loyalty I owed to Muriel, but because I was possibly taking advantage of or abusing, to use the appropriate verb, Beatriz Noguera's probable disorientation and confusion and fragility and, of course, her continuing unhappiness and even her accidental insomnia: she was much older than me and therefore more experienced in some respects, and she didn't seem to care about her lovers, but perhaps she used them consciously to comfort herself, to feel that she wasn't pure lard or a bag of flour or flesh, yes, solely for that reason and to avenge herself in her imagination, fictitiously ('If he knew' much more than 'When he finds out'), because there can be no real revenge if the victim doesn't know about it or doesn't suffer; but she was also someone who had recently experienced an unbearable sense of world-weariness or despair, who had just tried to slit her own wrists – those still bandaged wrists were an additional element, one of those details my future self would recall in many years' time, as I knew already because the sight of them only increased my desire – someone who was not always quite right in the head, as she herself had said, someone frustrated and rejected and who cared little what would come in the days that had been loaned or gifted to her following her attempted suicide, but then who does care what happens to them after death, and Beatriz had already died three times, at least in her mind; she was, inevitably, easy prey, beaten and will-less or weakened by indifference, the kind that would be capable of saying to anyone, not just to me: 'Do what you like, I won't resist, my time for resisting anything has passed.' It bothered me that the word 'prey' should have leapt into my head, since she was the one who had stood up and turned round and thrown herself into my arms or, rather, *at* my whole body, even treading on my toes, climbing on to them as if she were a little girl, and she certainly wasn't that. And yet, and yet . . . I couldn't help persuading myself that my conquest – another unfortunate word – had been the result of my emanations or pulsations, that they had provoked this almost overreaction; I couldn't help but see myself as the seducer, the opportunist, almost as the guilty party, perhaps that is always what the keener partner feels, although there's never any certain way of knowing who is keener than who, sometimes it remains hidden until it can remain hidden no longer. And that is perhaps when I committed the vilest of deeds, in order to shake off all those other possibilities, and I did so with my thoughts alone, but fully intending to act and not to stop: 'What does it matter, I saved her, I saved her from the blood and the water, because no one else would have known about it otherwise.' I dredged up that same miserable idea and this time formulated it in my head more or less as I've written it down now, while I was exploring or groping a new area – not in a humiliating way, but ardently, appreciatively – and feeling for her knickers underneath her silk nightdress, then pulling them down to mid-thigh level, one tug, two, and they no longer covered what they had been covering, I could use one finger or two to caress her, with nothing in the way now, or even slip them inside. 'The fact that she's here and breathing, that her skin smells so good and her flesh is still so abundant and alive, is all thanks to me, I have won the right to enjoy them; this woman who is neither memory nor ash nor decomposing flesh nor bare bone, this woman who survived is mine and will be tonight for a while at least; after all, these encounters are short-lived and then we'll both wash ourselves

359

clean and it will be as if it had never happened, apart from our wretched memory, which presents us with events of which no visible trace remains, which means that no one else knows, no one will find out if they weren't there, and if someone does talk about what happened later on, that's pure rumour. I'm an extension of Muriel, she herself said so, perhaps that's why she clings to me as she clung to him, in just the same way, as soon as she had the chance and it became a possibility; perhaps she's doing it in order to replace him and to deceive herself with her eyes shut, or perhaps to annoy him, although he will probably never know that I've screwed her, I certainly won't tell him and neither will she. But what do I care about the whys and wherefores, if there are any, and if she even knows what they are, it's time to get down to business.' And at this point, I grew impatient, hence the choice of language, which tends to be what passes through the mind when the feelings are superficial and the desire selfish. Vulgar terms, but they are never spoken out loud unless there is mutual trust and a liking for them or as a willing game between two lewd strangers, otherwise, they are only ever thought. There are no witnesses to our thoughts, and we don't have to be respectful or polite in them. And so I had no hesitation in saying to myself: 'I've got to screw her now, quickly and with no preliminaries, in case she takes a step back and has second thoughts midway through and what is just about to be won't be; I would never forgive myself, to have come so close and then to fail, to have brought the painting to life, to have endowed it with tremulous movement and volume only to let that likeness escape intact and unentered. Once I'm inside, there'll be no going back, I'll feel that warmth, that moistness and it will have happened and then I'll have that memory until the end of my days and be able to think about it whenever I choose: "I fucked Beatriz Noguera, who would have thought it, who could have predicted it;

that's how it was and no one can change it." Even if she still is in a disturbed state and not in control of her decisions, her actions; even if she forgets all about it or wipes it from her mind, even if she's dead and buried, even if she disappears from the world long before I do and hardly anyone knows who she was, still less remembers her, and even if no one tells the tenuous story of her private life even in whispers, this will have happened and no one will be able to take that away from me, and for me it will be an ineradicable piece of knowledge.'

Those are also thoughts appropriate to youth, when you are too new to the world to be able to believe in the things that happen to you or in your own actions, when everything seems improbable and as if it belonged to someone else, as if our experiences were not really ours and were simply on loan to us. It's not just a young man's heart that is on hold, it's also his consciousness. It takes a while, a long while, for it to find its proper place and settle in, and it's years before we realize that what is happening to us really is happening to us, and that we are not just spectators in the dark, staring at a stage or a screen or at a book lit by a lamp.

It had to be now, so that it would actually happen and not run the risk of failing to happen, for it to cease being a promise or the future or mere imminence. I proceeded cautiously – spurred on by my impatience – and gently, so as not to frighten her, I drew Beatriz towards my *chambre de bonne*, into the small room that would be almost unknown to her, for no one tended to visit me in my place of exile; it was best if the irreversible – although it was not as yet irreversible, not yet – didn't happen in the kitchen, where someone might come in or peer round the door, for wakefulness could assail any of the apartment's inhabitants who wanted to drink or eat something or stand at the open fridge door for a few seconds to cool off; we were too exposed there, it was a communal area, Flavia's territory and a transit point. I closed the door of my cubbyhole, but did not hear the usual click: I didn't bother to close it properly, though, since nothing could be seen from the outside, and matters were now urgent. Almost in the same movement – it's odd how we become so deft and efficient when it comes to preventing another person from reacting or retreating or waking – I removed her knickers and took off my jeans, but not my boxer shorts, there was no need, the fly was already open and in use, or indeed my shirt, since I hadn't buttoned it up, and my chest would touch whatever there was to touch without impediment. I gave her another gentle push so that she fell backwards on to the bed and let me do as I pleased, just reaching out her arms – the bandages visible, those bandages – waiting to clutch me to her again, as soon as I had completed my minimal preparations. I slipped off the straps of her nightdress so as to see her bare breasts and to touch them with whatever part of my body she or I chose. But I saw that she wasn't going to choose anything or guide me in any way. Then I drew back slightly and looked for a moment at her gleaming thighs, so close together. I parted them, carefully and resolutely, if such a combination is possible, and, while she once again enfolded me in a tight embrace, I thought: 'Now it's happened, my cock is inside her, nothing can now stop this happening, can prevent it from having happened.' I wanted to see her face, although she clearly wasn't interested in seeing mine, she couldn't, with her eyes tight shut as they had been when she was with Van Vechten in the Sanctuary, except that there, he had been behind her when I saw her face, while I was in front. I tried to drive away that image, but for a few moments, it remained unpleasantly vivid, troubling and distracting me. The first physical sensations succeeded in repelling it a little, as did my thoughts, which were intent on convincing themselves of what was happening with their coarse, crude language: 'Yes, I'm fucking Beatriz Noguera, my cock's inside her cunt and there's nothing to stop it now.' She had denied me her mouth and continued to do so, but she kept kissing my eyelids, thus obliging me to keep them closed. I could see nothing and perhaps that sharpened my other senses, definitely my sense of touch, but also my hearing. I heard rapid footsteps close by, as if someone were running. I stopped for a moment so as to hear better, Beatriz noticed this, but obviously didn't know the reason, lost in her own depths or thoughts, perhaps as she had been in the bathtub in the Hotel Wellington, who knows. Then I heard nothing more, they were evidently the footsteps of someone hurrying away – bare feet on the wooden floor – not of someone approaching. I turned my head to look at the door, it was closed, but not completely, it was open the tiniest crack through which no one could have seen anything.

'What is it? Is something wrong?' Beatriz asked quietly.

'No, no, it's nothing.' I didn't want to alarm her, to put her to flight, that would have been disastrous.

But someone might have heard something. There had been no words spoken between us, but perhaps some louder-than-usual breathing and a faint interjection or groan, despite Beatriz's discreet silence and my efforts to make not a sound, because I had not, for a moment, forgotten that there were three children in the apartment. I hoped desperately that the footsteps had been Flavia's and not the children's; she was of an age not to be shocked or to be less shocked, or perhaps she already knew or suspected or assumed. I was aware, though, that those fleet, barefoot steps were more like those of a child or an adolescent than of a grown woman. 'Damn,' I thought, 'one of them probably woke up and went looking for Beatriz, if so, I hope it was Tomás or, if not him, then Alicia, they probably wouldn't have fully understood what was going on, wouldn't have put two and two together; if it was Susana, though, she will have sized up the situation and will now be lying awake in her bed, her cheeks burning, listening for her mother to return to her bedroom. Whatever the truth, there's no undoing the situation; I'll feel embarrassed tomorrow, but today is not tomorrow. This is my moment, and I have to get back to the business in hand.'

The body lying underneath me required my attention, indeed it was demanding or hijacking it, and in those circumstances, it was impossible to remain absent for very long, not even after a brief fright. I took advantage of the fact that I had raised my head, thus preventing Beatriz from kissing my eyelids, and I looked down at her face, the better to retain the moment, the bold eyebrows, the very thick eyelashes, which were neither turned back on themselves nor curled, the straight nose so charmingly retroussé, the full, wide mouth that revealed – a dreamy half-smile – the slightly widely spaced teeth that unwittingly lent her a vaguely salacious air, in marked contrast to her otherwise childish face, one of those mouths that would instantly lead many men to imagine unexpected and inappropriate scenes, often quite against their perfectly respectful efforts to suppress such scenes entirely, except that I didn't need to suppress or imagine anything, I was performing one of those scenes with her, and she looked even more attractive than usual, as happens with so many women who, in such situations, grow more beautiful and more youthful, her lips fuller and redder and more porous, her skin so young and firm that I again had to curse those footsteps that had forced me to think of Susana, because for a few seconds I had the disquieting feeling that I was with her and not with her mother, of whom she was the very image: the same features, the same candid expression, the daughter already promising – already blossoming into — the same intimidating, explosive body that was now so closely connected to mine. And I was once more assailed by a feeling of incongruousness: when I looked at Beatriz's face and, where my perspective allowed, at her breasts, hips, thighs and buttocks, I realized that her features were not in keeping with her curvaceous body; they seemed to demand a less powerful, more moderate trunk, abdomen and legs, and her insolent curves a less innocent, ingenuous face. And in Susana, who was so much younger, that divergence would become more marked as soon as she was a little older. I don't know what was wrong with me: the mother led me to think about the daughter at that most inopportune of moments. However, I did not forget about the former, not at all, not for an instant: I carefully noted everything so that I could file it away in my memory. It's still there, as clear as clear, even though many years have passed, even though it's accompanied by many other memories, and even though she has been dead for nearly the same number of years.

'Thus bad begins and worse remains behind,' that is the Shakespeare quote Muriel was alluding to when he spoke of the benefits or advisability of – the comparatively minor harm involved in – giving up trying to know what we cannot know, of removing ourselves from the hubbub of what others tell us throughout our life, so much so that even what we ourselves experience and witness sometimes seems more like a story told to us, as it moves further off and becomes besmirched by time, or grows faded with the tick-tock of the passing days or grows dim beneath the breath of all those moons and the dust of all those years, and it's not so much that we then begin to doubt its existence (although occasionally we do), it's more that it loses its colour and its importance wanes. What was important no longer is, or only very faintly, and to retrieve that scrap of importance you have to make a real effort; what seemed crucial to us is revealed to be a matter of complete indifference, and what destroyed our life seems mere foolishness, an exaggeration, a piece of nonsense. How could I have been so upset or felt so guilty, how could I have wished to die, even if only rhetorically? It really didn't merit so much fuss – I can see that now – when its effects are on the path to dispersal and oblivion and there's barely any trace left of the person I was then. Of what significance is what happened or what happened to me, what I did, what I kept secret or failed to confess? What does it matter that a little child died, when millions of others have fallen without anyone so much as raising an eyebrow, apart, that is, from their progenitors, and sometimes not even them: the world is full of stoical mothers who say nothing and endure, and who perhaps press their grieving face into their silent pillow in the solitude of night, so as not to be seen. What does it matter if, one insomniac night, a young man went to bed with one of those mothers and what if a daughter found out and ran back down the corridor, troubled and barefoot, trying to erase that knowledge or, on the contrary, storing it away, so that it would have a determining effect on her own future marriage and, therefore, on her existence? What does it matter if a woman told a lie once, however much harm it did, or perhaps the harm attributed to that lie was exaggerated, for when all's said and done, lies form part of the natural flow of life, which is inconceivable without a dose of falsehood, without that equilibrium between truth and deceit? What does it matter if a decent, upright man should, for years, reject that woman and insult her? Households are full of rejections and slights and mortifications and insults, especially behind closed doors (and sometimes one gets shut inside with them by accident). What does it matter if one of those mothers kills herself, when she had already teetered along that knife-edge and when her nearest and dearest were expecting her suicide, which was even announced by the tick-tock of the metronome that she herself set in motion, when she was playing or not playing the piano? What does it matter that a twisted man abused his power and knowledge and behaved indecently with certain vulnerable women, almost all of them mothers and daughters? Just as now it doesn't matter in the least that a film producer for whom we work either was or wasn't involved in trafficking women in America in the Kennedy era, women who were vulnerable or invulnerable and stoical. What point is there in trying to stop, avoid, watch,

367

punish and even know all this; history is too full of minor abuses and major villainies against which nothing can be done because there is such an avalanche of them, and what do we gain by finding out about them? What happens has happened and is irreversible, that is the terrible force of facts, their unliftable weight. Perhaps it's best to shrug one's shoulders and nod and ignore them, to accept that this is the way of the world. 'Thus bad begins and worse remains behind,' that's what Shakespeare said. And only once we have nodded and shrugged our shoulders does worse remain behind, because at least it is over. And thus only bad begins, the bad that has not yet happened.

This, or something like it, is what Muriel must have thought when I finally had a stroke of luck and could provide him with information about what Van Vechten had done during the years when he'd behaved so well towards the people suffering persecution or reprisals under the Franco regime, and when he'd gained a reputation as a compassionate, understanding man who had refused to take any money for treating the whooping cough or measles or chickenpox of the children of those struggling to scrape a living. It's true, however, that we always arrive late in people's lives, indeed, we generally arrive late for everything: Muriel had decided not to hear what I had to say, not to listen to what I'd chanced to discover, whether I'd discovered it entirely by chance or thanks to my own persistence ('I don't want you to tell me about it, to test my curiosity. Keep it to yourself, say nothing,' he said) and he had ordered me to cease my investigations and my wheedlings, even to abandon my outings with the Doctor, albeit gradually. However, I found it impossible not at least to try to get him to listen, to tell him the story I'd heard not from Van Vechten, but from another doctor, a younger man, Dr Vidal Secanell, a family friend and my friend too, even though we saw each other only occasionally. If the story was true, it would have been inconceivable that Van Vechten would have openly admitted it to me, not even on a night of heavy drinking or endless boasting or contrite

369

confessions (the latter was hard to imagine); we could have gone out to discos and bars and so on thousands of times and have developed a profound sense of camaraderie, but still not a word about what he had done would have left his lips; it was the kind of thing you hope will remain hidden for ever, a secret you will take with you to the grave, although we all know which of our secrets would be best discreetly buried, if it were up to us. We don't, however, always get our way: as soon as someone else intervenes – and someone will always intervene, be it an accomplice, an intermediary, a witness or a victim – rumours, however subterranean, will start to spread, and nothing is ever completely safe. In the light of that story, Van Vechten had already told me a lot, and although I did pass on his words to Muriel, they weren't enough: 'And nothing gives one more satisfaction than when a girl doesn't want to do it, but can't say No. And I can assure you most of them do want to do it, once they realize they're obliged to.' Of course I couldn't understand the meaning of those words without knowing the story I was told by Vidal, who was scornful of and shocked by my friendship with Van Vechten. Muriel, on the other hand, would have understood, because he would probably have been told the same story by the person who had come to him or, rather, by a former lover, 'the love of my life, as people say'.

It didn't happen at once, but neither did I have to wait long for an opportunity to tell him. I mean that it happened immediately after Muriel's return from Barcelona. He came home only a few days later, looking very angry and annoyed and bearing bad news, an insult. Towers had got rid of him, sacked him, had refused to allow him to finish filming, and had turned instead to Jesús Franco to see if he, with his *sans-façon* and talent for juggling multiple projects, could bring the film into safe harbour. Jesús had said Yes, but that he wouldn't be able to take over for another week and a half, having other business to finish. The amazing thing is that he was able to find time at all, because I see from the Internet that no fewer than thirteen feature-length films by him are dated 1980 or 1981. And his trusted friend Don Sharp was busy too. Towers couldn't have Herbert Lom and the other actors twiddling their thumbs for another ten days and so he had sent them all home and suspended the production for the moment. Filming was never resumed, which is why, as I said, the title doesn't appear in any filmography and remains unfinished, a ghost work. I asked Muriel what exactly had happened, but he was in no mood for giving explanations.

'We had a falling-out. Harry's a slave-driver, of course, but I can hardly claim I didn't know that already,' was all he would say. Then he had the decency to add: 'In large part, it's my fault. And Beatriz's, needless to say, she couldn't have chosen a worse time for her "performance", and I fell for it; she really chose her moment. But don't ask me any more questions, I don't want to talk about it. Oh, and you'd better start thinking about looking for another job, Juan.' The succession of verbs indicated a certain delicacy, or a desire to break the news gently and not put me under any pressure. 'I doubt I'll be offered another project for a while, and I'm afraid you're not going to be needed. But there's no rush, I don't want to cause you any problems. You can stay here until you find something else, and when you do, tell me when it would suit you to leave, I leave it in your hands. I just felt it was fair to give you plenty of notice.'

His bad mood lasted for weeks. All consideration or concern, his sudden show of affection (if you can call it that), all solicitude ended. Instead, he was abusive and loathsome to her on the slightest excuse, as if he regretted the truce he'd called after the fright she gave him at the Hotel Wellington, after the panic that had obliged him to go haring down Calle Velázquez and suffer the indignity of having to run

371

even that short distance. Fortunately, he had few opportunities to wound her, because he was rarely at home; every day he summoned the telephonist-cum-accounts-clerk-cum-representative-cum-housekeeper, Mercedes by name, with whom he shared his office. He went there straight after breakfast, but I have no idea what he did or if he stayed there. I had the impression that Towers's insulting behaviour and his own foul mood had spurred him on, for far from giving up, he was in furious pursuit of finance for another film; perhaps he and Mercedes spent all day making phone calls and arranging meetings with more curers of ham and more breeders of fighting bulls, with canners of cockles and representatives of drinks manufacturers, whose drinks he promised would appear in every shot, with the label clearly visible, or perhaps he would again resort to the imperial Cecilia Alemany, to try to win her over with some clever and less pedantic tactic, as well as courting all kinds of professional and amateur producers, the former all thieving megalomaniacs, the latter all delusional megalomaniacs. Perhaps he spent the day chasing after such individuals. He didn't usually come home until late anyway, sometimes not until the small hours (poker games and nightclubs, I assumed), and he rarely took me with him. I didn't know if he preferred me not to see him humbling himself before the wealthy or if he wanted to get used to no longer having me there, or if his anger also extended to me, because I had been the unwitting instrument of his wife's salvation, perhaps he thought she might finally have succeeded on the third attempt. There were times when it occurred to me that Muriel would have liked to see her dead. This was doubtless a passing phase, but while it lasted, his fury and spite only intensified.

What there couldn't be, though, was any suspicion on his part that my relations with Beatriz had changed, because they didn't change at all. After that insomniac night, even before Muriel came back, Beatriz treated me exactly as if nothing had happened or as if that night had never existed. As though she had retreated into the painting again, into that flat, long-past dimension, and had never become flesh – texture and tremor – nor had pressed foot, thigh or breast against me in my present dimension. And I never dared to attempt another approach or to mention what had occurred: I sensed that, if I did, I might be confronted by a response along the discouraging, disconcerting lines of: 'I don't know what you're talking about, Juan. You must have dreamed it, young De Vere. You youngsters tell yourself such stories. Don't be silly.' I didn't find this so very hard to accept. Although I treasured and still retain the images and sensations of what went on in my little room and in the kitchen, I knew that certain looks and attitudes were not allowed and would be deemed inappropriate given my age, position or rank, and it wasn't that difficult to give them up, to dismiss rather than repress them, and to adopt a veiled, neutral gaze. Beatriz gradually went back to her normal life, resumed her teaching, her outings with Rico or with Roy or with her women friends, from whom she managed to conceal that suicidal episode, telling them that she had been away for a few weeks with Muriel in Barcelona. She also resumed her solitary walks, smartly dressed and in her high heels – the very image of misery, I always thought – but I felt less inclined to follow her, less curious, because I already had what I wanted, although up until then I had never admitted to myself that I did want what I now had – sometimes we discover this only once we have it. I imagined – no, I was sure – that she would continue occasionally to visit Van Vechten at the Sanctuary of Darmstadt – there was now an added link between them, that of saviour and saved, although not necessarily a very alluring one – and whoever it was in Plaza del Marqués de

373

Salamanca, or to drive to El Escorial or La Granja or Gredos on her Harley-Davidson; on some afternoons, I would watch her from the balcony as she rode off. She was, it seemed to me, doomed.

Needless to say, following that night of fantasy, I tried to detect any changes in the behaviour or looks or words of the three children or of Flavia, to see which of them might have been the owner of those fleet, barefoot steps, while I was inside Beatriz, deep inside without a condom or anything; as I said, AIDS was unknown at the time and it never occurred to anyone to take such prosaic precautions. I noticed no change in any of them – no hostility or reproach or distrust, no words open to interpretation – although I did occasionally have the feeling that the girls were looking at me with more curiosity or attention than usual, but that might just have been my imagination or simply that I'd never before stopped to look at them looking at me, as I then did. It was not so very odd that a couple of adolescent girls should fancy a slightly older young man who spent so much time in their home. There was nothing strange either in them having a secret crush on him, that's perfectly normal.

I bumped into José Manuel Vidal one day when Professor Rico had dragged me off to keep him company until his lunch date with two or three academicians whom he judged to be particularly stupid and with whom, for that same reason, he had to be helpful and flattering as long as his patience lasted, which was not very long at all, though he would probably achieve exactly the opposite effect and they would all be sworn enemies by the time dessert was served. These were academicians from the Real Academia Española, of which he planned to be a member within, at most, six years, despite his relative youth; there were other academicians whom he greatly respected, and since he considered them to be intelligent people, he assumed they would admire him equally unreservedly and so felt there was no need for him to win them round. He had dropped in at the apartment to while away the time, but finding that Eduardo was at his office and Beatriz was out teaching, he persuaded me to join him for an aperitif at the Balmoral, although I can't remember now if that was or is in Calle de Hermosilla or in Calle Ayala, or if it closed a few years ago or remains open, because it's been many years since I sat at its tables or its bar.

The Professor was in full flow, heaping elaborate insults on some of his Barcelona colleagues (some of whom he had once favoured, but now regretted doing so), when Vidal came over to us, friendly and smiling and slightly teasing, as was his way, at least with me. He was about seven years older than me (so he would have been about thirty at the time) and bore a remarkable resemblance to Paul McCartney: his nose, cheeks, even his eyes were rather like the ex-Beatle's, except that his skin was a little lined or pockmarked. His Republican family had always been good friends with mine, especially with my aunt and uncle, and he and I had known each other since we were children or, rather, since I was a child and he was an adolescent. The difference in age meant that, while we had never considered ourselves to be friends exactly, that same age difference allowed him to treat me in a fraternal fashion, taking on the role of older brother. He was like one of those people you've known all your life and with whom you tend not to make any special arrangements to meet up, but with whom there's always an immediate sense of deep trust and familiarity whenever you do run into them. His grandfather, an ophthalmologist and lawyer (the first career, oddly enough, didn't earn him enough to live on in the 1920s and 30s), had ended up in prison at the end of the Civil War, and on his release, he was further punished by being banned from exercising either of his two professions, and so in order to survive, he had to set up one of those agencies that helps people deal with labyrinthine Spanish bureaucracy. His grandmother, for her part, had had all her hair shaved off before being sent to clean the Falangists' latrines. As for their son, Vidal Secanell's father, he had been charged with sedition because, as a very young man, he had fought for the Republican side; luckily for him, though, the case against him was dismissed. Then, in the 1950s and 60s, he had set up a branch in Mexico of the record company Hispavox and made a fortune, which meant that he could send Vidal to a good school and to study medicine in Houston, which served him very well when it came to working towards his specialism, cardiology. Despite his family antecedents, Vidal had got on well and met with no difficulties, thanks to hard work, efficiency and a certain astuteness, that is, an ability to dissemble when necessary and not to antagonize those people he despised for professional or political reasons. Unlike Rico, who gloried in proud insolence or frank impertinence or gleeful arrogance, Vidal was one of those people who could put any antipathies, not to mention moral judgements, on ice. Such people reserve such judgements for when they're needed and bring them out at the propitious moment. And I clearly constituted a propitious moment, even if only because of our long fraternal acquaintance.

'Well, I'm very glad to see you in better company than of late. I was beginning to get worried,' he said almost as soon as he saw me. And holding out his hand to the Professor, who often appeared in the newspapers and even occasionally on the television, he added warmly: 'An honour to meet you, Professor Rico, author of *The World of the Small Man*.' Vidal was well read, or at least attentive and with a retentive mind.

Rico held out one languid hand (he had a cigarette in the other) without bothering to get up, and could not resist correcting Vidal:

'You mean *The World of the Small Man*. Why on earth would I write about a small man? I leave that to the author of *Tom Thumb* or *The Hobbit*, assuming you know what that is.' He was already being rude, or heading in that direction. *The Hobbit* was not particularly well known in Spain at the time. 'And you, sir, are?'

I made the necessary introductions. Vidal sat down with us, abandoning the two men and two women, possibly colleagues, whom he had been with at the bar. He waved his almost empty glass at a passing waiter, indicating that he should bring another beer to our table, where he was clearly intending to stay for a while.

'What do you mean "in better company"?' I asked anxiously, the

377

usual response to a brotherly reproach. 'We haven't seen each other lately, in fact, not for ages.'

'You may not have seen me, but I've seen you, two or three times. And the reason I didn't come over or make myself visible was precisely because I wanted to avoid the utter bastard you were with. What are you doing going around with a man like that? It's one thing me having dealings with the man, because we worked at the same clinic and he was a colleague, but you don't even have that excuse.'

Then the penny dropped. Vidal must have seen me with Van Vechten on café terraces, in discos or bars. As I mentioned earlier, in 1980, the whole of Madrid went out at night, regardless of age, respectability or profession.

I was slightly put out, but only slightly, after all, my mission, now cancelled, had been to ascertain more or less whether the Doctor was what Vidal had just said he was, or had been in the remote past. I was about to bombard him with questions and listen to his answers, but Rico, for whom the penny had not yet dropped, got in before me, filled with a doubtless prurient curiosity:

'So who is this utter bastard young De Vere has been fraternizing with? This is news to me. Come on, out with it, Dr Vidal, I love hearing about dirty deeds, even contemporary ones. They pale into insignificance beside the classics, of course, but it's better than a poke in the eye with a sharp stick, so chocks away and let the dog see the rabbit.' He had a penchant for idioms, sayings, proverbs and the like; some of which he invented or used in a way that was incomprehensible to me, I couldn't understand what those chocks, dogs and rabbits were doing there. He topped off his request with one of his indecipherable onomatopoeia: '*Fúrfaro*.'

'Why is he an utter bastard?' I finally managed to ask. 'As a doctor? That's not what people usually say about him. He's an expert in his field. And everyone says how well he behaved in the 1940s and 50s. I'm sure you've heard that too. It's true, isn't it, Professor? Isn't it true that Dr Van Vechten helped people who suffered reprisals after the War? Like your own family, José Manuel, you must know that. There are loads of testimonies to that effect.'

Vidal drew his chair closer to the table and lowered his voice a little, mainly, I assumed, given what he told us – although I assumed this only once I'd heard what he had to say – because we were in the Salamanca district, which, even now, is heaving with Nationalists nostalgic for the late dictator, even more at that time, when he'd only been dead for five years, which, to nearly all of us, felt more like twenty – so quickly, impatiently and eagerly had he been dispatched and forgotten.

'Yes, I know the story. That's the official version, the favourable version, the legend that has lingered on and which has suited him perfectly because it's meant he could be accepted everywhere. He's always played both sides off against each other, with no preference for either. He's clever, I can't deny that.'

'Come on, Dr Vidal, spill the beans. I'm all ears,' said Rico contentedly and as if the story were intended for him. He didn't seem to care two hoots or give a fig about his excellent relations with Van Vechten (those absurd idioms are as infectious as swear words, once they come into your mind).

'Look, Juan.' Fortunately, Vidal was still addressing me, with an expression that seemed genuinely concerned, even reproving. 'I don't know if you've heard, but I now work at the Hospital Anglo-Americano. Dr Naval took me with him when he was asked to take over as director there less than a year ago, and so we both left the Clínica Ruber, where he was the medical director and where I'd set up the ECG unit. Anyway, Naval had spent a lot of time in Chile.

He fled after the coup led by Pinochet because he was a prominent supporter of the Socialist Party, and he knows more than any of us about what people got up to here after the War. The people who left Spain after the War have put far more effort into finding out and remembering that kind of thing, whereas here we know almost nothing – well, it's so much easier to cover up uncomfortable facts. It's odd that Dr Bergaz, the owner of Clínica Ruber, who was an ardent *franquista*, should have appointed Naval as medical director, but that will give you some idea of how good he is. Lots of tales were told at the clinic, as happens everywhere, especially with a young man like me asking lots of questions. As you doubtless know, given your apparent friendship, Van Vechten worked as a paediatrician there for nearly twenty years; that's where he gained his reputation, and he still often drops by and he gets on very well with the staff there.' – That was the clinic Van Vechten had told Muriel to phone from the Hotel Wellington, because it was the closest one, saying: 'They all know me, I'll give any further instructions when I get there.' – 'Dr Naval is very discreet, but he couldn't even stand being in the same room with Van Vechten when he turned up at the clinic, slapping everyone on the back; he knew all about his past and couldn't resist telling me. Mind, he's not the only one who's told me things about him. I corroborated the stories later on, even with some of his biggest fans, who were full of admiration for what he'd done, at least for the first few years. Dr Teigell, for example.' Another foreign surname, it looked German to me when, later, I saw it written down. Vidal pronounced it Spanish-style: 'Teihell'.

'Listen, Doctor, I'm expected for lunch with three bores from the Real Academia,' Rico broke in rudely, looking at his watch. 'You'll either have to cut a long story short or I'll arrive late for my appointment and they'll have their claws out for me already. Which they tend to do anyway. So get to the point and don't stuff my head with a load of useless names I can't retain. So far, you've told me nothing new.'

Luckily, Vidal was a good-humoured fellow. He had instantly cottoned on to the Professor's style and rather liked it. He didn't take offence at all, but smiled.

'José Manuel,' I said, 'are you sure you don't mind the Professor hearing all this? I warn you, he's not known for his discretion.' This was a way of reclaiming the story, which was in principle intended for my ears only, Rico was merely a kind of stowaway.

Vidal laughed and happily agreed with him:

'The Professor is quite right, I'll get straight to the point. And if he hears it and tells other people, I have no problem with that. On the contrary, all the better. Van Vechten's hypocrisy is enough to rile anyone, as is that of his pal Arranz, another rich and famous paediatrician. There's not much you can do against such established reputations, but any reputation can be undermined a little, and the more people who know about his lies . . . well, at least then they'll have to think twice before boasting in public about their noble behaviour.'

'Arranz? Dr Carlos Arranz?' I couldn't help interrupting him, frustrating his promise to get straight to the point. I'd seen that name more than once, next to a doorway, on a plaque, followed by the words 'Medical Consultant'.

'Don't tell me he's a friend of yours too,' said Vidal. 'Things are worse than I thought. What are you doing hanging around with people like that? What world are you living in, Juan? Oh, I get it – it was because of their reputation as benefactors. A right pair of crooks, they are. They had everyone fooled, the bastards, I'll give them that.'

'That Arranz fellow, does he have a consulting room in Plaza del Marqués de Salamanca? At Number 2 to be exact.'

'I don't know, it's possible. I've never met the man, I only know what Dr Naval told me. And a couple of other people too, his name almost always crops up. He's not as famous as Van Vechten and he doesn't rub shoulders with society people, but he does pretty well, I'm sure. Do you go drinking with him as well? Just wait until you hear what I know about those two. Plus they're both about a thousand years older than you.' With this he only added fuel to the fire.

Rico sprang theatrically to his feet, cigarette in hand (he was a chain-smoker) and angrily flicked the ash on to the floor, despite there being two ashtrays on the table, or perhaps precisely because there were.

'Here ends my journey, which feels to me, gentlemen, to have lasted at least a thousand years,' he said. 'During the time I've been listening, six or seven doctors' names have emerged, if we include yours, Doctor, and you, to make matters worse, have two.' I had, it's true, introduced José Manuel as Vidal Secanell. 'Now I've no idea who Naval is or who Arranz is or Secanell or Vidal or even who Pinochet is or Teihell.' He pronounced the latter name exactly as he had heard it. He had, contrary to what he had just said, retained all the names perfectly and had made Pinochet a doctor. 'I'm off. I'm fascinated to find out more about Dr Van Vechten's dirty deeds, at least I know who *he* is, for my sins. But if you're never going to get started and keep going on about more medical nonentities, I can't allow myself to keep my pack of hounds waiting any longer just for your sake. The envious dimwits have got it in for me as it is. Enough said.' He pointed his cigarette at me as if it were a pencil and added: 'Young Vera, take note of everything your friend reveals and send me a detailed report. There's nothing like a list of crimes committed by a person one knows, whether true or false. Don't leave out a single detail.'

'A funny man, Professor Rico, very witty,' said Vidal once the Professor had departed, mumbling and grumbling. I watched him hail a taxi somewhat indolently despite his supposed haste, rather the way Hitler used to return the Nazi salute, with his hand bent backward instead of forward like the rest of the subordinate German populace. 'Is he always like that or was it just in my honour?'

'No, he's not always like that. He has a broad and varied repertoire. But you were telling me about Van Vechten,' I said, urging him on. 'Although, just to put your mind at rest, the only reason I've been going around with him at all is because I was asked to. He's a friend of my boss, Eduardo Muriel, the film director, who I've been working for lately as personal assistant, or, should I say, secretary. In fact, it was Muriel who asked me to draw Van Vechten out. Apparently, he had suspicions about something ugly in Van Vechten's past. I say "had" because not long ago, he told me to forget the whole business. He owes him favours old and new and has finally decided not to probe any deeper.'

'The usual story. He's got him fooled, as he has so many others. If you're the one who calls the shots and has absolute power, then you can dole out favours to your subjects and they'll be sure to gratefully kiss the hand of the tyrant for not being as cruel as he could be. So the idea here is that we shouldn't stir up the past. And that's probably

383

the sensible, more advisable approach. But these things should at the very least be known, don't you think? Sure, no one's going to be taken to court, that would be impossible and maybe it's just as well. But if I'm asked, I'm not going to keep quiet about what I know, so that at least they don't dish out the medals quite so easily.' Vidal was a friendly, rather benign fellow, but he was getting quite heated. Nevertheless, he still kept his voice low. 'Something ugly in his past, eh? You can't know for sure, nor can your boss probably, even though they know each other of old. Van Vechten has carefully buried any inconvenient truths, and he did so right from the start too, so he was very far-sighted really; it's the same with Arranz and so many others. You know that Catalan painter, what's his name now, the one they make all the fuss about, well, he was another card-carrying, gun-toting Falangist. No one knows that, or those who do keep it to themselves; we don't want to discredit one of our most acclaimed stars of the Left. People here have gone from being *franquista* to anti-*franquista* as if by magic, with the whole population believing them and applauding their sleight of hand, especially journalists. There's not much you can do about that. I mean, if it hadn't been for Dr Naval, who should take all the credit really (plus what my own family told me afterwards), I suppose I, too, would consider Van Vechten to be an example of generosity, reconciliation and decency in difficult times, always smiling and friendly whenever he visited the clinic. He used to slap me on the back too, even though I was a mere nobody. Yes, both men used to treat the families of those who, after the War, were stigmatized for having fought on the wrong side, right up until the early 60s, believe it or not, when the dictatorship eased off and those it had already destroyed had slowly been forgotten. Only those who benefitted from this know why and at what price. And of course part of the price was that none of this would ever

384

get out and only the public image would remain, the favourable image, the good reputation of those doctors from the winning side who treated children at home for free, without charging a peseta. The children of the enemy, no less, oh, they were exemplary men, Arranz and Van Vechten; and there must have been many more like them throughout Spain and in all kinds of professions (lawyers, notaries, policemen, judges, mayors, even minor civil servants). How many others must have taken advantage of that situation over the years, over the decades? Most didn't ask for money, they got paid in kind. Those two did anyway. They did very well out of those home visits. And they're the ones I'm talking about.'

'What do you mean "in kind", given that those families had little or nothing?'

'They had a past. They had secrets and they had women, Juan. That was quite enough,' said Vidal, and when he said this, a mist seemed to wrap about him, a mist of distaste, bitterness and long-postponed resentment, a resentment that would have to continue to be postponed, possibly for ever; he was exhaling that mist now, in private and almost in a whisper, as happens with very personal stories, which are the vast majority, and it's quite something to hear them at all, even in a whisper: very little is made public, little of what is of any interest, little of what people would like to know, we being so focused on our own lives, our own affairs, without much thought for others. Sometimes we do listen distractedly and with superficial curiosity or out of deference, but the affairs of others are never comparable to our own. Even if what is happening to them is desperate, sheer torment and what is happening to us is a passing petty triviality.

'I don't understand,' I said, but that wasn't really true. I was beginning to understand quite a lot or to piece things together and to imagine. Not only based on what Muriel had said to me before he changed his mind, but also on what Van Vechten himself had let slip on our nocturnal sorties, and the way he had behaved with my girl-friends (I suddenly wondered what he could have used to blackmail them), and on what I'd been told by the high-up civil servant with the glossy legs, Celia, about the time she went to him as a patient.

'Well, Van Vechten enlisted in Franco's army and stayed there throughout the War. He was very young at the time, he was born in 1918 or 1919, if I'm not mistaken. Apparently, when war broke out, he was at his parents' summer place in Ávila.' — Van Vechten's once-Flemish family, I recalled, came from Arévalo. — 'When the university was closed, he had already completed the first two years of a medical degree. As a university student, he was rapidly promoted to Acting Second Lieutenant. But I don't think he ever actually fought in the War. He was very young and thanks to the influence of his family, who were extremely right wing and well connected, he was immediately assigned to an intelligence unit, so he wouldn't have to risk his skin at the front. I'm not sure if he met Arranz there or later, it doesn't matter, perhaps they met at the so-called "Patriotic Exams" in 1940.' He made that awful gesture imported from America that people use to indicate quotation marks. I had no idea what those exams were, but I didn't want to interrupt him. 'He began collecting and filing away all the information he was given, some of which was passed to him by fifth columnists in Madrid when they could, or by others taking refuge in embassies and who received news from the outside world, and while some of this information was reliable, some of it was complete fantasy or a distortion of the facts. Much of that information was useless as long as Madrid remained in Republican hands, but would prove invaluable when the capital finally fell. He was one of the people in charge of storing, selecting

386

and ordering this information, and as soon as the city surrendered, he was able to do this unimpeded, all obstacles removed, and there was no shortage of the stuff either, because here, as everywhere, volunteers came crawling out of the woodwork to tell what had happened during the nearly three years of the War, both the true and the false, the population being eager to ingratiate itself and make amends. That's how he came to find out what numerous individuals had done and said; some had committed atrocities, others were merely sympathetic to the Republic or readers of a certain newspaper. The usual story of indiscriminate accusations. In short, when the War ended, Van Vechten was a man who knew a lot about a lot of people and, besides, it was easy enough to invent facts if you wanted to harm someone. If you could prove your loyalty to the regime, there was no need to provide proof of someone's misdemeanours; with very rare exceptions, an accusation was all it took. He collaborated with the police as necessary, giving them enough useful tip-offs for them to respect and believe him. Once the most urgent cleansing was done, I suppose he realized he could make use of his knowledge, long-term and for his own benefit, if he rationed it out. He went back to university and decided to specialize in paediatrics, and from then on it was plain sailing. In those "Patriotic or State Exams" in 1940' – Vidal again made the quotation-mark gesture presumably acquired during his time in Houston – 'after the university reopened in the autumn of 1939, those who had fought on the winning side and had, therefore, supported the Glorious Nationalist Movement, were given the "Patriotic Pass" for any exams they attended wearing their army uniform, some complete with cartridge belt and pistol. I learned all this from Dr Naval, who's about the same age as Van Vechten, maybe a couple of years younger, and who sat it out in Spain for a while until he was offered a post abroad and could leave thanks to a relative of his in the diplomatic service, who got him a passport. That's apparently how things worked, although nowadays it sounds like a bad melodrama or a caricature. Naval laughed a bit when he told me, imagining Van Vechten all got up in his second lieutenant's uniform for the exam, but, he thought, probably without his pistol, Van Vechten was canny enough even then to avoid such swaggering behaviour. Anyway, they gave him his degree, deeming him to have completed his studies.'

Vidal stopped speaking and took a long drink of his new and as yet untouched beer, and to give him more breathing space, rather than because I had anything to say that he didn't already know, or so I assumed, I said:

'Yes, I understand he had a brilliant career. I read that when he was only twenty-three, he was appointed Assistant Paediatrician at the Hospital de San Carlos and that, when he was only about thirty-one or so, in 1950, he opened a consulting room at the Clínica Ruber. Such precociousness could hardly have been the norm, not even then. With so many people dead or in exile or imprisoned and so many people like your grandfather, who was banned from practising as an ophthalmologist, they must have had to make do with whoever was available, plus, of course, they had to have a spotlessly *franquista* record. That would certainly have cut down the number of candidates. But that still can't be the whole explanation.'

'Yes, he was suspiciously precocious, but then he wasn't alone in that. Mainly, though, I'm just relieved to know that you're not completely in the dark about him, as I feared when I first saw you out partying with the bastard.'

'As I said, my boss asked me to befriend him and see what I could worm out of him. I have to say I didn't get very far. I gleaned all those facts about his life from *Who's Who*, and then Muriel pulled me up short, told me to leave him alone. That doesn't mean I don't want to know why, according to you, he's such an utter bastard. I did quite like him – sometimes – not that much, you understand, because there's also something chilling about him, something voracious, even when he's at his most friendly and paternal, offering fatherly advice. But then it's rare to meet anyone entirely devoid of charm. I even introduced him to a few of my female friends, but from what you say, I suspect they might not thank me for that. Am I right?' I suddenly felt alarmed and guilty. Perhaps I had unknowingly let a wolf in among the lambs.

'Yes, you are,' replied Vidal, frowning. 'Mind you, the man's older now and perhaps makes do with just looking. Let's hope so. What kind of relations did he have with those friends of yours? Do you know? Did you see for yourself?'

I was feeling increasingly uncomfortable.

'To my surprise, and if he's not lying and merely bluffing, he certainly got at least one of them to do much more than you'd ever imagine he could, given the enormous age gap. To be honest, I don't know how he did it.'

Vidal did not for one moment believe Van Vechten would have played by the book. His instant response was:

'He'll have threatened them with something, you can be sure of that.'

'With what though?'

'There's bound to be something. Do your friends take drugs? Do you all take drugs? Did he see you doing it?'

'In certain places, almost everyone takes drugs now, José Manuel, you know that as well as I do. Especially when you're out clubbing. I think Van Vechten himself, being a wealthy man, sometimes bought drugs for my various girlfriends or gave them drugs in small quantities, just as an enticement. It's a sure-fire way of winning people over or at least of wooing them. Well, a temporarily sure-fire way, because young people will flock to anyone who's got the stuff.'

'There you are, then. He'll have threatened to tell their parents: "As a doctor, I'm very worried about the company your daughter is keeping. I met her once through a young friend of mine . . ." etc. etc. And who are the parents going to believe, the famous Dr Van Vechten, celebrated paediatrician, or their crazy, nightclubbing daughter? He'll have taken care to give her the drug only when they're alone and with no witnesses. And if her parents are of the liberal variety, he'd threaten to report them to the police and get them into trouble, not deep trouble admittedly, but they might be frightened enough to want to avoid it in exchange for a small favour. The man's capable of anything. Or if a girl has had an abortion and been foolish enough to tell him about it, because you did say he offers fatherly advice, didn't you? He has the advantage of being a doctor, and I know from my own experience as a doctor that people do tend to ask your advice and even to confess. By the way, as a cardiologist, I would recommend giving up the drugs. Cocaine plays havoc with your blood pressure and your heart, if, that is, you're into coke. I'm not asking, mind. What you do is your own business. But people take these matters very lightly, and there are always consequences. Just so you know.'

I'm afraid I blushed a little, even though I took cocaine only rarely, if someone happened to offer me some, which was not that often. Van Vechten had never offered me any, of course, although I suspected that he used it himself, but I couldn't be sure. Perhaps he reserved it for those accompanied visits to the toilets and for when we did the home run in his car and he dropped off his final female passenger.

'OK, I'll make a note,' I said and rapidly changed the subject. 'But would he really go to the police? Would he be capable of that? Because girls nowadays aren't that easily intimidated.'

Vidal did not hold back. He really had it in for Van Vechten.

'It's the same now as it's always been, and fear doesn't take long to come back, you just have to feel exposed and helpless, or to be with someone who makes you feel afraid, and he's a past master at that. Look, I'm going to tell you what his so-called help consisted of, the famous solidarity that has given him such a good reputation among anti-*franquistas*, although you've probably worked that out for yourself. He would go and visit people he knew things about, people who had escaped the worst initially, but who still didn't dare poke their heads above the parapet. I'm talking about the 40s and 50s and even the very early 60s. People who had no money, who couldn't write anything under their own name, for example, even as translators, people who had to use a pseudonym on film scripts or articles, assuming any newspaper editor was brave enough to ask them to write one, or else they'd work illegally for someone just to earn a few pennies. Teachers who weren't allowed to teach, lawyers and architects and ophthalmologists, businessmen who had been barred from trading and had their business confiscated. As happened to people from my own family. It's true that he did tend and treat their children, but not in that legendarily selfless way, not for free. The stuff he could blackmail them with was far more serious than anything he might use against your young friends now, no, forget frigging drugs or parents.' Vidal was a cultivated man with a wide vocabulary, but this didn't mean he couldn't be foul-mouthed if the occasion called for it. 'He could threaten them with prison or even death, at least in the immediate post-War years, when the victors had no qualms about shooting people wholesale, in Madrid and elsewhere. He and Arranz swapped information and would take turns visiting when the other one got bored. And as far as I know, they didn't beat about the bush, they didn't bother with hints or innuendos. They were absolutely blunt about it, saying to some: "I know that, during the War, you did this and this, took part in illegal shootings or tipped off the militias, that you have blood on your hands," and to others: "I know you remained loyal to the Republic, that you wrote anonymous editorials for newspapers or broadcast propaganda programmes on the radio, that you worked for such and such a ministry, even if you were just a private and had been posted there and were simply obeying orders. That doesn't matter, it's enough for them to screw you good and proper. I pass on a lot of information to the police and what I say goes, it never fails. It's taken me a while to find you, but I know exactly what you did during the War. And even if you'd done much less it would be the same. In your case, I don't even need to invent very much, just exaggerate a little. I could easily say that you collaborated with the Russians or that you condemned half your neighbours to being shot and left in the gutter. Just as you might have done with me if you'd had the chance; who knows what would have happened if you'd caught me here at the time of the uprising. A few years have passed since then, but if I blab to the people who are always happy to listen to what I have to say, it's the firing squad for you or else life imprisonment, and why would I keep quiet? So it's up to you: you either have a bit of a hard time accepting my conditions or you stop having any time at all, either good, bad or indifferent. You certainly won't see your wife and children again, that's for sure. Never – or at least not for a very long time. You decide." '

Vidal Secanell fell silent for a few moments, staring down at the table, wide-eyed, at the ashtrays used by Professor Rico and by me, for we had been smoking as we drank. He had spoken almost without pausing for breath, as if he himself had once heard such a speech, but even though he came from a family that had suffered reprisals, this seemed unlikely. I had always thought of his father, Vidal Zapater, a friend of my aunt and uncle, as being very well-off and as having a certain Mexican arrogance (quickly acquired), a man with no financial problems and not easily intimidated either – quite the opposite. His grandfather was a different matter, although Vidal, who was born in 1950 or '51, would probably not have witnessed a scene like the one he had just enacted: parents then concealed everything from their children, especially the truly shameful things. Those were very different times: no one confessed to a humiliation, even if they had been repeatedly, horribly humiliated. Now there's nothing more profitable than declaring yourself to be a victim, subjugated and downtrodden, and to whinge on about your own misfortunes. It's odd that pride should have disappeared so completely, when, during the post-War years, those on the losing side were very proud indeed, and didn't even talk about their dead or those in prison, as if doing so – even in private – were a dishonour in itself, almost a recognition, an acknowledgement of the side that had humiliated them and of their continued power to do harm. They didn't keep quiet purely out of fear and so as not to refresh the memories of those who still had the capacity to inflict fear, to increase and augment it, but so as not to give their enemies that pleasure and not to have to bow their heads still lower by complaining.

'And what were those conditions?' I asked, in order to draw him out of that lost stare. 'Although I can well imagine.'

Vidal was by nature more pragmatic than meditative, and so he quickly returned from his momentary absence.

'You imagine quite rightly. The condition was that they could screw their women.' He used that crude verb as if it were the one Arranz and Van Vechten would have used themselves, as he immediately confirmed. 'That's what they proposed, apparently, with no beating about the bush, no circumlocutions, no attempt at delicacy. And with no hypocrisy either, although, in the circumstances, I'm not sure that was a virtue. They'd screw the wives or, later on, an older daughter. They converted them into objects, into money, which wasn't really that unusual at the time, I suppose, especially when one part of the population was so vulnerable. And they screwed them as often as they wanted and until they got bored. Always assuming they fancied the women, of course, found them desirable. If they didn't, then those families might well be left with no medical care for their children, because, as I said, these were people with nothing, with no other way of paying. They might have a valuable painting they'd managed to hold on to, a *bargueño* desk they'd inherited, a few jewels or antiquarian books they'd kept, although, after three years of siege, it was unlikely they'd have anything left, most people had

395

sold all their valuable possessions. And then, on top of all that, they had to agree not just to say nothing about the transaction, the blackmail, but actively to boost the doctors' reputations and spread the word that, despite being friends of the regime, the two paediatricians were altruistic and compassionate, conciliatory and civilized, and treated their children for free. I don't know about Arranz, although I imagine the same applies to him, but that arrangement has really helped Van Vechten socially. Well, you know how it is. It's the same with all those professors, historians, novelists and painters who supported Franco and served him during the cruellest decades of his regime, and who, with passing time, once it was no longer dangerous, have declared themselves, nominally at least, to be left-wingers. And now they claim to have been lifelong dissidents, to have lived in exile, to have been censored. I find that Catalan painter, whatever his name is, particularly infuriating. And that ugly, bald philosopher who preaches about ethics and whose name I can't remember either. Naval knows all about it, about what really happened, what each one did and said and where they were. And don't, whatever you do, consider denouncing Van Vechten publicly, because the left-wingers would be the first to leap like lions to his defence and throw it back in your face, accusing you of trying to discredit and tarnish the reputation of one of their own – one of their own since the day before yesterday. Can you believe it? People who have always known which side their bread was buttered on, both in the 1940s and now.'

At the time, I wasn't much interested in what he said; later on, I was, when it was too late to unmask anyone and, besides, who really wants to take on that role, even now, all these years after the War, after so many falsified biographies, embellished legends and deliberate or collective forgetting. Hardly anyone cares about all that now – certainly no one who's semi-young – or only in an artificial, dubiously idealistic way; and hardly anyone else who's alive today. The dead stop telling their stories once they are just that, dead.

'And the women went along with it?' I was much more interested in that part of what Vidal was telling me. Van Vechten couldn't have submitted Beatriz to that kind of blackmail: she had got married in 1961 or '62, and Muriel was a child during the War, and his anti-Francoism had always been more intellectual than active. But I couldn't help thinking about her. Why would she go and see Dr Arranz, Van Vechten's old sidekick, because it was probably him she visited in Plaza del Marqués de Salamanca, not Mollá or Deverne or Gekoski or Kociejowski. Perhaps it was merely a matter of habit: perhaps the two men continued to share women, even though the sex was now free and not some form of payment. And maybe Beatriz really didn't care, like certain vengeful women who have grown weary of their woeful bed, so long as she herself didn't have to go looking for the instrument of revenge, which can be very depressing.

Vidal rolled his eyes with their large Paul McCartney eyelids. I could see him thinking: 'God, you're naive.'

'Of course they did, Juan, don't you see? They had no choice. On the one hand, their husband or father could go straight to prison – if they were lucky – on the other hand, what mother wouldn't do whatever it took; what mother wouldn't see it as a blessing being able to call out a paediatrician, knowing that he would come at once whenever their child was burning up with fever or at death's door? I'm afraid many would have been willing to do as much even without the threats. Mothers are prepared to do anything, they're hostages to fortune, although there are always notable exceptions. Some might even have felt grateful . . . in a mechanical, reflex-reaction way. Having sex with the person who cures your children isn't the worst thing that

397

can happen to a woman, not from her point of view.' – 'And I can assure you most of them do want to do it', the few revelatory words the Doctor had let slip on one of our nocturnal sorties came back to me. – 'I assume they also counted on that, Van Vechten and Arranz, on the inevitable gratitude, the relief of seeing a sick child out of danger, the slow realization that he was safe. And, as time passed, on familiarity and habit. It wouldn't surprise me to learn that they had planted a child in one or two of those families, if they didn't get bored too soon and if they weren't careful. And too bad if the child was born very blond and the theoretical father was very dark.'

This reminded me of that brief encounter with the veteran whore in Chicote. 'I know you, don't I? I remember those blue, blue eyes and that blond hair,' she had said to the Doctor. He wasn't easy to forget, with that baguette on his head.

'What I don't understand is why Van Vechten was so desperate,' I said. 'Not that I consider him attractive, there's even something rather repellent about him, I think. But with that yellow hair and those pale, watery eyes, with that perennial, rectangular smile and his large build, he must have been very striking as a young man and would have been a hit with women. You wouldn't think he would need to use threats to get them into bed.'

This time, Vidal did not hold back. Like I say, he treated me like a younger brother with whom he had lived on and off.

'I didn't think you were so innocent, Juan. You've seen the way he behaves around women, haven't you? With your own friends, I understand, and they're young enough to be his daughters. He's an insatiable predator and always has been, that part of his reputation is true; he's the kind who keeps a tally of how many women he's had sex with. You surely don't think that in the 1940s and 50s there were many women prepared to go all the way, just like that and willingly.

Not for pleasure or love or anything. Do you honestly imagine that the sexual revolution was up and running and that the pill already existed? It was really difficult to get laid in Spain. You had to waste a lot of time and make a lot of promises, and even then. Ask the nurses at the Hospital de San Carlos and at the Clínica Ruber, even at the Hospital Francisco Franco, where he landed up when he was older, as Head of Paediatrics no less, with even more power, of course, and in more liberated days too, at the end of the 60s or thereabouts. He tried it on with all of them, those worth having, that is; tastefully and not so tastefully, forcefully and not so forcefully, and with more or less success; and he's still doing it in his sixties. He'll never stop.'

I suddenly thought of Celia the civil servant, the bullfighter Viana's girlfriend. Her verdict had been: 'He's a bit of an old lecher,' and she had gone on to say: 'It seemed to me that he touched me more than was necessary, a woman notices these things straight away . . . he'd stroke my abdomen as if his fingers were about to go where they shouldn't . . . and he kept brushing my breasts with the sleeve of his white coat or with his wrist, as though by accident . . . I felt sort of queasy when I left . . . I felt like I'd been groped.' And that had happened during a brief medical examination. And she wasn't the kind of woman to imagine such things, nor was she a prude.

'I see,' I said slowly. 'He's obviously not one to miss a trick.' And I blushed a little, thinking that perhaps already, at the age of twenty-three, I, too, was not one to miss a trick. I suppose I at least had the excuse of youth. And I had never blackmailed or threatened anyone.

'And never underestimate the added pleasure of domination, of humiliating the defeated,' Vidal went on, and his tone grew more bitter. 'Screwing someone's wife or daughter with his knowledge and with him unable to do a thing about it. The man's a complete and utter bastard. Have nothing more to do with him. Admittedly, he may have changed radically since then, I'm not saying he hasn't; maybe other people's false perception of him has led him to fit himself to that mould and become a genuine conciliator and even a very belated anti-*franquista*. Always remember, though, that at the time he wasn't. Then it was all a front and to him those cuckolds were the enemy, defeated, but nonetheless the enemy. He must have loved it. The very thought enrages me, but what can you do, that's how things stand now. And it's probably for the best. But I'm determined to tell the story, and whatever I know I tell.'

Vidal's eyes once again fixed on the tabletop, on the ashtrays and the beers the waiter had just brought us.

'Do you know a place called the Sanctuary of Our Lady of Darmstadt?' I asked suddenly. I could see he knew a lot of things. 'Not far from here –'

He looked up and, interrupting me, said:

'Yes, I've often walked past it. And wait, I've heard Dr Naval mention it, now what did he say exactly? Oh, I know. I think it's a branch or a replica of another sanctuary of the same name, in Chile. And it was founded by Germans, I believe, who settled there in the 1940s and 50s. Hence the name, I suppose; so the Chilean sanctuary is probably a replica too.' – I'd seen the name 'Father Gustavo Hörbiger' on one of the signs at the sanctuary: a Hispanicized form of an undeniably German name. – 'And it's run by some Apostolic Movement . . .' Vidal was trying to remember as he spoke. 'No, I don't know, I'd have to ask Naval, who mentioned it to me once, but I wasn't really paying attention and now I can't recall what he said. However, I've an idea that some of Pinochet's high-ranking officers and even some of his ministers belong to that movement.' – Pinochet's dictatorship was still going strong in 1980 and would for a while longer. Five years earlier, Pinochet had turned up in Madrid to attend Franco's funeral, wrapped in a sinister Dracula cloak and wearing the kind of dark glasses blind men wear, the living image of a humanoid bat in a peaked cap. – 'Why do you ask?'

'I've occasionally seen Van Vechten there.'

'What, as a member of the congregation?'

'No, in one of the outbuildings, as if he had a practice there, or an office. He seemed very at home.' – Vidal couldn't know just how at home, and I wasn't going to tell him.

He gave a mischievous smile, then let out a faint whistle. He hadn't once raised his voice, not even when he was at his most vehement.

'Well, I didn't know that, and Naval may not know it either. If it's true, then Van Vechten probably hasn't changed one bit and it's all a front. Or else he preserves certain old loyalties. The place is, of course, ultra-Catholic and probably ultra-right-wing, the two tend to go hand in hand. He may treat the children of the faithful now and then, as a favour or a contribution to the cause, or to the Virgin: doubtless the children of powerful families, pleased as punch to enjoy the services of the great paediatrician. Who knows? If you like, I can ask Dr Naval and report back. He'll be pleased to know anyway. He's interested in anything to do with Chile, for obvious reasons.'

He again sat staring into space, but this time he was smiling, as if anticipating how much all this would intrigue or amuse his mentor or teacher, who had fled Chile after the coup. Then he gestured to the waiter to bring the bill. It had grown late and his colleagues had left some time before, waving to him from a distance.

'One last thing, José Manuel.'

'What's that?'

'Do you know the name of any of Van Vechten's victims? If you wouldn't mind telling me, of course. I might be able to drop it into

401

the conversation one day, as if by chance, spontaneously. Just to see how he reacts.'

He thought for a moment, but only that.

'I don't imagine it much matters if you know it now,' he said. 'A cousin of my father's, married to a former anarchist who escaped the firing squad and the purges, she was one of their victims. A very sweet woman, whom I knew really well. Both of them had her, Arranz first and then Van Vechten. Like I said, they passed the women on to each other. They took turns, now you, now me, until they grew bored. Carmen Zapater was her name. Aunt Carmen. She's dead now. Although her children are still alive, the ones for whom she sacrificed herself with such repugnance. But with relief too, let's be fair.'

So that's how he knows, I thought. And perhaps that's why he feels so bitter too. His Aunt Carmen.

I didn't care about Muriel's instructions then, didn't care that he had so vehemently retracted his orders. What Vidal had told me seemed grave enough and coincided sufficiently with my boss's initial suspicions, and with the accusations he had heard, for me to feel obliged to tell him. And it was interesting enough in itself for me to impose my discovery on him if he showed no interest, if what I said didn't once again arouse his curiosity and convince him to listen to me. Strictly speaking, and legally speaking too, it was all rumour, but we tend to believe what we are told, and neither Vidal nor Naval had any reason to lie. I was burning to reveal all to Muriel, but in his frenetic activity – his response to being fired by Towers – he distanced himself from the apartment and from me, and so I barely saw him. He had been very generous, allowing me an indefinite period of time in which to find another job; I didn't want to abuse that generosity, though, nor have him pay my wages when it was clear he wasn't going to need me, or not very much. It was early July or so and, in August, everything would stop anyway, and so I gave myself until the end of September to dismiss myself. I visited various publishing houses to see if they would take me on in some role, most likely as a translator. Manuel Arroyo Stephens of Turner Books – who was fascinated when he found out who I was working for (he was an ardent admirer, of whom there were still quite a few) – suggested that I put together two bilingual anthologies of short stories by British and American writers, partly for students of English. It was better than nothing, and although it didn't guarantee a fixed income, it would do to be going on with and would provide me with a way into the world of publishing.

I held back and decided not to force that conversation with Muriel, but to wait a while. For Vidal to come back with more information if, as promised, he did consult the Spanish Chilean Dr Naval. And to sound out Van Vechten with the facts I now had to hand. He kept urging me to go out with him, almost every other night or indeed every night, he had acquired a taste for the partying ethos of the time and its effervescent bars and clubs. And although he could perfectly well have gone on his own, it wasn't the same, he said, as when we went together. I put him off for a few days. Until Vidal, true to his word, phoned me.

'Juan,' he said, 'I've spoken to Dr Naval. He confirmed what I told you about Darmstadt; the movement, whose name was on the tip of my tongue before, is known as El Movimiento Apostólico de Darmstadt. It has its remote roots in Germany, but it's now very firmly established in Latin America. There are replicas of the famous sanctuary not just in Chile, but in Uruguay, Brazil, Paraguay, Argentina and probably elsewhere. Along with a few in Africa and Asia, as well as in Europe. There are more than a hundred of them scattered round the world, so quite a number. They also run or control a few schools; in fact, there's one quite near here, in Aravaca or Majadahonda or Pozuelo, one of those wealthy areas, he couldn't quite remember which. And as I thought, among its so-called "Servants of the Virgin" or its prominent members are a couple of Pinochet's ministers, Chilean politicians and businessmen, as well as a cardinal and an archbishop; and it has some connections with one of the generals

404

responsible for the "Caravan of Death", which saw the cold-blooded murder of seventy or more prisoners in October 1973, shortly after the coup; you know, mass executions with no trial or anything, as happened here in 1939, which served them as a distant model. Naval could easily have met with the same fate if he hadn't managed to get out of the country immediately after the coup. That same "Caravan of Death" general has stated that what helps him sleep peacefully in his bed at night is knowing that the fervent folk in the Sanctuary of Darmstadt are all praying for him. A close relative of Pinochet's wife – a priest, apparently, who died some time ago – also belonged to the Movimiento Apostólico. Naval was delighted to learn that Van Vechten has an office there or whatever. Well, I don't know if "delighted" is the word. He thinks, as I do, that Van Vechten holds a more or less symbolic consulting room there, perhaps a couple of hours a week or a fortnight, just to keep in with them. He's going to investigate further, if he can, just out of curiosity. But you can see the kind of people your friend hangs out with. It's not hard to imagine what the faithful Spanish flock must be like, given its Chilean membership. Old loyalties and friendships on the part of your Doctor, if we're being kind. Old beliefs, if we're not. Who knows.'

That was the moment to start going out with Van Vechten again, at least one more time; that whole business weighed on me, for one rarely emerges clean or unscathed from such investigations. And he weighed on me still more: there are some people from whom you want to remove yourself at once, to erase them urgently from your life if possible. Regardless of whether or not it was all true, the stain described by Vidal contaminated everything, and even Beatriz and Muriel began to seem somewhat oppressive, despite my fondness for them both, my veneration for him and my growing affection for her – not just sexual, not at all, but always tinged with pity. They were the people who had got me involved, who had introduced me to the Doctor; Muriel had charged me with unpleasant missions only to relieve me of them subsequently, and Beatriz was having sex with Van Vechten and possibly with Arranz, the other doctor, and with me too, although just that once, and so I was vaguely like those two lechers, to use Celia the civil servant's word. As a couple, they had spotted me like one of those distant shapes on the ocean that can't be ignored and had afforded me a glimpse into the long and indissoluble misery that was their marriage. I thought it was no bad thing that Muriel should get rid of me and remove me from the social world in which I had felt welcomed as a fascinated and privileged guest. But I should first inform him, share with him my stroke of luck and reveal or confirm to him the kind of man his friend was, so that he, too, could remove himself from his company and say, 'I don't know you' or 'I don't wish to continue to know you', and perhaps Beatriz would then imitate him, she with far more reason, as the one who went to the Sanctuary and who allowed him to do to her what his former victims, mothers or daughters, had not been able to say No to.

I arranged to have a drink with Van Vechten at our usual bar, Chicote, as a preamble to a tour of various discos and dives, because some places only started to get lively very late and you had to kill time until gone midnight. However impatient he felt, we had to wait. He inquired briefly about Beatriz, whom he hadn't seen for days, to ask how she was doing. He inquired about my future and my plans, knowing that I would soon be leaving both the job and the apartment, the house in Calle Velázquez, which is always there in my memory, even after all these years, inhabited by the people who inhabited it then. He inquired after Maru and the sometime waitress Bettina, about García Lorca's niece and other acquaintances of mine, none of whom he had seen in the places he had gone to on his own or in the reluctant company of Rico and Roy: as if all my friends had disappeared during the few weeks I was keeping careful watch over Beatriz. I allowed him to ask me questions before I asked him anything or mentioned the names of people or places that might embarrass or disconcert him. I didn't know how to begin, I didn't dare. I could find no valid reason for leading the conversation in that direction, not at least in any natural way. And so I took advantage of a lull in the conversation to leap in without any preamble and to come straight to the point:

'The other day, a friend mentioned you and your heroic work helping people who, for political reasons, were having a hard time after the War. Apparently, you often visited an aunt of his, or, rather, her children. Her husband had been an anarchist and, by some miracle, had survived the War, but he couldn't find any work at all. My friend told me that, if it hadn't been for you, one of his cousins might have died all those years ago, when he was only a baby.'

Van Vechten broadened his almost fake smile, but I saw no sign of pleasure on his face. He seemed to be gritting his teeth, and his jaw looked even squarer than usual, his chin more protuberant, as if it had grown in size, his whole face flushed as his muscles tensed. He sat looking at me hard with his pale, cold, somewhat defiant eyes, as though he could see where I was going and wasn't about to fall into my trap. While others may have praised his past behaviour, he himself never mentioned it, or not at least in my presence. He, of course, knew what he had remained silent about and the price paid for each of those visits, and he knew that the families he had visited were the only ones who also knew that this was no rumour. It was only natural that he should be on his guard. Always assuming Vidal's story was true.

'Oh, please, let's not talk about that,' he said modestly, and gestured with his hand as if dismissing the importance of his past actions. His large hand. 'And there was nothing heroic about it. Others did the same.'

'Very few from what I've heard, and at the risk of losing your privileges too,' I said, and there I saw my chance to slip in the first name. 'My friend also praised a colleague of yours, with whom you took turns looking after his aunt, I mean, her children, a certain Dr Carlos Arranz. What became of him? You're really well known as a paediatrician and for what you did after the War, but I've never heard of him. Did things go badly for him? Was he punished?'

'Ah, yes, Arranz,' Van Vechten replied, as if he were travelling far back in time, and without once taking his inquisitive gaze off me. I was sure now that he was beginning to feel genuinely suspicious, that he already was suspicious; at that point, I didn't care since I had no intention of ever seeing him again on my own. 'I don't know, I lost touch with him years ago. But let's drop the subject, shall we? I don't care to remember those dark times. You weren't there, but believe me, they were very dark days indeed.'

I had decided that once I was on that path, I would keep straight ahead, and I felt it was the right moment to mention the second name I was holding in reserve. Who knows, I might succeed in unnerving him, in jolting him back into the past, or alarming or angering him, and his response, whatever it was, would be sure to betray him. Haste is very much a part of being young – wretched speed, damned haste – as is a lack of planning.

'The aunt's name was Carmen Zapater. Do you remember her? A very sweet, very pretty woman he said.' I added 'pretty' because I assumed she would have been: if Arranz had told Van Vechten about her and handed her over to him, there must have been a reason. Word spreads quickly among men. As if she had been another Mariella

Novotny to those two doctors, but not of her own choosing, against her will. There must have been many such women over a period of many years, when women tended not to earn their own money or to have it, and when they only had themselves. Although, I don't know why I'm talking in the past tense, because there are still thousands of women for whom the only way of paying their debts is to hire themselves out.

'No, I can't say that I do,' said the Doctor. 'The name sounds vaguely familiar, but I can't put a face to it. Besides, we tend to know only the husband's surname, not the wife's. And though I shouldn't say it myself, during that period, I did visit a lot of families in very similar circumstances, in my role as paediatrician, and I continued to do so into the early 60s. A lot of people had a really tough time of it.'

'Yes, I can imagine. People would have been prepared to do anything just to survive or at least for their children to survive.'

Van Vechten could have no doubt now as to what I was getting at. Perhaps I was showing my cards too quickly, but by then, I was sick to death of the whole business and didn't care. I just wanted confirmation from him, or some unmistakable sign, some clear indication, so that I could legitimately go to Muriel with the story. The Doctor's eyes were now almost colourless, glacial, yes, glacial, although they retained a certain southern intensity – a frightening and repellent combination. They must have looked like that, or worse, when he made his demands of the women he treated as mere objects. He had been in an intelligence unit during the War and had gone on to become an informer. He knew a lot, and he managed or used that information for his own blackmailing purposes, that was the sordid story. Perhaps he had looked at my girlfriends in that way too, certainly one of them, when the two of them were alone in the car after he had dropped off all the other partygoers.

'What exactly are you insinuating, young De Vere? Don't tell me someone has come to you with these ancient slanders.'

'Slanders? I don't know what you mean, Jorge?' I chose to call him by his first name so as momentarily to calm the situation. Or to assuage his Robert J. Wilke eyes, which were hard to bear.

'Yes, slanders spread by Franco's real hard-line supporters, who disapproved of what I was doing, I mean, the consideration I showed for my patients and my gradual withdrawal from the regime. They claimed I was being paid in kind for the favours I did. My pound of Red flesh, at least that was the running joke. What surprises me is that you should have heard it in 1980. It seems that nothing in this country ever ends or disappears, especially anything negative or harmful. Not to mention false. I can't understand why you gave it any credence. You young people are so impressionable.'

I tried to play the innocent and not give too much away. I hadn't heard those stories from Franco supporters, but from people whose lives those same supporters had made impossible, sometimes forcing them into exile; or from ordinary people like Celia and a suspicious Muriel or, indirectly, from that sometime actress, the love of Muriel's life. I didn't want to expose Vidal, of course, or his mentor Dr Naval, who had fled first Spain and then Chile. Van Vechten and he knew each other and had worked at the same clinic, although at different times.

'I'm not insinuating anything, Doctor, nor do I have anything to do with any hard-line Franco supporters. I don't know a single one.' I addressed him by his title this time, in a friendly fashion, but I wanted him also to feel a certain coldness on my part. 'I'm just remembering something you said to me once and making a few connections.'

'What did I say? I've never said anything of the sort.'

'You were speaking about women and how to get them into bed, Maestro,' I said. We forget more of what comes out of our mouths than what enters our ears, and so he had no idea what I was talking about. 'You said: "There's nothing more satisfying than when a girl doesn't want to do it, but can't say No." And then you spoke about the resentment they feel because "the very first time, they had no choice". That, more or less, is what you said. "Obliged", you said. "But can't say No", you said.' I repeated what he had said, underlined it. 'What other interpretation could I give those words?'

The Doctor hesitated for a few seconds. In the light of what I had been told and what he had guessed, in the light of the vengeful rumours spread, according to him, by former comrades, those words sounded very bad, even though they had been spoken at a different time and in another context. He must have realized that they sounded almost like a confession, an acknowledgement, he must have seen them as ugly and besmirching. He recovered at once, however, and laughed out loud, all congeniality and good nature, revealing his healthy, dazzling teeth in all their glory, his protuberant chin gleaming.

'What nonsense is this, Juan? I was just talking for the sake of it and we were joking, weren't we, you were pulling my leg. You've certainly got a good memory, though. I'd completely forgotten ever having said that. I was talking about the kind of girls who go all prudish and play hard to get and object if you insist, so as not to appear too easy if they're young, or adulterous if they're married. Every married woman will tell you: "It's the first time anything like this has ever happened to me, I can't understand why it's happening now." They need you to believe it or to believe it themselves. And of course you pretend to believe them, so that they can feel they emerge from the situation smelling of roses and generally feel relaxed about

411

the whole thing. Women may be less fastidious nowadays, but it was different in my youth. And young women, girls like your friends, for example, have to justify it to themselves before they give in to someone like me, a man twice their age or more, someone they consider to be an old man: he begged me, he insisted, he tricked me, he made me feel sorry for him. It's all a matter of flattering them. That's all I meant. And there you go putting a sinister interpretation on it. You and your conspiracy theories.' And he slapped me on the arm with his great hand, and either he misjudged it or else he did so on purpose, because it really hurt, and I saw that he hadn't intended it as a friendly gesture at all. He tried to pass it off as one, fixing me with his unvaryingly cordial smile, his large, rectangular incisors, that smile that had so eased his way with mothers and children and his superiors. But the smile wasn't cordial at all, it was angry and possibly alarmed.

I came very close to pitying him for having suddenly to consider himself an old man and having to admit it openly, someone reduced to spending what remained of his life merely admiring – or possibly entreating – not only young women, but almost any woman. Successful men take their decay very hard, it's not easy to recover from rejection if you're not used to it. I realized, too, that he was one of those men whom old age betrays by failing to teach them the usual lessons or quieting their passions and, instead, preserves their ambition and their energy rather than making them slower or more docile. And so it gradually undermines them, but without giving them any warning. I shook off that shadow of pity, however; after all, how could a man so unaware of the passage of time suddenly present himself as time's victim in the middle of a conversation that was highly embarrassing for him? I thought: 'He's resorting to trickery, he's defending himself. There is, as I've always felt, something voracious and troubling about him, and I mustn't allow myself to be deceived.' And in view of his denial, I decided, without further delay, to mention the third name and not bother waiting for some meandering path that would lead me to the Sanctuary:

'You're a religious man, Jorge.'

This was half-statement, half-question. And whichever it was, he was momentarily taken aback. His laugh lingered on a little, like a mechanism that takes a while to stop. But if it had been a cadaverous laugh to begin with, it was now the laugh of a dead man.

'What's that got to do with anything? What kind of a question is that?'

'I've seen you at the Sanctuary of Our Lady of Darmstadt, and so I assume you're very religious. You must be extremely devout to belong to the Apostolic Movement.'

His expression changed, he cancelled that now defunct smile and buried it once and for all, or at least for what remained of the night. He clearly didn't like me knowing that fact.

'You've seen me there? Seen me doing what?' His tone of voice was one of fear and scepticism.

'I often go to the Museo Lázaro Galdiano, which is almost next door.' I hesitated. I waited. What emerged from my lips next was not what I was planning to say at all, it simply escaped my wretched tongue. 'I saw you with Beatriz. I saw you in your consulting room.'

There was no jokey shove this time, that belonged to quite another sphere of behaviour. He took advantage of the fact that we were sitting on one of Bar Chicote's semicircular seats – almost like seats on a train or a tram – to place one of his large hands on my shoulder. As I said, when he did this apparently affectionately, it was as if his great paw had fallen from a considerable height and then gripped me like claws or talons, provoking in me an immediate urge to shrug it off and free myself from both its weight and grip. This time it was worse, I experienced a real pressure, an unmistakable threat. Van Vechten was strong and well built, he was, you might say, squeezing my shoulder, twisting it, bearing down on me, so much so that I felt I wouldn't be able to get up from my seat, that my whole body was powerless against that great weight. He was really hurting me, more than he had before and the pain was more prolonged. I imagined how that hand would have rested on the shoulders of the timid, while he gave them two options: 'So it's up to you: you either have a bit of a hard time accepting my conditions or you stop having any time at all, either good, bad or indifferent.' And he whispered in a very slow, unnaturally calm voice (but since he was normally such an expansive man, he was unused to whispering and his voice sounded like sandpaper):

'Listen, young De Vere, just watch what you say. Be very careful what you tell people. You wouldn't want to harm someone you shouldn't harm. Or even several people.'

I managed to slide sideways to the other end of the semicircular seat, beyond his reach. An old waiter with a napkin draped over one arm was keeping a watchful eye on us, he must have been sensitive to any tensions, able to sniff out a brawl before it happened. Van Vechten wasn't going to intimidate me, young people are such unconscious beings that they often fail to notice when they're in danger. And I was convinced I was in charge of the situation. I even thought he might offer me something in exchange for my silence, once his anger had passed and he had recovered from the shock.

'If you mean Beatriz, forget it. Who could possibly be interested?'

'Exactly, who could possibly be interested?'

And I replied coolly:

'No one, as far as I know. Absolutely no one. It's that curious place that interests me. A strangely neat and tidy place, with a devout, almost fundamentalist air about it; a Germanic air from another age.'

He was still preoccupied by the carnal aspect of the matter and by his friend's wife, and hadn't realized that this was a secondary issue for me, part of his private life, about which one should never speak – a rule almost no one obeys. It was as if his amazement at my having seen them together prevented him from making the connection between the supposed calumnies about his remote past to which I had only alluded – I hadn't actually *said* anything – and his duties there in the Sanctuary in 1980. Maybe that connection was an indication that he had never entirely changed, I mean that he hadn't even changed sides, despite his reputation and his friends and despite appearances. At the time, people in Spain lived in permanent fear that a *coup d'état* might, any day, return us to a dictatorship. Indeed, later on, there were two attempted coups, the second being the most famous.

'What did you see? And how did you see it?' asked the bemused sandpaper voice. Even though we weren't as close to each other as before, he was still speaking in a whisper. He must have assumed that no one could possibly have seen them from outside.

'I saw everything. Not exactly romantic, I must say.' I added that last impertinent comment so that he would know I wasn't bluffing. 'It was pure chance. I just happened to look in. And there's a particular corner . . .' I wasn't going to tell him the truth, nor that I had climbed a tree, although if I hadn't done that, I doubt I would have seen his face. And then I returned to the important, revealing fact: 'As I understand it, that place, the Sanctuary, is a branch office of Pinochet's supporters. And you know who their allies are here in Madrid. I'm sure Muriel would like to know about those connections of yours, Doctor. And with good reason. So as to know where he stands.'

Van Vechten turned pale, finally understanding the intent behind my possible indiscretion. First, he came up with an excuse, then he got a grip on himself. First, he felt afraid, then he tried to make me afraid.

'I'm just doing a favour for an old friend of mine, a priest, and he has absolutely nothing to do with politics. I'm not religious, but neither do I interfere with other people's beliefs. Nor do I have to answer to a little squirt like you.' That was when he recovered his sangfroid. He slithered over towards me, his great paw outstretched, doubtless intending to grab me again, though who knows where. However, before he could reach me, I leapt up and removed myself from the semicircle. The waiter shot us another glance. 'I'm warning you, Juan, be careful what you say. There's a good and a bad way of telling things and a good and a bad way of listening – *and* of understanding. So best not say anything, all right?' And when I said nothing at all, but just stood there looking him up and down as if dumbstruck, he added: 'Do you understand me, boy?'

I left no money on the table, he was much richer than me. That night's odyssey was obviously not going to take place, unless he went alone.

'Still doing people favours, eh, Doctor?' I said as I was about to make for the bar's revolving doors. 'From 1939 until now. How very exhausting.'

VIII

When you're impatient to see someone or to reveal what you've discovered, you also tend to put off the moment for as long as possible.
Although only, of course, when you're sure that sooner or later you'll
see the person and be able to tell them your story. If there's any doubt
about this, then haste takes over and things happen in a rush, usually
with disappointing results, anticlimax and frustration. I could afford
to postpone my encounter with Muriel, to prepare for it and savour it
beforehand; to wait until that period of frenetic activity ended and he
spent a little more time at home. Besides, during those febrile days,
full of brief entrances and continual exits, it wouldn't have been a
good idea to force him to stop, to sit or lie down on the floor and then
listen to me for a good long while, entirely against his will. (A prior
period of boredom is vital to awakening curiosity and invention.) If,
that is, he would agree to hear what I'd found out about Van Vechten,
and I thought he would if I insisted and managed to intrigue him. I
had to wait for him to calm down, for him to sort out the financing of
this new, angrily urgent project or for him to give it up as impossible
and resign himself to that for the moment and perhaps until after the
summer. The delay suited me, since I was in no particular hurry, but
was rather enjoying that pleasurably expectant, alert state of impatience when you feel absolutely certain that your impatience will
finally be assuaged.

I had felt uncomfortable about not being upfront with the Doctor when I took him out with me at night in order to observe him and try to get him to open up about his past, and I felt equally ill at ease having to behave like an informer and denounce him and his now proven indecent behaviour to his friend, with all too foreseeable consequences. Many years had passed since his blackmailing activities, if that was true, of course: I had been very slightly persuaded by his explanation that these were slanders put about by his vengeful former *franquista* comrades, who felt betrayed by his clemency and lack of venom, because everything we are told leaves a faint mark and sows a tiny seed of doubt, which is why it's not so very odd that sometimes, when we have already composed our own picture of events, we would prefer not to hear any more or to allow the accused to speak, so that he cannot gradually convince us of his innocence and the truth of his story. Yes, many years had passed and people do change and do repent, and they look at their past selves with a feeling of horror, but at the same time are unable to recognize that primitive self, as if they were gazing into a distorting mirror: 'Was I that person? Did I do that? Was my former self so very bad? If so, there's no way I can alter it. Guilt is stronger than my desire to make amends, guilt prevents me from even trying, and all I can hope for is that the guilt will pass or grow so old that its remnants will dissolve into the mists in which everything that has ever happened fades and vanishes, until its shape blurs and becomes indistinguishable: the good and the ambiguous, the contradictory and the bad, the crimes and the acts of heroism, the malevolence and the generosity, the honesty and the deceit, the never-ending rancour and the forgiveness finally wrested from the weary victim, the self-sacrifice, the promises made and the cunning acts of exploitation, all, in the end, will be greeted with an oblivious shrug of the shoulders by those who come afterwards and succeed us, preoccupied with their own passions, which are quite enough to cope with, indifferent to everything that happened before they trod the earth, where they will merely be superimposing their footprints on those of their infinite predecessors and peers, not knowing that they're merely imitating them and that nothing is new under the sun, that everything is doomed to become confused and mingled and homogenized, to be forgotten and left to float on a repetitive magma of which, nevertheless, no one tires, or is it just that none of us has ever found the path that will lead us out?' (That's why history is full of Eduardo Muriels and Beatriz Nogueras, of Dr Van Vechtens and Professor Ricos, of Celias and Vidals and Juan de Veres and identical extras, determined, one after the other, to perform the same play and rewrite the same melodramatic plot. There's nothing original about my character, nor, I suppose, about any of the others.) 'But until that happens – and however brief a life, it will take a while – there is a terrible, hateful interlude that belongs to us alone, and during which we have no alternative but to cope with what we have done or omitted to do and to distract or placate our feelings of guilt, and sometimes the only way of achieving this is to increase that guilt, to heap up new guilt to cover the old, to overshadow or blur or minimize it, until finally all guilt has passed and there isn't a soul in the world who can remember what we did, no quick, wicked tongue to talk about it, not even a tremulous finger to point us out as having been the cause of anything.'

I imagine there were various factors that overcame my natural and general reluctance to squeal on someone else. First, what I had learned was precisely what Muriel had asked me to find out and, as an unconditional admirer of his, I had wholeheartedly set about doing just that. Second, what Vidal had told me coincided all too closely with my boss's suspicions: he had never been explicit about these, but had mentioned the possibility or rumour that Van Vechten had behaved indecently with a woman, or possibly more than one, as seemed to be the case ('That, to me, is unforgivable, the lowest of the low'). Third, the Doctor's actions had been so despicable that, once discovered, they deserved to be exposed. Not that anything would happen to him: there was no proof, it didn't constitute a crime and, in Spain at the time, no one was in a mood to denounce anyone. The Amnesty Law had been passed, that is, an agreement had been reached according to which no one individual would begin an endless chain of accusations or bring out anyone else's dirty linen, however filthy – murders, summary executions, betrayals provoked by envy or revenge, show trials, military tribunals condemning to life imprisonment or death civilians with little or no access to a lawyer (and that went on until the final, far milder years of the dictatorship): not even the crimes common to both sides during the War or those perpetrated afterwards by the winning side, which was

422

free to continue soiling its own linen. It wasn't just that there could be no judicial consequences for any abuse or crime, it was even frowned upon to talk about them in public or write about them in the press; as I mentioned, the few people who tried this were met with the instant disapproval not just of former Franco supporters who had a personal interest in the matter – in reality, there was nothing 'former' about them – but of anti-*franquistas* and committed democrats too: as Vidal had pointed out, it suited some people perfectly to have the slate wiped clean like that, so as to conceal their own remote pasts and polish up their less than immaculate biographies. It was decided rather too soon that all guilt was gone, that such ancient history should be left to dissolve into those blurring mists, as if a whole century had passed not just four or five years. I thought it likely that the Doctor's misdemeanours would have been known by some in private, that they would at least have cost him one or, with luck, two precious friendships. Fourth, I was troubled now by that routine relationship between him and Beatriz Noguera, by those prosaic fucks at the Sanctuary; it wasn't, I think, that I was jealous exactly – that would have been absurd when nothing between us had changed, certainly not on her part: the night spent in my cubbyhole must have been a mere caprice as far as she was concerned, or a remedy for insomnia, or perhaps a delirium she scarcely remembered or was unaware of the following day; she was, to use her own eloquent and simplified words, not always quite right in the head. But young men – or myself at the time – need to believe that every one of their experiences or actions is unique and all it takes is for something unthinkable – not to say impossible – to happen for them to embellish it in their memory and cleanse it of any ugly accretions, and Van Vechten was a vulgar and now very ugly accretion. And lastly, I had found his behaviour in Bar Chicote altogether disagreeable,

423

unconvincing and evasive: he had begun by denying everything, then tried to make a joke of it, presenting himself as the victim of other people's defamatory remarks, before becoming threatening and aggressive, planting one large hand on my shoulder, warning me that I could get hurt, calling me 'boy' and 'little squirt'. As to his present-day links to and relationship with El Movimiento Apostólico de Darmstadt, he had not even attempted an explanation, indeed, had avoided doing so. In the light of all this, my desire to do him harm prevailed over my reluctance to squeal on him.

I could still not bring myself to be like Vidal, though, ready to unfold what I knew from the orient to the drooping west, to tell anyone who would listen. I ought to reserve that particular exclusive for Muriel and so, that same afternoon, I had to dodge Professor Rico's questions as best I could. He was in such a foul mood after his lunch with the mummies that, initially, he forgot what had happened earlier and that he had ordered me to make detailed notes about why Van Vechten was an utter bastard and to inform him of his crimes.

'What a bloody awful lunch,' was his first comment. He removed his glasses and breathed on them furiously as if intending, after the fact, to poison his loathsome lunch companions with his breath. Such was his annoyance and frustration that he had dropped in at Calle Velázquez in order to vent his feelings on whoever happened to be there. 'The three of them behaved like absolute piranhas and did nothing but raise objections and throw past insults in my face, insults I'd heaped on them, you understand; they were like the three witches in *Macbeth* at their most doom-laden or *tricoteuses* huddled round the guillotine. It's true that in certain academic articles I did describe them as inept, superficial, obvious, ill-informed and obtuse, and even called one stupid. Not that I did so directly, mind, but it was implied; the fellow had dared to criticize my conclusions about *Lazarillo* in an impeccable study of mine that deserved, certainly in his case, open-mouthed reverence. But they're just hell-bent on getting their own back. These were, in short, mere skirmishes; and since my arguments were unassailable, he immediately clammed up so that I wouldn't lay into him if he attempted a riposte. Well, what does he expect when I have an unerring eye – or should that be aim? – and always get what I want? Those semi-cadavers know that all they're good for is correcting exam papers with a chewed red pencil. *Érforstrafó.*' – He came out with a possibly rage-fuelled onomatopoiea, longer than usual and with two stresses. He continued to breathe hard on his glasses as if he were a fire-breathing dragon, until the lenses were completely fogged; then, with remarkable dexterity, he removed a lens cloth from his glasses case and unfurled it with a flick of the wrist just as magicians do with their vast handkerchiefs. – 'They made it clear that they have no intention of voting for me when my sponsors propose me as a candidate. Since they're a meddlesome trio, I fear they may succeed in convincing some of their duller or dimmer colleagues, of which there are quite a few. They were clearly thrilled at the thought of having their revenge. The most irritating thing was that I could barely remember what it was I'd written that had so put their respective noses out of joint. That's the trouble with dispensing blind justice, one doesn't notice who one's victims are.' – He applied himself to polishing the lenses with painstaking brio, and they were so damp by then that they were sure to turn out spotless. Then he put the cloth away with a suave gesture (in this respect, he reminded me of Herbert Lom), lit a cigarette, and his gaze grew calmer as he added with jovial optimism (he was not a man to harbour resentments, he got bored too quickly for that): 'Perhaps it would be best to wait until they kick the bucket before presenting myself as a candidate. I shouldn't think any of them are going to last

425

very long given the way they were coughing. Several times they came close to choking – it quite put me off my food. I hardly ate so much as a chickpea.' – And it was then, to drive away this unpleasant thought, that he remembered I owed him a piece of gossip. – 'Ah yes, what news of the Doctor, young Vera? When I left, that vehement, well-read friend of yours was about to tell you all about his horrendous crimes.'

'Oh, it turned out to be a fuss about nothing, Professor. Hardly worth mentioning. Vidal was exaggerating, he just regaled me with a lot of hospital tittle-tattle and conference gossip. Well, you know what doctors are like, always at each other's throats.' – This was completely untrue, or at least I had no evidence to back it up, I knew nothing about their quarrels and rivalries. I imagined, though, that these did exist, as they do in any profession in Spain: even chimney-sweeps have their differences, to mention a trade that ceased to exist centuries ago.

Rico regarded me suspiciously. I could see his eyes perfectly now, not a speck of dust marred the lenses.

'Enough of this namby-pambyism, young Vere. You're not going to bamboozle me, I'm not your gull.' – He had resorted once more to his outdated vocabulary, and although I didn't understand a word, I knew exactly what he meant. – 'If you don't want to tell me, then don't, but I'm sure your friend wasn't talking about nurse-chasing or plagiarism or stolen accreditations. Nor even groping any female patients who come within range or mothers accompanying their children. It's as clear as day that the Doctor is an old lecher and we all know it, but that doesn't make him an utter bastard.' – He used the same word, 'lecher', that Celia had used, although it sounded less damning on his lips; neither of them knew just how right they were. – 'The country would be full of utter bastards then, well, it is already: you need only look at those three old fossils who've just given me the go-by.' – And he resumed his attack on those ancient academicians.

This continued to absorb him in the days that followed, hatching plots and inventing insults. However, he did not forget about Van Vechten either, and from time to time would return to the charge: 'You owe me a salty tale of treachery, young De Viah, and you owe me a verbatim report of it,' he would say as soon as he saw me. 'Just when will you deign to keep your promise? If there's one thing I can't stand it's being in the dark. Not having the foggiest. Not a clue. So be warned.'

If only Muriel had felt the same mischievous curiosity, for it proved to be a terrible disappointment when, at last, a week later, he eased up slightly on his frantic fund-raising and spent a little time at home. This was in part due to his friend Jack Palance, who immediately agreed to co-star in this new film – if it was new, or had Muriel simply pulled it out of a drawer of old projects that had failed or been delayed or gone astray? He often had difficulty bringing his plans to fruition, and there may well have been as many films in the making as there were actual films. Not that Palance was exactly at the peak of his career, indeed, he was probably at his lowest ebb. If you look at his filmography, you'll see that from 1981 to 1986 inclusive, he didn't make a single film, and during four of those years, his sole artistic activity was presenting an American TV series that was never shown outside the States. So it was perhaps not so very strange that he should be happy to participate in a phantom production, be it Spanish or any other nationality; after all, in the 1960s, he had been quite happy to work with Jesús Franco, Isasi-Isasmendi and a handful of insignificant Italians (even though, in that same decade, he had worked with directors like Godard and Brooks, Abel Gance and Fleischer). However, Muriel's unbounded admiration for Palance meant that his promise to take part in the film calmed Muriel's spirits and filled him with hope. Not that, at the time, the presence of the great Jack Palance in a cast was any guarantee of financial backing or success, rather the opposite, embarrassing though that may seem now. But Muriel felt it was a good omen being able to count on Palance and possibly also on Richard Widmark, with whom Palance had worked on two feature-length films in 1950 or thereabouts, and whom he had promised to persuade to take on the other leading role. I had and still have no idea what the film was about or even if Muriel ever began shooting it. I only know that Volodymyr Jack Palahniuk – to use Palance's original Ukrainian name – was already sixty and Widmark would have been about sixty-five.

I also had the feeling that Muriel was feeling happier because he was in frequent contact with the impresaria Cecilia Alemany. I don't know how he managed to get her to take an interest or what kind of interest that was exactly, but now they spoke almost daily on the phone and he would always turn away when he received one of those calls and speak in a murmur so as not to be heard by whoever happened to be in the apartment, including me. He also stopped making derisive comments about her inaccessibility. He no longer spoke of her as a demi-goddess, he no longer said things like 'What a remarkable woman; what a business brain she has; why, compared to her we are mere microbes.' When we stop exaggerating and stop joking about someone we revere, it's usually a sign that that someone has finally descended to earth and become less remote. I didn't dare to think that perhaps they both now chewed gum together or even shared the same piece, but one night when Muriel came home late and I was still up, I noticed that he gave off an intoxicating, almost narcotic whiff of perfume, and he had definitely not applied it himself. I was sure that the owner of the chic boutique no longer addressed him as 'my dear man', which Muriel had found simultaneously so humiliating and so amusing at that now far-distant first interview.

The following morning, he was, I suppose, in such a good mood that he summoned me to his office and, with one thumb tucked under his armpit and in the other hand his pipe, which he pointed at me as if he were Sherlock Holmes or, perhaps, Walter Pidgeon, who sometimes sported a moustache like his, he said:

'Young De Vere, now that it seems things have taken a turn for the better, and the new project appears to be going ahead, forget what I said to you. If you haven't taken on another job and prefer to stay here, I think I can find you something useful to do. The script, once it's ready, will need to be translated.' And he added with a kind of prematurely compensatory pride: 'I can't wait for Towers and a few others to hear the news.'

I had become accustomed to his changes of mind, to his commands and countermands, as well as to his variable moods. And so it occurred to me that this was perhaps not a bad day to see if his position regarding Van Vechten had changed at all.

'Thank you, Eduardo, for your confidence in me. Working for you is, as you know, a pleasure, although I'm not sure I'm always that useful. Could you give me a little time to think it over? I'd got used to the idea of moving on in September.'

As I mentioned earlier, I was beginning to find the atmosphere in the apartment somewhat troubling, not to say troublesome on occasions. Beatriz was now going about her business in a relatively normal fashion, but during the hours she spent at home, the music-less, insistent tick-tock of the metronome had returned, and it seemed to me more ominous than ever, as if she were always doing a slow-motion countdown to an end that never arrived or that only she could see in her personal fog. I imagined her sitting staring at the piano keys, mechanically counting the black keys and the white and noting the time passing, letting it tick on without filling it with a single chord or melody, and unfilled time tends to be accompanied by static, repetitive thoughts, for example: 'Not yet, not yet, not yet, it's not yet the right moment.' And she also seemed more depressed; even though Muriel and she barely exchanged a word, she must have noticed his sudden good humour and might perhaps even, from a distance, have smelled that distinctive perfume. As far as I knew, she no longer made any nocturnal incursions or stood guard outside his bedroom door, as if she had finally abandoned all hope. As for me, although she and I continued to treat each other with the same deference and affection as before, as if there had never been any kind of intimacy between us, I still felt guilty and so uncomfortable sometimes that I blushed, and my impulse was to leave the apartment and allow my transgression to dissipate; I couldn't help thinking that I had behaved indecently, as regards Muriel, I mean. And I didn't quite trust Beatriz or myself either, fearing that one day she or I might be tempted to reoffend. As everyone knows, what happened once can easily happen again; however, fewer of us seem to be aware that precedents are, in fact, of no importance: what has never happened before is just as likely to occur.

'Yes, you decide,' he said. 'You're under no obligation either way. I told you that you could take your time leaving, well, you can also take your time deciding whether or not to stay. Let me know when you've made your decision. The offer is there and will remain open. So keep me posted.'

I looked at the eye that was speaking and saw in it an expression of affection. Then I looked at the silent eye, and, as so often before, felt an urge to drum on the patch with my fingers, and felt, too, the attraction of that affection. I would miss him a lot when I left, that much I knew.

'As it happens, there is something I'd like to tell you about,

431

Eduardo, if you don't mind. Some things don't matter so much to me, but I don't like to leave unfinished any commission or order you gave me. Now, I know you revoked your commission regarding the Doctor' — I think I chose that pedantic word 'revoked' to give my words a more solemn tone — 'but I feel you should know what I've found out recently. It chimes so completely with your own information, with your suspicions, that I really have to tell you —'

Muriel raised the hand holding the pipe and brought me up short, an imperious, prohibitive gesture. He pointed the bowl at me, I could see the glowing embers: as if he were showing me a red light.

'Stop right there, young De Vere. What did I also say? I said that I couldn't prevent you from continuing your investigations on your own account, if that's what you wanted. I was wrong to reveal my doubts to you and alert you to them, that was a weakness on my part, and then, once activated, there's no way of deactivating that alert. But I warned you that if you did continue, then you mustn't come telling me or anyone else what you had learned. If the Doctor has confessed to you or you've discovered something on your own account, keep it to yourself. And best take it to the grave with you, although that, I realize, is a lot to ask. With me at least, though, keep schtum. I refuse to hear it. I don't want to know.'

I was standing up, since he hadn't asked me to take a seat. By then, it's true, I didn't need to be asked, because I was perfectly at home there. But he had probably only summoned me to inform me that I could keep my job, not to chat or to discourse on anything. I decided to insist; one always does when faced by a refusal, at least once. A regrettable habit shared by most of us.

'But you did want to know at the time, enough to get me involved. You were tormented by uncertainty and unable simply to ignore the matter, as I suggested you should. I remember you saying to me: "I

432

need either to have in my possession or to acquire some clue . . . some way of orienting myself that will allow me to say: 'That's a downright lie' or 'Oh dear, it must be true'." You found the accusations so disturbing, so discouraging, base and stupid. "More incongruous than grave," you said. Well, it turns out that what I've learned is both those things. And not just in the past either, there may be some murky business in the present too. You can't ignore it now, just when I've found the clue that will give you the orientation you wanted.'

Muriel got up and came over to me. He folded his arms sternly as he had when he opened his bedroom door to Beatriz, when he appeared in the doorway in his white pyjamas and dark dressing gown. He looked at me, too, rather as he'd looked at her, the poor woman standing there in her nightdress. Any affection he may have felt for me had vanished from his blue eye; now there was only irritation, a little festering anger and even a slight hint of scorn, the scorn due to anyone who tries to impose his will. I realized that I wouldn't be able to tell him what I knew.

'Of course I can ignore it, why shouldn't I? So what if, at one point, I sought your involvement? I've told you already, I've changed my mind. I owe the Doctor a great deal and he has just saved Beatriz yet again. He's a very old friend and I don't want to lose him, nor for my view of him to become further tarnished, it was tarnished enough by what that other person told me. I wish she never had. I can still pretend it never happened and, as you suggested, ignore what she said. I don't need orientation, I don't need any clues, because when I cancelled your mission, I'd already decided to tell myself: "It's a lie or should be." We lose far too many people in a lifetime, they either drift away or die, and it doesn't make sense to get rid of those who are left. So what if he committed some vile deed in the past or took advantage of someone or other? Here, during a very long

433

dictatorship, almost everyone did at some point. So what? We just have to accept that this is a grubby country, very grubby. For decades we've rubbed along together, what else could we do, and we've been obliged to get to know each other. Many of those who behaved badly then, behaved well in other circumstances. Things can change a lot over the years, it's very hard to behave badly all the time, as it is to behave well. Who hasn't committed some vile deed (not political, but personal), and who hasn't also performed acts of great kindness? It wasn't like that forty years ago, there were no half-measures then. But this is 1980, and those forty years have mixed everything up far more than we think, and you can't go back to those long-lost days. Contrary to what some may think, time didn't stop then, but continued to flow, however hard the *franquistas* tried to make it stop. Anyone who was a bastard in 1940 probably remained a bastard, but he also had the chance to temper his bastardly nature and to become something more. Revenge has its sell-by date, evil grows wearisome, hatred gets boring after a while, except among the real fanatics, and even then . . . We all need a break from those things. People go to the bar and talk and joke, and in the midst of the laughter none of us feels or believes ourselves to be evil, even if we're telling the sort of cruel jokes we Spaniards tend to tell. No one is seamless or all of a piece, or very few of us are: even Franco loved the cinema, just like you and me; he probably genuinely empathized with the characters' many vicissitudes. While he was watching a film, he probably stopped making decisions and stopped plotting; he was perhaps completely engrossed during those ninety minutes, in a parenthesis from normal life. Needless to say, that's the worst possible example, but I've only seen the Doctor in normal life, and that's all I know of him. I've seen him curing my children and saving Beatriz and being kind and attentive to me. I've seen him laughing, having fun, joking. So I

434

don't care what he did or didn't do all those years ago before I knew him. He has been and still is something more than that to me, Juan. That's all I have to say.'

He unfolded his arms and retreated a few steps, as if he had finished his lesson or his warning. I couldn't force what I knew on him. Well, I could, I only had to say a few words, spoken in wretched haste: 'The Doctor abused various women and blackmailed their husbands or fathers, he threatened to send them to prison or the firing squad if they didn't agree to his demands.' You can't help but hear, and auditory stains cannot be cleaned up, unlike sexual stains, which can all be washed away. I was so emboldened by the situation that I was even tempted, for a fraction of a second, to say the unthinkable: 'Did you know that, for quite some time now, the Doctor has been screwing Beatriz?' (That disrespectful verb would once again have escaped my lips, because it was the right word to use.) I had done the same thing, although it had only been once and, besides, and this I will never know, it might not have bothered Muriel that I had screwed her or that she'd been screwed by Van Vechten or Arranz or who knows who else, perhaps someone outside Madrid. And I could have let slip other equally swift words, to lend more weight to the information: 'They meet in an ultra-Catholic place, which apparently has links to Pinochet and his followers.' But you don't say such puerile things, not even when you're twenty-three. Not to someone you admire and respect and are fond of, not to someone who has, moreover, forbidden you to tell him anything and insists that he doesn't want to know, someone who has resolved to renounce all passing curiosity. And so I asked two questions, one after the other, and understood from his response that he considered these puerile too:

'But what about justice, Eduardo? What about what actually

happened, what took place?' He had probably forgotten the comments he had made to me once about that last expression.

'Justice?' he retorted, quick as a flash. 'Justice doesn't exist. Or only as an exception, just a few stern lessons to keep up appearances, but only in the case of individual crimes. And woe betide those who receive those lessons. But for collective or national crimes, there is no justice, not even an attempt at it. Justice is always terrified by the magnitude of those crimes, overwhelmed by their superabundance, inhibited by the sheer quantity, paralysed and frightened. It's naive of us to appeal to justice after a dictatorship or a war, even after a mere lynching in some one-horse town, because there are always too many people involved. How many people do you think committed crimes or were accomplices to crimes in Germany, and how many were punished? I don't mean tried and sentenced, because that was even rarer, but something easier and more feasible: how many were punished socially or on a personal level? How many found themselves marginalized or excluded, how many found themselves rejected, as you are asking me to do now with the Doctor because of what you've found out about him? A tiny, insignificant proportion. And it's the same in Italy, in Hungary, Croatia, Poland, France, everywhere. A whole country is never brought to justice, not even half or even a portion of the population. (All right, this does happen in dictatorships, but who wants to go back to that?) And just supposing that we could do it here, what sense is there now in putting those people on trial, which is neither possible nor appropriate, and on that we pretty much all agree – but ostracizing the majority of the population? You can be quite sure that we, the foolish avenging angels, would be the ones to end up spurned and isolated. No one denounces his peers, no one accuses someone who is like himself.' Muriel paused and sat down on the sofa, but I still didn't dare follow suit. He looked

436

up at the painting by Casanova's brother, of which he never tired. He turned his one eye on me again and added: 'Look, young De Vere, Spain is full of bastards large and small, individuals who oppressed and plundered, who flourished and took advantage of others, or who, at best, were merely accommodating. And you want me to turn against a friend because he might once have done something similar? Come on. Yes, I did involve you in the matter and, yes, I did have my doubts, it's true: remnants of another age, of the person I once was; remnants of rectitude. But frankly, the way things are going here in Spain, I'm not about to be the one idiot who harms himself by dispensing his own personal justice.' He drummed with his fingers on his eyepatch as if he had guessed that this was precisely what I was then tempted to do (I had to content myself with that pleasing sound) and he concluded with a half-smile and an unexpected lightness of tone. 'Because that doesn't exist either, Juan, disinterested, personal justice.'

It was those two things that annoyed me, both his denial that personal justice existed and the light, even paternalistic tone in which he spoke. Not that I found the latter unacceptable in him, on the contrary, it was understandable that Muriel should treat me like that, given that he exceeded me in age, knowledge and government, and then there was also the unconditional loyalty I felt for him. This had perhaps diminished a little, for no enthusiasm, however fervent, can survive continuous contact and proximity, being a witness to how someone conducts his personal life, which is rarely spoken of because such tales are so tenuous, so similar to other tales, that the more ambitious storytellers tend to scorn them and barely pay them any attention at all. I *had* paid attention to the atmosphere in that apartment, possibly more than I should have done. And perhaps that's what angered me.

'Really, Don Eduardo?' I sometimes reverted to addressing him as 'Don', the form of address I had early on and rather reluctantly abandoned; but this time I did so on purpose. 'So personal justice doesn't exist either? And you, of all people, are telling me that?'

He noticed the sarcasm, if it went that far; for I never entirely lost my respect for him.

'And why shouldn't I? What do you mean, young De Vere?' For the moment, he didn't feel offended, only intrigued.

'I've spent long enough here, Don Eduardo, I mean, Eduardo, to see that you're subjecting Beatriz to something that seems very like a kind of personal justice. Or rather, a punishment, a personal punishment. You tell me you're not prepared to lose a friend because of something he did years ago, that you won't even alter or modify your relationship with him one iota; and now you won't even hear what I've found out about him. On the other hand, you've spent years, at least I assume it's been years, making your wife pay for some past misdemeanour. I know that, in principle, it's none of my business, as you've occasionally informed me yourself when I've asked you other questions, not that I ever asked with any ill intent, just out of normal curiosity. But when I've had to witness certain unpleasant scenes and sharp remarks, then it begins to be my business, wouldn't you agree? One can't remain indifferent to what's there before one's eyes, nor, in my opinion, should one; and you certainly don't hold back. Forgive my boldness, but I've heard you say quite a lot of things that are, to be blunt, unbecoming to you. Things about Beatriz. You don't exactly keep your feelings to yourself.'

His expression hardened. That hardness, though, was not yet directed at me, but perhaps at what had happened in the past, at what had one day led him to take against his wife and send her into permanent exile, if not from his affections (it was clear that the embers, or more than that, still glowed) then from conjugal life.

'You pride yourself on your attentive and retentive abilities, Juan, and yet you're missing out an important part of what I've just said. I said that *disinterested*, personal justice doesn't exist.' And he stressed that first adjective, which I had, indeed, omitted. 'There's a fundamental difference between what the Doctor may have done and what Beatriz did, however worthy of censure his actions may be; however systematic, repeated and despicable and on quite another scale, it

439

doesn't matter. At the time, you asked if it constituted a betrayal of me, and I told you that what I'd heard about him was unrelated to me, had nothing to do with me, and didn't directly affect our friendship. – 'And what I saw from the top of a tree in the Sanctuary of Darmstadt,' I thought, and in my thoughts I addressed him familiarly as *tú*, 'and that you also wouldn't let me tell you about – not that I would tell you – would you consider that to be a betrayal?' – 'Whatever the Doctor did he certainly didn't do to *me*. Beatriz, on the other hand, did. She did it to *me*, she changed the course of my life, she determined it and ruined it; and ruined the life of another person too. The accusations I heard against Jorge were unpleasant. Most distasteful. And I did wonder about them. But now I can see (all the more so when I look around me) that I needn't worry about the thousands of filthy things people have done over the decades out there. Or, rather, here. I don't have to take steps, still less against someone to whom I feel indebted, and even more so now.' – 'What you don't know is that you might also feel yourself to be his creditor,' I thought, 'or perhaps not, perhaps you simply don't care.' – 'I've no wish to sit in judgement on the past, no one does, as we've seen on a daily basis since Franco died. Not even the professional judges want to do that. Everyone is furious and resentful about what was done to them or to their loved ones or their forebears, but not about what was done "in general". Tackling "the general" would be a mammoth and absurd task, one that no age and no nation has ever undertaken. One fit for the idle or for fanatics, self-obsessed individuals longing to find a mission in life. Let's not deceive ourselves, we are all concerned solely with our own affairs; we want our revenge or our compensation, we each have our own personal grudges, and have neither thought nor time for those of others, unless joining together with those others is of some benefit to our cause and our plight. And yet, even in those strategic unions, deep down we're thinking only of ourselves, each of us is in pursuit only of our own redress, the success of our particular suit. Only a few weirdos are prepared to set themselves up as the policemen or judges of other people's misdemeanours, of what is wrong per se.' – 'According to Muriel, Vidal would be one such person,' was my first response, 'and yet he doesn't seem weird to me at all, but very normal.' Then I thought again and corrected myself: 'Ah, no. Vidal isn't entirely disinterested either, there's his Aunt Carmen, whom both doctors screwed, Van Vechten and Arranz; so perhaps Muriel is right.' – 'What's more they're always very pretentious and self-important. There's a megalomaniac quality about that inability to tolerate impunity in matters that have nothing to do with us, don't you think? Those avenging angels hang a medal round their neck, look at themselves in the mirror and say: "I'm incorruptible, I'm implacable, I will not allow any injustice to go unpunished, whether it affects me or not." ' – I didn't think Vidal was like that at all; he was equally angry with the Catalan painter and the ugly, bald philosopher, neither of whom had affronted him personally; he simply chose not to keep silent in private about what he knew, but he had no desire to dispense justice or take anyone to court or expose him or her to the public gaze: conversations over a few drinks or at the hospital, advice and warnings given to an inexperienced friend, tales told while sharing a beer or two, that was all. But I let it pass. His family *had* been directly affected. Not irreversibly, because his father had become a wealthy man, although he had, admittedly, had to make his fortune abroad. But perhaps that first factor was enough for Vidal's anger to be impersonal, all-embracing. – 'I myself succumbed to the temptation of behaving like that, so it's not that I don't understand the attitude. The younger you are, the more likely you are to suffer those attacks of "objective" indignation. That's why, on a juvenile impulse, a resurgence of my former self, if you like, that's why I asked you to do what I asked you to do. But one isn't young any more; those youthful remnants don't last, they fade with each day that passes . . . And then one considers and thinks: What has that got to do with me? Did he ever hurt me? No. The Doctor has never harmed me in any way.'

Muriel had forgotten the purpose of his speech, his riposte or defence. This happened more and more often. It wasn't his age, he was only in his fifties after all. Sometimes he spoke at length and, at others, was brusque and laconic, and this had been so since I first met him. But the two tendencies had become more marked: when he spoke at length he spoke for longer and when he was brusque he was even brusquer. Now he stopped, as if disoriented, as though asking himself: 'Why the devil are we talking about this?' And I took advantage of this pause to try to lead him in the direction I wanted:

'But Beatriz did harm you,' I said. 'Beatriz did something unforgivable to you.' His eye flashed into life, as if he were shooting an arrow at me, albeit not as yet a very sharp one. 'You see, Eduardo, while you were in Barcelona, Beatriz and I talked more than usual; that was my role, I was here as her companion, her guardian, her protector.' – 'Don't let your tongue run away with you,' I thought, 'and be careful what you reveal, you don't want to betray yourself: Muriel has seen far too much cinema.' – 'Since I came to work here . . . well, I can see you feel a kind of retrospective affection for her, I don't know how else to put it. For old times' sake. She remembers them as having been very good times, or more than that, she holds them close and clings to them, as you well know. And I saw how alarmed you were that night at the Hotel Wellington, your panic at the possibility that she might have killed herself. But I also see that you find her unbearable. You almost always treat her badly, very badly. Perhaps

442

you have good reason, but I don't know that reason, and it's really not at all pleasant to see.'

Muriel's eye softened, now it was only sarcastic. With two rapid movements, he rolled up his sleeves still further; the sun was getting higher and it was beginning to get hot.

'And did she not tell you the reason during one of your long chats? The lady of the house complaining to the innocent boy, with her as the poor victim.'

'No. She said she was ashamed to tell me, because it was so ridiculous. That it would be better if you told me yourself and then I would see how disproportionate your reaction had been. All I could get out of her was that she once told you a lie that you took very much to heart. Something really stupid, a childish thing, was how she described it. She never imagined you would react in such a violent, exaggerated fashion.'

'And you believed her?'

'How can I believe anything when I still don't know the facts? But unlike you with regard to the Doctor, I *would* like to find out what lies behind what I've witnessed. Don't worry, you've made it quite clear that whatever the Doctor did doesn't affect you in any way; if it happened, you weren't there to witness it, so why should it interest you? Don't worry, I won't insist. But in exchange for my silence, why don't you tell me once and for all? I think I've been very respectful of your reserve since I've been working here. I've asked you very few questions. But all reserve has its limits, as does all respect. Forgive me for being so direct, but what exactly did Beatriz do to you?'

Muriel did not respond at once. He was, it seemed to me, pondering my words. Then he looked at his watch, tapped its face with his finger, as I had seen him do on other occasions and as if he were calculating whether or not he could afford to devote a little time to me, time that had not been part of his plan for that morning. His eye changed again: it again looked at me with a certain fondness or understanding or patience; perhaps also with a degree of interest. I assumed that he had heard my request and accepted it, that he understood my curiosity and did not reproach me for it. Perhaps he realized that he had kept me too much in the dark. By bringing someone into your home, you are inevitably obliging him to be a witness to your life. And while there's no reason why you should have to explain anything to him if he's being paid to work for you, inevitably the employee will silently pass judgement and ask questions, it happens with even the most invisible and sporadic and insignificant of employees. He would never know to what extent I had become established and involved in his world, and I hoped he never would. But he did know that I had served him as spy and vigilante and had saved his wife from death, although not as purely by chance as he believed, for he knew nothing about my unseemly habit of secretly following her on some or quite a number of afternoons, a habit I had since abandoned. Perhaps Muriel had never stopped to think that I might have

444

made any silent judgements or had questions that remained unasked. Now he was discovering that I had both and perhaps discovering, too, that they were not a matter of indifference to him, but of some importance, and that he needed to give me his version of events in order to influence those judgements, those questions, that it was no longer appropriate to answer me brusquely: 'Let's get one thing straight: I don't employ you to ask me questions about matters that are none of your business.' That time had gone or been replaced, but he hadn't noticed until I voiced my discontent, until that moment.

'Give Mercedes a ring and tell her I won't be coming in this morning after all. Tell her to get on with whatever needs doing. And then sit down. This is going to take a while.'

I phoned from the desk in the office, right there. Meanwhile, he went over to the door separating his side of the apartment from the corridor and carefully pulled it to: it was a high door with two leaves that had become warped so that they never quite clicked shut; the lower half was painted white, while the upper half was made of frosted panes of glass framed in white wood, typical of those old Madrid apartments.

'Where do you want me to sit?' I asked absurdly, to make his job easier, just in case he had a preference.

'Wherever you like,' he said. 'I'm going to lie on the floor, in keeping with your possible opinion of me, if you're of the view that Beatriz is right and that I have fallen very low. That it was all ridiculous, a piece of childish nonsense.' He said this with a faint smile, which seemed to me somewhat forced. It can't have been easy to start talking about what he was going to talk to me about, or perhaps he was reluctant to revisit those distant events, or still felt so embittered by them that they had extinguished any underlying joviality in his character. 'Don't go thinking you're the first person she's told this to, her

445

women friends can't stand the sight of me, my sister-in-law, for example. Beatriz genuinely believes it, so either she's an idiot or I'm very wicked. You might incline to the latter view. But she's not normally an idiot and I'm not naturally wicked. One of us has changed.' And once he was lying down on the floor, one arm under his head as a pillow (when he was already staring up at the ceiling or at the topmost shelves of the library or at the painting by Casanova, and at me out of the corner of his one half-closed eye), to my surprise, he added: 'I'm sorry you've had to witness those embarrassing scenes these past months. And you're quite right, I should have been more careful, more discreet. It took me no time at all to get used to having you around and I've come to think of you as an extension of myself.'

This was the same diagnosis Beatriz had made on that insomniac night. She had added: 'Which is both good and bad.'

'Don't worry, it wasn't so very terrible.' I felt obliged to play down the importance of those scenes. He had unexpectedly apologized and that only increased my feeling of betrayal and baseness, at least nominally. I'd had sex with his wife in his absence and couldn't apologize for that, if, indeed, I needed to, given that he didn't want her in his own bed. That's the trouble with secrets, one can never ask forgiveness.

'Beatriz, as you know, was largely brought up in America. But she often spent whole summers here as well as the occasional school term, living with her aunt and uncle, and that's how we first met, when she was almost an adolescent and I was a young man. And when she was a young woman and I a slightly older young man, we got engaged. I suppose it was inevitable that she would fall in love with an older friend of her cousins; with a Spaniard, like her father, rather than with an American. And that she would have the patience to wait until she'd grown up enough to be noticed and to win my heart. Yes, although I'm a few years her senior, which mattered more then than it does now, that is the right expression. Girls are very determined and stubborn, and tend to want to see their childhood dreams come true. Until they reach a certain age or until they see them crushed for ever. That wasn't the case with us. As soon as she reached adolescence, which she did very early, I began to look at her differently, and the other person's enthusiasm does tend to persuade and carry you along, and I've almost always been the passive type. It wasn't hard to love her. Besides, Beatriz wasn't the great fat cow you know now. On the contrary.'

At the risk of revealing my secret – when you've something to hide, you're afraid to utter even the most innocent of words – I broke in, driven by an urge to do her justice and defend her – which I was finally in a position to do – more than by a need to justify to myself my carnal baseness on that insomniac night and my occasional visual baseness on other nights.

'You do exaggerate, Eduardo, you do blow things up out of all proportion. It's hard to believe that you don't intend to wound her when you come out with things like that. How can you possibly describe Beatriz as a fat cow? Or a cask of amontillado.' It had probably never occurred to him that I might remember his insults, but it was time he realized that I'd memorized nearly all of them. 'She's still a very attractive woman, whom many men would find desirable. As you well know.'

Muriel laughed unexpectedly. He was doubtless amused to be reminded of his own wounding insult, with its incidental homage to Poe. I preferred not to remind him of other outrageous comparisons to the hot-air balloon from *Around the World in 80 Days* or Hitchcock's silhouetted figure, still less Charles Laughton.

Buah, he said, or was it *Bué*? 'There's no accounting for taste.

447

I imagine there are some men who like voluptuous women. The ones who only want to get them into bed. The lechers of this world.' Again that word that had been used before to describe Van Vechten, one of the men who did find Beatriz attractive, in however utilitarian a fashion, or, given his age, perhaps he couldn't afford to be choosy. But I was nearly forty years his junior. Perhaps I was a bit of a lecher at the time too, it's not uncommon among young men, beginners don't have much taste.

'I think you're wrong. I think that one day you made a decision and put a veil over your eyes that you've chosen not to take off. A distorting veil. But I interrupted you. You were saying she wasn't a fat cow then, on the contrary.'

'Quite. I don't mean she was scrawny, not at all. No, she was always on the voluptuous side, but in proportion. She was striking. She was very pretty and sensual, with those slightly widely spaced teeth of hers. She smiled a lot. And she certainly filled her clothes, but in a good way. To put it bluntly: she was an absolute dish, if that's an expression you still use nowadays. And, yes, any man would have fancied her then, especially me. She was a real gift in that respect. And since she set the pace, I just let myself be carried along. Looking back, and despite all that, it's possible that I might not have taken the initiative, or wouldn't have gone so far as to get engaged. Engaged to be married, you understand. But she was so determined and so strong, and tried so hard to please me . . . You'll have noticed that she knows as much if not more about films as I do. She made my interests hers and moulded herself to my tastes and my eccentricities, I some-times think that this was a task she set herself, a programme, as if, even when she was a girl, she'd said to herself: "I'm not going to let this man be bored in my company. I don't want him not to be able to share a part of his life with me because he thinks I won't be interested or won't be up to understanding it. I don't want him to find me

448

lacking and to look elsewhere. I don't want him to exclude me from anything." She was not only happy to see all kinds of films, from masterpieces to the utter tripe I sometimes dragged her along to – because to get a real grasp of things, you need to see the full range, the old and the new, the good, the bad and the bizarre – she also read all the books I recommended, and quickly overtook me in that regard. The young Beatriz wasn't the woman you see now, apathetic and unstable, spending hours at the piano without so much as playing a scale. She brimmed with energy and curiosity, she was unstoppable. Of course I'll never know to what extent she had her own life, or if she merely lived her life through me. She took all the weight, she did all the heavy work demanded by any loving relationship when it's just starting out, and afterwards too, as it develops.' He paused very briefly, then added: 'It wasn't hard to love her. Another person's love is inevitably touching. It arouses pity too, like the love of children. So much so that it seems cruel not to accept it, not to welcome it. It's the kind of pity that melts the heart. Even though there was no passion on my part . . . not that I missed it at the time, having never experienced it.'

He remained silent for longer this time and fixed his gaze on his beloved painting of the retreating horsemen and the one man turning round, dressed in red and possibly one-eyed, in order to cast a final, stern backward glance at the fallen he was leaving behind and whose deaths he and his men had probably caused: 'At least remember *me*.'

'And what happened then?' I didn't want to give him time to have second thoughts, to regret telling me about something that was still no business of mine.

'She moved here when she was about eighteen, to live with her aunt and uncle, who thought of her almost as a daughter. I'm afraid I was the reason for that move, so that she could be close to me. Or,

449

rather, she reversed the order of her visits, going to Massachusetts once a year to spend two or three months with her father, her solitary, disastrous father, and look after him a little. During those visits, we would write to each other – well, phoning was just unthinkable then, we're talking about 1959 or 1960 remember. No one could afford it. Then, about six or seven months before the wedding (she had just turned twenty-one, I think), she had to go to America urgently, some serious incident, some grave problem. Her father . . . I don't know how much I should tell you about him, Juan, it's not really up to me . . .' He gave a sigh of annoyance, drummed his fingers on his eyepatch, pondered for a few seconds, then opted for indiscretion. 'Her father was a homosexual. There you are, I've said it. He may always have been, and it may not have been a belated discovery, as Beatriz at first believed. Perhaps that's why his wife left him shortly after Beatriz was born and chose not to accompany him into exile. That may have been part of the reason why he chose exile, who knows? He was a Republican by conviction, but hadn't done anything very significant during the War and wasn't, therefore, at risk of being persecuted. But for a man with that problem (and it was an enormous problem then, your generation has no idea) and with a child to take care of, you can imagine what it would have been like for him in Franco's ultra-religious Spain, with the Church having been given carte blanche. If he'd been found out, they would, for a start, have taken his daughter from him. So he went first to France, then to Mexico and ended up teaching in Massachusetts, thanks to some contacts he had there; he had a thorough knowledge of Spanish literature and was a pretty decent translator from German and English, in fact, you can still find some of his translations in second-hand bookshops. Not that there was much, if any, tolerance of homosexuality in 1940s or 50s America or even in the mid-60s, but it wasn't like it was here, where all queers were sent to prison – no, almost anywhere was more civilized than here. I don't know how he coped. A lot of self-imposed abstinence, I suppose, and a few weekend escapes to Boston or New York, where he wouldn't be noticed (on a campus it was impossible), to visit the odd clandestine or semi-clandestine club and have some fun. There would have been bars like the one Don Murray goes to in *Advise and Consent*, with men dancing with each other, you've seen it, haven't you?' I shook my head. 'You haven't? You're mad. What are you waiting for? It's wonderful. It was made in 1962 and is based on fact, so there must have been something of the sort at the time. Whatever the truth of the matter, poor Ernesto Noguera would have had a much harder time of it having a bit of modest fun in America than Towers did setting up his prostitution racket in the headquarters of the United Nations, because that coincided more or less with the final part of her father's life.' He raised one hand to his chin, stroked it repeatedly with his thumb and smiled: despite his humiliating dismissal from the Towers film, and given his excitement about his new project with Palance and hopefully Widmark, his most furious fury must have passed. 'Harry's a nasty piece of work, isn't he? I'm sure what Lom told us is true, about the worst of his dirty tricks, I mean. What did you think?'

'Yes, I felt he knew more than he was telling us. But then it's only normal that he should tread rather carefully, always allowing for a degree of indiscretion. After all, he's often worked with him.' Muriel shook his head, amused by the memory of that conversation, distracted. Yes, he had probably forgiven Towers, just as he had completely forgiven Van Vechten, without knowing exactly what he was forgiving, which always makes things easier, and without *wanting* to know either. If he wasn't a man to bear a grudge, or to pass judgement on matters that didn't affect him, and was even playing down the importance of having a film taken away from him, then his gross behaviour towards Beatriz for all those years was utterly inexplicable. But he had been about to explain and had got diverted. I grew impatient, afraid again that, at any moment, he might think better of it. I decided to lead him back to the matter in hand. 'But you were saying that just months before your wedding, some grave incident occurred, some serious problem. I presume involving her father.'

He raised his head a little to look at me more directly. I had a sense that he was enjoying keeping me hanging on: now that he had agreed to tell me the story, he would do so at his own pace and in his own way. That is the prerogative of the one doing the telling, and the person listening has none at all, or only that of getting up and leaving. But I was not going to leave just yet.

'I don't know what could have got into the man. By this time, he was in his late forties, so hardly in the first flush of youth, but ardour takes a long time to fade. Or perhaps he just got fed up and lowered his guard. Anyway, after all those years of moderation, a university colleague caught him in Boston giving a blow-job to a man in some public toilets or maybe it was a cinema toilet, I'm not sure. Like any good liberal, this colleague didn't rush off and report him to the police, but to the Board of Professors or whatever it's called, or to the Chairman, although now I think they call him, absurdly enough, the Chairperson, so as not to seem sexist. Those New England colleges are so proud of their moral rectitude they end up being positively inquisitorial. You can imagine the scandal. Not that it was leaked to the press or anything, college rectitude wouldn't allow that, and, besides, they didn't want to frighten off any future students. But in those isolated places, in their little bubbles of lakes and woods, everyone knows everything. Not only was he dismissed, other universities in the area were warned about him, making it impossible for him to find a similar post. He was left without a job and without an income, depressed and stuck at home, shunned by most of his friends. And so Beatriz flew there urgently to see what she could do, not quite knowing what had happened. The telegram she received left her no choice; I can remember it clearly: 'Dismissed from university.

453

Situation desperate. Long story. Don't phone. Come quickly.' Her aunt and uncle helped her out with the air ticket, I couldn't help much at the time because I still hadn't come into the family money and lived more or less from day to day. She didn't find out the details until she got there, and the people at the college had no alternative but to explain what had happened and her father had no alternative but to own up to her about his sexual proclivities, and about the fact that her mother wasn't dead, although we've never found out anything more than that, because Beatriz never wanted to go looking for her. The lady, who would be in her sixties now, is probably out there somewhere, perhaps having had more children. Beatriz told me all this by letter, because, at first, we wrote to each other almost every day, or she did anyway. Her father was in a dreadful situation: either he had to move to the other side of the country, to some insignificant university that his colleagues had failed to notify, or . . . in short, disaster. We even discussed bringing him to Spain to live with us when we got married. Not the ideal start to married life, but we had to consider it as a possibility. Her aunt and uncle, her father's sister and brother-in-law, who were both loyal *franquistas*, were outraged when they learned the nature of the offence. They made some comment that included the word "incorrigible", so they must have known about him before, about his tastes, I mean. Anyway, probably as a result of the shame and the shock, Noguera had a heart attack about a week or so after Beatriz arrived. He survived, but was left very weak and in need of care. She stayed by his side, well, she was always a devoted daughter and continued to be, as daughters brought up solely by their father tend to be, regardless of how that father may have behaved. At least they weren't in dire financial straits initially: they drew on the savings Noguera had accumulated during years of earning good American wages and making only modest expenditures, and hoped he would recover sufficiently for him to try his luck in Michigan or Oklahoma or New Mexico, or to return to Spain; no firm decision was made, and, besides, he was in no fit state to travel. Months passed. Her father was very slowly and gradually recovering, but he was still very frail, and Beatriz's return continued to be postponed. Hand me a cigarette, will you, and an ashtray.'

He paused and I handed him my pack of cigarettes and put an ashtray on the floor beside him. He put aside his pipe, now extinguished, and took a cigarette, which he lit, inhaling deeply, then exhaling and aiming a couple of smoke rings up at the ceiling. He was one of those men who knew how to do that, like Errol Flynn and those other actors whose moustache he had copied as a young man and kept. He had combed his hair back with water, a clear parting through his thick hair. He lay there in silence, thinking. I decided to give him a prod, just in case:

'Poor Beatriz,' I said. 'I still can't see that she did anything deserving of punishment. On the contrary, she seems to have been an affectionate, loyal young woman.'

He propped himself up on his elbows and looked at me rather haughtily, as if I'd said something impertinent.

'You don't see because we haven't got there yet. If you're going to be impatient and prejudge the situation, we'd better just drop the whole subject.' I raised both my hands, palms open, as if surrendering or as though to protect myself, meaning: 'I'm sorry, I'm sorry' or 'Truce, truce' or 'Take no notice of me.' Again, in that gesture so characteristic of him, he tucked his thumb under his armpit like the tiny riding whip of a British officer, and added: 'Of course, when we do get there, you, like her, will doubtless consider it to have been nothing, mere nonsense. You're perhaps expecting something dramatic or terrible. Possibly even a crime, like in the movies. Well, it's nothing like that. Just a lie and her vengeful, no, her impetuous subsequent revelation, far too many years later, when she would have done much better to keep it to herself. The tenuous facts of married life can also be very serious. And there are hundreds of such facts, so many that people often overlook them, because otherwise the relationship would collapse. I'm not one of those people. Well, I've overlooked others, like everyone else, but not that one.'

'Tell me then, go on. Don't worry, I'm not going to prejudge anything. I have no reason to, no right.'

He lay down again, feeling reassured, and it was then that I saw the smudge of a face, or someone's head and shoulders, through the glass panes of the door, and because the panes were frosted I couldn't make out who it was. When Muriel had summoned me to his side of the apartment, there had been no one else at home. The children had gone to a swimming pool, Flavia was out shopping and running various errands, and Beatriz had left as soon as she'd had breakfast without saying where she was going, certainly not to me. From Muriel's supine position on the floor, that face lay outside his field of vision, that pink stain, which was not pressed against the glass, but a step or two away, so as not to attract attention or in the belief that it would remain undetected. But I could see it from where I was sitting at the desk. I wondered if that person could hear us, the doors were closed, but not completely; it was possible. I wasn't sure whether to warn Muriel of that ghostly, distorted presence. 'He'll stop talking at once if I tell him,' I thought, 'and I still won't know the story, and he may never again be in storytelling vein. I mustn't risk it.' When I looked harder at the pink smudge, I seemed to recognize the oval of Beatriz's face, which I had seen once before through glass, except that then her face had been squashed against it and the glass had been clear, and her eyes had been tight shut while someone fucked her from behind:

it hadn't been me on that occasion, but the two memories combined and filled me with sudden shame – for Van Vechten in the Sanctuary and for me in my cubbyhole – so much so that I may have blushed. 'Even if it is Beatriz,' I thought, 'there'll be nothing new about Muriel's version of events, nothing that he hasn't flung in her face a thousand times for eight long years, it will be an old wound, if it is a wound.' She had even admitted her guilt on that night of prowling and pleading, my first act of espionage: 'I'm so sorry, my love, I'm so sorry I hurt you,' she had said, and she had perhaps been sincere, or was it just a ploy? 'I wish I could turn back the clock.' That's what we all wish sometimes, my love, to go back, have our time over, to change what that time held, all too often we're the ones who decide what time holds and who determine how time will see us once it's gone and has been definitively relegated to the past, and yet, as it's happening, we can't see it and can't, therefore, picture it. In the end it will become an immutable image, full of hasty, random, twisted lines, and that's how it will always appear to our eyes, or to the one eye in the back of our head, maritime blue or midnight blue. I decided not to warn him, not to tell him about the smudge, the face, the stain.

'No, you don't have the right,' said Muriel, 'but you won't be able to help yourself. You will make a judgement, even if you don't pronounce it. It doesn't matter. Anyway, what is it that you keep looking at?' He had noticed that I kept staring to my right, at the door.

'Oh, nothing. There are a few books over there that need putting back on the shelves. You know what a fiend I am for order. I'll just go and tidy them up. Sorry.'

I got to my feet and went over to a small revolving bookshelf to the left of the door, where Muriel, who was something of a bibliophile, kept a few of his favourite first editions, or ones signed or inscribed by the author. The bookshelf was on a lower level than the glass panes I was looking at, but my excuse worked. As I walked past the door, the figure on the other side immediately retreated or disappeared briefly from view. I was pretty sure it was Beatriz; she must have come in without our noticing, and when she heard the murmur of our voices, she must have stopped to see if she could glean something of our conversation. I pretended to put the books back on the shelves and then returned to my place at the desk. A moment later, I saw the pink smudge reappear, like an unfinished pastel portrait.

'For heaven's sake, leave them be.'

'Sorry. Do go on, please. What happened? What fault did she commit?'

'Um,' he said, 'um', as if he were a hesitant Englishman. 'Well, the first fault was mine, if falling in love is a fault, given that it's almost always involuntary. It can sometimes be deliberate, but that's pretty rare. Months passed and more months, and Beatriz still couldn't leave her father on his own. We postponed the wedding or decided, at any rate, not to fix a date, not until the situation was resolved, although it was quite hard to see how that would happen. Her father was feeling weak, bewildered, ashamed and indecisive. He had aged ten years, according to Beatriz; his hair had turned white, lines had appeared on his face as if by magic, he had lost both his physical and mental agility and seemed to be making no progress at all. And of course I carried on with my life here, you can't go on endlessly waiting for someone, especially when they're such a vast distance away and you can't see them or even hear their voice from time to time, something that's so easy now . . . I must confess, too, that misfortunes have a cooling, distancing effect, and if they continue for too long, you end up fleeing them : . . I was given the chance to make my second film and threw myself into that – films were made very quickly then, in three or four weeks, sometimes less, but five at most, apart from the editing and all that . . . Anyway, I fell madly in love with another woman, it doesn't matter who she was.' – 'A woman who deserves my complete confidence. A former friend, a former actress, although she wasn't an actress when I met her, that came later,' I remembered or thought. 'A former love. The love of my life, as people say,' he had said. But I preferred not to interrupt him with an unnecessary question. – 'I experienced a passion I had never known until then. I'm not going to explain to you what it feels like. If you haven't yet experienced it yourself – and it rarely appears before you're thirty – it will sound to you like certain fervid pop songs, shrill ballads, cheap, trite literature. And if you have, well, you'll know what I'm talking about. It's very dull to describe, just as sex is. Actually experiencing those things is fascinating, but talking about them is tedious, the same tired old story, with the occasional change of character or cast, but few variants. It's a very bothersome thing, when you look back at it, when you've got beyond it. Later on, it's even hard to imagine yourself in that state. But while it lasts, it's all-absorbing. You feel sucked in, you're under the illusion that real life consists entirely of that, and everything else pales into insignificance. You even rather look down upon those who don't feel passion, you fall into a kind of hubris. I was quite clear that not only did I want to be with that woman, I wanted to be with her for ever, imagine that. And she felt the same. Our passion grew and showed no signs of diminishing. I had no choice but to break off my engagement and put an end to our relationship. Once I had discovered passion, staying with Beatriz would have meant unhappiness for us both. It would not be a pleasant task, it never is. But, given her situation, it became a mountain I couldn't climb.'

Muriel was not studying the painting now, but the ceiling. He was speaking almost as if to himself. He stopped. I glanced to my right, quickly so that he wouldn't notice. The smudge was still there behind the glass, Beatriz's legs must have been getting tired, weary of standing, she had been there a while. Although she did have strong legs, which would help; and she had probably taken off her shoes too. She must have been able to hear some of our conversation, she would hardly have stayed there all that time, if, as well as being barely able to see us, she couldn't hear us either. I thought she would probably catch only fragments, for Muriel's voice scarcely rose above floor level and I hardly spoke. 'It must be worth her while though,' I thought, 'to catch the odd thread of this story that she knows already.'

'And I assume you didn't climb it, the mountain, I mean,' I said.

'And what makes you think that, may I ask?' Muriel retorted angrily.

'Well, Eduardo, because you married Beatriz. You had children together. You've been married for years. What other conclusion could I come to?'

'Don't push your luck, young De Vere, don't push your luck,' he repeated, audibly offended, and he sat up again like a spring; I thought he was going to get up altogether, and that he would then notice the blurred face at the door and not finish his story. 'Do you really think

460

all my resentment stems from my having lacked the courage to speak, that I ruined my life out of delicatesse? That I avoided an unpleasant scene out of cowardice? How could I possibly have blamed her for that situation, man? Who do you take me for?' I said nothing, and he calmed down and resumed his supine position on the floor, his liking for which never ceased to surprise me. He recovered his serene tone, grave, almost mournful, a feeling he could barely disguise. 'No, I behaved honourably, as far as I could, although no one can be expected to do so indefinitely. I wrote her a long letter explaining what had happened, what was happening to me. I tried to word it as affectionately as possible, regretting the pain I was causing her, explaining that this was the last thing I would ever have wanted, well, the usual things one says when giving someone painful news. I couldn't conceal it from her. I told her to stay in America, not to come back. Or not to come back because of me, because I wouldn't be here for her, that it was all over between us. I assumed that if she stayed in America, she would soon forget about me and get on with her life. After all, she'd been brought up there and it was more her home than Spain was. The very people who had ousted her father would con-sider her an innocent victim and help her with scholarships or find her a job or whatever. Not that I felt comfortable about it, how could I? I marked the letter "Express" and prepared to wait. I half-expected an urgent call, not that it would have made any difference, you can't talk about something like that with the meter ticking implacably onwards. In those days, you thought carefully before making a long-distance call, and tended to speak as quickly as possible, "You're going to bankrupt yourself," you'd say if someone was dragging things out. When I assumed the letter must have arrived, though, there was no phone call, but after a few days, I received a telegram. I opened it, convinced it was her reply, a scream, an insult, an entreaty,

461

a reproach, a threat, a plea to wait until we saw each other again, to give her a chance to win me back, because distance distorts and displaces. But no. The telegram said: "Dad died last night. Another heart attack. Things to sort out here. Home in two weeks. Get everything ready. Love you." '

'So the letter hadn't arrived,' I said.

'Obviously not. Letters did sometimes take ages to arrive, however many times you wrote "Express" on them. Some got lost. Well, it's not so very different today, I suppose. I hadn't sent it registered mail, though, it simply hadn't occurred to me to do so. My heart sank. She would receive the letter any day, adding despair to grief; she would feel as if her world had fallen in on her. If only I could stop the letter. Not in order to cancel it, but to wait for a more opportune moment, to postpone it a little, even if only for a week, and not add blow upon blow. But it was already flying to its destination, indeed, it must already have arrived. "Get everything ready." She would leave behind her dead past, and I was her only future, her life. I didn't know what to do. I was tempted to phone her briefly about her father, so that she could at least hear my voice. But that would have contradicted my letter. In the telegram, she sounded fairly calm. The way her father had been heading, stuck in that cul-de-sac, death was almost a solution. But she adored him and that hadn't changed, I mean not since the most recent, shocking revelations: for many women, the father of the little girl they were survives intact and unchanged, they forgive him everything. She would be lost. And more or less alone. In the end, I judged the most prudent course of action would be to send another telegram: "Deepest condolences. Urgent letter on way. Important. Read first. Best wishes." '

Muriel could recall exactly his words and hers in that telegraphic exchange. He was quoting verbatim, he must have read and reread

462

them many times, and I imagine that isn't something you forget. 'He didn't even write "Lots of love",' I thought, 'still less return her "Love you". "Best wishes" is what you would say to anyone, especially if they had just suffered a loss. He was watching his back, he must have thought about what he was writing; he didn't want to be abrupt, to add blow upon blow, but neither did he want to give her any room for hope. Yes, in that respect, he acted honourably.'

'And what happened?'

'Nothing. She never answered. Not that there was really any need for her to answer that last telegram. It was simply a matter of waiting for the promised letter. And she would have been busy arranging the funeral, closing up their no doubt rented house, sorting out his will, not that he would have left very much, but there might have been something. Or so I assumed. Besides, she had already said that she needed two weeks to get everything done before she could fly back. I just had to await her reaction to my letter. It would happen sooner or later, but it didn't. Every day, troubled and fearful, I expected that reaction and wondered how I would deal with it; but the day passed and no response, nothing. I was getting desperate and, at the same time, why deny it, I felt a kind of illusory sense of relief, well, no one wants to face up to the tears he has caused. But she didn't even take those two weeks of extra time. She hurried everything along as if the devil were after her, as if she were fleeing persecution by the FBI, like Harry and his posh totty.' He laughed abruptly at the thought of the two of them. 'She left a lawyer friend to deal with the paperwork, and just nine days later, I received another telegram: "Arrive Barajas tomorrow Wednesday. TWA NY 7AM. Meet me there. Love you more than ever."'

'So she still hadn't read your letter,' I said. 'Arriving from New York the following day, and really early too. She wasn't giving you

463

much time to make a decision, to get things ready. And what was happening with the other woman meanwhile?' I couldn't help asking about her, the love of his life, who, either before or afterwards, had fallen victim to Van Vechten, or so she had told Muriel, when she discovered he was a close friend of the paediatrician.

'You're such a pest with your inquisitiveness,' he said. 'Hand me another cigarette and pour me a drink, will you? My mouth's gone dry with all this talking.' I did as asked and poured myself one too. I placed his on the coffee table, where he could easily reach it from the floor and put it down again. When I got up to go over to the drinks cabinet, the smudged figure again retreated from the glass panes or perhaps crouched down. Muriel took a sip and went on. 'It doesn't matter about her, she's not relevant. She was extremely important once, but she's ancient history now. She was erased completely and absolutely, at least for many years.'

'You gave her up.'

'What else could I do? It didn't take me long to consider once I received that telegram. There was, quite simply, nothing to be done about it. My letter had got lost somewhere or would only arrive after she'd set off. Beatriz knew nothing of its contents and was flying back to me like someone travelling towards her salvation, to all that she'd left behind, in the belief that nothing had changed, that everything was just as it had been when she flew off to America. It was what had sustained her for all those months, and, although she was a grown woman, she was only twenty-one. I'd written the letter when her father was still alive, although he hadn't yet recovered from his first heart attack and his future as a teacher was pretty much non-existent after the scandal. But Beatriz was still then in a position to stay put and had a very good reason to remain in America – a mission even – and make a life for herself there. Now, though, she had burned all her boats. She would have spent much of her remaining money on the air fare; she had closed the house in Massachusetts, so she couldn't go back, she would have nowhere to live; there was nothing to keep her in that country, no strong bond. It was a fait accompli. I could have stood my ground and hoped she would get over it in Madrid. We do eventually recover from everything, and her aunt and uncle would have taken her in, at least initially. Later, who knows? People have, of course, found themselves in far worse situations. Dickens's novels are positively teeming with orphaned children.' A remnant of good humour almost always surfaced from his basically jovial self. 'I didn't have the courage. I had tried, but it hadn't worked. I felt that I'd made a commitment, and was in her debt. She was travelling towards me entirely ignorant of what was happening, of what had happened to me; full of excitement and hope, despite her grief, despite several consecutive hard blows. I just couldn't bring myself to deal her yet another blow, the definitive one, or so I thought. The inconveniences of an old-fashioned upbringing, young De Vere, and I was young then, too close to my childhood self. I'd been brought up to have a sense of responsibility, to believe that one must keep one's word. The notion of behaving like a gentleman sounds so ridiculous now, but it didn't twenty years ago. Everything disappears so quickly.' – 'Wretched haste,' I thought; 'it doesn't afflict only tongues; time, too, is constantly driving out people, customs, concepts.' – 'The belief that you shouldn't cause any harm if it's in your power not to.'

He raised the palms of both hands to his face and squeezed his cheeks, distorting his mouth. I didn't know if he was cursing that old-fashioned upbringing or embracing it retrospectively, if he was struggling to find a place for it again in his heart; after all, we can do little to protect ourselves against what befalls us. Or against our character if we can't change it. There are, though, more and more people who, every now and then, do reconfigure themselves.

'And how did the other woman take it?' I was still interested in the abandoned woman, despite Muriel's reluctance to talk about her.

Removing his hands from his face, he gave a long sigh, and his mouth returned to its usual shape; then he touched his eyepatch with two fingers to check that it hadn't shifted.

'I spent the whole night with her. I told her what had happened, I explained everything, and she cried and cried, but she also understood in part, she didn't become aggressive or hysterical. She wasn't even filled with self-pity, she just cried. But as I said before, best leave her out of it, since that's precisely where she was left, poor thing.' Muriel had doubtless forgotten that he'd already told me a little about this, and in another context. 'Do what you think you ought to do,' I remembered him saying that she had said. 'Do what will cause you least pain, what you'll find easiest to live with. But never think of us, of you and me. Never think of us together if you don't want to be filled with regret day after day and, still more, night after night. Never even think of us apart either, because, by remembering that, you'll bring us together again.'

'Yes, you've told me about that before.' And I repeated those words back to him from memory.

He sat up again and looked at me for a moment in amazement, then quickly collected his thoughts.

'Hmm, very good.' There was a slight quaver in his voice and he sounded a touch irritated by my perfect recall. 'You've always boasted about your retentive memory. I'll need to be careful what I tell you, because you register it all like a tape recorder. Yes, she did say something of the sort. But that was at the end. That night, believe me, was very long. It had its ups and downs and I did occasionally waver. But the decision I had made prevailed. I said goodbye to her just after six in the morning and went straight to the airport, straight from her apartment. I closed the door behind me so that she wouldn't watch me waiting for the lift to arrive, although she may have watched me through the spyhole, I've no way of knowing. I closed that door in the knowledge that I was letting passion and the love of my life slip from my grasp. That rarest of things: passion . . . When I arrived at Barajas, I probably still smelled of her, but it didn't matter. No one was going to call me to account, that would have been the final straw; and Beatriz was too astute ever to make such a blunder, not after so many months apart.'

'And how did it go, your re-encounter with Beatriz? Given where you'd just come from, I mean.' I spoke again because he had fallen silent. I shot a quick glance at the glass door, where the pink face had resumed its vigil.

'The flight arrived punctually, almost on the dot, and I got there just in time. When Beatriz appeared, she looked really lovely, I would be lying if I said otherwise, nothing at all like the way she looks now. Not that it was any kind of compensation, but it was better than nothing. It's best if you like the person you're going to spend a long time with, in the most elemental, epidermal way, I mean. She flung her arms around me with a smile the like of which I've never seen in my life, radiant, luminous. I've tried to get a few actresses to reproduce that smile in my films, but, however good, they've never managed to come up with anything but a pale reflection of it. She smiled as if she couldn't believe her luck, as if she couldn't believe that she was back with me again. And then she burst into tears, buried her face in my chest and stayed like that for a while; I remember she left a wet patch on my raincoat. She must have been really longing to see me again. And that can't fail to touch your heart, the other person's ignorance and their happiness too, I mean, when it's clear that you're the cause of that happiness. You feel responsible, or more responsible. When we collected her luggage and she'd recovered a little, one of my first questions – I couldn't help myself – was: "Didn't you ever receive my letter? The one I mentioned in my telegram?" "No!" she said in a pained voice. "And I was so looking forward to it. I thought it would be a real consolation, that you would talk to me about my father, about his death, that it would help me to accept it. I was so furious that it got lost, the letter I most needed to read." She had assumed my letter would be a letter of condolence in a way. That I'd written it as soon as I heard the news, quickly, so that she wouldn't be left with just a few compressed, laconic sentences. If I had sent it then, though, too few days would have passed for her to give it up as hopelessly lost: nine or ten at most. I hadn't been explicit enough in my telegram. "Urgent letter on way. Important. Read first," I had said. At the time, she wouldn't have been in any state to decipher subtleties or ponder meanings. I should have added "before you travel" or "before you make any decision". "Read before you travel"; I imagine that would have been enough to bring her up short, to make her think, to investigate further and not rush into anything; or even to phone me when the letter failed to arrive.' He paused, took a sip of his drink and smiled, this time with a certain self-mockery or a touch of bitterness. 'But everyone then saved on words when sending telegrams.'

'You don't think then that things would have turned out very differently if you hadn't saved on words?' I said.

Then he grew weary of lying down or else wanted to see me face to face, because not only did he get up, he gave himself a good stretch, arms taut, sat down on one of the sofas, the one with its back to the door (when he got to his feet, the smudge, doubtless startled, again disappeared), and told me to leave my post at the desk, indicating that I should sit on the other sofa.

'Sit over there, will you, so that I don't have to crane my neck. Why is it that you always forget that my field of vision is not the same as yours? As if this eyepatch wasn't enough of a clue.' And he drummed on it briefly. And when I'd done as he asked, he said, 'Who knows? Probably not. She would doubtless have found another way to play the innocent, to feign ignorance. I know that now, but I didn't then. Well, the idea did occur to me, and even more so to the other woman, but I thought that was just her despair speaking and dismissed it out of hand. To be honest, I didn't think anyone so young would be capable of acting in such an underhand, cold-blooded manner.' – 'I'm slightly older than she was then,' flashed through my mind, 'and I've acted in an equally underhand manner, but not, I think, cold-bloodedly.' – 'Especially not in the midst of her grief, but we often confuse vulnerability with innocuousness and believe victims are somehow harmless – a widespread misconception. I didn't believe she was capable of basing her whole future life on a lie. Of mortgaging her life and placing it on such a precarious footing. Of course, the more all-embracing the lie, the more likely the liar is to forget about it. She knew me intimately, had spent years studying me from when she was a child, when I was too distracted to even notice or realize. I was too ingenuous, too trusting. I always felt that one couldn't go through life full of suspicion and mistrust. It took me a long time to learn my mistake. I'm not even sure I've learned it now. But what can you do? Life may teach you some bitter lessons and force you to be more cautious, but if that's not in your nature, those lessons may have an attenuating effect, but little more.'

'And it was years before you found out.'

'Twelve years more or less,' he said, 'imagine that. Twelve years and four children later. And I didn't find out for myself either, she blurted it out in a fit of anger, to wound me. I could have died without ever knowing, which would have been better, I think.' – 'If only you'd never told me. If only you'd kept me in the dark,' I recalled him saying.

'Do you really think so? Are you serious?' However precocious in other respects, I was too young to understand that. Young people are overly attached to the truth, the truth that affects them, that is. They themselves are frequently rather less than truthful, but you can't expect them to question those truths that concern or touch them. They can't bear to be mocked or taken for fools, when that, in fact, is a minor matter and the common fate of all men and women, without distinction.

'Yes, I really do. I had, after all, made an effort, a huge effort. I'd taken absolutely seriously the advice of that other woman, whose words you recalled. Hers was a rhetorical, not to say dramatic recommendation, yes, a final theatrical flourish. Quite right, given the abrupt, unexpected nature of that farewell, a way of preserving her dignity. But I took it literally, I saw the sense in it. And so I did exactly as she said, I forgot all about her and me, insofar as that was possible, that is, superficially: a nostalgia for the life you discarded always lingers on in the inner depths of your being, and, during bad times, you seek refuge in it as you might in a daydream or a fantasy. But once I'd made that decision, or on that morning when I left the airport with Beatriz on my arm, as if we were a real couple setting out towards our future, I decided that I would follow that path. "I'm going to love her," I told myself over and over, "I'm going to be always by her side. I'm going to be faithful to her, I'm not going to fail her or abandon her. I didn't choose her, but she's the person who it's fallen to me to marry. It doesn't matter, though, I'll stay by her side, I'll protect and support her and care for her children, and I'll love her as if I had chosen her. I'll forget what was lost along the way, it's too late to go back and, besides, that path is no longer mine to follow. I will walk this path without looking back and will try not to complain." That's what I told myself and repeated to myself endless times, over many years.'

'And did you keep that promise?' I asked, although I knew the answer, because I'd heard it that night when Beatriz rapped timidly on his bedroom door with one knuckle: 'How stupid of me to love you during all those years, love you with all my heart, as long, that is, as I knew nothing,' he had said, placing his hands on her shoulders, before disdainfully, crudely groping her body, with perhaps a vague or concealed lust he had long since forbidden himself to feel. And after a while, after the groping, she had answered: 'No, it wasn't stupid of you. On the contrary, you were quite right to love me during all those years, all those past years . . . You've probably never done anything better.' Then I felt sure that her eyes must have filled with tears, because that's the only explanation I could find for Muriel's surprising reaction. 'I'll grant you that,' he said. 'All the more reason for me to

471

feel I've thrown away my life. A part of my life. That's why I can't forgive you.' And he said this in a gentle, almost regretful voice.

'Of course I kept my promise, perhaps excessively. As I said, it was easy enough to love her, but without passion. But then passion isn't essential. And I found it easier still after her revelations about her father, his convalescence and subsequent death, I saw her as helpless and rootless, alone and without a place in the world. It was easy enough to desire her too, until I felt repelled by what she'd done, and it was then that she began to neglect herself. I'm not saying I didn't have the odd flirtation during those twelve years, because we often spent time apart, when I was filming in America or not so far afield. But they were very few and were just that, occasional flirtations that were never any threat to her and left no mark on me, still less nostalgia. I can barely remember them now. Then the children came along, and that always strengthens ties. Then our oldest child died, and we got through that together. I won't even attempt to describe what the death of a small child means, there's far too much cheap, opportunistic literature out there, too many films exploiting that misfortune as a guaranteed way to move people to tears and pity, it's easy enough in fiction and in autobiography, it's cynical, indecent. Even Thomas Mann resorted to it, I believe, in his famous *Doctor Faustus*. Anyway, it's something you never forget. It's not just the child you don't forget, but the person who was by your side, who experienced that misfortune with you, who you watched suffer and struggle to keep afloat, who you sustained and who you yourself clung to so that she could sustain you. You can't cancel out everything that happened, Juan, even if the origin of it all turns out to have been a lie.'

He broke off, remained sunk in thought. He was no longer looking up, but staring downwards with his one fixed and penetrating eye, as if trying to see right through the wooden floorboards. I didn't dare go over to the photo of Beatriz and the little boy, which was my first impulse; not that I really needed to, I knew it well and had studied it carefully. I took a moment to glance over at the glass door, where there was not a trace now of the blurred face; perhaps she was hiding behind the door frame or had left, not wanting to hear any more (if she could hear) or not wanting to be discovered there by her old and current love who had so wholeheartedly rejected her ('I'm so sorry, my love,' she had said).

'Why did she tell you after all those years?'

'Oh, the reason is the least of it. Not long after Tomás was born, we had an argument. There was an actress . . . She wasn't important then, none of them were, not even the woman I left for Beatriz, and by the time she reappeared briefly in my life, I had carried out her advice to the letter. And one time cannot supplant another . . . Anyway, I turned very nasty, you've seen me do it, I can be very provoking. And that's what I did to her on that occasion, and she blurted it out without a thought, without considering the possible consequences. We so often gauge things badly, thinking erroneously that the words we say are less harmful than anything we might do with our hands. So much time had passed, so many things and events had intervened, children, films, our marriage, that she saw her earlier trick as mere childish nonsense, at least that's what she always says in her defence. I see it too as prehistory, something that our life together should have buried ages ago, beneath the weight of the present, the weight of events, of irreversible time. But the worst thing wasn't that she told me, but that she actually brought me the letter to show me. She went straight to a shelf, took the letter out of a book and handed it to me. There it was, opened, but still in its stamped envelope, the name and address in my handwriting, I'd written "Express" on it in red pen and tremulously entrusted it to the postal service, taken it to

473

the central post office in Cibeles so that it would get there more quickly. I'd sweated blood over writing it, spent a whole sleepless night, weighed every word, trying to be honest and at the same time not to hurt her, or as little as possible. As far as I was concerned, it had got lost in some limbo and never arrived, and yet there it was, it had travelled all the way to America and come back with her in her suitcases or perhaps in her handbag or already tucked inside the book she had perhaps read during that long flight. It had spent twelve years in her grasp and, what's more, she had kept it. Why else would you keep something like that – when it would make more sense to destroy it, burn it – if not to show it to me one day, in order to gloat, in order to rub it in, not content with having changed the course of my entire life, with directing my life as a director would an actor, imposing herself on my life and occupying it against my express wishes, which she had known from the start. She must have wanted me to find out one day, must have wanted me, one day, to be undeceived, when deception is sometimes the best state to be in if you're resigned to your lot. And I was pretty much resigned to my lot. I'd certainly forgotten all about passion, which is not that difficult, given what a rare thing it is.'

I remembered then what he'd said to me on another morning, when he talked to me about their firstborn who had died and how much Van Vechten had done to save him, and how much he'd done for all of them over the years. Those were the words of someone who knows what the balance of probabilities is in people's lives and who doesn't consider himself to be an exception: 'Far too many lives are shaped by deceit or error, it's probably always been like that, so why should I be any different, why shouldn't my life be the same? That thought gives me some consolation, convinces me that I'm not the only one – on the contrary, I'm just one more on an endless list of those who tried to act correctly, to keep their promises, those who prided themselves on being able to say something that sounds more and more like a piece of antiquated foolishness: "My word on it" . . .'

He took a sip of his drink, lit another of my cigarettes, and crossed his legs, so long that the foot of the upper leg easily touched the floor. He felt in one of his trouser pockets, took out his compass and brought needle to eye or eye to needle, as if the latter contained all of past time or all of time as yet unhappened, or as if he had grown tired of remembering and was leaving the rest for me to deduce. However, I asked:

'Why didn't you separate? Weren't you tempted to just leave at once?' I wanted to know why he had opted instead for that long and indissoluble misery. As I've mentioned, divorce didn't exist in Spain then and wouldn't be made legal until a year later, but from 1940 on, people used to separate discreetly, without making it official or telling anyone, especially if it was the husband who decided to leave. It had always been like that in subjugated Spain, with people finding ways of getting around the laws, or some of them.

'Certainly not.' He reacted at once, his one eye bright with anger, and looked up from his compass. 'When she showed me the letter, I understood that the radiant smile with which she had greeted me when I went to meet her at the airport, the smile I'd tried to get actresses to emulate, was not one of mere unknowing happiness, blithely unaware of the risk she had run, but the knowing, triumphantly happy smile of someone who has got her own way and seen her performance crowned with success. She had to pay for that, and leaving her would have been too benign a thing to do. She would have recovered sooner or later, and since she was still fairly young, she might have met another man. However, if I was still around, even if only periodically, that would have been impossible. As has proved to be the case.'

'She still *is* young, Eduardo, although you don't want to see that.' Either he didn't hear me or he ignored me.

'I insisted on having separate rooms and closed my door to her for ever. If nothing else, ours had always been a very sexual relationship. But I haven't touched her since, not for . . . how old is Tomás now? . . . eight years. Nor have I gone back to loving her in that easy, celebratory, superficial way in which I always loved her, and which, for her, was enough.' And yet I had on a few occasions seen them laughing together perhaps without realizing that they were; and after the Hotel Wellington incident, he'd behaved kindly and almost affectionately towards her: we can't entirely suppress old habits, I suppose, however hard we try. 'She put on weight, became depressed, began gradually to lose her mind, every day a little more. All her suicide attempts have occurred since then and are doubtless a consequence of that, or were to begin with. She would never even have considered suicide before, she had nothing to complain about. No, there was nothing benign about what I did, but it was just.' – 'Forgiveness doesn't last as long as vengeance,' I thought or recalled. Or perhaps I only think or recall that now.

'Yes, but at the cost of staying bound to her. It reminds me of that expression that so perfectly defines us Spaniards: *Quedarse uno tuerto por dejar al otro ciego* – "To put out your own eye while trying to make another man blind."'

He looked at me with a mixture of severity and irony.

'I was already one-eyed, young De Vere, or hadn't you noticed?' And he again tapped on his eyepatch. But this time he didn't mean this only in the literal sense, he was referring to his own ingenuousness, his good faith, his credulity of twenty or so years ago. 'Since then, I do as I want, I don't have to account to anyone or to bother inventing truths. And it's the same for her, I suppose, I don't care how she conducts her life, I've washed my hands of her; but she does what she wants because she has to, not because she wants to; she does it reluctantly, I oblige her to enjoy a freedom she doesn't want at all,

476

because she would much prefer to be tied to me. Besides, I haven't missed anything: I haven't met anyone else who interested me enough to make me consider running off with her. That's all over, out of the question. Although who knows, soon . . .'

'Soon what?' The words just slipped out, and my pushiness doubtless prevented me from finding out what he was about to announce, what tempting future beckoned.

'Nothing.' He clammed up at once. 'Just as the past isn't really any of your business, the future certainly isn't.'

I didn't insist, I prudently let it pass. 'Just as well,' I thought when I saw the recognizable oval face, the pink smudge behind the glass panes, she obviously didn't care now if Muriel saw her or not, although he still had his back to her, while I was facing her. 'It's best if she doesn't hear, assuming she can, it's best if she doesn't hear him, that poor unhappy woman, sad and affectionate. Poor soul, poor wretch.'

'But you obviously do care how she conducts her life,' I said, returning to what he had said earlier, 'given how terrified you were on that night at the Hotel Wellington.'

'Ha,' he said. And after a few seconds, he made the same sound, not so much a laugh as a sign of faint disappointment or superiority: as if he needed to make himself superior to me. 'Ha. So much for being the memory man. As you yourself said: I don't care how she conducts her life, but I do care how she conducts her death and I don't want her to succeed in that. I care a great deal about her dying, about her killing herself. That's the last thing I want. It would be terrible for my children, and for me as well. Of course if she does succeed one day, there's nothing I can do about it. But if that does happen, be in no doubt, it will be a real tragedy for me and I will weep for her. As I said, you can't just put a line through the past to erase it. Even once you've decided that you no longer want that past.'

477

Yes, I had heard him say something along those lines, and he had put it more elaborately to Beatriz at the door to his bedroom: 'What is the point of setting the record straight? That's even worse, because it invalidates or gives the lie to everything that went before, it obliges the deceived person to look at their whole life in a new light, or else deny it. And yet that *was* your life, and you can't unlive what you've lived. So what do you do? Strike out your whole existence? That's impossible but neither can you simply discard all those years, which were what they were and can be no other way, and of which there will always be a remnant, a memory, even if it smacks of the phantasmagorical, something that both happened and didn't happen. And what do you do with something that both happened and didn't happen?' His tone had been one of lamentation, not scornful or aggressive, although there was still perhaps a hint of rancour. Beatriz Noguera had immediately adopted that same tone, wishing she could turn back the clock and asking his forgiveness; perhaps knowingly, perhaps sincerely.

Then she opened the door, revealed her presence. She wasn't barefoot, she was wearing the high heels she almost always wore when she went out and that accentuated her voluptuous figure. When Muriel heard the door open, he got up and turned round, and when he saw her, his one eye glinted. She remained on the threshold with one hand held out, looking at him pleadingly, as if she were asking him to take her hand and lead her into the room, as if she were again calling him 'my love'. Hearing him say that her death was the last thing he wanted, hearing him say that he would weep for her, must have seemed to her a motive for gratitude, or perhaps for unreasonable hope. However, the gesture he made was unequivocal. A gesture of rejection repeated several times, driving her away, ordering her to leave at once, as if he were scaring off a cat. I felt he was repeating the words he'd been saying to her for eight years: '*Non, pas de caresses*. And no kisses either.'

IX

And he did weep for her, I saw it with my own eyes.. He wept for her when he heard the news and wept copiously during the burial at La Almudena cemetery, one sunny Madrid morning; I saw how the irrepressible tears flowed from his speaking eye – not from the silent one, which presumably had no tear duct or maybe the tightly fitting patch acted as a dam – while the gravediggers were finally lowering the coffin into the grave and covering it with the first spadefuls of earth. No one stayed behind to see the last spadefuls nor for the gravestone to be lowered back into place, after it had been removed to make way for the new coffin; there was still room though in the family tomb – presumably for Muriel himself; and their ill-fated son, Javier, who had been resting there for a long time and took up very little space, having died so young, would now be wrapped in his mother's imaginary embrace. However hard Muriel found it to say goodbye, he didn't stay behind and was so unsteady on his feet that he had to be supported, and Susana, Tomás and Alicia, who provided that support, didn't stay behind either, more concerned about their living and temporarily aged father – a sudden ageing that lasted only a day – than about their mother who was now only abundant, inert flesh that would soon be lost, a process which, fortunately, we would not see: we, very sensibly, do not impose witnesses on the dead, but leave them in their deathly pallor to continue dying. Neither Rico nor

Roy nor Van Vechten stayed behind, nor Gloria nor Marcela nor Flavia, nor Beatriz's colleagues at the school where she used to teach her American English, nor the few students who attended as representatives, nor the two or three private students who also came. Still less Muriel's acquaintances, who came out of obligation or out of *vergüenza torera*, the bullfighter's fear of what the public will say if he holds back: maestro Rafael Viana and other gambling pals, the former accompanied by the civil servant Celia, who shot me a veiled and neutral glance; a couple of diplomats and a few people from the film industry, among whom I spotted a wine-producer whom Muriel was trying to cajole into financing his latest project and, very briefly, Jess Franco, who left almost at once, taking short, hurried steps, doubtless hoping to finish shooting half a film in what remained of the day. I was not exactly surprised to see, standing at a discreet distance, the impresaria Cecilia Alemany, who I recognized despite her dark glasses, partly because she was chewing gum, unaware of how inappropriate her mandibular movements were in that place and that context. A brazen woman, as very wealthy women tend to be, and as confirmed by her recent close relationship with my boss. I didn't stay behind either to see the coffin disappear completely beneath the earth; it wouldn't have been right and would have seemed strange. However, I promised myself I would visit the grave now and then, although I haven't done so in all this time, or only once, years later, to accompany the dear departed and to support Susana, who was then the person unsteadiest on her feet.

Shortly after my conversation with Muriel, he and Beatriz, the children and Flavia went to spend the summer in a house they often stayed at in Soria, a cool, breezy town with Romanesque churches, memories of the poet Antonio Machado, a river you can swim in and a beautiful park. They had been going there for years, or else, if it got

482

too hot there, and depending on the highs and lows of their finances, to a hotel in San Sebastián, and since Soria was less than three hours from Madrid by road, Muriel could drive back if any urgent business cropped up. I don't know what happened during their time there, if anything did. It probably didn't, apart from Muriel's usual foul behaviour, possibly exacerbated by a lack of escape routes: I imagine that Muriel was only there occasionally, his presence being required urgently in Madrid or in other places, whether on genuine business or not or perhaps summoned by the first woman in many years to exercise a real hold over him. And when they came back at the end of August, I stopped working at the apartment in Calle Velázquez and said goodbye to my cubbyhole, as I had more or less decided to do anyway. I'd become too involved in everything, or perhaps that troubled marriage had got in the way of my own life, the life of a mere beginner. Another deciding factor was the invariable presence of Van Vechten, who continued coming and going as usual, although with me he was no longer friendly and chatty and relaxed, but stiff and severe. Muriel was grateful enough and fond enough not to care much about what the Doctor might have done, and after those wretched, tormenting doubts of his – which were the reason he had involved me in the whole sordid story in the first place – he preferred to know nothing about it. Van Vechten, he said, hadn't done whatever it was to him, whereas Beatriz had. But after what Vidal had told me and after my meeting with Van Vechten in Bar Chicote, after his far-from-veiled threats ('Be careful what you say . . . Do you understand me, boy?'), I didn't even want to be in the same room as him.

This meant that I couldn't be there to follow Beatriz or to guard or keep watch over her, to set off after her when she went out alone, which was when we should have been worried, according to her husband and as I myself discovered later on. On the other hand, I gave up that furtive and hard-to-explain habit more or less after I'd had sex with her – only on that one night and unbeknown to anyone, or known only to the someone who had run down the corridor and then said nothing or behaved no differently towards me afterwards or never looked at me reproachfully – not a sign – whoever that was, I've never been certain, although I have my suspicions. And even if I had been there, I wouldn't have been able to follow her that afternoon, I never could when she got on her Harley-Davidson and disappeared off who knows where or with whom or to see whoever, if such a whoever existed. Muriel never talked to me about the two suicide attempts she had made before I came on the scene, or not in detail, but if they failed they must, like the one attempt I thwarted, have been less drastic and less rapid, less brutal and less hesitant, with a chance that she might be saved. Beatriz Noguera crashed into a tree in September, as it was getting dark, on a minor road near Ávila, a couple of kilometres from where Muriel's brother, Roberto, had been killed, along with a young Frenchwoman, both of them in a very unbuttoned state. I don't know why, but I imagined it would have been one of those trees – there are long rows of them – with a white line painted round them to make them more visible at night, although it may be that, by 1980, they'd stopped painting those lines, I can't be sure, I don't remember. Even though with motorbike or car crashes there is always the possibility that it wasn't intended, that it happened by chance, the result of the driver's distraction or imprudence or something quite unforeseen, we all thought that she had driven into the tree on purpose, at least we adults did. (The children, of course, were given a version involving a fallen branch, a patch of oil or an animal suddenly running out on to the road, the kinder story of cruel fate and bad luck, which Susana, wise as she was when she was fifteen, pretended to believe out of pity for her two siblings.) The crash had been so head-on that it seemed Beatriz must have chosen the tree with great care: that one and no other, even though they all look the same, perhaps thinking: 'My guilt has passed, but the punishment remains. If not now, then when is the right time to die? I will not return to my woeful bed, I don't want to be haunted by sorrow any more. The readiness is all.' As I learned from Rico and Roy and Flavia and, days later, from Muriel himself, she had presumably stopped the Harley-Davidson at some point on the road and taken off her helmet, which not many people wore at the time, although she did sometimes: it was found on the grass, not on the road itself, and some metres from the site of the accident, as if it had fallen off or been thrown from that head that didn't always feel quite right, thinking perhaps: 'I wouldn't want a new life with another man. I want the life I had for quite a number of years and with the same man. I don't want to forget or get over it or move on, but to carry on in exactly the same way, like a prolongation of what was.' Probably few cars passed at that hour, and she could have taken her time before getting up enough imaginary momentum and setting off again and accelerating to top speed, could have looked around her a little to accustom herself to that dark, leafy place, which would be her last, and perhaps, as she waited, she wondered: 'Why should we be loved by the person we have chosen with our tremulous finger? Why that one person, as if he were obliged to obey us? Why should the person who troubles or arouses us and for whose flesh and bones we yearn, why should he desire us? Why should we believe in such coincidences? And when they do happen, why should they last? Yes, why should it last, this rarest of conjunctions, something so fragile, so held together with pins?' She perhaps took one last look at herself and her clothes, or even took a small mirror from her handbag, now that she was about to become definitively the past, a fixed portrait; although, by then, she may not have cared at all about the state in which she would be found or seen, feeling instead very much as the poet Bécquer wrote in a letter: 'By then, I won't care if they place me in an Egyptian pyramid or throw me in a ditch like a dog.' She may not even have bothered to look up at the incipient moon, all too familiar with its bored, impassive eye, she herself bored with its insistence, and may have thought: 'Soon I will cease to belong to the foolish, unfinished living and will be like falling snow that does not settle, like a lizard climbing up a sunny wall in summer that pauses for a moment before the lazy eye that will not even notice its existence. I will be what was, and once I am no more, I will be what never was. I will be an inaudible whisper, a light, passing fever, a scratch you barely notice and that heals up at once. In short, I will be time, which no one has seen and no one ever will.' And when at last her eyes finally grew used to the dim light, or perhaps when she started to feel cold, and she turned on the headlight again to see more clearly and not miss the tree chosen by her tremulous finger, and pressed down on the pedal to start Muriel's bike, which ended up being more hers than his, perhaps her last thought, as she raced along, was shorter and simpler and very much like this: 'Thus bad begins and worse remains behind.'

I waited a few days after the funeral before going to see Muriel on my own, a kind of tacit, individual presentation of condolences, and, I suppose, to keep him company for a while, although most of the time he was with other people, because in those circumstances, people do tend to flood in for a short period, never leaving the bereaved person alone for a minute, visiting him, taking him out, trying to distract him and keep him so busy and buzzing with activity that he doesn't think about the one thing occupying his thoughts, and feels less keenly the absence of the person who has irreversibly absented herself. Then those same people grow weary in unison and leave him alone, as if there were a social expiry date for mourning, two or three weeks at most, and as if they then considered the widow or widower to be in a fit state to get back up and running again and resume her or his normal life and habits, when it is precisely normal life that has ended, never to return. Muriel was clearly deeply affected and doubtless disconcerted, he seemed slightly shrunken and hesitant, as though the loss of Beatriz had uncovered a certain vulnerability, although I didn't imagine this would last. But when a situation ends, you miss it, even the worst possible situation, even one you'd wished would end countless times. That paradoxical nostalgia doesn't last very long, but initially you get the same empty feeling as when you've achieved an objective that has cost you great effort and patience,

487

closing a deal or getting a job, for example, or finishing a film or putting the long-delayed full stop to a novel.

Muriel probably didn't even remember the words I'd heard on that night of supplications, just before he ran his hands over Beatriz's body roughly, crudely, pointlessly, before groping her breasts and grabbing her crotch like someone picking up a handful of earth or a clump of grass or catching a thistle head in the air before blowing it away and leaving it to float, not even noticing where it's going. 'When the hell are you going to understand that this is serious and for good, until you die or I do?' were the words that had vomited forth from his mouth. 'I just hope I'm the one who'll carry your coffin, because I could never be sure you wouldn't rub yourself up against my still warm or already cold corpse, because warm or cold it would be all the same to you.' Superimposed on that memory, though, was another more concise, more poetic version: 'I hope to be the one to bury you, the one to see your lifeless body, your deathly pallor.' His wish had been granted, but the trouble was he didn't even remember saying those things (we forget more of what comes out of our mouths than what enters our ears), whereas they still reverberated in my mind as they would have in Beatriz's, possibly right up until the evening when she stopped in that dark, leafy spot on the road; and perhaps she would have said to him in her thoughts, when she was already astride the Harley-Davidson and had her gaze fixed on the target: 'Now you'll have to rub yourself up against *my* corpse.' Muriel hadn't gone that far, of course, but he had been visibly shaken when he heard the news and at the cemetery too, and it was clear, in his perplexity, that at first he missed her irritating, uncomfortable presence, irksome and even exasperating at times, the size and the shape and the footsteps of the person who had been his wife both for too many and possibly too few years, because when something ends we

488

almost always feel that it wasn't enough and could have lasted a little longer.

'You know sometimes, Juan, I think I can hear the tick-tock of the metronome,' he told me. 'Especially when I'm here alone, when the children and Flavia go to bed and the others leave, or when I come back from having supper out with a crowd of people. The fact is that, lately, my friends have obliged me to lead a life of almost obscenely frenetic activity, as if I were at a fiesta or something, and they've done so with the very best of intentions, because they don't want me to be left alone with my thoughts, imagining all too clearly what those thoughts will be. In fact, they have no idea what my thoughts will be, but they're pretty sure what they'll be about. It's absurd of me in a way to agree to all this, since I'm hardly an inconsolable widower. Don't get me wrong, I *am* sad. However much you expect it and even though you can do nothing to avoid it; however many warnings there have been and even though you're not entirely sure you want to avoid it; however much you harden yourself and accept the probable consequences of your . . .' he stopped, looking for the right word '. . . your impermeability, nothing prepares you for the event itself. I'm sad because we were together for a long time, and suddenly what resurfaces in my mind are the earliest years, when Beatriz was still almost a child and neither of us knew what the future might hold. But I'm not inconsolable in the sense of having suffered the loss of someone crucial to my life. There's an element of unreality about it all, and that's why I think I can still hear the tick-tock of her metronome, as if its echo had not yet faded and I could still hear in my head its music-less music, that beat which had become a permanent background feature here. It's the same with everything else, as if it took longer for Beatriz's footsteps or her smell to disappear than for her herself, people are survived by the traces they leave behind, that's been my experience at least, and it's perfectly normal, and then those traces will gradually evaporate too. But while they last . . . They seem to need a bit of extra time before they can leave altogether, time to clean up and collect their things. They're never given notice so that they can prepare for the move.'

He fell silent, and I didn't know how to respond, and there probably was no appropriate response.

'I see,' I said, just to say something.

That day, he was still looking a little older, but it didn't last; they soon disappeared, those signs of the old age that would return to stalk and haunt him without ever daring to take full possession of him, to take root in his mind or make any real incursions into his appearance. The dark shadows under his eyes, his lined, weary face, his slight stoop, noticeable even when he was seated, were purely circumstantial, the product of that event for which nothing prepares us however much notice we're given; the product of shock and corroboration. Then he suddenly sat up and looked at me with his one alert eye.

'You know she was pregnant.'

I was so taken aback that all I could come out with was a quite nonsensical question, possibly an instinctive attempt to gain a few seconds and recover from that revelation.

'Who, Beatriz?'

'Of course, who else? I mean, who are we talking about here, young De Vere?'

'No, of course not, how could I possibly know? Had she said anything to you?'

'Not a word. I found out just now from the Doctor. Fortunately, he managed to have a young colleague of his from the hospital carry out the autopsy, the bare minimum, very superficial, which was all that was needed. Enough, though, to detect that pregnancy. But the fact that she said nothing to me is hardly surprising. Needless to say, the child wasn't mine. The Doctor says that she herself may not have realized either. Although given that she'd had four children, that seems unlikely to me, but who knows? Perhaps she couldn't believe it, the possibility may not even have occurred to her. Anything is possible.'

'And do they know how many months gone she was?' I asked, a touch apprehensively.

'A couple of months or so.' Then he fell silent for a few moments and studied his nails as if he suddenly found the situation highly embarrassing. But what he found embarrassing was what he was about to ask: 'You wouldn't have any idea whose it might have been, would you?' I must have blushed a little, but perhaps he, too, was blushing inside and so didn't notice; or else he attributed my slightly flushed cheeks to what was causing him to blush under the skin, because before I could respond, he felt obliged to explain: 'As you can imagine, I didn't care tuppence about what Beatriz got up to. It was none of my business and I certainly never asked any questions, in case she took that as evidence of a certain interest on my part, or even jealousy, who can say? But if she was going to give my children a brother or sister and that child was going to live here, I would obviously feel a certain curiosity. You don't have any idea, do you?'

I realized that I needed to answer very quickly and without hesitation, that any pause or vacillation wouldn't necessarily point to me, but would indicate that I might know something or have my suspicions. I wanted to think – no, I was sure – that he was only asking because a couple of months or so before, I had been Beatriz's custodian while he was in Barcelona filming his final sequences with Towers and Lom; I had been closest to her and her main witness. He wasn't the suspicious type, it hadn't even occurred to him that I could have anything to do with it. For him I was almost a callow youth. I summoned my wretchedly swift tongue, the tongue that both condemns and saves us, and said confidently:

'No, Eduardo, Don Eduardo, I haven't the slightest idea. How would I know who it was?'

And since I really couldn't possibly know, I didn't even have to lie.

Afterwards, I saw him less and less frequently and, in the end, almost not all. I wouldn't say that we had become friends exactly, but while he may not have felt friendship for me, I felt it for him, and even though I no longer worked for him, I would have gladly continued to please and help him in anything he might reasonably have asked of me. But one quickly ceases to depend on someone who is no longer present on a daily basis, let alone at all hours and prepared to do any task. He never phoned me, and although I occasionally phoned him, I perhaps felt I was bothering him and didn't want to insist, and so my calls became fewer and further between until I was just another person who had passed through his life and not stopped.

Despite his dislike of photos – which is why, for years, there had been so few full-face portraits of him – I began to see him appearing more in the press, but not because of any cinematographic projects or productions. In fact, he made only one more film and it wasn't the one with Palance and Widmark, which took its place in the vast, crowded limbo of not-to-bes, and for which, I assume, he never managed to get the necessary financial support. He appeared in gossip magazines, doubtless reluctantly and unwillingly, first as the new partner and then as the husband of the impresaria Cecilia Alemany, who was attractive and wealthy enough to arouse more interest than him, for he, as he had once commented to me jokingly, was becoming a bit like Sara Montiel, only with an increasingly minority audience of archaeologists and film buffs and experts like Roy. I thought, too, that she was attractive enough to have made Beatriz lose all hope, had she ever known of her existence, or would always have been a threat. Someone who would have prevented her from taking any small trophy back to her woeful bed, saying to herself as she returned from her nocturnal incursion: 'We'll see.'

Muriel married for the second time just a year after he was widowed, in a discreet civil wedding to which I was not invited, not that there was any reason to include me in the cast, a mere former employee, a fleeting young man to whom he had given a job opportunity. Divorce had finally arrived in Spain when Muriel no longer needed it, and if Beatriz had lived, he might not even have made use of it, I sometimes think that the bonds of deceit and unhappiness are the strongest of all, as are those of error; they may bind even more closely than those of openness, contentment and sincerity. In the few pictures of the wedding available, I saw Van Vechten and Rico and Roy, as well as maestro Viana who adorned the ceremony – well, a bullfighter always lends colour to an occasion. There was no Gloria or Marcela or Flavia, the first two would have considered it a betrayal and the third perhaps preferred not to attend. I also saw the three children, older now, and all still identical to Beatriz. I looked for a long time at Susana: when she was just a little older, she would be the very image of her mother in those youthful photos that Beatriz kept on show out of nostalgia and persistence and which I had so often seen, the one with the dead child still alive in her arms and the one of her wedding to Muriel some twenty years before. I had a better understanding now of the expressions of both of them on that day: she smiling broadly and directly at the camera, revealing her obvious euphoria – or was it triumphalism? – a child disguised as a bride. He,

494

on the other hand, seemed anxious, almost sombre, like a man convinced he's taking on an enormous responsibility. She was playing at getting married, while he was seriously contracting a marriage, as if aware of the appropriateness of that verb when applied to obligations, debts and diseases. To her the world was a lightweight affair, as were the consequences of her actions, which, once over, were mere childish nonsense, the past; he was someone who already knew what it means to renounce something or who was aware that love always arrives late for its appointment with people, as he once gloomily told me, a phrase he had read in some book, although I don't know which. In the pictures of his second wedding, there's no trace of that, his one eye looks distracted and patient, with not a hint of seriousness. He seems merely to be going through the motions of a social formality and to be looking – without looking – at his watch.

I wondered how this new, artificial family would manage, if they would all live together in the apartment in Calle Velázquez or would start anew in another apartment; if the impresaria would gladly accept having an adolescent and two children – or two adolescents and one child – permanently around, especially when their father was away travelling, absorbed for months on end in the making of some film; if Flavia would leave them or be forced to emigrate to the new address. I considered phoning Muriel to congratulate him, but discovered to my surprise that even I felt that was a kind of betrayal. Absurdly enough, it would, it seemed to me, be like heaping more earth on Beatriz, regardless of the fact that she had chosen to be the first to start digging her grave on that lonely, shady road. Perhaps carnal bonds, however ephemeral and unmemorable and basically unimportant, oblige us to feel a certain irrational concern for the people with whom we have established those bonds; or perhaps it's imposed on us by a ghostly personal sense of loyalty.

495

I went to see Muriel's last film when it opened. It wasn't generally well received, but I liked it. I phoned to tell him so, but he wasn't in, and then I let the matter slide, because he didn't exactly need my opinion. He hadn't managed to make another film until five years after Beatriz's death; and two years later, seven years after her suicide, I learned that my former boss and maestro had suffered a devastating heart attack while lunching with a group of boorish bankers from whom he was trying to extract a little small change for some new film project. As soon as I heard the news on television, I called Professor Rico, the only one in that circle with whom I'd remained in contact and with whom I'm still in touch today. By then, he was already a member of the Real Academia: his enemy papyruses – or were they mummies? – had all pegged out at a rate of knots and he'd been elected with more than enough votes, almost by acclamation, although he's since acquired a few more splendid enemies, without whom he cannot live or only at the risk of getting royally bored. He was about to catch a plane to Madrid to attend the funeral, and he told me the hour and the place. That's the only time I've heard a tremor of emotion in his voice. No, I lie, that tremor is always there whenever we speak of Muriel or Beatriz – he's basically an old sentimentalist – even though it's ages since they bade farewell to life without first bidding farewell to either of us.

The following morning, I went to La Almudena cemetery and stood before the grave I'd first seen some years before, although to me it felt like only yesterday: time vanishes when you return to a place you rarely visit and where you only go in sorrow or for some other exceptional reason. There were a lot of people and a fair number of journalists, and I kept well to the rear, not daring to push my way to the front. For most of those present I was a stranger, an interloper, an intruder, no one they need say hello to. Some distance away

I saw Susana and her siblings with their backs to me, I recognized them at once despite the intervening years and despite how much the two younger ones had grown. Susana looked round now and again, perhaps so as to see how many people had come, how respected her father had been, until on one of those occasions, she spotted me and came running over to me. I was thirty by then and she was twenty-two, but she immediately hugged me hard and wept silently, in the wholehearted way one embraces someone who belonged to old, imperfect but far less sad times, when all those who should have been there still were; then she took my hand and led me over to the front row, along with Alicia and Tomás and Flavia and other people I didn't know, including Cecilia Alemany, who doubtless found a moment to look at me from behind her dark glasses (she wasn't chewing gum this time) and wonder indifferently who the hell I was: I don't think she was much interested in the past of her short-lived and now late husband, and it occurred to me that she would probably now simply shake him off, like someone leaving behind her an episode that had been the fruit of weakness or seduction. During the rest of the ceremony, the lowering of the coffin and the replacement of the gravestone for the last time (no one else would fit in), Susana kept her hand in mine, squeezing my hand hard so as to steady herself, for as I said, she was far unsteadier on her feet than the widow or than anyone else. Or perhaps she clung to my hand like a stubborn child.

I've been married to Susana for so long now that she's older than her mother ever came to be and I am more or less the age reached by Muriel, who survived his wife by seven years; more or less the same number of years, seven or eight, that separated him from her, and me from Susana, so in total, he lived about fifteen years longer than Beatriz. She seemed mature to me in 1980, like a painting in comparison with me, when I was twenty-three and she was forty-two or possibly forty-one – I never knew exactly – but she was about two decades older than me, which is a lot for a mere callow youth. Now, on the other hand, Beatriz seems very young in retrospect, and not just too young to have died, but too young for everything. It wasn't, therefore, so very odd that she should still have nurtured hopes and that, on the nights when she was defeated, she would temporarily abandon the field in order to gather renewed strength and valour and withdraw to her room, thinking: 'Not tonight, no, not tonight, but later perhaps. My pillow will receive my tears and I will learn how to wait just as the insistent moon waits. A time will come when his offensive groping will, out of inertia, slide into a different territory, where it will suddenly become yearning or irresistible caprice or primitive desire, for nothing can be driven away like that by pure mental effort, by a punitive decision, not for ever or not entirely – such things are mere suspensions of activity, mere postponements.

He might come back one day or one night, and, besides, who can resist being wanted and loved?' As far as I know, he never did go back either by day or night, but I can't be sure.

Yes, she was young when she killed herself, and fertile enough to be expecting another baby, that's what Muriel told me, that's what Van Vechten told him, that's what the young colleague at Van Vechten's hospital told him; so all of that is merely a rumour that stopped with me, never even reaching the drooping west, or his daughter Susana, not through me at any rate, and it's best that it stays in the orient. Over the years, I've often remembered the whisper that Muriel transmitted to me in the form of a rhetorical question ('You know . . .'). And I often shamefacedly congratulate myself – in one aspect, but only one – that Beatriz did kill herself and that the child was not born, and had perhaps not even developed enough for its future, distracted mother to notice. I don't know which man was the cause of that new shoot, if it was Dr Van Vechten himself in the Sanctuary of Darmstadt or Dr Arranz in Plaza del Marqués de Salamanca or some other lover she visited on her Harley-Davidson, in El Escorial or the Sierra de Gredos or in Ávila. I often stubbornly tell myself that there must have been a third man, just to share out the responsibility. But I can't deny that the new shoot could also have been my work on one hot, insomniac night in Calle Velázquez, which would have been very bad luck, of course, but then neither of us took any precautions. Whenever that nightmare possibility crosses my mind, I shudder and cannot help but feel glad – rather despising myself as I do, but I can take it – that that projected being did come to nothing, because it might have spent its whole existence as an impostor, unaware of its own imposture, or would have prevented all the good things that came later in my life and, I think, in Susana's life too, and our daughters would not exist. Had that child, a girl say,

499

emerged into the world, it would have been a half-sister to my wife, a kind of stepdaughter, both my daughter and my sister-in-law, and the children I've had with Susana would have been both her sisters and her cousins, and it's usually at that point that I stop these ramblings, because the whole hypothetical chain of relationships makes me dizzy, but also because it evokes the dreadful thought that my marriage to Susana would then have been almost impossible. (How little it takes for what exists not to have existed.) Nothing could have been proved at the time, and Beatriz might have kept quiet about the identity of the father, if she had managed to deduce it or know for certain. However, there's no getting away from the fact that I once had sex with the grandmother of my daughters, that is, with the person who would have been my mother-in-law had she lived long enough. But who can possibly know who is going to be what in the course of a lifetime, and we shouldn't hold back because of conjectures or predictions that are beyond our grasp, we only have what we know today and never what we might know tomorrow, and yet we do sometimes give ourselves over to such prognostications.

For many years, the memory of that night remained very dim. It was as if that tenuous story had never happened, for as long, that is, as Susana was young and, despite her striking resemblance to her mother, as long as her youth kept at bay the image of her mother, the image I had known personally, not so much the one in those old photos that had led me to think – although it wasn't only the photos that led me to think this: 'She must have been very alluring, I can understand why Muriel would have wanted her at his side day and night, I'm sure I would have too. Even if only for her sheer carnality, which counts for a lot in a marriage. But I wasn't Muriel then, nor am I now.' However, since Susana has grown older, that memory has taken on colour, it slips into my bed and troubles my sleep. She has come more and more to resemble the Beatriz I knew when I was twenty-three, although I certainly don't see her as fat and she isn't fat at all, indeed, I've noticed only very tiny changes in her – but then I'm biased – since, at Muriel's funeral, she appeared to me as a grown woman, newly and fully formed and with the same intimidating, explosive body, in full bloom now and no longer the adolescent girl I'd forbidden myself to look at – another inanimate representation – and I didn't look at her, while she perhaps, without my noticing, couldn't keep her eyes off me, the young man who spent so much time in her home, like one of those very stubborn girls determined to see her childhood dreams come true, until she reaches a certain age or sees those dreams crushed for ever. Muriel once said that the other person's enthusiasm helps a lot, persuades and carries you along. And another person's love is always more touching and provokes more pity than the love you yourself feel.

Of course I never saw the forty-something Beatriz as fat, it was my boss who insisted on that or who had decided to compare her with the most rotund of film stars simply in order to wound her. Lately, though, when I'm making love with Susana, I've found that remote image slipping into my mind to trouble and disturb me, to almost paralyse and strike me dumb. The past has a future we never expect, and just as, on that distant night, Beatriz's unexpectedly youthful face – her face embellished as happens with many women in that state of semi-oblivion – momentarily suggested that of her daughter, the same features and the same candid expression, so now the daughter leads me back to the mother at the most inopportune of moments, and even becomes overlaid by that scene watched from the top of a tree in the Sanctuary of Darmstadt, which now I find utterly repellent (fortunately, I can drive that scene away at once, it's gone in a flash). What is perhaps most regrettable (or, perhaps, disquieting because impossible to assimilate) about these intersecting images is that I am now that older man who, in our youth, appears in our unconscious mind and whispers mysteriously to us, like a ghost from the future: 'Remember this experience and note every detail, experience it with me in mind and as if you knew it would never happen again except in your memory, which is my memory; you won't be able to preserve the excitement or relive it, but you will recall the sense of triumph and, more especially, the knowledge: you will *know* that this happened and you always will; grasp it firmly, take a long look at this woman and keep that image safe, because later on, I will ask you for it and you will have to offer it to me as consolation.'

I don't want to ask for it, but the images blur together and that's what I end up doing. And when this happens, I can't help feeling that Susana notices that something odd is going on, can sense the incongruousness of what's happening in my mind, or in that uncontrollable thing – the mind's eye. She pauses for a few seconds, observes me with one half-open eye, and waits for the malaise to pass. And I sometimes wonder if she hasn't always known exactly what happened, if the barefoot steps I heard in the corridor were, in fact, hers and whether her cheeks burned with a daughter's indignation or with the childish jealousy of the young girl in love or with a combination of both those things, if those were her footsteps. She has never mentioned it, however, and I certainly haven't; some secrets are best left secret. That's also why I've never told her what I found out about her mother when I followed her nor what Muriel told me later on. What would be the point? She witnessed the results and her father's wounding, punishing behaviour, and I don't think she wants to delve into what happened in the lost past, before she was even born. However, I'm always afraid that one day, in a fit of anger, she'll reveal what she knows and reproach me for what I did that night, that she'll throw it in my face and say: 'How could you?'

Or that I might angrily reveal my secret, as Beatriz did with Muriel, showing him the letter she denied having received and thus, after long years of careful concealment and deceit, unleashing her own misfortune. The two situations can't really be compared, and it wouldn't necessarily be a misfortune if we managed to laugh about it, anything is possible, and I'm not Muriel and Susana isn't her mother, although, like Beatriz, she takes a light-hearted view of her own actions and those of other people and often considers things to be ridiculous or mere childish nonsense, and rarely gives any importance to what isn't important at all. I was right to wait to love her, until she chose me with her tremulous finger and I was capable of seeing her; and how right I've been to love her during all these years, all these past years. I've probably never done anything better.

That's why I find it so worrying when the image of Beatriz suddenly, and however fleetingly, comes into my mind in the middle of some intimate moment. Then I try to summon up that remote foreshadowing, which disquieted and troubled me at the time, the ephemeral, intrusive vision of an adolescent Susana. Now, on the other hand, I'd like to recover that vision, so that, through the memory of that vision, reality can be restored and that forgotten yesterday can return the today, which, just for an instant, has slipped away from us. It isn't only Susana who, with one half-open eye, stops to observe me suspiciously, or is it questioningly, curiously? I stop too, become distracted, absent, turn my face away as if I didn't want to be kissed on the mouth by a ghost who also once turned away her face and denied me her mouth when she was still flesh, brimming, moving flesh. And then there's a moment when one of us, either Susana or me, I'm not sure, must be thinking: 'No, no kisses.' We look at each other without saying anything, and perhaps what we're saying to ourselves is something on which we both agree: 'And no, no words.'

Translator's Acknowledgements

I would like to thank Javier Marías for all his help and generosity, and, as always, Annella McDermott and Ben Sherriff for their unfailing support and advice.